A Funny
Thing
L

Rebecca Farnworth has worked as a writer. She lives in Brighton with three children. *A Funny Thing About Love* is her second novel.

Also by Rebecca Farnworth
Valentine

rebecca farnworth

A Funny Thing about Love

Published by Arrow Books in 2010

2 4 6 8 10 9 7 5 3 1

First published in Great Britain in 2010 by
Arrow Books
The Random House Group Limited
20 Vauxhall Bridge Road, London, SW1V 2SA

www.rbooks.co.uk

Addresses for companies within The Random House Group Limited can be found at:
www.randomhouse.co.uk/offices.htm

The Random House Group Limited Reg. No. 954009

A CIP catalogue record for this book
is available from the British Library

ISBN 978 0 099 52718 3

The Random House Group Limited supports The Forest Stewardship Council (FSC), the leading international forest certification organisation. All our titles that are printed on Greenpeace approved FSC certified paper carry the FSC logo. Our paper procurement policy can be found at www.rbooks.co.uk/environment

Mixed Sources
Product group from well-managed
forests and other controlled sources
www.fsc.org Cert no. TT-COC-2139
© 1996 Forest Stewardship Council

Typeset in Baskerville by Palimpsest Book Production Limited,
Falkirk, Stirlingshire
Printed and bound in Great Britain by CPI Cox & Wyman, Reading, RG1 8EX

For J

Acknowledgements

Thank you to everyone at Random House, particularly my editor Gillian Holmes and Kate Elton for all their input and enthusiasm for the book. And thanks to Amelia Harvell and all in publicity, marketing and sales.

Thank you to my wonderful agent, Maggie Hanbury, clever, witty and wise and always to be relied on and of course to her team Stuart and Henry (Wobbly Worms and Peanut Grigiot all round!).

Thank you to my family for keeping my feet well and truly on the ground and for making me realise what's important.

And thank you to Brighton, a brilliant city.

1

Carmen Miller was horribly late for work. Late and hungover. She'd been up until two the night before getting outrageously drunk with Sadie, one of her closest friends. She should have known that ending the night on sambucas would be a major mistake. She was thirty-three for goodness' sake! She didn't even like sambuca! Where were reason and common sense when the decision was made to crack open the bottle? On a mini break together apparently, leaving Carmen free to throw caution to the wind and enter that state of drunkenness where you feel invincible. That king-of-the-world, Leonardo di Caprio standing-behind-you, emotive-music-playing feeling. She certainly didn't feel invincible right now. She had hit the iceberg and gone down.

She adjusted her sunglasses. It was a breezeblock-grey cloudy day with no hint of sun at the end of September, but Carmen needed the cover-up. She crossed Oxford Street, narrowly avoiding being squished by a bendy bus, and headed up Great Portland Street W1, towards Fox Nicholson where she worked as a comedy agent. According to their kick-ass blurb, Fox Nicholson were one of the 'cutting-edge agencies, specialising in representing talent in comedy and drama'. There was nothing kick-ass or cutting-edge about Carmen today. Her mind was a woolly fog with only three thoughts bleating in it: coffee, can of coke and croissant.

She stumbled into her favourite Italian café which had been run by the same family for donkey's years. As soon as Rico, the shiny black-haired, good-looking-and-he-knew-it eldest son, clocked her staggering through the door he started firing up the chrome coffee machine for her skinny latte. Not that she was a creature of habit or anything. Well, not much. She'd been coming to the café for the last four years and always had the exact same thing – skinny latte and a croissant. No doubt the croissant cancelled out any benefit of the skinny latte, but Carmen loathed cereal and figured that if slim-hipped French women lived off croissants and coffee then it couldn't do that much harm. She neglected to recall that they probably didn't eat anything else for the rest of the day, whereas she would be back at Rico's at lunchtime ordering a jacket potato and cheese.

'*Ciao, bella!*' Rico called out. Rico carried something of a torch for Carmen, which at times threatened to burst into a towering inferno, but then again as he flirted with all his female customers she didn't take it personally. She certainly did not feel terribly *bella* at this moment. What was the Italian for raddled old hag with seriously dehydrated skin? *Hagissima*?

'*Ciao,*' she mumbled, then opened the fridge and

grabbed a can of coke and put it on top of the glass counter, trying to avoid looking at the array of sandwich fillings. The sight of the lurid yellow egg mayonnaise next to the tuna and sweetcorn was turning her stomach quicker than a ride on a waltzer.

'Rough night?' Rico asked. God, even her sandwich man could read her like a book! And she'd spent bloody ages doing her make-up, piling on practically every single product she owned to conceal the dark shadows, brighten her eyes and put some colour into her pallid complexion in an attempt to look more girl-about-town and less night-of-the-living-dead.

'I did get a bit carried away,' Carmen admitted, handing over the money.

'Lucky him,' Rico replied wistfully. Ever since he had found out that Carmen was separated from her husband he had become blatantly inquisitive about her love life.

'There is no lucky him, Rico,' Carmen corrected. 'Just single, embittered me and my mad friend.'

Rico popped a croissant into a brown paper bag and snapped the lid down on Carmen's coffee. 'You know, I could take you out sometime,' he said quietly, a hopeful edge to his voice. He shot an anxious look in the direction of his mother, a vast, fifty-something woman, perpetually dressed in black, who occupied the seat by the till and who was rumoured to be psychic.

Carmen raised an eyebrow. 'Yeah, right, I'm sure your wife would love that.'

'She wouldn't mind,' Rico persisted.

Carmen picked up her coffee and stuffed the croissant and coke into her bag. 'Yep, she would. *Ciao*.'

'Quite right, Carmen, of course she would!' came a booming voice. It was the Italian *mamma*, whom everyone unoriginally called Mamma Mia behind her back. Her real name was Carla. She must have hearing like a bat or else she really was psychic.

Rico looked startled and his '*Ciao*' had a slightly nervous ring.

Carmen had loved working for Fox Nicholson when it had just been Nicholson, one of the smaller agencies representing comics and also a select number of actors. Carmen specialised in comics. She'd become a comedy agent completely by chance after meeting Matthew Nicholson, the owner of the agency, at the Edinburgh festival in the late nineties where her boyfriend Nick, later to be her husband, had been performing as a comic. Matthew had signed Nick up and offered Carmen a job as PA at his agency.

Back then she'd had no real idea of what she wanted to do. After her English degree she'd done TEFL and the travelling thing, and had even appeared on stage with Nick in a comedy sketch show. Her secret ambition had always been to write her own comedy drama. She'd even written the first episode, but she'd never been confident enough to take time off paid work to complete it and somehow she had never got round to working on it in the evening – there was always a comedy gig to go to or a DVD to collapse in front of with a bottle of wine. God only knew how T.S. Eilliot had written *The Waste Land* while working in a bank. Sheer will power, no doubt, and being a better person with no addiction to DVD box sets. And while Nick had encouraged her writing, he had always seen it as a hobby and never really taken it seriously.

After a couple of years as a PA Carmen worked her way to the position of agent. Once there, she discovered that she didn't especially like it. She lacked the killer instinct and thick layer of skin that were the essential requisites of being a good agent. However, there were compensations. Matthew was a brilliantly witty bon viveur who was great fun to be around. He had always run the small agency as an eccentric extended family, and whenever Carmen was having a tough time nego-tiating fees, she could always rely on Matthew to step in for her, leaving her free to do the nicer, less stressful parts of the job, like spotting talent and reading scripts. But then the recession had changed everything. Matthew had been forced to accept a buyout from Fox, a much larger, more corporate-style management company, whose sole mantra seemed to be money.

Since then Matthew had been sidelined and the company had grown from just five agents to twelve, who had to account for practically every minute of their day. The clients were given new terms and some of them left, including Nick, which was probably for the best as it had been more than slightly awkward since the break-up. Marcus Taylor, a comic Carmen had championed, had also left and gone on to be huge in TV. Now her boss was a scary, tiny, thirty-something Australian called Tiana, who was one of those passive-aggressive types who seem to be lovely on the surface but underneath have all the compassion of a great white shark smelling blood. She knew very little about performers. All she cared about was the bottom line.

Wearily Carmen pushed open the heavy glass front door and walked into the minimalist lobby, which had recently been refurbished. Despite being the size of a small football pitch, it was furnished only with one blood-red leather sofa and a glass coffee table at one end for visitors and a white glass reception at the other. There was an enormous, stainless-steel light fitting, which resembled a series of knives radiating out from the ceiling. No doubt it was supposed to act as a visual metaphor for how cutting-edge the company was, but to Carmen it looked like a piece of rather dangerous scrap metal. She always avoided walking underneath it, fearing that it would fall and she would be impaled by one of the vicious-looking spikes. Tiana had been behind the design, which to Carmen said everything you needed to know about her new boss. She privately thought that if Tiana had deliberately set out to design an intimidating space for the lobby she could not have done a more effective job. Not that some of the comics who came to the agency didn't deserve a bit of intimi-dating – in fact, many of them deserved a lot more. Mild torture, perhaps, if such a thing existed.

'Hiya,' she called out to Daisy, one of the girls on reception – her favourite, in fact – a pixie-haired blonde

6

who always wore black and who hated the general public. Carmen knew for a fact that she had a card pinned to her computer screen that read, 'Do I look like a fucking people person?' Daisy did not. She did not look like a Daisy either. She had recently morphed from a goth to an emo. Carmen wasn't entirely sure what the difference was, but as she had already asked Daisy twice to explain it to her and had forgotten the answer, she hardly felt able to ask her again. Daisy raised her hand in greeting but didn't take her eyes off her computer screen, where she was most likely playing *Grand Theft Auto*.

Carmen knew she ought to take the stairs as a token gesture to burn off some of the thousands of calories she must have consumed the night before. She had a vague, guilty recollection that she and Sadie had eaten *two* bumper bags of Doritos when they'd got the two a.m. munchies; Alas, she had the will power of a gnat, and so she found herself pressing the button to the lift. She would probably end up with the thighs of an elephant, but hey, at least she would have a good memory.

As the lift door pinged open on the fourth floor she sneaked a look along the corridor. *Please don't let me be seen by Tiana*. It was nearly midday and she had no explanation for her lateness. And she'd already been ticked off last week for turning up late and missing a management meeting. She should have been sitting at her desk beavering away from the dot of half past nine. To her left was the open-plan office occupied by the three PAs and Colin the accountant, who were all focused intently on their screens. Connor the postboy was doing his rounds and he caught sight of her and winked. Carmen pretended not to notice, not wishing to encourage him. Recently he'd acquired a tattoo of Johnny Depp's face on his shoulder in homage to his favourite actor, which he kept threatening to show her. Carmen had no desire to see a half-naked, possibly pimply eighteen-year-old, even with the lure of Johnny. But apart from Connor, the coast was clear.

Carmen turned right towards her office and careered along the corridor at high speed, past the succession of glass-fronted mini offices occupied by other agents. The cubicles offered no privacy whatsoever to the worker inside, unless you pulled down the blinds, and then it looked as if you were up to something you shouldn't be. Which if you were Dirty Sam, you most likely were. She had nearly reached the safety of her office when Sexy Will, Tiana's deputy and chief comedy agent, called out her name. Bugger! She was busted! She backtracked and leaned nonchalantly against his door frame.

Will was mid-thirties with jet-black hair, stunning blue eyes and pale skin. It was a combination that hinted at Irish ancestry, and one that Carmen had always been partial to. He was only a little taller than she was, and at five foot seven herself she usually liked her men way taller, but his gorgeous eyes and sexy smile more than compensated. There was something undeniably compelling about him. He was totally ruthless as an agent and she shouldn't fancy him, but he had a kind of knowing, sexy sleaziness that almost made her want to go there, plus he was clever and funny. Unfortunately he was just a bit too much into toeing the company line for Carmen's liking.

Will was putting on his Tom Cruise, show-me-the-money act now, his blue shirt cunningly making the blue eyes seem bluer, a hands-free headset clamped to his ear as he wound up a call, telling the person on the other end, likely to be some hapless BBC Radio producer with a tiny budget, that they had to offer way more money before he would even consider mentioning their project to his client. If it had been her, Carmen knew that she would have sounded apologetic, but Will was a much smoother operator.

He pointed to his watch, and raised an eyebrow. 'Half day, Miller? Very naughty. I might have to discipline you.'

They'd been exchanging flirtatious banter along these lines since Will had joined the company three months before, but it had never gone further. Carmen was still too raw from the break-up of her marriage, and she could never quite make up her mind whether Will was more smarmy than sexy. Plus she had made a vow a long time ago never to have a relationship with anyone she worked with, not after what had happened with Nick. Plus too the fact that she never exactly knew what Will's relationship status was. Carmen reached for a packet of M&S Wobbly Worms from her bag with studied insouciance. Once a week, or twice on a bad week, she treated herself to the wriggly wine gums, but as she loathed the green ones she always gave them to Will. She held the packet open for him now.

He walked over and extracted five. 'Do you think the worms are going to distract me from my mission to find out what you've been up to? And if this is meant to be a bribe, couldn't you do better than confectionery? A drink, now that would be more like it.' He returned to his desk, sat back in his chair and put his feet up.

At the mere mention of alcohol Carmen's stomach lurched. She would *never* drink that much again. No, in future it would be a couple of white wine spritzers and then she'd switch to water. *As if.*

'You really should have more faith in me, Will. I've just been seeing a potential client. We met in North London at his house as he couldn't come into town. He's agoraphobic, but the meeting was very productive actually.' She fervently hoped Will couldn't smell alcohol on her. She had sprayed on liberal quantities of Tom Ford's White Patchouli, which she usually reserved for special occasions, but this morning had been an emergency.

'Could you actually see him through those shades?'

No wonder everything had seemed so dark! She slid the glasses on to the top of her head, careful not to mess up her fringe. She might have the hangover from hell but at least her black bob looked immaculate.

Will studied her, a sceptical expression on his ruggedly handsome face. 'What's his name? Maybe it's someone I've seen? Although if he's agoraphobic I'm guessing he's not big on doing live gigs.'

Rats! Why had she said that? 'Oh, did I say agora-phobic? I meant arachnophobic. Apparently at this time of year there are lots of spiders at large, which is why he prefers to stay at home in his spider-free zone.' She felt pleased with herself for thinking on her feet.

'His name, Carmen?' Will asked, a slight twitch to his mouth betraying that he did not believe her. 'And if I've seen him we could compare notes. You know two heads are always better than one.'

Oh God, her head hurt too much to be able to lie convincingly. She decided to drop all pretence. 'Actually, Will, I'm just late because I'm late.'

'Night on the tiles with some guy?' Will asked. 'I wondered why you had that sexy, husky voice, redolent of a hangover and not going to bed until the early hours.'

'Maybe . . .' Carmen decided to play him, just a little, rather pleased that he thought her hangover voice was sexy. 'Actually, I'm completely *shagged*.' Big emphasis on *shagged*.

Will rearranged the folders on his desk. Was he bothered? It was hard to tell with the banter they'd built up. 'I thought you said you weren't seeing anyone, needed space, that kind of bollocks.'

Hmm, maybe he was a teeny tiny bit bothered. 'Well, let's just say I found a window. Anyway, must dash.' She swung her bag over her shoulder, ready to saunter off.

'And I can't believe you've forgotten what day it is.' Will was glaring at her now. 'If I was you I would have my hands on my hips, a petulant curl to my lip, and be stamping my little red-Converse-shod feet.'

The woolly fog got denser. What on earth was Will going on about? Then her eye fell on the birthday cards fighting for space on his desk. Oops! She'd known there was something she needed to remember this morning. She foraged in her bag again, having a vague recollection that last night, before she'd fallen into the abyss of oblivion, she had managed to put in Will's present and card.

'Ta da!' she declared, pulling them out. 'As if I would forget! Celebrating you getting even older has been one of the highlights of my social diary. Remind me how old you are again? Was it thirty-six? In four years' time it will be the big one! Have you planned your midlife crisis yet? I'm thinking a Harley-Davidson motorbike and red leathers for you.'

Ow! That diatribe had caused her head to throb outrageously. God knew how many little grey cells had been consigned to dust last night. She had visions of her cranium being littered with miniature grey crosses to mark their demise. And they would never be replaced, even if she took up Sudoku as her dad was always urging her to do.

Will pursed his lips fractionally. 'I'm thirty-five, let me remind you. And people in glass houses on the wrong side of thirty – thirty-four if I remember rightly – are in no position for stone throwing.'

Touché. 'I'm thirty-three!' Carmen hissed back.

'Whatever. Either way, sweetie, you'll never see

twenty-nine again. You're past your prime, but that's okay. I like old birds.'

Carmen found herself with her hands on her hips, a petulant curl to her lip, all ready to stamp her Converse-shod feet.

'Anyway, what have you got me?'

Carmen handed over the gift. She had actually spent ages agonising over what to buy Will. She knew he was a huge fan of Sinatra, so in the end she had bought a new biography of the singer, figuring he might not have it yet. First Will ripped open the card. She'd gone for a typically cheeky one of rodents dressed up as members of Abba, with a message alluding to his grand old age. Will rolled his eyes, then turned his attention to the present.

For a few seconds after he had ripped off the paper to reveal the book, he was silent, then he looked up and said seriously, with no trace of flirty Will, 'This is my best present. I've wanted to get this for ages. Thank you, Carmen.'

'Well, I was going to get a year's supply of Viagra online but thought you would appreciate this more, even though your lady friends might have appreciated the other.'

'Miller, if only you knew. I have absolutely no need of any help in that department. I can be at it all night.' At this he stood up and performed the kind of double macho hand gesture of exultation beloved of footballers when they score, at the exact moment that tiny, scary Tiana walked in.

Carmen bit her lip to stop herself from giggling. The irony of Tiana being boss of an agency representing comics was that she herself was renowned for her absolute absence of a sense of humour. Her nickname behind her back was Comedy Bypass.

'I was just telling Carmen about a stand-up routine I saw the other night,' Will blustered.

'It sounded hilarious!' Carmen added helpfully. 'All about a thirty-six-year-old man who can't get it up.' Okay, it wasn't the funniest comeback ever, but it was the best she could muster in the hungover circumstances.

Will scowled at her. But Tiana was busy emailing on her BlackBerry and barely registered them.

'Anyway, Carmen, you are coming tonight, aren't you? Drinks at the Ship and then dinner at Rico's?' Will had managed to compose himself enough to ask the question.

'Yep, see you later.'

Carmen tried to avoid being around her boss wherever possible and was all set to retire to the relative peace of her office when Tiana addressed her. 'Oh, Carmen, can you drop by my office at one? I need to go through your appraisal with you.'

Of all the days to go through this particular form of mental torture, today was without doubt the worst.

'Sure, Tiana,' Carmen said breezily and slunk off to her office. That had well and truly taken the shine off her flirty banter with Will.

* * *

14

Once in her office she collapsed on her chair and switched on her MacBook. She'd just drink her coffee before she faced the day's barrage of emails. For about the hundredth time she wished she could open her window, but when Fox had taken over they'd insisted on a complete refit of the offices – hence the glass cages and the air con. Carmen had tried to personalise her cell with photos of friends, her collection of snow globes, ranging from the predictable New York skyline right through to a quirky family of meerkats; and hot-pink cherry blossom lights to counteract the harsh overhead lights, which were a friend to no woman. Still, it was pretty hard to make your mark on such a sterile environment.

Carmen was about to tuck into her croissant when the phone rang. It was Trish, Tiana and Matthew's PA, who ran the office, remembered everyone's birthdays, did the expenses – in other words, was completely invaluable.

'Hiya, Carmen, just to let you know that Karl Fraser has been on the phone. He wants to come and see you tomorrow.'

'Oh no!' Carmen groaned. 'Couldn't you have said I was on holiday?'

'I said that last time he called.'

'Gynaecological appointment?'

'I said that the time before last.'

'Funeral?'

Trish tutted. 'You really shouldn't tempt fate like that, Carmen.'

'Oh, I know. Thanks anyway, Trish.' Carmen sighed and sipped her latte.

Karl Fraser was her least favourite client. In fact he was one of her least favourite people. He was egotistical, and yes, that was only to be expected in a comic, all her clients were, but Karl took it to another level. He was monstrously egotistical. He was also a misogynist, mean and had bad breath. Possibly Carmen could have forgiven those three flaws, but for one thing. In her opinion, Karl actually wasn't that funny. His humour was aggressive and laddish, like a punch in the face rather than a tickle in the ribs. Carmen adored clever performers like Eddie Izzard, Stewart Lee, Harry Hill and Bill Bailey, but Karl was so relentlessly cynical, charmless and crude. She had inherited him after he'd managed to alienate every other agent in the group and Tiana had ordered Carmen to take him on, promising her a bonus if she did. Funnily enough, she had never had the bonus, but she'd had more than enough of Karl.

She made inroads into her croissant and tried to push thoughts of noxious Karl out of her head as she wondered what fresh hell her appraisal would contain. Before Fox they hadn't really had appraisals. It had been a pretty informal system, where Matthew decided who would get a bonus largely on the basis of who hadn't had one the year before.

She looked up as Lottie knocked on her door, walked in and flopped down on the chair opposite her. 'Bloody bollocking hell!' she exclaimed. 'I've just been done over by Comedy Bypass.' Lottie was another agent who, like Carmen, had been with Nicholson. She was in her late thirties but seemed younger, as she always looked as if she'd just been on a brisk country walk and had a constant healthy glow about her. She never wore make-up except the occasional flick of mascara. She had cropped, brownish-blonde hair, always wore jeans and white shirts, bit her nails, was gay and was also a fantastic agent.

'Oh God!' Carmen wailed. 'If she gave you a hard time, what is mine going to be like? She'll make mince-meat of me!'

'You'll be fine,' Lottie replied, but both she and Carmen knew that was not true.

'So what kinds of things did she say?' Carmen asked tentatively, thinking forewarned was forearmed.

'Oh, the usual crap about meeting targets, getting more clients, charging them more. Honestly, the woman knows nothing about comedy.' Lottie shook her head and chewed a nail before changing the subject completely. 'So I reckon tonight will be the night that you and Will get together.'

'Lottie!' Carmen was outraged. 'No way is that going to happen, especially not in front of all you lot, who'll be sitting there like a bunch of hyenas eyeballing our every move.'

'So perhaps it will happen when we've all gone home,' Lottie persisted. It was why she was such a damn fine agent, she was ruthless in pursuing a point.

'No, it won't! There is nothing going on between me and Will. We're just friends.'

Lottie let out a snort of laughter, 'Come on, Carmen, there is so much suppressed lust between you two, I'm surprised you haven't both combusted!'

Carmen curled her lip. 'I have no further comment to make.'

'I think you'd be good together.' Lottie was not going to give up. 'You know that I didn't like Will when I first met him, but I really like him now.'

'Right, this is the last thing I'm going to say on the subject. I am not going to go there. He might even have a girlfriend for all I know.'

'He hasn't got a girlfriend. He split up with her four months ago. He's ready for you, fully primed. A Ferrari waiting to be switched on, a panther ready to sprint, a—'

Carmen cut across her. 'Out, now,' and pointed at the door. Reluctantly Lottie got up. She was almost out the door when Carmen called, 'Wish me luck with my appraisal.'

'Good luck, and don't cry. Remember, Tiana thrives on weakness.'

Carmen rolled her eyes by way of an answer.

She tried cracking on with some work after that. She took a call from a producer interested in one of her acts and sent off a few emails, but she was really suffering from attention deficit disorder – first the hangover, then the appraisal, and then Will. She wouldn't admit it to Lottie, but she was right, there *was* so much suppressed lust between her and Will. There had been from the first time they met, but both had been wary about going beyond flirtation. They had never even been for a drink together on their own, always with colleagues. The only time they were alone was in the office. But the truth was she knew she liked Will. Liked him very much. Fancied him like crazy, in fact.

She looked at her watch. Five minutes before her encounter with Comedy Bypass. She pulled her make-up bag out and did a quick check. *Hallelujah, praise the Lord for cosmetics*, she thought as she registered that, despite having the hangover from hell, she didn't look too bad all things considered, though her green eyes had a slightly world-weary air about them. Carmen had never been a woman for the natural look. She had decided aged eighteen that she would never leave the house without lipstick. She had worked her way through a rainbow of colours before deciding her favourite was red, or, to give it its proper name, Fire by Chanel. With the red lipstick she wore black eyeliner and lashings of mascara. She loved make-up, loved its transforming powers, loved the feeling that she could look like someone different today.

Right now she really was wishing she could *be* someone different as she made her way along the corridor to Tiana's office – say Lara Croft, who wouldn't be intimidated by a passive-aggressive executive, although the leather catsuit would probably not be such a good look for size-twelve Carmen, making her more porn star than action heroine. Will was on the phone when she walked past him, but he gave her the thumbs up.

Trish was on duty outside Tiana's office, typing away at her computer. Carmen adored Trish. In her late twenties, she was a beautiful Ghanaian woman with the kindest, sweetest nature. The window ledge and filing cabinets surrounding her were covered in brightly coloured pots containing cacti of every shape and size – fleshy, star-shaped cacti, pointy cacti like the ones you always saw in westerns, and small, ball-shaped cacti, which looked furry rather than spiky. It was safe to say that Trish loved cacti.

She gave her warmest smile when she saw Carmen, and Carmen caught a waft of uplifting geranium – Trish was a great believer in essential oils. 'Hi, she'll be a few minutes.'

Typical mean boss tactic of Tiana to make her wait.

Carmen shrugged. 'You're coming out tonight, aren't you, Trish?'

'Sure am!' she replied, flicking back her long black hair which she'd just had braided. 'Biscuit?' She held out a tin of home-made shortbread. 'Mum made it.'

Carmen shook her head, while Trish popped one into her mouth. She caught Carmen looking at her and said guiltily, 'Yes, I know I said I'd join Weight Watchers, but I've just been so busy organising all the appraisals that I haven't had time.' Trish was always making excuses. She'd been a size eighteen for as long as Carmen had known her, and she was permanently starting diets and abandoning them. The trouble was she still lived at home and her mum was forever feeding her comfort food.

'Trish, I'm not judging you, but you did say you really wanted to this time. I'll come with you to the sessions if you can find one near here.'

'Okay, thanks. I would appreciate that, Carmen, though are you sure you won't get lynched for being a size zero?'

'I'm a size twelve, Trish.'

'Oh, it's just that you all seem so skinny to me.' Trish looked sadly at her magnificent, ample figure which was threatening to spill out of the black wrap dress. At that moment her phone gave a single ring.

'She's ready for you. Have a quick whiff of this, it's supposed to help you centre yourself.' She thrust a small vial of tea tree, menthol and eucalyptus under Carmen's nose, which smelt so strong it made Carmen's eyes water. Damn it! She would look as if she was crying before Tiana even got started on her.

Tiana's office was at least five times the size of everyone else's, with a pleasant view of London rooftops instead of the yard with bins and a motley crew of pigeons that comprised Carmen's view. Tiana was sitting on one of the lilac leather sofas, looking like the model executive as she tapped daintily away on her BlackBerry. She looked up briefly. 'Hello, Carmen, do take a seat?'

Carmen had quite liked Australian accents until she met Tiana; now she wasn't so sure. On the one hand there was her image of Australians, which tended to be on the clichéd side – happy-go-lucky, maybe a little worried about skin cancer but on the whole saying yes to life while having a barbie and cracking open the beer – and on the other there was Tiana with her passive-aggression. Every time she spoke with that Antipodean lift at the end of her sentences which suggested a question but actually was not, it set Carmen's teeth on edge as much as someone raking their nails down a blackboard.

She sat on the sofa opposite Tiana and shivered. Her boss always had the air con up to the max. Tiana continued tapping away on her BlackBerry. Carmen couldn't recall ever seeing her without it – she was bound to be one of those people who slept with it under their pillow. She tried to cheer herself up by imagining Tiana in the throes of passion with her partner and hearing her BlackBerry ring. Faced with the choice of interrupting the passion or ignoring the call, Carmen reckoned coitus interruptus every time. She looked round the office, taking in the gigantic glass vase of white lilies and the flickering Diptyque candle on the desk, then looked back at her boss.

Tiana had shoulder-length honey-blonde hair which was her pride and joy. Carmen knew from Trish that she had it blow-dried twice a week. Along with the salon-perfect hair, her nails were always immaculately French manicured. She favoured fitted jackets with pencil skirts to show off her trim figure. Navy or black were her preferred colours and she always wore killer heels. Today she was wearing a black suit and a pair of black patent Louboutins. Somehow that iconic red sole which Carmen had always adored looked menacing as Tiana uncrossed and recrossed her legs. She had the sudden image of Tiana walking all over her, the red of the soles mixing with Carmen's blood. Oh God, stress really could do terrible things to a mind.

Tiana finally dragged her eyes from her beloved BlackBerry and gave the briefest of smiles. 'Before we get down to the nitty-gritty, how do you think these past months have been?' Okay, that was a question, so she was allowed her Antipodean lift.

'Well,' Carmen began cautiously, 'I would say that I've really been consolidating my relationship with my clients and finding new projects for them – in TV, radio and live gigs.' She reeled off the names of several of her clients, outlining what work they were doing.

'And what about any new clients?' Okay, she was allowed the lift there as well.

'There are two possibilities. Will is going to see them as well before we make a final decision.'

Tiana looked at her. 'I would have expected more?' Ha, there she went with the spurious question-asking voice. The session went downhill from there. Tiana didn't let up with her criticism of Carmen's performance. She hadn't been proactive or hardworking enough. She was late at least once a fortnight. She seemed to lack direction and drive. Did Carmen realise how many other people there were out there who would jump at the chance to be a comedy agent in the prestigious Fox and Nicholson? This was less an appraisal and more a character assassination. The only way Carmen could stop herself from crying was to recite the lyrics from *West Side Story*'s 'Somewhere' in her head. Beautiful, uplifting words which told her that there was a truth beyond Tiana and her brutal words as she battered relentlessly at Carmen's self-esteem.

'So we'll give it another month, Carmen, and review your performance again. I really need to see an improvement?' Not a question but a command.

Somehow Carmen managed to get up from the sofa and walk out of the office. Her cheeks were flaming with a mixture of mortification, humiliation and resentment. She knew, in spite of Tiana's dressing-down, that she did have some redeeming qualities as an agent. Trish looked at her with concern. She silently held out the tin of shortbread. Carmen took two and crammed them into her mouth. Through the crumbs she managed to mumble, 'Is Matthew in?'

Trish nodded and Carmen knocked on his door and hearing a muttered, 'Enter,' she walked in. Instantly she was assailed by whisky fumes and presented with the sight of Matthew lying stretched out on his battered brown leather sofa. He had resisted a refit to his office, which was messy, full of books and papers, and a million times more welcoming than Tiana's. But it didn't seem so welcoming right now. Matthew was pissed. 'Carmen, lovely to see you! What can I do for you, my angel?'

Carmen had been hoping for an uplifting pep talk but there was no way she was going to get that from

Matthew. His pale blue eyes could barely focus on her. Matthew was sixty-five but looked at least ten years younger. He had a full head of silver-grey hair and his eyes were usually sparkling with mischief, as if he was permanently amused. He must have been a very good-looking man when he was younger, along the lines of the actor Terence Stamp, and he was still striking. Carmen nicknamed him Silver Fox. But he was not looking so good today. His cheeks were flushed and his eyes bloodshot. The silver hair was dishevelled and his purple silk shirt had a large stain on the front.

'Oh, I was just popping by. Are you okay?'

'I'm fine. You must have had your appraisal. I said lovely things about you so hopefully that will have registered with Comedy Bypass. You really are one of my favourite agents. Super agent Miller.' He raised his whisky glass to her.

Carmen didn't have the heart to report that Tiana had failed to say a single favourable thing about her. Matthew seemed such a wreck. He'd always drunk a lot but usually only after work. He also had an emergency supply of alcohol in his office open to anyone who'd had a bad day. It looked as though Matthew had helped himself to the entire stash. Since Fox had taken over, Carmen had noticed that Matthew's alcohol consumption had risen dramatically and he had lost some of his joie de vivre.

'Anyway, I'm just nipping out and wondered if you wanted me to get you anything. A sandwich or a coffee?' Matthew would need an urn of coffee to get sober. She couldn't bear the thought of Tiana seeing him in this state and further sidelining him.

'Thanks, but I'm fine and dandy.'

'Are you going to Will's birthday drinks?'

Matthew shook his head. 'Going to the theatre with Penny – it's her birthday too.' Penny was his wife. Carmen couldn't imagine that Matthew would be capable of going anywhere other than straight to bed. She walked wearily back to her office. Everyone else was out at lunch. She really should sit down and do some work, but she couldn't face it. She grabbed her bag and jacket. There was only one thing for it, a spot of retail therapy to take away the blues. Besides, she needed something to wear tonight, something a little more exciting than jeans and Converses.

Oh, the bliss of walking out of the office and going into shops where assistants were actually nice to you and didn't tell you that you should work harder, that you were a loser and needed to buck up your ideas or else. Swept up on a wave of post-appraisal misery, Carmen ended up in French Connection buying a gorgeous green silk tunic dress, which made her eyes look even more intensely green. And because that was never going to go with her Converses – Agyness Deyn she was not – it inspired the purchase of a pair of patent shoe boots from Kurt Geiger. All better now, she thought, as she returned to the office and managed to sneak in without anyone seeing her. Tomorrow's another day and all that. She would work hard the next day, take on board Tiana's harsh words, but today she was too tired, she just needed to sit quietly and decide what to do about Will.

Speaking of the devil, Will knocked on her window and wandered in. 'How did the appraisal go? Were you pleased with all the nice things I said about you? How creative you are and good with clients, even the ones who suffer from arachnophobia?'

'You are joking! I didn't receive a single shred of praise or constructive criticism. It was like being in the water with a pack of piranhas and having your flesh ripped off. I had to go out and spend money to try and make myself feel better, which I know is a stupid, shallow, girlie thing to do. It was either that or score some blow off Connor, which as I hate blow and I don't want to give Connor any ideas, was never an option. I haven't recovered from last Christmas when I had to kiss him – he used his tongue and everything.'

Will frowned. 'But when I filled in your three-hundred-and-sixty-degree appraisal I said really positive things.'

A 360-degree appraisal was when colleagues were asked to comment on each other – another of Fox's innovations, something else which Carmen loathed. The whole 360 bit just reminded her of the scene in *The Exorcist* when Regan the devil child spins her head round and spits out something very rude, which maybe wasn't the intention behind the scheme.

'Do you want me to have a word with Tiana?' Will continued.

Carmen shook her head. 'I don't know, I can't think straight right now. Maybe when I see what she's written I could show it to you and you can let me know what you think. Maybe I am just a work-shy loser.'

'Miller, pull yourself together. It's the alcohol slump, you're getting depressed. Quick, have a Wobbly Worm, or better still,' he looked at his watch, 'in two hours' time I will buy you the largest vodka the Ship can provide.'

'Thanks, but you're the birthday boy, *I'll* buy *you* a drink.'

Will was about to leave when his eye fell on the carrier bags propped up against Carmen's desk. 'Ahh, I'll have to get out the muttonometer.'

The muttonometer had been devised by Will practically in the first week of meeting Carmen when he discovered her penchant for lunchtime clothes shopping. After one particular spree she'd come back with what could only be described as mutton fodder – a zebra print tee-shirt dress, suitable for fifteen-year-olds, some ill-advised wet-look leggings which had gone straight back, and a pair of tiny denim shorts. Carmen had a fantasy of wearing them with bare golden brown legs, a white shirt and havaianas, and drifting about like Jennifer Aniston, sipping a skinny latte. In reality she could only wear the shorts with black tights and very high heels, so it was less about dressed-down easy chic and more about looking like a ho.

Will reached for the French Connection bag and carefully unwrapped the layers of white tissue paper to reveal the silk dress. There was something deliciously sexy about Will handling the dress. A vivid image popped into Carmen's head of Will slipping it off her body. Steady on.

'Come here, Miller, I have to see it against you.'

'Aren't you going to say, if I said you had a beautiful body would you hold it against me?' She couldn't resist coming out with it.

'No, because that would be corny.' Will looked away as he added, 'But you do have a beautiful body.' And just as Carmen was about to exclaim that was the nicest thing he'd ever said to her, Will qualified it with, 'For a thirty-three-year-old.'

Carmen stomped over to where he was standing, grabbed his hair and pushed it back from his forehead, trying to detect a receding hairline. 'Yeah, well, you might lose your hair one day.' It was a very intimate gesture, probably the most intimate she had ever made with him. They were standing so close that she got a blast of his Jo Malone Amber and Lavender cologne which had long been a favourite of hers. And she could feel the heat from his body. For a second they held each other's gaze.

'You'd still love me if I was bald,' Will finally said.

'I wouldn't count on it,' Carmen shot back. 'I only tolerate you as it is.'

Phew! There were so many pheromones whizzing about she was surprised the glass walls didn't steam up. She let go of his hair and Will instantly smoothed it back.

'Okay, shoes next,' he ordered and Carmen opened the box to reveal the shoe boots. Even she couldn't help smiling as she saw them. Will was suitably impressed. 'No mutton for a change. So is this my birthday treat, seeing you in all this?'

'This is to cheer *me* up after Tiana's vicious savaging.'

Will frowned and looked sympathetic. 'I really will speak to her if you want. Yes, your timekeeping is not great and you have got those mutton tendencies, but you're a good agent – all the clients love you, and apparently so does Connor.' He paused. 'Did you really kiss him?' There it was again, a slight, almost imperceptible flash of jealousy.

'He kissed me. I had no say in the matter.'

'I bet he waxes his chest. He's good-looking, I suppose, in an obvious, *Hollyoaks* sort of way.'

'If you like eighteen-year-olds. Now be gone, birthday boy, I have to at least go through the motions of doing some work before I leave in two hours.'

Incredibly, after that Carmen actually managed to confirm two of her clients as guests on a TV comedy quiz show and read a script another client had written. Incredibly, because Will's flirtatious banter seemed to have gone up a gear and Carmen was having a hard time thinking of any reason why tonight should not indeed be the night that she got it together with him.

2

Everyone else had already left for the Ship before Carmen finally made her way to the Ladies to get ready, which was just as well, as she didn't think she was up to Lottie, Trish and Daisy doing their will-she-won't-she-do-Will speculations in her face. She was actually running nearly an hour late, because just as she was about to leave, her good friend Marcus had phoned and they'd spent a while catching up. Still, late was good, it showed that she wasn't too keen. The Ladies had also had a makeover with Fox's takeover and now every time someone walked in, or so it seemed to Carmen, the automatic air freshener dispenser squirted out poisonous chemicals, which were supposed to smell like spring flowers. *Spring after a nuclear winter*, Carmen always thought; she loathed the smell. She eyeballed the white machine, where it clung to the wall like a malevolent albino bat as she set out her make-up by the mirror. 'Don't you dare do it!' she exclaimed out loud. Silence from the dispenser. Carmen began reapplying eyeliner and was congratulating herself on having escaped the evil squirter when it let out a particularly noxious blast. 'I'm wearing Tom Ford! Enough already of your putrid smells, you vile machine!' she

31

shouted, just as Tiana pushed the door of one of the cubicles and trit-trotted out, her Louboutins clicking emphatically against the tiled floor.

'Everything alright, Carmen?' Tiana asked.

'Fine,' Carmen blustered. 'I was just going over some lines one of my comics sent me, I wanted to see how they sounded out loud.'

'That's good then?' Tiana replied, with her spurious question-asking voice, looking at Carmen as if she should be sectioned, before washing her hands and trit-trotting out.

A large vodka now seemed like the only possible answer to the day. Carmen rallied slightly as she took off her jeans and tee-shirt and slipped into a pair of black twenty-denier tights – so forgiving to the legs – the silk dress and the shoe boots. *My career might be on the verge of imploding but I can still rock a silk tunic dress*, she thought, as she swept out of the office and headed towards the Ship.

There were many pubs and bars to choose from around work, but somehow everyone – with the exception of Tiana, who didn't drink and never socialised with colleagues – invariably gravitated to the Ship, a resolutely old-fashioned London pub, with lots of dark wood panelling and a faded, swirly mustard and green carpet which seemed to mourn the days of smoking. In fact, even though Carmen didn't smoke she quite mourned it too, as at least the nicotine had the effect of blocking out other unsavoury odours. The Ship was mainly staffed by Australians who were the Antipodean antithesis of Tiana, being mostly cheery, friendly and seeming to have no real concerns other than what country they were going to visit next. Desi, a bubbly girl, with a big black bow in her hair, not unlike Minnie Mouse, was working at the upstairs bar. She waved to Carmen and pointed at the far corner where Will and the gang were sitting in their usual spot. As she walked over Carmen was aware that butterflies had taken up residence in her stomach at the prospect of seeing Will. *It doesn't mean anything*, she tried to tell herself, but as she drew closer to Will those butterflies really went for it.

He was sitting on the sofa next to Lottie and Trish, opposite Daisy and two other agents. One was Dirty Sam, who rumour had it had been caught being orally pleasured on the fire exit by the girlfriend of one of Dirty Sam's comics. Sam was in his late twenties, cute in a laddish way with spiky brown hair and a cheeky grin, though after finding out about the fire exit incident Carmen had never found him cute again. Sam had once fancied himself as a stand-up, but it hadn't gone well, and so he had become an agent. Next to him was Lovely Christina, who was in her mid-fifties but could pass for considerably younger on account of her beautiful peachy skin. She represented actors and could out-luvvie the best of them.

'I was going to ask if you wanted a drink, but you look as if you're okay,' Carmen said, clocking the three pints in front of Will.

He looked up at her. 'Took your time, Miller. Were you canoodling with Connor?'

'With who?' Dirty Sam always wanted every salacious detail of every encounter.

Carmen wrinkled her nose, wondering what he was on about, then remembered she had told him about the kiss with the postboy. 'Don't be daft, I was getting changed. You like?' She did a quick spin around.

Lottie gave a wolf whistle, Dirty Sam leered at her breasts, Christina called out, 'Fabulous, darling,' and Will gave her the thumbs up. A slightly wobbly pair of thumbs, it had to be said. Carmen realised that Will was already a little drunk.

Lottie stood up. 'Sit down, Carmen, I'll get you a drink, sounds as if you need one after the appraisal.' This was blatantly part of Lottie's cunning plan to get her and Will together but Carmen sat down anyway. What she hadn't bargained for was how close she would be sitting to Will. She was practically on his lap as Trish, on the other side, was taking up a considerable portion of the sofa.

'It's a gorgeous dress, Carmen,' Will said softly in her ear.

'Thank you,' she replied, they were sitting so close that she could see how his eyes weren't light blue throughout as she'd always thought but had a dark indigo ring round the iris. So close that she could see the dark stubble on his face. 'So how much have you had to drink?'

'I had a couple of shots and pints. Desi and the guys had them lined up when I walked in, and it would have been rude not to. But I'm not pissed. I'm ready for whatever you've got planned for me tonight.' And he winked.

'You *so* are pissed!' Carmen exclaimed, delighting in the fact that for once she had the upper hand, being sober.

'Get this down you, princess.' Lottie handed her a double vodka and tonic.

'Why, thank you, Lottie, but you know how rarely I allow alcohol to pass my lips.'

'You don't mind kissing Connor though, do you?' Will put in.

Lottie sat down at the table and immediately began a conversation with Trish, Daisy, Dirty Sam and Lovely Christina. She might as well wave a banner saying *I am trying to get Will and Carmen to get off with each other* and be done with it!

'What is this fixation about Connor? It was one kiss, one time, forced upon me!'

Will took a long drink from his pint before replying, 'So what kind of kisser was he?'

'Bad.'

'What's bad?' Will demanded. They were shoulder to shoulder, thigh to thigh. The butterflies were multiplying.

'It's bad you've got to ask. Don't you know what a bad kiss is?'

'Course, I was just checking, but tell me anyway.'

Carmen sipped her vodka. 'It's all teeth and tongue and too much saliva.' She gave a mock shudder. 'Though in fairness Connor wasn't such a bad kisser as Sean Maxwell.' Sean was a stand-up comic whom she'd ended up kissing after one of his gigs.

'You kissed Sean Maxwell! Did you have a thing with him? God, Carmen, he's slept with everyone!' Will actually sounded quite heated.

'I did not have a thing with him! I snogged him one night just after I separated from my husband. A never-to-be-repeated mistake – I've had more sensual oral experiences at the hygienist. He was a sucker.'

Will looked slightly more appeased. 'So aren't you going to tell me what a good kiss is?'

Carmen put her head to one side and without thinking clearly came out with, 'That's easy, a good kiss makes you want to go straight to bed.' What had made her say that? She blamed the hangover, blamed the appraisal, blamed Will sitting so close to her. Blamed the fact that she hadn't had sex for nine months.

She reached for her drink again to avoid looking at Will, but he wasn't going to be put off now. 'Perhaps you can show me later,' he whispered in her ear, nearly causing Carmen to drop her drink.

This was going beyond their usual flirtation and Carmen suspected she was supposed to come back with something equally smouldering but instead she squeaked out, 'Hey, Lottie, when we are eating? I'm starving!' Food was the last thing on her mind but she had to say something to break the spell.

Lottie looked at her watch. 'I've booked the table for eight. Drink up.'

On the way to the restaurant Lottie once again organised everyone so they were walking ahead of Will and Carmen. Honestly! The woman was unstoppable in her mission, the matchmaking equivalent of a Panzer tank.

'So, is there anyone else I should know about who you've kissed?' Will asked, going back to dangerous territory.

'I never kiss and tell,' Carmen batted back. 'Well, except about Connor and Sean. But no, Will, I haven't seen anyone since I split up with my husband. I'm thinking of entering a nunnery so long as I can shop, drink wine, read *Grazia* and see my friends – oh, hang on, that *is* my life!'

'Was it an acrimonious split?' Will stumbled over acrimonious – he was definitely on the wrong side of sober.

'Well, I wouldn't exactly say it was amicable, though we get on okay now, so long as we don't see each other.' Carmen would rather talk about kissing Connor than her failed marriage. That was like opening the chamber of secrets and she really didn't want to go there. There would be no good outcome, no happy ever after.

Usually Will never asked such personal questions, but alcohol had clearly liberated him from his usual caution and his next question completely floored Carmen: 'So why did you split up?'

37

For a moment she was speechless, then she said quietly, 'I know we have this banter thing between us where we laugh at each other and flirt, but I can't talk about this. Really, cannot talk about it.' She was genuinely rattled now, the fizz of lust replaced with the all-too-familiar feeling of bitter anguish.

Will seemed to realise he'd overstepped a line. He lightly touched her arm. 'Sorry, Carmen.' He was serious for once, looking at her intently. 'I guess I want us to move beyond our banter.'

Just a few minutes ago Carmen would have said exactly the same, but right now his questions about her marriage had made her clam up, fold in on herself. 'Sure,' she said curtly. 'Let's catch up with the others. I don't want Dirty Sam speculating about what we're up to.' And she walked briskly towards her friends.

Rico's restaurant was downstairs from the café. It was small with just ten tables, decked out with red-and-white tablecloths. Italian flags adorned the walls, along with black-and-white photographs of Sophia Loren and various players from AC Milan. It was unpretentious and the food was delicious. Mamma Mia adored Will and in his honour had decorated the entire restaurant with balloons. There was even a silver-and-blue banner emblazoned with 'Happy birthday, Will!' over the door. As soon as she saw him she enfolded him in a great bear hug, nearly smothering him with her formidable bosom. 'Happy birthday, my darling boy!'

Carmen smiled as she watched Mamma Mia fuss

over Will, demanding that he order the most expensive items off the menu and insisting on pouring him a very generous glass of Barolo. Carmen had foiled Lottie's plan to have her next to Will by sitting at the opposite end of the table to him, next to Trish and Lottie. She felt subdued and barely ate any of her penne arrabbiata, though she knew she risked incurring the wrath of Mamma Mia who would demand to know why she hadn't finished her signature dish. Every now and then she would catch Will looking at her and she could tell he was wondering what had happened to flirty Carmen.

'What's the matter?' Lottie whispered, while Will's attention was taken up with Dirty Sam recounting his recent trip to a lap-dancing club, which he claimed was for research for one of his clients. No one believed him.

'Nothing,' Carmen muttered. 'Just the appraisal. It was really awful, Lottie.' This was only partly a lie – the appraisal *had* been awful, it was just that the marriage question had been worse.

'Forget about it!' Lottie urged her, then checked Will wasn't looking over as she added, 'Will really likes you, Carmen. He spent the whole time we were in the Ship wondering where you were and then his face lit up when he saw you.'

'"His face lit up"! Lottie, have you got a night job writing for Mills & Boon?'

'Well, it's classier than saying he's got the horn for you, isn't it?' Lottie demanded.

'Though he has as well, like a massive—'

'Lottie!' Carmen cut in. 'You're not supposed to know about such things, let alone talk about them!'

Lottie shrugged. 'I can still appreciate the male form objectively, and I imagine Will has a very fine male form.'

'What are you talking about?' Will demanded from across the table. Mamma Mia was continuing to pour Barolo into his glass as if it was Ribena.

'Your member, actually.' Carmen couldn't resist it. It was too perfect a comedy moment, even sunk into a decline as she was.

She got a disconcerted look from Will in return.

'Lottie reckons you've got a fine one. And yes, I know it sounds as if we're objectifying men, but she started it. And as she's gay I think she's probably allowed to.'

Dirty Sam had been eyeing up a female diner on another table, but he pricked up his ears. Any whiff of talk about sex and he was in like a Jack Russell down a foxhole. 'What did you think of mine, then?'

'Sorry, we didn't get that far,' Carmen replied, regretting her cocky comment if it was going to get Dirty Sam all excited.

'Well, we could do a comparison now.' He took a quick look round the restaurant. 'Come on, Will, stand up. I reckon I could take you any time.'

This was precisely why Carmen usually avoided going anywhere with Dirty Sam where alcohol was served, because when drunk he invariably wanted to drop his trousers. His hand was actually on his fly right now. Carmen put her head in her hands, but before Dirty

Sam could flash the room, Mamma Mia appeared and said in a booming voice, 'Samuel, sit down and don't even think about what you were about to do if you *ever* want to come into my restaurant again. And that includes the café. There will be no more bacon butties for you.'

Suitably chastened, Samuel sat down. But as soon as Mamma Mia was out of earshot he said, 'Mine's bigger than Will's, I swear.'

Everyone ignored him and started talking about Lottie's recent trip to Goa.

A few minutes later the lights dimmed and an expectant hush fell in the restaurant. On cue Mamma Mia walked across the room, stately as a galleon, bearing a chocolate birthday cake blazing with candles and sparklers, and everyone burst into a raucous rendition of 'Happy Birthday'. Will looked faintly mortified but still made a big show of blowing out the candles and giving Mamma Mia yet another hug and a kiss.

'So, what did you wish for?' Lottie asked him, just after he had cut into the cake.

'He can't tell you!' Trish exclaimed in genuine outrage. 'Or it won't come true.'

Carmen smiled at Trish and as she did so caught Will looking at her – a searching look, and one that she couldn't hold right now.

Mamma Mia insisted everyone have a glass of Strega on the house. It was a strong Italian liqueur and an acquired taste in Carmen's opinion – on a par with glugging a glass of petrol – but no one wanted to risk

41

upsetting Mamma Mia, so they all raised a glass to her and knocked it back.

At midnight Lottie took charge of asking for the bill, overruling Will's comment that he should pay, even though Dirty Sam, who was mean as well as filthy, perked up at the suggestion. Then, with a few last hugs from Mamma Mia, the party were out in the cool September air where, in one last, desperate match-making act, Lottie corralled the others, leaving Carmen and Will alone, and practically frogmarched them towards Oxford Street before anyone could protest.

Carmen made to follow them, but Will put his hand on her shoulder. 'Stay with me a minute. I want to talk to you. I really didn't mean to upset you earlier.'

'You didn't, it's fine,' Carmen lied.

'I don't believe you, but I think you're not going to tell me.' He put his other hand on her other shoulder. 'You know, there was one thing you forgot to do today.'

Carmen looked blank.

He drew her closer. 'You forgot to give me a birthday kiss. I've had one from Trish, Lottie, Christina, and even Daisy kissed me, and you know how she feels about physical contact; I've had about twenty-five from Mamma Mia, but not a single one from you. And you're the only person I've wanted to kiss all day.'

Wow! Even in her present state of decline Carmen was not immune to such a comment – her stomach went into free fall and the hyperactive butterflies started flapping again. Despite this, she checked her watch, desperately trying to play it cool. 'It's not your birthday any more.'

'You're so picky, Miller, but you're not going to get away with it. I demand my birthday kiss.' And before she could stop him he had steered her into the doorway of Ryman's, which wasn't the most romantic location ever, unless you had a fetish for office stationery, but it didn't matter, as there in the soft blue glow of the lights he took her in his arms and kissed her. And it was a very good kiss. A firm, sexy kiss that demanded the same response back. A kiss that almost made Carmen forget all the horrible things about the day – and oh, how she wanted to. But the chamber had been opened, some of the bad stuff had leaked out and she couldn't ignore it.

'That was a good kiss,' Will murmured. 'D'you know where I want to go now?'

Carmen shook her head and stepped out of his arms.

'So you think that was a bad kiss!' Will exclaimed.

'It was a good kiss, but here's where it ends tonight.' And in a very rare moment of serendipity, because usually it took her ages to get a cab, Carmen saw a black cab hurtling down Great Portland Street with its light on and she successfully hailed it. Retreat was essential now.

3

Mamma Mia clearly didn't need much sleep, as she was at her place by the till at quarter past nine when Carmen walked into Rico's the following morning. At least she wasn't hungover, but her head was all over the place as she struggled to process the events of last night, specifically *that kiss*. That kiss that burned into her consciousness; it had been so beguiling, so enticing. So, so sweet. That kiss threatened to be her undoing.

'*Ciao*, Carmen,' Mamma Mia greeted her, then made a big deal of looking around. It didn't take rocket science to work out the meaning of the look.

'Will's not with me, Carla,' Carmen replied. Ignoring the curiosity on Mamma Mia's face, she turned to Rico and placed her usual order. She was just about to leave the café when Mamma Mia appeared beside her – for someone so large she could certainly move quickly and stealthily when she wanted.

'Carmen, you must realise that Will is in love with you,' she declared theatrically. 'I know it as clearly as if he had told me. I feel it here,' at this she planted her plump hand over her heart. Perhaps Mamma Mia was still drunk from all the Strega she'd consumed the night before.

Carmen tried not to show how surprised she was. 'We've just got a flirtation going on, an office romance.'

Mamma Mia shook her head emphatically. 'You feel it too, I know you do. You felt it when you kissed him last night, under the blue lights.'

OMG, Mamma Mia really was psychic! Carmen looked at her in awe but Rico piped up from behind the counter, 'She saw you on the CCTV monitors last night. We've got them in the office as part of the neighbourhood watch scheme. We can pretty much see the whole of Great Portland Street.'

Never mind Big Brother watching you, it was Big Mamma!

Carmen raised an eyebrow, then simply said, '*Ciao*,' and marched purposefully out of the café. She slowed as soon as she was a little way down the street, suddenly feeling incredibly nervous about seeing Will again. The butterflies were up to their old tricks.

Daisy did an unsubtle double take when she saw Carmen walk into the foyer alone. 'We did *not* spend the night together, Daisy. Will you please let everyone know?' Carmen said as she walked past her.

'As if I ever pass on gossip!' Daisy said in outrage. Carmen glared at her, but Daisy was now taking a call. 'Good morning, Fox Nicholson, how can I help you?' she said in a sing-song, insincere voice (subtext: *Why don't you just fuck off and leave me alone to play on* Grand Theft Auto?)

Carmen took the lift, and as she got out at her floor

and tried to walk nonchalantly towards her office she felt as if she had a large sign pinned to her back: 'I kissed Will and I liked it!' Her nervousness increased as she drew near his office and she steeled herself for the encounter. But Will wasn't there. *Damn*! It would have been better to get seeing him out of the way sooner rather than later, otherwise she was bound to obsess about it all day.

She sat down and switched on her MacBook, but there was no chance of any peace as one by one Lottie, Christina and Trish all found excuses to troop into her office and interrogate her. Dirty Sam was the last to just happen by. 'So, good night, Carmen?' he said, leaning against her door frame.

Carmen tried to fob him off. 'It was great, wasn't it? Mamma Mia does a mean penne arrabbiata, doesn't she?'

Dirty Sam was not to be deflected. 'Will seemed to have a good time didn't he?'

'You'll have to ask him.'

'Well, I thought you might know after last night. Did the birthday boy get his wish?'

'I don't know what you're talking about.'

'I think you do, Carmen. Come on, give it up for Sam.'

He was insufferable! Carmen shook her head. 'No idea.' But then, as Dirty Sam was about to head off, she called out, 'Oh, for God's sake, Sam, I kissed him but that was it. I didn't sleep with him, so can you please tell everyone so I can get on with some bloody work?'

'Didn't sleep with whom?' Matthew wandered into her office.

'Oh, Matthew, not you as well! Will, I didn't sleep with Will Hunter, okay?' She had raised her voice. Probably the entire corridor had heard her.

'Well, that seems to have cleared that up, doesn't it?' Matthew said drily. He looked especially dapper today in a navy-blue pinstripe three-piece suit, complete with a violet orchid buttonhole. He always wore a suit, but this seemed extra smart.

'Let's forget I said that,' Carmen groaned. 'Anyway, you look particularly lovely. Is someone getting married? Are you being presented with an award for being such a super-fantastic silver fox agent?'

Matthew gave a wry smile. 'Not exactly.' He paused and adjusted the buttonhole. 'I wanted to let you know before the management meeting, where I'll announce it formally, that I'm resigning. This is my farewell-cruel-world suit.'

Carmen looked at Matthew in total astonishment. He loved his job, loved the company, which he'd founded. It was his life. 'Why on earth are you doing that? You're too old for a midlife crisis!'

'I suppose I should take that last comment as a kind of backhanded compliment,' Matthew replied, folding his long, thin body into the chair opposite Carmen's desk. 'It's time for me to go, Carmen; I can't fit in with these new people. Penny's online furniture business is going well and we're lucky to have a fairly decent pension. I'd like to leave while I still have fond

47

memories of the company. I simply can't go on like this, with Tiana on my back every two minutes, wanting to know about figures. It's all spreadsheets this, projections that, it's sucking the life blood out of me. I've been drinking too much, you must have noticed.'

Carmen thought back to the day before, when Matthew had been lying drunk on his sofa, and it wasn't the first time that she'd gone to his office and discovered that he was half-cut. In spite of the dapper suit, Matthew looked exhausted, a man at the end of the line, with huge bags under his eyes that a small hamster could have cheerfully slept in.

Carmen gave a heartfelt sigh. The thought of work without Matthew's wit, kindness and emergency bottle of red wine was a deeply unattractive one. How much longer could she go on herself? She knew she wasn't ruthless enough to be a really successful agent, but Matthew had always protected her, seeing other qualities in her. However, on the basis of her appraisal, Tiana saw the lack of ruthlessness as a weakness and a failing.

'What will you do?' Carmen asked. 'You *promise* you won't drink yourself to death?'

Matthew made the cub scout salute. 'I promise. I'm actually going to finally pull my finger out and write a novel. I've only been thinking about it for the last thirty years. Procrastination is my middle name. And I'm going to be on your case, demanding to see the next episode of your sitcom. I love what I've read so far.

You're a really good comic writer, with a great ear for dialogue and brilliant grasp of character. Don't let this place bleed you dry.'

At this, Trish poked her head round the door, blasting the room with geranium. 'Sorry, guys, the meeting's about to begin and Tiana has asked me to get everyone together.'

Matthew stood and held himself straight up to his impressive full height of six foot three. 'Those who are about to die salute you,' he said ironically, raising his hand.

'I'd have felt a whole lot better if you'd said, "At my command unleash hell",' she replied, as they both began walking towards the boardroom.

'We can't all be Russell Crowe in *Gladiator*, Carmen. I would look bloody awful in a leather miniskirt.'

At the mention of Russell, Carmen got a dreamy look in her eye; she did have a thing about the actor. Then she pulled herself together. 'I don't know,' she said, surveying Matthew's long legs. 'There's probably a niche market for spindly-legged men in leather skirts. I can google it later if you like.'

Carmen was sure it was entirely deliberate that Tiana was sitting on one side of the vast, glass-topped table coolly looking out at all her employees. Will, as her deputy, was sitting at her right. Carmen suddenly felt shy. He caught her eye and gave the briefest of smiles before looking down at his notes. Maybe he felt embarrassed about last night. To hide her discomfort, Carmen joked to Trish, 'Do you think she's going to do a "Suralan" and tell us we're fired?'

Trish glanced at her and smiled. 'No way, you look too smart to fire today.'

They both considered Carmen's pearl-grey fitted shift dress and shoe boots – after the casual look yesterday, she'd thought she'd better pull her finger out style-wise. 'But I'm sure she'd like to,' she muttered back. Trish, usually so positive about everyone, had nothing good to say about Tiana.

Matthew took his place next to Tiana. The mischief was entirely missing from his eyes. Tiana gave him a tight little smile and then launched into her speech.

'Thank you all for coming here?' The Antipodean lift was in full swing. 'I won't take up too much of your valuable time, I know how busy everyone is, but I have a special announcement?' She looked round the room, making sure she had the full attention of the twenty or so people there. 'Matthew has decided to step down as deputy director of the company.'

There was an immediate mass intake of breath and exclamations of 'No way!'. Clearly Matthew had only told a select few.

'You can't leave!' Trish wailed. 'You *are* Fox Nicholson!'

'Hear hear,' came a chorus. But not from Tiana or Will, it had to be said. Carmen shot him a WTF look which he ignored. He was doing his bland corporate, expressionless act, and he was rather too good at it for Carmen's liking.

Matthew smiled. 'Thanks, but it's time for me to take a bow. I've worked in this business for over twenty-five years and really you can't teach an old dog new tricks. I can't help wanting things to be the way they were, and that's just not helpful to the company right now. But I love all of you and hope you're going to stay in touch. I might even join Facebook.' At this there was an audible chuckle from the room, as Matthew was a notorious technophobe and had only just got a mobile phone, and he detested using email. He was so dignified and courteous and such an all-round lovely person, Carmen could feel tears prickle her eyes, and she knew she wasn't alone as she scanned the room and saw the expressions of shock on her colleagues' faces.

'Anyway,' Matthew continued, 'I want to go with a bang and not a whimper, so I'm having a party at home at the weekend. You're all invited.' Matthew's parties at his house in the leafy suburb of Thames Ditton which overlooked the river had been wild annual events that usually took most of the office at least a week to recover from.

'Speech!' Lottie piped up, beating Carmen to it.

Matthew shook his head. 'Not here, Lottie, I'll do it at home.' Matthew's hatred of the boardroom was also legendary. It had used to be a cosy, shambolic room with a large wooden table and mismatched chairs, until it too had undergone a makeover and all the furniture had been swept out and replaced with the impersonal glass-topped table and black leather and chrome chairs, which were desperately uncomfortable.

After a few more platitudes from Tiana about how much Matthew would be missed, everyone shuffled out of the room and slunk back to their offices.

Carmen wanted to ask Will if he'd known about Matthew, but he was deep in conversation with Tiana. *Traitor*, she thought savagely, and stomped out of the boardroom. Yet again as she sat down at her desk it was impossible to work. There were too many thoughts swirling around her mind for her to concentrate on what she should have been doing, which was to prepare for the meeting with Karl Fraser. After some ten minutes she couldn't resist the impulse to see Will any longer. She just had to find out if he had known about Matthew.

He was in his office this time, busy writing something at his computer. He radiated stress and seemed a million miles from the Will who had kissed her last night, but Carmen ploughed on regardless. 'That was nice of you to speak out for Matthew at the meeting,' she said sarcastically. 'Did you know he was leaving?'

Will looked up. He seemed pretty annoyed at her tone. 'Yes, I knew, and what was I supposed to say? I've only known the man three months and I am Tiana's deputy. She's the one who gets to make the speeches.'

Carmen scuffed her shoe boot on the wooden floor, deliberately making an irritating squeaky noise. 'I just think you could have said *something*. Matthew founded this company, people are going to be really sad to see him go. *I'm* really sad to see him go.'

Will pushed his hair back. He seemed distracted and there wasn't a smidgen of flirtation. Carmen was starting to feel distinctly awkward about last night. Maybe Will had lied when he'd said it was a good kiss, maybe he thought it was a terrible kiss and was now trying to put as much distance between them as possible.

'I know you're upset about Matthew and I'm sorry, but there's nothing I can do about it. Anyway, I've got to get on, I have a meeting to prepare for.'

Carmen felt horribly rejected. 'Yeah, well, so have I,' she said defensively.

'Like flirt with the postboy?' Will asked, a slight twitch to his mouth.

Okay, so that was a slight improvement. 'No, like see that fuckwit Karl Fraser.'

'Look, if he gives you a really hard time, you can always refer him to me.'

It was actually a sweet thing to say, but Carmen couldn't help feeling patronised. 'No, no, I can handle him. Anyway, must get on.'

'Laters, Miller,' Will called after her, adding, 'I really am sorry about Matthew. And liking the dress — rock that sexy governess look.'

Will's flirty comment could not dispel Carmen's feeling of gloom as she slouched back to her office. She couldn't face the prospect of work, all those emails to follow up, all those calls to make extolling the virtues of her clients, trying to screw out the best deal for them. It all seemed pointless. Instead she sat at her computer and clicked through photographs of the last time she reckoned she'd really felt happy – on holiday over two years ago on the Greek island of Zakynthos with Nick. There they were beaming away on one of the beautiful beaches, blissfully unaware that a year later they would have split up.

'Oh God,' she said out loud, drinking in the brilliantly blue sea and the radiant happiness. Just then her mobile rang. It was Nick.

'That's a coincidence,' she told him. 'I was looking at pictures of us.'

There was a pause, during which Carmen could detect Nick's unease at the mention of the word 'us'. 'No, no, I'm not harbouring thoughts of getting back with you, it was just to see Greece – you know how I feel about it.' Carmen loved Greece – the sky, the clear seas, the smells, the people, the heat, the cicadas, the sunsets – she had to go there at least once a year or suffered withdrawal. 'My soul needed a shot of happiness. Matthew's just resigned and I'm due to see fuckwit Karl and you know how much I detest him.'

She expected Nick to launch into some expletives of his own – he too loathed Karl – but none came. 'I wanted to see you, Carmen, but I've got to fly out to Germany tonight for the tour and there's no other time, and I really didn't want you to find out from anyone else.'

Suddenly Carmen was on high alert. She and Nick had promised to do the two-year separation and then divorce – both hoped it would be less acrimonious, less painful, and after all, it wasn't as if they didn't still care for each other, if not as lovers then as friends. 'You don't want to get married already, do you?' she asked accusingly. For the last four months Nick had been seeing Marian, a French hairstylist he had met at one of his gigs, but Carmen hadn't realised it was serious.

'No, it's not that.' Nick had his uptight, you're not-going-to-like-this voice on. 'Oh God, Carmen, I'm really sorry to do this to you. Marian is pregnant.'

'Oh' was all she could manage. Dropping the phone, Carmen lunged across the office and retched into the bin. She could hear Nick calling her name. 'Sorry,' she wanted to say in that disembodied voice you hear when you get someone's voicemail, 'the person you are calling is unavailable, please try later.' Nick's calls grew more urgent. She staggered back to the chair and picked up the phone.

'I'm sorry, Carmen, really sorry, I know how this must feel to you, really I do, even though you must think I'm the most insensitive bastard in the world.'

'When's the baby due?' Carmen didn't know why she asked this – it would only pain her further.

'The eighth of March or around then,' Nick reluctantly replied.

'So Marian must have got pregnant practically straight away?' Oh, the bitter, bitter irony after all that trying with Nick, when sex became the last thing in the world you wanted to do but you forced yourself, for a baby that was never going to happen.

'Something like that.' Another reluctant reply. 'Anyway, take care, let's speak properly when I get back.' Nick spoke in a rush, so quickly she couldn't have got another word in even if she'd wanted to. Poor Nick, the bearer of what would be to anyone else the best news in the world, no wonder he wanted to get off the phone.

Carmen very carefully clicked the hang-up button on her mobile and put it on her desk. She felt as if she might shatter at any moment. Shock pulsed through her. Nick was having a baby. She struggled to take in the news. But then again, how could she not have seen this coming? It was, after all, the whole children thing, or rather her not being able to have them, that had done for her marriage. Unexplained infertility, *her* unexplained infertility, the doctors called it. Two years of trying and then a year and a half with three cycles of IVF later the couple were broken financially and emotionally. They had not pulled together in the crisis, as she had hoped, they had been driven apart – Nick straight into the arms of another woman, Carmen into the arms of despair. She suddenly had a pounding headache. *Oh my God, on top of everything else, I've probably got a tumour*, she thought grimly. *Still, at least I've spared my children the sight of me dying young. Always look on the bright side and everything.*

She picked up her bag. There was absolutely no way she could stay at work now. She had to get away, somewhere she could give vent to the pain. Her office door burst open. Of all the people in the world right now it was safe to say that Karl Fraser was the very last person Carmen wanted to see.

'Michael Evans has got a fucking Channel Four quiz show and he's not even funny!' he roared, sending a shower of spittle Carmen's way, causing her to flinch.

'Actually, he is funny,' she corrected him. Karl was too wound up to sit and paced like a caged rhino up and down Carmen's tiny office, which only took three paces each way. He kept bashing into her cherry blossom lights. If he broke them she would bloody kill him as they'd been a present from one of her best friends, Jess.

'He is not!' He stopped pacing and leaned across the desk. Carmen contemplated putting up her umbrella as defence against the rain of spittle. 'Where is my fucking quiz show? I won the fucking Eddie two years ago, the world should be my fucking oyster.'

'Maybe it's because you've alienated every single TV producer you've ever met with your enormous, over-weening, unbearable ego.' Carmen thought, or rather she thought she'd thought it but judging by the look of sheer astonishment across Karl's fleshy face, Carmen had actually said it out loud. Nick's shocking news seemed to have freed something in her. She felt swept along on a righteous tide of anger herself. It seemed all the pain, anguish and bitter disappointment were being channelled right at Karl, like a wave gathering momentum as it reached the shore. She was powerless to resist.

'*What* did you say?' he roared.

'I think you heard me. You are egotistical in the extreme and impossible to work with.' Carmen stood up.

'What do you know about *anything*? You're just a fucking agent!' Karl snarled.

'I know talent when I see it,' Carmen shot back, the wave of anger rearing up and breaking now. 'And I know that you have an appalling case of halitosis. I also know that I loathe you and no longer want to represent you. In fact, I no longer want to represent *anybody*, so if you'll excuse me, I'm going to hand in my resignation and get as far away from all you egotistical fuckwits as possible.'

'You'll never work in comedy again!' Karl shouted.

'*Unoriginal*, egotistical fuckwits. Oh, and I thought your last stand-up set was deeply derivative. Frank Skinner was doing all that aeons ago. So do me a favour and piss off, and do everyone else a favour and buy some Listerine.'

Carmen marched out of the office and along the corridor. She heard Will calling her name but ignored him and, blatantly disregarding all company protocol and Trish, who was shaking her head and saying, 'No!', she burst into Tiana's office. Tiana was perched on her desk, yacking away on her inevitable BlackBerry.

'I really need to talk to you,' Carmen interrupted. Tiana held up her hand and then pointed at the lilac sofa.

Carmen sat down and waited for Tiana to stop

tormenting her with her voice. Finally Tiana ended the call and swung round to face Carmen.

'So, Carmen, what can I do for you?'

'Actually, Tiana, I've decided to resign. With immediate effect.'

'Really? That is something of a shock announcement, isn't it?' Alright, she could have the lift as it was a question. 'Are you sure you aren't overreacting to the news about Matthew?' And that one as well. 'I know how close you guys are. And I know your appraisal left you a lot to think about, but I am sure you can make the requisite improvements?' But not that one.

Carmen shook her head. She felt as if she was about to dive into the deep end and the water looked very dark and very scary, but she had to do it. 'I think it's time for me to do something else, Tiana.'

Tiana clicked her Mont Blanc pen on and off, another intensely annoying habit. 'Usually I would ask you to work a month's notice? But I feel under the circumstances that it might be best if you clear your desk now? The company really can't have agents working for it who can't give a hundred and fifty per cent?' Another pet hate of Carmen's was people who came out with this percentage as if it meant something, instead of being utter nonsense.

It wasn't a question. Carmen nodded. This really was it.

'And you can say your goodbyes at Matthew's party. It's been nice working with you, Carmen?'

There, she was dismissed. She was about to reply,

but Tiana was already on another call. Carmen had just torpedoed her own career. Way to go.

She spent the next hour in a complete daze. Trish helped her pack up her books and snow globes, all the while bemoaning the fact that she was leaving. Carmen also had the humiliation of having Dex the security guard hovering in the doorway, making sure she wasn't going to steal anything – though quite what she would steal was anyone's guess, seeing as the only valuable thing was the MacBook, and that belonged to her. Or maybe he was stopping her from seeing her colleagues, in case she spread ill will and discontent and was bad for morale. Dex kept shifting his weight, which was considerable – too much time spent sitting in front of a CCTV monitor, eating Danish pastries – from Doc Martened foot to foot and apologising, 'I'm just doing my job, Carmen.' His plump white face was quite pink with embarrassment. Carmen ended up feeling sorry for him. She'd always thought he'd probably suffered enough by being the one who caught Dirty Sam on the fire escape, and he was decent enough not to report him.

Connor the postboy was on his rounds and looked equally devastated to see what was going on. 'I'll have to have a goodbye kiss, Carmen,' he said, managing to squeeze past Dex and popping his head round the door in expectation.

That really would be the icing on her day. Carmen took a step backwards and blew him a kiss. 'Let's not spoil the memory of the one we had at Christmas,' she said. 'Dex, you'd better get Connor away, I don't want him to get into trouble.' Connor looked reluctant to budge without the full tongue-on-tongue experience, but Dex was bigger and managed to extract him.

'Are you really sure you're doing the right thing?' Trish asked for about the twentieth time.

'I need a change, Trish,' Carmen told her. She was disappointed not to have seen Will, but Trish said he'd been called out of the office on urgent business.

'I'm sure he'll be in touch,' she said as she caught Carmen gazing wistfully out of the door in the direction of Will's office.

'I doubt it,' Carmen muttered, 'but I guess he'll be at Matthew's.'

'Oh, he'll ring you, Carmen, he really likes you. He's always really down when you're not in. And the kiss last night seals it, doesn't it?'

Although Carmen had always admired Trish's ability to run the office, unjam the photocopier, remember to buy fresh coffee and organise Matthew, she had never placed much significance on Trish's matchmaking abilities, seeing as Trish's longest relationship that she knew about to date had been with her collection of cacti. Still, she didn't want to be rude, and gave Trish a hug goodbye. Trish then insisted on giving her one of her favourite cacti. 'This is Basil, he loves it if you sing Motown songs to him,' she declared. 'He likes them all, but I always feel "Papa was a Rolling Stone" is his favourite.'

'Are you sure?' Carmen replied. Clearly Trish really, *really* should get out more.

'Yes, he needs to be free from here as well, he hates the air con, they all do. In fact, I might have to take them home, but then what would I look after?' Trish said sadly.

'What about some tropical fish?' Carmen suggested, reasoning that fish were pretty low maintenance and calming to watch.

Trish fiddled with her braids. 'Fish, I like it. I'll write up a proposal for Tiana.'

'Can't you just ask her?'

Trish shook her head. 'No, she has to see everything in writing.'

Carmen felt that she had definitely got out of the company at the right time.

It was only when she was walking towards Oxford Circus Tube at the, for her, unusual time of three o'clock in the afternoon that the enormity of what she'd just done hit her like walking into a brick wall. She carefully placed Basil on the pavement while she scrabbled for her phone. 'Marcus, is there any chance I could see you? Nick's having a baby and I've just resigned.'

'Oh, for fuck's sake, Carmen! You mad bridge burner, get a taxi. I can see you for a bit before I have to do the pre-record of the show.'

4

Marcus was riding high on success – both as a stand-up comic and now as a presenter of a Friday-night chat show on Channel 4. He had been one of Carmen's first discoveries and they had quickly become friends, though Carmen was always aware of the client/agent divide. In a way it was a relief when Marcus left the agency, as it made their friendship uncomplicated. Carmen hoped that Marcus would have some words of wisdom for her as she was shown to his dressing room by an ultra-efficient male PA, complete with headset, walkie-talkie and clipboard. Just once, she thought, she would like to meet an ultra-inefficient TV PA.

Because she had known Marcus pre-fame, it never failed to amuse her watching him being given the star treatment. Right now he was sitting in front of a large mirror while Tara, his make-up artist, blended foundation into his practically perfect skin. Marcus was achingly good-looking, with dark blond hair, brown eyes, and lashes so long that people were forever asking if they were fake. They were not. But under that oh-so-pretty exterior was a sharp mind and an even sharper wit, and you dismissed him as a pretty boy at your peril. Carmen had met Tara many times and always figured that make-up artists had heard it all before and that nothing phased them, so she prepared to launch herself into her tale of woe.

'Hey,' she said, moving a pile of newspapers and celeb mags and plonking herself down on the sofa with Basil next to her. 'Meet the unemployed saddo.'

Marcus arched a perfectly shaped eyebrow in her direction. 'I suppose you're waiting for me to give you a lecture so you can justify yourself, but actually I think it's the best thing you've ever done.'

'I don't know what happened to me,' Carmen babbled. She was surfacing from her dive into the deep end and panic had taken hold. 'I mean, I've only got that ten grand I was left by Nana Lesley. I don't know what I'm going to do next. Nick is having a baby, so that means I'll probably have to sell the flat. My pension is probably worth all of fifty pence. I'll have to work at Asda forever when I'm old, and yes, I know they sell lots of organic products, but it's not Waitrose, is it? And they'll probably have to bury me in that black and fluorescent green fleece because that's the only item of clothing I'll own. And I still haven't paid for that Alexander McQueen biker jacket that you made me buy because you said it was an investment piece. Gok Wan wouldn't have made me buy it. He would have sourced something for me from the high street but, oh no, I had to be friends with a high-end-designer fashionista gay. And I bet you'll drop me now I can't go out to all those expensive restaurants, or buy designer clothes.

And I'm such a fucking cliché having a gay best friend and being single. And last night Will kissed me but today he seems to barely want to know me. And did I tell you that Nick's having a baby?'

Tara handed Carmen a large handful of tissues. For a second Carmen couldn't think why, and then she realised that she was crying, huge, fat tears spurting out of her eyes and cascading down her cheeks.

'I'm going to get a different foundation, I'll be back in a bit,' Tara said diplomatically, heading for the door.

'Oh God, I must sound deranged if I've made Tara leave the room. I thought she'd heard it all.'

Marcus came and sat next to Carmen on the sofa and put his arm round her. Now his tone was serious, sympathetic. 'Stop making light of what's happened. The Nick news is big, you're bound to be reeling. I'm so sorry, Carmen.' He paused to allow Carmen to mop up the tears and blow her nose. 'You must have known it would happen sometime, though?'

'Sometime,' Carmen sniffed. 'Not so soon. I thought I would be more sorted in my head, in a place where I could accept it. It makes me feel like such a failure.'

'Don't be silly, you're', – 'Marcus switched to his American accent – 'intelligent, talented and gifted.'

'Just don't say "go girlfriend",' Carmen replied, managing the smallest of smiles in spite of the situation.

'Well, it was you who said you wished you'd been friends with Gok. Seriously, Carmen, leaving Fox Nicholson is just the best thing you've done in ages. You were ossifying there in that horrid little glass cage, and you know it. Give yourself six months and go off and write that drama – you'll regret it forever if you don't. As for Will, he probably felt awkward because of work, but by the sounds of things he likes you.' Marcus paused. 'As for the baby thing, what can I say? It's not fair, it's wretched and cruel and I wish more than anything that it wasn't so.'

'I know,' Carmen said in a small voice. 'There is nothing more to say.'

Marcus gave her another hug. 'You can always talk to me, even if we have the same conversation over and over and over, you know that.' He checked his watch and frowned. 'Except now. I'm sorry, the show starts recording in ten minutes, I'm going to have to get on. Is Sadie around? I don't want to think of you on your own.'

'Actually, I think I just want to be on my own right now.'

'Alright, Greta Garbo, I'll call you later. By the way, what's with the cactus?'

'This is not just a cactus. This is Basil, he likes Motown.'

That comment received another arch of the eyebrow, 'You've named a plant? Sweetie, you really need to go home and rest. Everything will seem better in the morning and you'll realise that Basil is just a plant with attitude.'

Back at her North London flat Carmen's instinct for self-preservation kicked in. She was suddenly exhausted, barely able to put one shoe-booted foot in front of the other. The adrenalin which had been firing her up all day had drained away. There were several messages from Will on her mobile and on her home answer-phone asking her to call him urgently, but she really wasn't up to speaking to him. Instead of hitting the vodka, which was what she had intended as soon as she left Marcus, she made herself a hot chocolate, put on her pyjamas and listened to her all-time favourite Victoria Wood CD, whose comedy always made her feel as if the world was not quite as bad as she feared it was, as she retreated under the duvet. Maybe in the morning her troubles would have melted away like lemon drops.

But in the morning her troubles felt like bloody massive boulders as not one but three bills landed on her doorstep – including the credit card bill with the unpaid jacket. 'Bloody Marcus!' she exclaimed to Basil, who had pride of place on the desk in the living room. He did look a little lonely, though. Perhaps she should download that Motown track and get him a little friend? She was all set to google cacti pals when she stepped back. That way madness lay. She also had another new message on her answerphone. It was Nick. 'Hi again, hope you're okay. I'm sorry to load this on you as well but when I get back from the tour we really need to talk about the flat. I'm sorry, Carmen. Speak soon.'

When Carmen and Nick had separated it had been agreed that she should have the flat for the time being. Somehow the time being had always felt as if it should be longer than nine months. It wasn't as if she liked the flat that much, as it overlooked a busy main road and was in a sort of in-between place – on the borders of trendy Crouch End and the not-so-upmarket Hornsey. It was next to a fire station, so evenings were frequently punctuated by the beep-beep-beep of the station doors opening and the whoop-whoop of a siren. Though the location also had its perks as in the summer the firemen would sit outside playing cards and some were really rather lovely. The best features of the flat – a third-floor Victorian conversion – were the fireplaces, high ceilings and a roof garden with a great view of the local park and of the aforementioned fire station (not that she was stalking the boys in uniform in any kind of pervy way, but pickings had been thin on the ground since her separation). For all its shortcomings, this was her home and she really didn't think she was up to dealing with Nick's baby news, leaving her job and losing her home all at once. That would surely count as stress overload.

She emailed her parents in Melbourne where they were staying with her twin brother, Toby, figuring it would be easier to break the news that she was unemployed that way and be spared the emotional phone call where her mum would be bound to go off on one. (How was she going to support herself? Didn't she realise there was a pension time bomb coming up? Did she want to be an impoverished old lady? And so on.)

Carmen spent the next hour fielding calls from her concerned friends. First was Jess, one of her oldest friends from uni: 'Carmen, Marcus rang me, how are you?' Jess was mother of one son, married to Sean, also a friend from uni. She lived in Brighton where she worked as a part-time English teacher at a sixth-form college.

'Oh, you know, just doing the usual positive things one does at a time like this – not getting dressed, wallowing in a pit of despair, watching daytime TV.'

'I know things seem bad right now, and I'm really sorry about Nick and the baby. But you will feel better for leaving your job, I'm sure. Why don't you come down to see us at the weekend? Sean could babysit and I could take you out for dinner. It's been ages since I saw you.'

Jess was right, it was a good four months. Since she and Sean had moved to Brighton Carmen had seen much less of her friend. 'Thanks, Jess, but it's Matthew's farewell party, and apparently mine. Another time would be great, though.'

The next call came from another good friend, Sadie, an actress. Given the roles were quite thin on the ground and she was yet to land a much-coveted part in *Spooks* or *Waking the Dead*, Sadie often worked for BBC Radio 4 as a freelance continuity announcer. She had a deep, sexy voice that conjured up dark chocolate and velvet. The news never sounded quite so bad when she delivered it. People, for that read men, always assumed that with such a voice Sadie was some kind of sex siren; Carmen had been to many a party with Sadie where married men were stopped in their tracks and came over all dreamy when she opened her mouth. And she was forever receiving emails, letters, poems and gifts from her admirers, several of which were treated as suspicious packages by the BBC post room but were subsequently X-rayed and found to contain nothing more dangerous than racy underwired bras. But Sadie was no temptress. If you had to sum her up you'd say she was ditzy, obsessed with fashion and dating comedians. She was pretty, with wild, curly blonde hair, brown eyes and a dimple on her left cheek. 'Darling Carmen, are you okay? I heard from Marcus. You should have called me last night, I would have come round.'

'Thanks, Sadie, but I needed to sort it out in my head.'

'And have you?'

Carmen sighed. 'Not really, and especially not about Nick and the baby. I keep thinking about him and Marian going off to the first scan and doing all those things that expectant parents do and—' here her voice caught.

'And it's really tough for you,' Sadie said gently. 'Which is why we're all here for you.' Indeed, Carmen's friends had been there for her throughout the awful roller-coaster ride of fertility treatment. At times she must have driven them mad by going over the same ground, and she couldn't bear for that to start up again. She wanted to be there for her friends now, didn't want to be poor Carmen again, wanted to be the happy, carefree Carmen she had been some five years ago, back in the day, when she imagined her future included a baby.

'I know you are, and it means a lot. But I need distraction now, so tell me how things are with you and Dom.'

Dom was the latest in a long line of comics Sadie had gone out with. She had a weakness for them and persisted in a naive belief that because they made her laugh when they were performing, they would make her laugh in the relationship. They seldom did. Carmen realised that Nick had been an exception, as he was relatively well balanced, not prone to bouts of depression, and no more egotistical than any other man. But Nick aside, dating a comedian was rarely an amusing experience. As the girlfriend you were expected to go to all their gigs and hear them recite the same routine, massage their egos that were generally the size of a continent and invariably pay for everything because they were broke. Once Sadie had gone out with a comedian who had mined their sex life for source material, and even then it had taken her an entire month to dump him for it. Any other woman would have got rid of him on the spot, or sewn prawns into the hem of his curtains or cut off one leg of each of his suits − not that the comedian in question had any suits or indeed any curtains, and Sadie was allergic to shellfish, but that wasn't the point. A dramatic act of revenge had been called for, and Sadie had flunked it.

A deep sigh from Sadie. 'Well, he asked me out for

dinner, so I was hoping for somewhere lovely, as I have paid for the last three meals. Guess where he took me?'

'The Ivy?' Carmen said hopefully, knowing Sadie loved going there.

'He took me to KFC because he was doing some research for one of his jokes. K fucking F fucking C!' Now that was a Sadie the Radio 4 listeners had yet to be treated to.

'I had chicken in a bucket and I was wearing my brand new Miu Miu red suede platforms.' Sadie's velvety tones were turning a tad screechy-meets-estuary; she would end up on Radio 1 if she wasn't careful.

'Just tell me you didn't go back and have sex with him after that?' Sadie's compulsion to pick complete and utter tossers as boyfriends never ceased to amaze Carmen. It was almost as if she had been genetically programmed to only ever go for the wanker.

Another sigh. Which Carmen took to mean yes.

'Well, don't tell me you did that thing for him again, did you?'

That thing involved Sadie recounting an imaginary shipping forecast, while Dom got down to business. Dom had apparently been fantasising about Sadie long before he met her, having heard her on Radio 4. Apparently he especially loved hearing her read out the shipping forecast and gale warnings issued by the Met Office. Carmen didn't like to imagine what Dom was doing as he listened but she bet checking the forecast for factual information was not part of it.

Another sigh. But then a giggle. 'He only got up to

Rockall. And I felt like saying, at least you got your rocks off, which is more than I did.'

'*Please* tell me you're not going to see him again,' Carmen implored, with all the hopelessness of King Canute trying to stop the tide.

'Oh, he's quite sweet really.'

Carmen ended the call agreeing to meet up soon but felt that further warnings about Dom were fruitless.

Will called her mobile again but as soon as she saw his number flash up she switched her phone off. Along with her job at Fox Nicholson she might as well kiss goodbye to that little flirtation. She very much doubted Will would be interested in her now she was unemployed, and she wasn't up to hearing him trying to be nice but inside pitying her.

Flopping down on the sofa, Carmen let out a long sigh. She felt so crushed by Nick's news, she just wanted to lie down and cry. It brought back so many unwelcome memories of the last two years of her marriage. The whole trying for a baby thing had left her feeling so drained that she supposed she had never really looked to the future and thought about what would happen to Nick. She'd been totally wrapped up in herself. And now as Nick made his way into a baby-filled sunset, there really was no escaping the fact that it had been her fault that she couldn't get pregnant. She was left behind feeling like a defective being, the reject.

On the second day of unemployment the reject finally got out of her pyjamas. She caught the W7 to Finsbury

Park. Carmen always remembered Nick pointing out that backwards Finsbury Park spelt krapy rubsnif – only a man would ever bother to work that one out. She caught the Victoria Line to Oxford Circus to find a suitably stylish leaving present for Matthew. She found it in Liberty's – always good for calming the soul even if she couldn't afford anything in there – in the shape of a wonderfully flamboyant tie which was over her budget but which she put on her card, because it was so Matthew. Then she decided to say goodbye to Rico and Mamma Mia.

As soon as Carmen walked in Rico exclaimed, 'Carmen, is it true you have left your job? I have so missed seeing you!' His handsome face was indeed quite scrunched up with concern.

'Yep, so there will be no more croissants and lattes for me, I'm afraid.'

'Maybe not here, but somewhere else?' Mamma Mia joined her at the counter.

'Yes, somewhere else,' Carmen said and suddenly felt terribly sad that she would no longer see Rico, even though his flirting had got on her nerves at times.

'So you will sit down with me and have a latte?' Mamma Mia said. 'It'll be on me now you're unemployed. Temporarily, I'm sure.' She clicked her fingers at Rico. '*Un espresso e un latte.*'

Carmen slid on to the red leatherette bench at one of the white formica tables. Mamma Mia managed to wedge herself in opposite. Her girth was impressive but she carried it well and somehow looked formidable and solid rather than, well, fat. Maybe it was the black dress.

Rico came over with the coffees and two glasses of Strega, hardly Carmen's first choice of a mid-morning beverage, but she was going to have to knock it back. Mamma Mia would be offended if she didn't. Rico hovered nearby, clearly expecting to be asked to join them. Mamma Mia shooed him away, with some more orders in Italian.

'Children!' She rolled her nut-brown eyes. 'Not always a blessing, Carmen. I know as an Italian I am not supposed to say that, but sometimes it is true.'

'I wish I could find that out for myself,' Carmen replied sadly. The feeling of lethargy and hopelessness was once more settling on her like an unwelcome blanket.

'Maybe you will one day,' Mamma Mia said wisely.

'Not going to happen. Can't have them. It's a fact.' There, she'd said it. Usually she never told anyone, except her very closest friends, but there was something about Mamma Mia that demanded total honesty.

Mamma Mia smiled. 'Nature can be a mystery sometimes. We think we have all the answers, but she can still surprise us. I see you with children, Carmen.'

If it had been anyone else Carmen would have been tempted to say, 'Mind your own business', but Mamma Mia had at least seven stone on her. And so she simply smiled and sipped her coffee.

Mamma Mia held up the glass of Strega. 'Cheers, Carmen, to your new future by the sea.'

Carmen was so intent on knocking back the liqueur without choking that she almost didn't register what Mamma Mia had said. But once her throat had stopped burning she asked, 'What do you mean, by the sea? I live in Crouch End.' Mamma looked at her quizzically as if she knew that wasn't strictly true. 'Alright, near Crouch End, more Hornsey, I suppose, but it's definitely not near the sea.'

Mamma Mia shrugged expansively, causing her massive bosom to rise up like a giant pillow. 'I don't know, it just came into my head, these things happen to me sometimes. Ah, look, there is lovely Will. *Ciao*, Will.'

Oh shit, it couldn't be, could it? She hadn't returned any of his calls. Carmen turned round and saw Will at the counter. As soon as he saw her he raised his eyebrows and wandered over. The butterflies, which she had thought had packed their bags in the spate of bad news, came fluttering back.

'Miller, I thought you must have died. Do you never return calls?'

'Sorry,' Carmen mumbled, 'I had a lot on my mind.'

Mamma Mia managed to prise herself up from the seat, which made a sucking noise that would have had schoolkids in fits, as her buttocks unpeeled from the leatherette. 'I will leave you two to chat, I'm sure you have much to talk about.' As she went past Carmen she planted two hefty kisses on her cheeks. '*Ciao*, Carmen.'

'*Ciao* and *grazie* for everything.'

76

Will slid on to the seat vacated by Mamma Mia. 'So do you want to tell me what happened? I came back to find your office cleared – it was like a scene from bloody *Nineteen Eighty-Four*. I can't believe you left like that. You're such a good agent. You were a real asset to Fox Nicholson.'

Carmen rolled her eyes. 'Oh, please don't give me that company-speak bollocks, Will! This is me you're talking to and not she of the Antipodean annoying sentence construction.'

Will frowned. He had pretty much bought into the corporate set-up and it clearly jarred hearing it dissed. He tried again. 'I could put in a good word at Brand's, I'm sure they'd snap you up.'

Carmen shook her head. 'Nope, I'm going to take six months off and write my comedy drama.'

Will looked seriously at her. 'I think that's great, Carmen, but are you sure you should give up the day job? Lots of people do both. Couldn't you write your drama in the evenings and at weekends?'

Carmen shrugged. 'I've just had enough, Will. I don't think I'm cut out to be an agent and I really want to give my writing a go, and now seems like the right time.'

'Do you know something about the current economic climate that I don't? Like, is the recession over? Because I'd have thought that leaving your job right now, with nothing to go to, counted as a pretty high-risk strategy.'

Carmen was not enjoying Will's comments. Where was the flirtatious banter? What about the kiss? She really didn't need his insights into the wisdom or folly of her course of action.

'Thanks for the vote of confidence, Will,' she said sulkily. 'Like, big me up, why don't you?'

Will distractedly ran a hand over his black hair, which was in need of a cut. It kept falling into his eyes, which usually Carmen would have found quite adorable but now it was annoying her. 'Sorry, I didn't mean to be negative, it's just I reckon if you'd hung on a little longer there might have been the chance of redundancy. Tiana wants to lose at least three agents. I really wish you'd spoken to me first before you went off on one.'

No wonder Tiana had been so keen to get rid of her on the spot. Will carried on, 'But you must be okay financially. Didn't you get the flat from your marriage?'

Carmen just couldn't bear to admit the truth. She was also curious about Will's interest in her finances. 'I'm fine, Will, my nan left me some money last year, but I don't know why you're so bothered. Is this so you can find out if I'm still worth knowing? I mean, if I'm just some impoverished would-be writer living in a bedsit in, say, Finsbury Park, am I going to be deleted from your BlackBerry?' She couldn't help sounding so defensive.

Will frowned. 'No way, I was just concerned about you, is all. You've done quite a radical thing and I thought we were friends'. He hesitated. 'More than friends on the basis of that kiss.'

Just the mention of the kiss caused the colour to rush

into Carmen's face and the butterflies swooned. She was about to reply when Mamma Mia bustled over with Will's espresso, breaking the moment. 'A double one, just how you like it, my darling,' Mamma Mia said dotingly.

Carmen waited until Mamma Mia had moved away before she mumbled, 'Sorry, I didn't mean to sound so arsey. I'm probably a little bit uptight at the moment because of the whole leaving-job thing.'

For a second they held each other's gaze, then Will smiled and said, 'You're not really living in a bedsit, are you? It doesn't quite go with your Alexander McQueen jacket or with being called Carmen.'

'Not yet,' Carmen said grimly.

'Anyway, I've got you a little something. I was tempted to buy you an outfit but then I know how fussy you are, so I've got this instead.' He reached into his jacket pocket for a small package wrapped in pink tissue paper and slid it across the table to her.

'You really didn't have to get me anything!' she exclaimed, though she was touched that he had. She unwrapped the package to discover a delicate silver swallow for her charm bracelet. She'd had the bracelet for years and always wore it.

'It's perfect, Will, thank you,' she said, holding it against her bracelet to see how it looked. 'Is that because I'm like a free-spirited bird?' she said teasingly, wanting to get back in flirtatious mode.

'Nope, it's because you already had a silver love heart.'

Wow, Will had nearly bought her a love heart? That seemed intimate.

His BlackBerry then vibrated with an incoming message. He frowned as he looked at the screen. 'Got to get back to the office, Miller, some of us have work to do.' He quickly drained his coffee, then stood up and just as Carmen thought he was going to clear off, he leaned down and kissed her lightly on the cheek and said softly, 'We still haven't talked about *that* kiss, but we will. I'm up in Manchester for the rest of the week but I'll see you at Matthew's. Take care of yourself, kid.'

Carmen was left disarmed by the further mention of *that* kiss. She lingered for a few minutes, thinking about Will. He'd revealed a much sweeter side lately. Maybe they could carry on their flirtation outside work, and maybe more. Then she snapped out of it. Frankly she had too much on – like the fact that she would most likely end up in a bedsit pretty damn soon . . .

5

It was easy to spot Matthew's house on the upmarket residential street, as his was the only one where the trees were decorated with flashing blue fairy lights, flickering tea lights lining the path, and the only one with 'Ziggy Stardust' blasting out (Matthew was a huge Bowie fan). Clearly the leaving party had already kicked off. Carmen crunched along the gravel path in her heels. She was looking forward to seeing Matthew and her former colleagues. But most of all she was looking forward to seeing Will. After their encounter at Rico's she hadn't been able to stop wondering what exactly he thought of her, and for that matter what she really thought of him, and she was hoping tonight might resolve her dilemma one way or the other. If he liked her then wasn't tonight his chance to show it? And indeed hers?

All this speculation had not helped her writing one little bit. It had been going spectacularly badly – in fact, the most coherent thing she had written so far had been her shopping list for Sainsbury's. Tormenting herself about Nick's baby news hadn't helped either. She'd read somewhere that no one could write if they were really happy, that it was essential to know the dark side in order to be creative. After the last few days, though, Carmen could truthfully say that feeling wretched was not the greatest spur to writing.

Matthew opened the door to her, resplendent in a purple velvet smoking jacket, which set off his silver fox hair beautifully. 'Thank God for that,' she said with feeling, after she and Matthew had hugged. 'I was dreading that you might be wearing some kind of smart-casual retirement ensemble in pastel colours.'

'The day I wear a sweatshirt is the day I am put into a home for the mentally bewildered,' Matthew declared. 'You look sensational, and I'm glad to see you haven't gone on the downward spiral either. Now come on in and get partying!'

Carmen had in fact spent much of the week on the downward spiral but had put in the effort for Matthew's big night in a fitted red dress that did wonders to her curves and skimmed over any problem areas – a definite case of va-va-voom to dispel the gloom. 'Let me give you your present first,' she replied, handing over the slim box.

'That's so sweet of you!' Matthew exclaimed, opening the purple Liberty tie box to reveal a midnight-blue silk tie, splendidly patterned with pink flamingos.

'Absolutely no way will that go with a sweatshirt,' Carmen said sternly.

'I hear you, sister,' Matthew teased her. 'And here are your presents.' He grabbed two parcels from the hall table. Carmen ripped open the first to discover a thesaurus.

'I know you can get one online, but nothing beats a book, does it?' Matthew declared.

'The second one was trickier. I hope you haven't already got this one in your collection.'

Carmen opened the square, rather heavy parcel to discover a snow globe containing the characters of *The Wizard of Oz*.

'Wow, that is so kitsch, I love it!' she exclaimed, giving the globe a shake and watching the fake snow cascade on the yellow brick road and on Dorothy et al. Dorothy had found her Somewhere over the Rainbow, would Carmen find hers? And what kind of kitsch thought process was that? She definitely needed alcohol.

'Come on through,' Matthew said, taking her arm and leading her into the large living room which was decorated with more fairy lights, Japanese lanterns, bunting and balloons – an eclectic mix but that was Matthew – and packed with guests. He certainly was going out with a bang and not a whimper. Casper, his twenty-two-year-old son, was the DJ. Matthew's fifteen-year-old daughter Molly and two of her friends were waitressing in uniforms of short black skirts and fishnet tights, and a great deal of make-up that wouldn't have looked out of place in *The Rocky Horror Show*.

Molly approached Carmen and offered her the tray of champagne. 'Take two, I can't be arsed to keep coming round!' At fifteen Molly had attitude with a capital A.

As Carmen moved round the room saying hi to her

former colleagues, she felt so proud of Matthew for throwing such a party. It was like giving two fingers to the whole corporate horror. He deserved so much better, they all did. Well obviously not Tiana, there were no words for what she deserved. Carmen scanned the room, wondering if her boss had dared to turn up, and her gaze fell on Will, standing at the far side of the room, chatting to Lottie. As soon as he noticed Carmen he made a beeline over and made a big show of kissing her twice.

'Just watch the champagne!' Carmen exclaimed, holding on tightly to her two glasses. 'I don't know when Molly will next be passing. She's most likely going to hide out somewhere and diss the grown-ups.'

Will folded his arms and looked at her consideringly. He was dressed in a black shirt and jeans and had just had his hair cut. The hair looked good short. Carmen, who never thought she had a particular type when it came to men, did love short hair; in fact, she would go so far as to say she really didn't like long hair on a man. 'So how was the rest of your week? Have you finished the series yet? When can I read it?'

Carmen shrugged and said, 'Okay. No. I'll think about it. I certainly don't miss Fox Nicholson.'

'Not even flirting outrageously with me?' Will demanded.

'I never flirted outrageously with you!' Carmen protested, while thinking how very much she did in fact miss flirting with Will.

'Well, I miss flirting with you, Miller. I miss you

84

coming back from your shopping expeditions with all those little numbers from Top Shop, practising walking in your new shoes. You always had such a glow about you. Materialistic, yes, and sometimes we have to say a bit more mutton than lamb, but always sexy.'

Carmen glared at him at the mutton reference, then remembered the zebra print tee-shirt dress, wet-look leggings debacle. But she liked the sexy bit.

'And sweet,' Will added, catching the look. 'And no one else eats Wobbly Worms and lets me have their green ones.' He paused and moved closer. 'It's good to see you, Miller. In fact, I've never seen you looking so lovely as you do tonight.' He smiled and waited for her to get the reference.

'Lady in red, that's me,' Carmen replied. 'Except wrong colour hair, obviously, I don't have highlights. I always thought that line was really cheeky, like, would the lady want him to notice her highlights or would she rather be thought of as having naturally lovely hair?'

Will shrugged. 'Maybe the lady in red with naturally lovely hair will be dancing with me later cheek to cheek?'

Ordinarily if any man had quoted a Chris de Burgh lyric at her she might have laughed, and she wanted to make a joke but found she couldn't, because yes, actually, she would like to be dancing cheek to cheek with Will. There was a beat when they both looked at each other, one of those moments when the rest of the room recedes into the distance. Maybe seeing Will again was just what she needed, and maybe more than seeing . . .

'So what do you think of Carmen leaving as well?' Matthew had joined them. He put his arm round her. 'Has Fox Nicholson crumbled yet? Has Tiana learnt to speak properly?'

'Everything's fine, Matthew,' Will said smoothly, switching in Carmen's mind straight from sexy to smarmy. It was disconcerting just how rapidly he could do that. 'Of course you're both sorely missed, but life goes on, doesn't it?' He was so smooth he could easily have been a spin doctor; truly he was wasted in entertainment – politics was where he could have excelled.

'Well, glad to hear it.' Matthew smiled but Carmen knew that he had never really seen eye to eye with Will. They were just too different.

'Sushi?' Molly demanded, thrusting the platter in front of Will and narrowly missing his chest.

'Not sure if you're going to get your silver service award, Molly,' Matthew said drily, 'or even get paid.'

'Whatever,' Molly shot back. Carmen knew that in fact she had a huge crush on Will, hence was being extra rude to him.

'Thanks,' Will said, taking a portion of sushi. 'Like the get-up, Molly.' Molly turned as scarlet as her lipstick. Carmen winced in sympathy: who would be a teenager again?

Then Carmen and Will were alone once more. 'Okay, this is me being serious for a minute, and I don't want you to laugh at me or tease me.'

Carmen put on a mock-innocent look. 'When do I ever do that?'

Will rolled his eyes. 'When do you not? I wanted to ask if you'd have dinner with me next week. Now we're not working together it's going to be much easier to see each other. You know Tiana had that problem with inter-colleague fraternising, as she called it, but now we can do what we like, can't we? Not that I ever needed her permission.' The 'do what we like' was practically dripping with suggestion.

Carmen liked the suggestion, liked being asked, in fact was wildly flattered. 'Are you asking me out, Will?'

'I think that's pretty obvious, don't you? I have to after that kiss.'

That kiss! Carmen got the free-fall elevator sensation again and the butterflies batted their wings in anticipation, but she still couldn't resist playing him. 'I'll have to check my itinerary,' she said loftily, 'and get back to you on that.'

'Come on, Carmen, you're unemployed, you're going to have shedloads of free time – there's only so many episodes of Jeremy Kyle the spirit can take.'

'I'm not unemployed!' Carmen shot back. 'I'm a writer, remember!' Oh God, now she had said it, she had better bloody get on with it. But it wasn't just the work issue; she actually hadn't been out with anyone since she split up with Nick. She wasn't sure if she was ready, whatever that meant.

Will was stopped from pressing his cause any further as Molly enthusiastically rang a gong, declaring, less enthusiastically, 'Dad's going to make his speech thing now.'

'Don't worry,' Matthew called out from his position by the fireplace, crammed with family photos, Penny at his side, resplendent in a black sequinned flapper dress – neither she or Matthew did understated. 'I'm not going to witter on, I know there is valuable drinking time to be enjoyed and liaisons to be struck up.' Carmen was sure it wasn't her imagination that he seemed to glance over at her and Will.

'I just really wanted to say a massive and heartfelt thank you to everyone in this room. Thank you to everyone I've worked with over the many, many years; it really has been the most tremendous fun. It never felt like work to me to be alongside you all and signing up such marvellous acts and watching their talent flourish. Only lately.' He paused. Everyone knew what he meant.

'I have to thank Trish especially for looking after me so wonderfully,' at this he raised his glass in Trish's direction; tears were streaming down her cheeks. Poor Trish, Carmen wondered how long she would last with Tiana. Matthew revelled in people's quirks, but she had a feeling Tiana would not tolerate Trish's enormous collection of cacti for long. 'And for this lovely cactus,' Matthew gestured at the giant cactus on the mantelpiece. 'Apparently she's called Fifi and her favourite song is "You're All I Need to Get By".' He smiled at Trish.

'I also have to thank my family, especially Penny.

My work took me away from home a lot, but I think it's my turn to make it up to her, and I'm going to be the domestic rock for a change and support her in her work.'

He raised his glass to Penny, who said, 'Don't worry, kids, I'll still cook.' Matthew was known to be able to make macaroni cheese and that was it. But there was real warmth in her voice; theirs was a marriage that had weathered many a storm.

'And this is of course also Carmen's leaving party, so I'm now going to hand over to her.' Matthew ignored Carmen's frantic gesticulations to the contrary. What the hell was she going to say? She hadn't prepared anything and she hated speaking off the cuff.

'Thanks, Matthew,' she replied through slightly gritted teeth, aware of everyone in the room looking at her. 'Before I say anything, I think we should all give a toast to Matthew. He's been a fabulous boss, an inspiration. I'm sure we're all going to miss him greatly. Here's to Matthew, and good luck in his new career as a writer and apparently a domestic goddess, though I'm guessing Nigella doesn't have anything to fear just yet.'

'I protest!' Matthew called back, 'My macaroni cheese is without compare.'

'To Matthew,' the room took up the chorus. Then looked at her expectantly.

'So as you know I also resigned last week. I'm going to miss all of you, but I felt it was time for me to have a change. I'm absolutely terrified about it, but it had to be done. Thanks for all your support over the years, the gossip in the ladies' loos, and the many laughs.' She ground to a halt, not knowing what else to say.

'To Carmen,' Will declared next to her. 'Funny, impetuous, gorgeous Carmen. We're all looking forward to the comedy drama.'

'To Carmen,' the room echoed.

Carmen smiled and Will raised his glass to hers. She rather liked his toast, but wasn't so sure that she wanted him to know that yet. As she was now surrounded by Lottie, Trish and Daisy, Will touched her briefly on the shoulder. 'I'll catch up with you in a bit,' he said, moving off to talk to Janie, one of his clients, a female comedian whom Carmen was convinced had the hots for him. It had been one of the many things she'd teased him about.

'He's not interested in Janie,' Trish told her, seeing Carmen looking at the couple.

'He's been pining for you,' Lottie said, 'in a state of depression.'

Carmen looked at the pair of them in disbelief. 'No way.'

'It's true.' Daisy actually spoke. Usually she restricted herself to glaring, eye rolling and vigorous gum chewing. 'He really hasn't been himself.'

'You see,' Carmen exclaimed, 'this is exactly why I always said I wouldn't have a relationship with anyone at work. I don't need the analysis!'

'Oh, shut up,' Lottie said good-naturedly. 'And tell us if he's asked you out yet.'

A pause, which Carmen milked for dramatic effect, then she came out with, 'He might have.'

'Carmen!' the trio exclaimed in exasperation.

'Okay then, yes!'

'That's so romantic,' Trish sighed. 'Will is lovely. I know he has that tough exterior, but underneath he's so kind and warm and passionate, I'm betting.'

'She's just pleased that Will managed to get the fish for her,' Daisy said.

'They're tropical – I've got some guppies and angelfish,' Trish said proudly. 'Do you want to see the pictures of them?'

'Could I get some more champagne first?' Carmen replied. She really could not be expected to look at Trish's fish sober.

Conversation then moved on from Will and fish, and Carmen didn't hold back on the champagne. She felt happier than she had all week and she wanted to hold on to that precious feeling, which had been in very short supply lately. The bubbles went straight to her head as she'd barely eaten anything that day, because she was so nervous about seeing Will. Then Casper turned up the music and dimmed the lights and people began dancing. Carmen found herself being led on to the dance floor by Matthew as they all danced to 'We Are Family'. He spun her around and they both energetically threw some shapes. She was slightly worried about Matthew's dodgy hip, but it seemed to be holding up well.

'So have you and Will got a bit of a thing going?'

Matthew shouted in her ear over the music. Carmen was surprised. Matthew didn't usually comment on people's private lives. She shook her head. Matthew looked sceptical. 'Just be careful. Will is pretty ruthless. I think he only really cares about work, and I don't want you to end up getting hurt, especially when you're feeling vulnerable. I know how much the news about Nick and the baby has upset you.' Matthew was one of the very few people at Fox Nicholson who knew about that, and his reference to it took the wind out of Carmen's sails. Right now it was the very last thing she wanted to be reminded of.

'We're just having fun, Matthew, and I might go out for dinner with him sometime. It's really no big deal.'

Matthew put his hand lightly on her arm. 'Good girl, you deserve it.'

He made to spin her around but she smiled. 'I'm going to get a drink.'

She wove her way through the dancers, trying to block out Matthew's words. Molly was passing out shots of tequila. Carmen waylaid her and downed two in quick succession. 'Respect.' Molly said, looking at her in awe.

'Rubbish,' Will replied, appearing at Carmen's side. 'It's not big or clever.'

'It's my leaving party and I'll get drunk if I want to,' Carmen replied, taking a third shot. She stumbled slightly and Will reached out to steady her arm.

'Are you too drunk to dance?' he asked. 'What about dancing cheek to cheek, my lady in red?'

'I'd like to see Casper's face if you requested that particular number,' Carmen replied. She was definitely feeling wobbly.

At that moment The Cure's 'Lovecats' came on. Molly let out a snort of disgust. 'What is it with this old timers' music? I want a bit of Kasabian.'

'It's a classic, young lady,' Will told her. 'And anyway, it's your dad's leaving party, you've got to let him have his tunes.'

Molly gave him the face version of 'whatever' before one of her waitress friends joined her and they both did that teenage girl thing of huddling together and giggling.

Will turned to Carmen and held out his hand. 'Come on, let's show these teenagers how it's done.'

Now this was a testing moment in any courtship. How did the man dance? Would Will sway from foot to foot as if he had concrete in his shoes, or would he throw some foxy moves that would have her wondering if he was entirely straight? Or would it be a version of Michael Douglas dirty dancing in a V-necked sweater with Sharon Stone in *Basic Instinct* that had the power to give any woman nightmares?

She took Will's hand and followed him to the dance area. Once they were in the throng she was all set to let go, but Will kept hold of her hand and they performed a version of an energetic jive to the music, with him spinning her round and performing some smouldering moves with his hips that would have had the judges on *Strictly Come Dancing* combusting with delight. Will was a good dancer, he had rhythm. He went up further in Carmen's estimation.

After 'Lovecats' came 'Wake me Up Before You Go-Go', where Carmen and Will deliberately camped it up and strutted around the floor, occasionally catching each other's eye and giggling, then Casper dramatically slowed down the pace with Sinatra's 'One for My Baby'. Carmen looked at Will and smiled. 'Did you pay Casper to put this on?'

Will shook his head. 'So will you dance with me?'

Carmen stepped into his arms. They moved slowly to the music, which was steeped in regret and loss. 'Funny that we should be dancing to this,' Will said softly. 'As this is about the end of something, and I really hope we're at the beginning.'

There was a moment at the end of the song when they held each other's gaze, then Casper segued into 'Smack My Bitch Up', which had the consequence of clearing the dance floor as Molly and her posse took over along with Casper and his mates.

'It's one a.m.,' Will said as they watched the teenagers do their thing. 'D'you want to share a taxi?'

Here was a dilemma. Was Will just proposing a taxi ride? If he was, would she be offended at his lack of interest? If he wasn't, was she really in the right frame of mind? Was she too vulnerable for Will? She looked into his blue eyes, 'I'll just have one more drink, one more for the road.' She reached for a glass of red wine from a tray Molly had abandoned on the top of the piano in her haste to get down on it.

'Champagne, tequila and now red wine. Miller, you are hardcore and you are going to be so hungover. Come to mine and I'll make you a cup of tea and feed you paracetamol.'

Carmen glugged back some wine and then pulled a face; she really had drunk too much. She was getting the blurry, spinny-head feeling.

Will took the glass out of her hand and put it back on the tray. 'Come on, let's call that taxi.' He took her arm and they wove through the partygoers.

While Will called for a taxi on his mobile, Carmen found that she had to cling to the banisters for support, swaying gently from side to side like some kind of drunk orang-utan. This was not good. Orang-utans were cute but not sexy. She tried looking down but the black-and-white tiles swam in front of her eyes. Looking up was no better as the light, table and Will started to perform a slow waltz in front of her. It was actually rather delightful but she wasn't in her twenties any more, she knew perfectly well what this signalled – the descent into drunkenness and the certainty of a humdinger of a hangover. She had to ask Will if he had peppermint tea. She always drank peppermint tea after a night on the lash as if it was supposed to offer some miraculous cure. It never did, of course.

Will finished the call. 'Are you very drunk, Miller?'

'Very,' she smiled at him. 'So did you mean what you said about me? That I'm funny, impetuous and gorgeous?' She swung out one of her arms and nearly lost her balance. Will put his arms round her waist and she sort of collapsed into him.

'And drunk, but very lovely with it.' He was definitely being Sexy Will now, not smarmy. He leaned towards her and lightly kissed her lips. Yes, very sexy. Carmen lightly kissed him back, lord, how she hoped it was lightly and not a drunken slobber. And then Sexy Will slid his arms round her neck and she slid her arms round his waist, his very satisfyingly hard abs – all those sessions in the gym before work had definitely paid off. Got to love a man who worked out. She breathed in slightly. The only workout her abs had been getting lately was digesting Oreos and salt and vinegar Hula Hoops. And then the heat turned up on the kiss as it went from PG to a definite 18 certificate, a steamy, sexy, take me, devil-may-care kiss. Even drunk, Carmen registered how good the kiss was, even better than their first, and as Will pressed his body into hers she registered something else pressing into her at a very pleasurable angle – perhaps him being only slightly taller than her had its advantages after all. Except now the something was vibrating, which seemed a little freaky.

He pulled away and scrabbled in his pocket for his phone. Ah, that explained it. 'The taxi's here. Are you coming?'

I practically just have, Carmen did not reply. 'I should say goodbye to everyone,' she said instead.

She and Will walked back into the living room. Music was still blasting out, this time 'Let's Dance', and Matthew and Penny were dancing with their kids. Everyone else was slumped on the sofas and chairs. Carmen went up to Matthew and shouted, 'I'm off now.'

Matthew raised his eyebrows when he noticed Will standing behind her.

Carmen ignored the look. 'I'll give you a ring next week. Let's have lunch – us writers should stick together.'

'I'd love to,' Matthew replied, then reached for her hand and kissed it. 'Look after her, Will,' he said in a decidedly cooler tone than he had used with Carmen.

In the taxi Carmen's inhibitions had long since left the building. No more was she too-cool-for-school Carmen; she was drunk-as-a-skunk Carmen. 'Lovely Will,' she said, snuggling next to him. He really was lovely, why had she held back for so long?

'Lovely Carmen,' Will replied, putting on her seat belt for her. And safety-conscious too. She laid her head on his shoulder. She'd just rest her eyes until they got to his place and then she'd feel refreshed and up for whatever Will was. Tea and paracetamol! Ha, she knew what his real agenda was! He really was lovely and smelt lovely too. She liked Jo Malone, they both loved comedy, liked coffee, they could share a packet of Wobbly Worms, they were a very good match, they were bound to be great in bed together. She just needed to conserve her energy for that bit.

'You okay?' Will asked.

'Hmm,' she murmured. 'Lovely.'

*   *   *

'Are you okay?' Will was speaking to her.

'Hmm,' Carmen murmured back, snuggling deeper into the duvet. Hang on a minute, why was Will talking to her in bed? A montage of images flashed up in her mind: the party, the flirtation, the dancing cheek to cheek, the kiss, the − what the bloody hell happened next? Carmen had absolutely no recollection of how she had ended up in Will's bed. Naked, apparently, except for a pair of briefs. She cautiously opened her eyes. Will was up and dressed and sitting on the edge of the bed. He looked as fresh as a daisy. Carmen felt as fresh as a dung heap.

'What am I doing here?' she croaked, sounding as if she'd spent the night chain-smoking unfiltered Gitanes.

'You don't remember? Well, young lady, you wanted to ravish my body, every inch of it, apparently, to do the dirtiest, naughtiest things. Really, Miller, I was shocked. I always thought you were a nice girl, but then they're always the dirtiest, aren't they?'

'We didn't, did we?' Carmen croaked tentatively.

Will rolled his eyes and left a pause before putting Carmen out of her misery. 'I like to think I'm a little more memorable than that! Nothing happened because in the taxi you fell asleep, which is really the polite way of saying you passed out. You were still passed out when we arrived back at my flat and I couldn't wake you up. I had to carry you inside with the taxi driver, and do you know what floor we're on?'

Carmen shook her head, then winced as the hangover kicked in with a vengeance.

'The second. My back may never be the same.'

'Oh God!' Carmen exclaimed, mortified, pulling the duvet up so only her no-doubt bloodshot eyes were visible. 'It's like a scene from a bad rom com. I'm so sorry.'

'D'you mean about my back or about being a cliché?' Will sounded amused.

'Both,' Carmen muttered.

'Well, I know you'd had a pretty stressful week, so I'm not too offended. You're always going on about what a tough bastard I am, but as you can see, I'm a total gentleman.'

'But why am I practically naked?' She fervently hoped that Will had not undressed her in her state of drunken stupor – talk about blowing her air of mystery!

'Because in the night you suddenly sat up, declared that you were boiling hot and pulled everything off. But it was dark, I promise I didn't see anything. And yes, I slept in the same bed as you because my sofa bed is knackered and I really didn't want to sleep on the floor, and it *is* my bed. It was the least you could do after failing to carry out your threat to ravish me like a beast.'

'I did not say that!' Carmen exclaimed. 'However drunk I was, I would never say such a thing.'

Will looked at her then smiled. 'You're right, but you did tell me I was lovely, which I take to mean that you wanted to ravish me like a beast. I learned something else about you last night – you are an appalling duvet hogger and at one point you were muttering to yourself about having to have the duvet folded under your feet because of the foot monster.'

Carmen *was* an appalling duvet hogger, she had been told this on countless occasions by Nick and she did indeed have a thing about having the duvet folded under her feet because of the foot monster – a mythical creature from her childhood which she had never quite managed to shake off. But that hardly said sexy, independent woman, did it?

'I don't know what you mean,' she replied.

Will clearly decided to be gentle with her. 'Anyway, cup of tea, toast? Paracetamol?'

'All of the above please,' Carmen said. As soon as Will walked out of the room she shot out of bed and headed for the ensuite bathroom, ignoring her pounding head. The reflection looking back at her in the mirror was a dishevelled study in the-morning-after-the-night-before. Her mascara had smudged, her hair was all over the place. She looked rough as an old boot. Oh God, Will was never going to fancy her again after this, unless he had a weird fetish thing going on for old boots.

Quickly she washed her face with some of Will's Clinique face wash.

That got him a tick. She liked a man to take care of himself; she definitely wasn't interested in a man who couldn't even bring himself to use moisturiser or face wash because he thought it was poofy. Her view was that she made the effort and she expected something in return. Face wash and moisturiser were the minimum, she didn't mind a bit of tweezering round the eyebrows to avoid the Neanderthal mono-brow and maybe even a back wax. She cleaned her teeth by using the trusty late-night stop-out method of squeezing toothpaste on to her forefinger and rubbing hard. She just hated not flossing, but this would have to do. Then she dived into the shower. Even more brownie points for Will for the Jo Malone shower gel.

Five minutes later she emerged, cleaner in body but still mortified in spirits, and tracked down her clothes in Will's bedroom. Even in her hungover state she registered how tasteful the room was. One wall was taken up with a bookcase crammed with books; the other had a stylish cast-iron fireplace with art nouveau tiles round it, and a print of the Edward Hopper painting of a late-night diner which had always been one of her favourites. Her dress, red bra and tights were all neatly arranged on the black velvet armchair. Carmen blushed as she thought of Will picking up her clothes – it felt just the wrong side of intimate. Although she felt a bit of an idiot putting on her sexy red dress from the night before, she rallied enough to slap on some tinted moisturiser and mascara. By some miracle her hair didn't look too bad, apart from a slight kink to her fringe. She might have the hangover from hell, but she didn't want to look like hell.

Taking a deep breath, she exited the bedroom and headed along the corridor towards what she thought must be the kitchen judging by the aroma of toast. It was clear that Will had a lovely flat. She glanced in at

101

the living room, a large airy room, then went on to the kitchen, which was small but functional, with shiny red units. Will was reading the *Observer*, to the accompaniment of Frank Sinatra on his iPod station. He looked up.

'Ah, the creature has emerged! How are you feeling, Miller?'

'Okay,' Carmen muttered, sitting down on one of the stylish black Philippe Starck Ghost chairs that she had always wanted and never been able to afford.

'Right, Dr Hunter to the rescue, take these,' he handed her a packet of ibuprofen, 'and drink this.' He poured her a glass of orange juice. He was being so sweet. Carmen suddenly felt incredibly self-conscious.

'So, what plans do you have today?' he asked, as he passed her a plate of toast already buttered and cut into triangles (another tick for the butter – Carmen loathed low-fat spread).

'What day is it?' Carmen only half-joked.

'Sunday, and I would suggest we did something . . .' he paused, 'but I've actually got to work. I've got to prepare a presentation for Tiana and a group of potential investors. She just called me to say it had been brought forward to tomorrow.'

Oh no, take the shame! Will was trying to get rid of her by pretending he had to work! Carmen had thought she couldn't be any more mortified than she already was, but apparently not. 'No worries, I think I'm supposed to be seeing my friend Marcus.' She quickly shoved a triangle of toast into her mouth, determined to have one slice and then be on her way. She knew when she wasn't wanted.

'Marcus Taylor? Say hi from me, I've met him a couple of times. I'd love to entice him back into the agency. I think Tiana made a real error of judgement letting him go.'

'She certainly did,' Carmen replied through the toast.

'And she made a mistake with you, too. I could have a word with her if you like, see if she'll reconsider.'

Carmen shook her head. 'Thanks, but no, I really am going to give my writing a shot. Anyway, thanks for breakfast, I'm going to grab my stuff and head off.'

'Hey, have some more toast?' Will called after her as she practically jogged back to the bedroom, her stockinged feet skidding on the shiny wooden floor.

'No thanks,' Carmen shouted back as she quickly strapped herself into her heels, trying to ignore the pulsating blister on her baby toe, which was screaming please don't make me wear these again! She ineffectually shook out Will's duvet, and nearly had to lie down again from the effort, picked up her bag and clattered into the living room. Will had relocated there and was already sitting at his desk, typing away at his laptop. He didn't have to put on a pretence. She was going, for goodness' sake! She reached for her Alexander McQueen jacket.

He looked up. 'Shall I book you a taxi?'

She shook her head. She couldn't bear to be in the flat another second. 'I'll get the Tube.'

Will's mouth twitched. 'Do you actually know where you are?'

Carmen reached into her pocket for her lip balm and dabbed some on her lips, as realisation dawned. 'Nope.'

Will stood up. 'I'll walk you to the Tube – we're at Ravenscourt Park.'

'You don't have to do that if you've got work to do.' Carmen felt defensive now.

'I can take ten minutes out.'

Outside the sky was a miserable grey, heavy with rain. 'Kind of makes you want to go back to bed, doesn't it?' Will said cheekily as they turned out of his flat and walked through a small park.

'Oh, I'll probably do an hour or two of writing before I meet up with Marcus,' Carmen said airily, thinking longingly of collapsing on her sofa and fretting that Will must think she was a complete lush.

'I admire your self-discipline, Carmen,' Will replied. 'I know I couldn't do what you are. But I'm sure it will pay off. Trish sent me the first episode and I loved it.'

'Oh my God! I can't believe she did that! It was just a draft, it's rubbish.' Carmen felt even more exposed than she had lying in his bed. She moodily shoved her hands into her jacket pockets.

'I made Trish do it. I threatened to stamp on one of her cacti and kidnap her favourite angelfish. Stop panicking, it was really good. And I wouldn't say that if I didn't mean it. You may need to rethink your pitching skills as I don't know if the expression "it's rubbish" is going to cut it with producers. Seriously, Carmen, you should think about letting me represent you.'

'Hah! I know how much Fox Nicholson screw their writers, remember!'

Will looked at her and gave her his naughtiest grin before lowering his voice and saying, 'How much they like to screw their writers. But only the select few.' The butterflies did a loop-the-loop of lust, and despite wanting a career as a comedy writer, Carmen could not for the life of her come back with a witty riposte.

'This is you,' Will said as they reached the Tube. 'I'm really sorry that we can't spend the day together, but I've got to get this report done.' He paused and the flirtatious tone was gone. 'The company's in a real mess at the moment. I'll call you to arrange that dinner, I don't want you starving in your garret.'

In my bedsit, more like, Carmen thought as she click-clacked her way towards the ticket barrier after a PG-rated kiss with Will.

6

'Day seven of unemployment for Carmen Miller of Crouch End slash Hornsey and Carmen is finding it tough,' intoned the morose Geordie voiceover in Carmen's head. 'No, no, not unemployment! Day seven of being a writer! And it is more Crouch End than Hornsey,' piped up the more optimistic American voice, let's say in the manner of John Barrowman. Was there anyone more optimistic than him? Those dazzling teeth, those scrumptious cheekbones, that lovely jet-black hair . . . Hmm, why wasn't *he* her gay best friend? Why did she end up with cynical Marcus, who loathed musicals, probably as much as John adored them? And why was she wasting time having this debate when she should have been writing? Carmen looked over to where her MacBook sat on the desk by the window, waiting for her to get started. She couldn't help thinking that it had a slightly accusing air about it. Oh my God, she was ascribing feelings to inanimate objects, perhaps this working from home, pretending to be a writer (five scenes so far) was sending her crazy. No wonder so many writers drank. This was hard! The hardest thing she had ever done.

She sat down once more at the desk and clicked

open the document. She would write for at least three hours, then go out and have lunch. No, hang on, she couldn't have a late lunch as she was meeting Will for dinner tonight; she would have to have an early lunch, which meant working for less, say an hour and a half.

At the thought of Will she found herself gazing, not at the expectant screen, but out of the window and at the stately horse chestnut tree, whose leaves were already turning golden. She still didn't know what to make of their relationship. Her instinct warned her to steer clear, to get on with writing. Matthew had told her to be careful, but she couldn't deny the attraction. Those three kisses had been intoxicating, and the feel of his body against hers had been quite something as well. And they did get on, the flirtatious banter was delicious, but more than that she felt Will was also a friend, she felt connected to him. The truth was she was looking forward to seeing him that night. She was determined not to drink; she hadn't since Matthew's leaving party. She almost felt proud of herself for achieving this unprecedented spell of abstinence until she remembered that she had probably consumed a month's worth of units at the party.

Carmen fidgeted some more, wrote a few more lines, then went on Facebook and sent a message to Matthew. Then she gave her profile picture an American year-book style makeover, emailed Sadie, Jess and Marcus, googled the new Vivienne Westwood collection on Net a Porter and spent a wistful few minutes wondering if she could afford anything, maybe a trinket such as the crystal orb pendant? That would be a lovely pick-me-up. Maybe if she didn't eat for a couple of weeks? Maybe not. Maybe she would have to disable her broadband connection to stop this random googling and emailing, never mind twittering, which Marcus kept telling her she should do though she was yet to be convinced. She made a coffee and wrote a few more lines – admittedly she was slow, but hey, Rome wasn't built in a day, was it? Her mobile rang. It was Nick. Carmen hesitated. She hadn't replied to his message about the flat the other week, but she was going to have to speak to him sometime.

'Hi,' she couldn't stop herself from sounding curt.

'Hi, Carmen. How are you?'

'Great,' she snapped, sounding far from it.

Nick sighed. 'Look, I'm back now and there are things we need to talk about.'

Carmen steeled herself. 'Like what? My tips on motherhood? After all, I read all those baby books, didn't I? I'm very well up on the subject, I could give Marian plenty of useful advice.' Her voice was now brittle with pain.

'Carmen, I'm so sorry to put you through this,' Nick said gently. 'I'm sorry for everything; I'm sorry we couldn't have children together, I'm sorry we broke up, but we've got to face it.'

Carmen took a deep breath and tried very hard to be brave. It wasn't Nick's fault. It was no one's fault. It just was. 'Okay, go ahead, I'm sorry.'

A pause, 'It's about the flat.'

'My home, you mean,' the brittle voice had turned bitter.

'I know, Carmen, and believe me I don't want to put you through this, but I'm really strapped for cash at the moment – we're bursting out of Marian's one-bedroom flat and with—'

'Yes, I know what's on the way,' Carmen interrupted. 'So what do you want to do?' She picked away at the Rouge Noir nail varnish on her nails, ruining the look.

'I need you to get the flat valued and see if there's any equity which you could give to me, then I'd take my name off the mortgage and the flat would be yours.'

It was a generous offer and if Carmen was still working it would have been entirely possible, however she doubted she could take on a mortgage on her own with her conspicuous lack of income.

'Actually, Nick, I just resigned, so I'm not sure if that would work.'

'Oh,' Nick paused, clearly taking on board the enormity of Carmen's statement. 'So we might have to think about selling the flat.' He said it quickly, as if somehow that would make it hurt less, like ripping a plaster off a wound. Carmen would much rather have left that particular plaster stuck on.

'I suppose we might,' Carmen replied, trying to keep her voice steady. Everything suddenly seemed uncertain, unstable. She was a little girl again trying to avoid stepping on the cracks in the pavement, and right now she had fallen down a bloody great chasm. She was still falling.

'Look, I know this is tough for you, do you want me to set up the valuations?'

Carmen looked around the living room, painted a shade of pale green that she and Nick had debated over endlessly, down at the honey-coloured floorboards that Nick had spent an entire weekend stripping and then varnishing – badly, it had to be said – and nearly having a major bust-up with their neighbours over the noise. The maroon velvet Habitat sofa that she didn't think they'd even paid for yet, where they'd hung out watching films, made love, consoled each other when yet another month went by without Carmen getting pregnant. Towards the end it was the battleground where she sat at one end, Nick at the other, and they'd fired off accusations and recriminations at each other. The flat wasn't grand, it wasn't stylish, but it was hers. But not any more, it seemed.

'Yep, if you could set it up that would really help. I'm going to have to go now, Nick, so take care and just let me know the arrangements.' She sounded businesslike, calm and collected on the outside. But inside she was screaming with hurt, pain and despair. She looked at the computer screen, wanting with all her heart to escape into her fictional world.

But of course after that conversation writing was out of the question. Instead Carmen alternated crying with pacing round her flat, even opening the drawer she wasn't supposed to open *ever* which still carried a selection of baby books, relics of a life which would never be hers. She pulled out the week-by-week planner to work out what Nick's baby looked like for maximum pain. At twelve weeks Nick's baby was about twenty-two millimetres long. It was fully formed; all its organs, muscles, limbs and bones were in place. Nick's baby was already moving about, but Marian wouldn't be able to feel it yet, that would come at around eighteen weeks, along with the baby's finger- and toenails, eyelashes and eyebrows. Nick's baby and her tiny, not-yet-grown fingernails needed the flat more than Carmen did. It was time for the barren, childless woman to get out.

The pain of not being able to have a baby was like a raw wound inside her, which most of the time her brain cordoned off for her own self-preservation. From her early twenties she had longed to have a child, and because she and Nick had decided to try in their late twenties it never crossed either of their minds that there would be a problem. She was not playing Russian roulette with her fertility and precious eggs by leaving it until she was forty to try. Their failure to conceive took them both by surprise. For a few hours Carmen was back in the dark place. It wasn't one of those things she could just shake off; it clung to her as she got ready for her night out with Will, hardly caring what she wore and what she looked like, was there as she sat on the Tube, staring mindlessly at her reflection in the opposite window, and was why she was already over half an hour late meeting Will. What did it matter if Will flirted with her now? He surely wouldn't if he knew that she couldn't have children. He would simply feel sorry for her.

* * *

111

It felt strange charging up Great Portland Street, her old stomping ground. It had only been a week since she was last there but already she felt so detached from it. The workers were heading off for post-work drinks at the variety of bars and pubs lining the street. She turned down a small side road and headed to the Ship. Desi gave her a cheery wave as she walked in.

Will was sitting at their usual table.

He smiled when she bowled up to him. 'Miller, you have the worst timekeeping of anyone I know.' He pointed at his watch. 'Shall I introduce you to this invention? It's called a watch and it's really useful.'

'I'm sorry, Will, I just got held up.'

'Was it all those creative juices flowing?' he asked, lightly kissing each of her cheeks.

'Something like that.' Carmen knew she was expected to banter back but in her present mood couldn't manage it. Now she was with him she realised it was a mistake seeing Will tonight, she should have stayed at home. She just felt too bleak. 'So what can I get you to drink?' Will asked. 'It can only be a quick one as we're meeting the others in fifteen minutes.'

'What others?' Carmen asked, sitting on the sofa next to him and pulling the sleeves of her black sweater dress over her hands to cover up the ruined nail varnish. She'd thought she was seeing Will one on one. She could just about handle that, but having to make small talk with strangers was really pushing it.

'Sorry, I meant to tell you, I'd double-booked. It's just some friends slash former work contacts of mine, you don't mind, do you? I didn't want to cancel you; I really wanted to see you.' He gave her his most smouldering look.

In spite of the look Carmen wasn't at all sure she liked the fact that *she* was the one who might have been cancelled. She had never been into that pack-as-many-people-into-an-evening-as-possible scenario – having drinks with one set of friends then going on to dinner with another. It reminded her of people who graded guests at their weddings, where some only qualified to be invited for the evening, for drinks and dancing. It seemed to Carmen as if they were saying, we like you, just not that much. You're not an A-list friend, just a B-list. Poor old you.

Will went off to the bar to buy her a vodka and tonic; she had been sorely tempted to ask for a double. She picked more nail varnish off and wondered how quickly she'd be able to leave the meal. Will returned. He looked as good as ever, though his eyes looked tired – no doubt Tiana had been keeping his nose to the comedy grindstone.

'So how's it going, Miller? Have you finished it yet?' Will was in full flirtatious mode.

Carmen shook her head. 'Give me a chance, Will! I've had other stuff to deal with.'

Will looked at her curiously. 'What's that then?'

God, why had she mentioned it? There was no way that she wanted to let Will know about the emotional minefield that was her life right now. Keep it light was going to be her mantra for tonight.

113

'Just stuff. So do you still miss me at Fox Nicholson? Give me all the gossip. How's Trish and the fish?' And as Will chatted away Carmen did her very best to look animated and smile.

But as soon as she walked into the restaurant with Will and was introduced to his friends, she just knew she was not going to be able to sustain the act. There was Didi, a polished blonde who was very high up in publicity at the BBC and her husband, Patrick, who was an agent working at Brand's. They were perfectly charming to Carmen as Will introduced her, but as soon as they found out that she had given up her job and was now a writer Carmen sensed their condescension.

'So have you had the sitcom commissioned?' Didi asked. She was one of those twitchy, skinny, neurotic types who looked as if they never ate anything, and true to form she was shredding a piece of bread into tiny pellets on her side plate. 'Just shovel it in!' Carmen felt like saying as she slathered butter on her own bread – well, she was an impoverished writer, she had to eat!

Carmen shook her head. 'Nope, I haven't finished it yet – just the first one and a half episodes.'

'Wow! That's so brave to give up your job before you'd actually got a deal in the bag!' Didi exclaimed. 'And it is so hard to get anything actually commissioned, especially in the current climate, where channels are even more cautious about new projects. I was talking to a producer only the other day who said he had never known things as tough as they are now. And he's been around the block a few times, so he would know.'

Didi was enjoying her role as the grim reaper a little bit too much. Carmen was surprised she hadn't accessorised her navy Diane von Furstenberg wrap dress with a scythe and a cloak.

'I do have a few contacts,' Carmen replied, sounding more confident than she felt.

'She certainly does,' Will joined in. 'And Carmen is very talented. I think she's going to be a great success as a writer.' He gave her a reassuring smile. She couldn't help thinking that he was just saying it to be nice.

'So how's your work going, Will?' Didi asked. Cue a long discussion about what was happening in the industry, who was changing agents, who was hot, who was not. Did you see so-and-so's last show, disastrous, wasn't it? Didi and Patrick seemed to revel in bad news; perhaps their second name was *Schadenfreude*. Carmen's interest waned after ten minutes or so of insider gossip, and she moodily knocked back her Sauvignon Blanc, disregarding her earlier resolution not to drink. Hey, what else was there for it? She had thrown away her career and was about to be thrown out of her house.

'Are you okay?' Will asked her quietly when Didi and Patrick were caught up with comparing main courses. He looked so warmly at her that Carmen was almost tempted to confide in him; then Patrick commented, 'Your job must be so much easier now Nicholson's gone.'

Carmen bristled at the dismissive way Patrick used Matthew's surname and at the idea that Matthew's departure had been for the best.

'Yeah, things have been running more smoothly,' Will conceded.

Carmen was not going to sit there and listen to her dear friend being discussed like this. 'What exactly do you mean, Will? Matthew was a brilliant boss. Infinitely better than Comedy Bypass.'

'Where do I start?' Will muttered. 'Matthew's a lovely guy but he had no idea about managing a company in the current climate. If he hadn't accepted the buyout, Nicholson's would have gone under ages ago. His world of a gentleman's handshake is so long gone.'

'It's practically from the Jurassic era,' Patrick quipped, smiling broadly at his comment.

Wankers! Carmen thought as she sawed into her tuna steak. She wasn't wild about tuna, it had to be said, but she had to keep her strength up. Maybe that was why she felt so on edge: she was suffering from a lack of protein, too many Hula Hoops and not enough omega-3.

Didi clicked her fingers at the waiter. Carmen loathed people who did that. 'I'd like a green salad, dressing on the side.' She didn't even look at the young male waiter, as if he was too insignificant for her even to bother acknowledging his existence.

'No problem,' he replied.

'Thanks,' Carmen added, when it was clear Didi wasn't going to bother.

He nodded and was halfway across the room before Patrick held up the bottle of Sauvignon Blanc and called out, 'And another bottle of this.'

'Please,' Carmen again felt obliged to add.

Patrick looked at her blankly then carried on talking to Will and Didi. Now the conversation had turned to property prices. Apparently Didi and Patrick were having an *absolutely horrendous* time selling their house in Chiswick. *Good*, Carmen thought bitchily. Maybe *her* second name was *Schadenfreude*. They'd had to drop the asking price by a hundred and fifty.

'Your house is massive, why do you want to move?' Will put in.

There was a pause as Mr and Mrs *Schadenfreude* looked at each other. 'Shall we tell him?' Didi asked.

'Go on,' Mr *Schadenfreude* urged her.

Didi beamed at Will and Carmen, showing off her tiny, perfect white teeth, then she reached for Mr *Schadenfreude*'s hand and squeezed it. 'We're having a baby!'

'Congratulations!' Will exclaimed, and then stood up and raced round the table to kiss Didi and give Patrick a big manly hug.

Well, wasn't this just perfect? Carmen thought. 'Congratulations,' she managed, raising her glass. 'Guess you'll have to lay off the old vino.'

'Surely you can have a glass of champagne?' Will put in. 'We've got to celebrate, guys!'

And he summoned the waiter over to order a bottle. Carmen was only slightly pacified by the fact that Will actually thanked the waiter.

'So now you see why we want a bigger house,' Didi put in.

Patrick turned to her. 'Shall we tell them the best bit?'

Didi nodded, and took a deep breath before she burst out, 'It's twins!'

'Oh my God! I've got to do the hugging and kissing thing all over again!' Will leaped out of his seat.

Luckily he was putting in double the effort, which made up for Carmen sitting there like an ancient crone of misery. She suddenly felt she knew exactly how Maleficent the evil fairy felt at the christening of Sleeping Beauty. Everyone else is having a ball, and she is just a ball of bitterness.

'It's so incredible, isn't it! Twins aren't even in our family, so you can imagine how completely stunned we were at the scan.'

'Gobsmacked.' Patrick beamed.

There then followed a ten-minute barrage of when were they due, were they identical, girls or boys, how was Didi feeling? Carmen's face was hurting from the fixed grin she had on it, she most probably looked like the Joker in *Batman*. She made a few 'that's great' noises, but inside she was reeling. This was too much. Way too much.

'Carmen's a twin,' Will said.

'Oh are you?' Didi turned to her, her face radiant with pregnancy hormones and curiosity. 'Brother or sister? How did you get on? Did your mother breast-feed you both at the same time, I think it's called tandem feeding? It's a bit scary, isn't it? And Patrick is trying to be right-on about it but thinks it looks weird, as if you've got both babies in a rugby grip. But I want to breastfeed as I know that way you are absolutely giving your children the best possible start in life. I'm also wondering if the twins should sleep in the same cot, and for how long. Did you? You must be so close.'

When Carmen could finally get a word in she replied, 'Actually, we loathed each other for years. We were always bickering, drove my mum and dad to distraction – put her off having any other kids, though I think she would have liked more.' She really was channelling Maleficent. She just needed to cackle and declare that the twins would prick their fingers on a spinning wheel on their sixteenth birthday and die and be done with it.

That wiped the look of enraptured radiance right off Didi's face. Carmen almost felt sorry for her, *almost*.

'But you get on really well with your brother now, don't you?' Will the peacemaker put in.

'*Now* he lives in Australia,' Carmen said and laughed. 'And we only see each other every other year.' Didi's chin gave a slight wobble. Oh God, what was she playing at being so mean? It wasn't Didi's fault that she was having twins; the poor woman was probably terrified. Carmen quickly softened. 'We email each other all the time. And from the age of ten we got on great, we were best friends.'

She had drained her glass of champagne quicker than anyone else. Will frowned slightly as he refilled it and when Didi and Patrick were talking he whispered, 'Are you sure you're okay? Has something happened?'

'I'm fine,' Carmen muttered back. Will did not look convinced.

'Sorry we got a bit carried away on twin talk,' Didi put in. 'Just promise you'll come round and see us lots, Will, when I've had them?'

She looked at Carmen. 'Will is absolutely fantastic with kids, they all love him. He's amazing with all his nieces and nephews. A complete natural. He's going to be a brilliant dad one day.' Didi must have thought that this was something Carmen would love to hear – after all, so many men were terrified of commitment and being tied down with kids. How could Didi know that she was saying the one thing that would depress Carmen even further?

'So you want kids then?' Carmen turned to Will, asking so casually a question that was nearly killing her to voice.

Will could of course have no idea why his answer to this question would be so significant to Carmen, and so it was that he bantered back, 'Are you propositioning me, Miller? What kind of combination would that be? Your mutton tendencies, my egomania and ruthlessness according to you. But so long as they had your beautiful green eyes I wouldn't mind.'

Will was even looking at her flirtatiously. Oh God, not this, not now. She could have told the truth, she could have lied, she could have bantered back, but she was paralysed.

She appealed to Patrick, 'Please, someone change the subject! I think I'm baby-talked out!'

Patrick politely obliged, with not the most original question of the night but at least it was safe: 'So which part of London are you from, Carmen?'

'A rather nondescript part of North London.' She simply couldn't be bothered to enter into her Crouch End borders repartee.

'Which part?' Didi asked.

'Hornsey,' Carmen replied.

'I always thought you lived in Crouch End, Miller,' Will teased her. 'Have you been lying to me all this time?'

Carmen simply looked at him. She had not been impressed by his dissing Matthew, she'd been sent on a journey into hell with the baby talk; the feelings of lust he usually aroused in her had been temporarily doused with cold water. She shrugged. 'I was being economical with the truth. You know what I mean. It's what you do at work most of the time, isn't it?' Oops, she sounded a little too passionate.

Will frowned. 'What are you getting at?'

'You know, you talk the talk, give your clients that spiel – we'll work our bollocks off for you, get you all the best gigs, you're our number-one priority and our percentage is very fair, blah blah blah.'

She had spoken sarcastically, but Will took her words at face value. 'Well, we do work really hard for our clients and our percentage *is* very fair.'

'You'll need someone like Will when you're struggling to sell your script!' Patrick exclaimed.

'I'd never give it to Will's agency,' Carmen shot back. 'I hate what they stand for. It's all about money and nothing about talent or integrity.' A comment that stunned the three into silence. It was possible that Carmen had gone too far, but she felt there was no going back. She was having one of those off-at-the-deep-end moments again and she couldn't stop. The revelation about the twins and Will wanting kids was the final straw. She had an overpowering urge to speak her mind. 'I mean, I like Will, he's a good kisser and I could probably shag him but I wouldn't trust my work with him.'

Didi and Patrick both stared at the tablecloth. Will looked at Carmen, an expression of utter disbelief on his face. 'God, if this is what a week of unemployment does for you, I'd get a bloody job!'

'I'm not unemployed, I'm a writer!'

'Yeah, well, when you've actually produced something then you can say it. Until then I think you're having an early midlife crisis, Carmen, and you need to take a fucking chill pill.' Clearly any lustful thoughts Will had been harbouring towards Carmen had been similarly doused in cold water.

Suddenly Carmen wanted very much not to be there. She had gone too far. She had behaved appallingly. She had been unforgivably rude to a pregnant woman and vile to the man she fancied. Really it was time to leave. She reached into her bag for her wallet, pulled out thirty quid and left it on the table. 'This should cover my share, let me know if it doesn't.' And she got up to go.

'Are you serious?' Will said, looking and sounding severely pissed off.

'Yep.' Carmen slung her bag over her shoulder. 'Enjoy the rest of your evening.' She addressed Didi and Patrick, 'And congratulations about the twins. I didn't mean to be negative. Twins are a blessing. It's wonderful news and I'm sure you'll be wonderful parents. I love my brother and I'm really glad I'm a twin – there's something really special about our relationship. And my mum didn't get on with tandem feeding, but she breastfed us in rotation and got my dad to give us bottles at night. And we slept in the same cot until we were three months old. So good luck.' With that she marched purposefully out of the restaurant, only pausing to thrust a fiver into the hand of their waiter. 'Sorry that lot were so offhand.'

The waiter smiled ruefully. 'Oh, I've had way worse.' He held the door open for her and Carmen exited with her head held high, trying to ignore the feeling of hot shame that was rushing through her. She really did like Will and she had just humiliated him in front of his friends. Way to go, Miller, she sighed, and headed down Oxford Street to her bus stop on the corner of Tottenham Court Road and desolation. She couldn't face the Tube right now. *At the number 134 bus stop I sat down and wept*, she thought miserably as she reached her stop. Actually the pavement looked too icky and she would ruin her dress. Grand Central Station was altogether a more desirable location to break down and weep by.

As she pulled out her mobile to text sorry to Will, she discovered a message from Marcus: 'Had brilliant idea, the tenants have just moved out of my Brighton flat. It's yours rent-free for three months. Just say yes x.'

It was starting to rain now – not the dramatic fat raindrops hammering down that would have fitted Carmen's mood, but a fine drizzle that seemed pointless but soaked you anyway. The traffic was swishing by, people were standing at the bus stop with those set Londoner faces that said, don't talk to me, I am in my zone. The lad next to her was shoving a Big Mac into his mouth, a homeless woman of indeterminate age was talking to herself as she pushed a battered Tesco's trolley full of newspapers. Carmen texted back 'yes x'.

The following two weeks were a fever of packing and putting furniture and books in storage, of getting the flat valued, and trying and failing not to think about Will. She had texted 'sorry' but heard nothing back. His silence was hardly surprising, given her behaviour. Every time she replayed her comments from the evening they seemed to take on a new, more toe-curlingly mortifying layer of horror. It was as if she'd had an outbreak of Tourette's for the night. Why oh why had she made that cringey comment about shagging him? And talked about his work so negatively? Will was a great agent. The words kept going round and round in her head until she wanted to sit in the corner with her hands over her hot, shameful ears chanting 'la la la la!' until the feeling went away. Will must think so badly of her. On top of the shame was the even more painful realisation that she missed him, missed their chats, their banter, their flirtation that now never would blossom into anything else. Even though she was still coming to terms with Nick's news, devastating as that was, somehow she actually felt worse about being so foul to Will. Thank God for Marcus and his Brighton offer. Perhaps a change of scene might bring some perspective.

On the night before she was due to move Marcus and Sadie took her out for dinner at Carluccio's, which turned into a grilling. She was starting to sympathise with the grilled sea bass the waiter had just put in front of her.

'Why can't you call him?' Marcus, cutting into his steak with gusto.

Carmen shook her head. 'I've said sorry, what more can I say? The ball's in his court.'

'Well, in fairness you were the one who was bloody rude to him. Poor bloke, takes you out to dinner, introduces you to his friends, and you turn on him like a demented Rottweiler with PMT.' Marcus adjusted his latest toy – a Cartier Santos watch. He had a thing about watches, especially Cartier. He was always joking that it was just as well he'd made it as a comedian and could now afford them, otherwise he'd have to go on the game to fund his passion.

'I did not have PMT!' Carmen shot back. 'God, I bet Gok wouldn't drag a woman's hormones into an argument! You're such a sexist, Marcus!'

Sadie, who was daintily arranging her gnocchi on her plate, said, 'You were a bit of a mentalist. I mean, there was Will thinking he was going to get his end away after a pleasant dinner with friends, and there you were laying him to filth.'

'Yes! All he wanted was a filthy lay!' Marcus crowed. 'Not for nothing do they call me the King of Comedy.'

'Don't you mean the Queen?' Carmen scowled at him. 'And anyway, Sadie fed you that line.' But oh my God, if even Sadie thought she was in the wrong, Carmen really was in trouble. Sadie was usually outside any norms and existed in her own parallel universe of kookiness.

'And you said he was a fantastic kisser.' Marcus again. 'He is bound to be dynamite in bed.'

'I'll send him a Christmas card or something,' Carmen muttered into her glass of Pinot Grigio. Would they just give her a break!

'I expect he will have moved on by then,' Marcus continued. 'He's a bit of a catch from what I've seen. And I can tell you now, if he was gay and I was single I'd snap him up. He's just so damn manly. In fact,' he mused, 'maybe I should try and turn him anyway, perhaps Leo wouldn't mind.' Before Marcus had got into a serious relationship with his current boyfriend Leo, he had made a point of seducing straight men. It was his opinion that all men could be turned. It was just a question of opportunity on his part and a feeling from the straight man that they wouldn't be found out. He had been proved right on many an occasion. He caught sight of Carmen's scowl. 'You know I'm kidding, I don't do that any more. He's all yours.'

'Knock yourself out,' Carmen replied gloomily. 'He probably hates me now. And you're prettier than me anyway. My eyelashes could never compete with yours.'

'It's a thin line,' Sadie agreed. 'But I'm sure you could turn him round in that Vivienne Westwood dress.'

'I may well have to sell it,' Carmen said sadly, looking down at the red drape dress that she adored.

'Oh no! You could never sell Vivienne! That would be like selling one of your children.' Carmen raised her eyebrows. Sadie had the grace to look ashamed. 'Sorry, Carmen, wrong comparison.'

'Lucky for you I really like you,' Carmen said, but she instantly forgave Sadie her slip. Humour and friendship were always needed and never more so than now.

'So will you come and see me in Brighton?' Carmen demanded. 'At least once a week − it's only forty-nine minutes on a fast train. And that's practically the same as going from North to South London.' She fixed Sadie with a beady eye, as she had an appalling reputation for never leaving the capital.

'Of course!' Sadie said brightly. 'I love the seaside, especially Brighton. It's so sexy and brash, like a Jean Paul Gaultier perfume ad. I always expect to see sailors in tight Breton vests and white bell-bottoms strolling along the promenade, arm in arm. And there were those marvellously surreal marshmallow penises for sale everywhere last time I was down, and men in tiny gold hot pants dancing on floats.'

Parallel universe, Carmen thought, *I rest my case*.

'You're thinking of Pride, sweetie, it's not always like that.'

'Oh, isn't it?' Sadie was disappointed. For her, a sailor came a close second to a comic. Ironic, really, as they at least would appreciate her gale warnings for their content and not just as a sex aid.

'There are lovely shops, though,' Carmen wheedled. 'Space NK, Mac and various designer boutiques.' God, what was she? A representative from Brighton tourist board?

'Chanel?' Sadie said hopefully. She didn't recognise anywhere as being civilised without those iconic two ccs of approval.

'I'm not sure, I'll find out.'

'It's just that you know I wither if I'm not within ten miles of a designer store.' It wasn't that Sadie could afford to buy designer, she couldn't; she just liked to go into such stores and try things on, just for the thrill of it, much to the annoyance of the *über* snooty assistants. Sadie stroked her pillar-box red quilted Chanel bag protectively. She also had one in black, which was why she could only afford one chair in her living room and had a very large credit card bill, but 'Who needs furniture when you can be fabulous?' was her motto. It was not one Carmen shared after enduring one-too-many bum-numbing nights at Sadie's, sitting on an ancient bean bag that had spilled most of its beans.

'I'll come and see you lots and lots, Carmen, I promise.' Marcus was being extra nice now; he realised he had gone too far with his threat to seduce Will. 'And you'll have Jess down the road.'

'Does she still hate me?' Sadie asked, looking at her gnocchi and trying to seem casual.

'Pretty much,' Carmen replied. The three of them had been great friends when they'd shared a flat in Tufnell Park. Carmen knew Jess from uni, and Jess had been at school with Sadie. Three had been the magic number until one fateful week nine years ago when Jess and her boyfriend Sean had been on a break. In a night of drunken, never-to-be-repeated abandon Sadie and Sean had ended up sleeping together. A month later Jess and Sean had made up, but when Sean fessed up about Sadie all hell broke loose. Jess refused to speak to Sadie, who ended up moving out. Nor would Jess ask Sadie to her wedding or invite her to see her baby son Harry. They'd met over the years at various friends of friends' but had never patched things up – Jess's nickname for Sadie was 'the bitch whore from hell'. Indeed, Carmen often felt as if she was torn between two lovers as each of the two former friends was fiercely possessive of her and always monitored how much time she spent with the other.

Talk then turned to Marcus's latest stand-up tour, which was due to kick off the following year, to Leo being a workaholic and how rarely Marcus got to see him, and to Sadie's burgeoning relationship with Dom. In spite of Carmen's warning, Sadie had gone out with him again. She had paid for the cinema as he was skint again, and afterwards he had lasted until South East

Iceland, which at least was an improvement. Sadie persisted in thinking he was sweet as he had given her the complimentary Twinings tea bags from the hotel he'd been staying at in Doncaster while doing a gig.

'But they were free!' Carmen told her.

'Yeah, but it's nice that he was thinking of me,' Sadie replied, a tad defensive.

She was a moth to the comedy flame. Carmen and Marcus just looked at each other, too despairing of Sadie's addiction to tossers to expend energy on an eye roll or arch of a brow. And then it was time to say goodbye and for Carmen to return to her flat for the last time.

As everything was in storage she had to kip down on a lilo in a sleeping bag, with only Basil for company. She found herself humming 'Papa was a Rolling Stone' as she tried to get comfortable. *Goodbye Hornsey/Crouch End borders, Goodbye sexy firemen. Hello, Brighton.*

7

Carmen had not been to Marcus's seaside pad before, as he'd always rented it out. So when she walked in she was stunned by the size of the living room, the neck-cricking high ceilings, the huge bay window giving a fantastic view of the sea. Today, this was admittedly not looking its best as it was a relentless steely grey, the colour of old-lady curls, but still impressive compared to Carmen's old view of the fire station, even if the firemen were cuties. But she was also struck by the terrifying minimalism of the flat – just a fireplace, an elegant Venetian glass mirror above it, glass shelves, a single glass coffee table, an Arctic white leather sofa, a chandelier. The only splash of colour was a bottle-green velvet armchair. That would have to be her seat, she couldn't imagine chilling out on a white sofa. Carmen loved clutter and bohemian touches. In fact, she could feel panic setting in as she viewed the vast expanse of highly polished dark wooden floorboards and the large white rug occupying the middle of the room like some kind of designer cloud. What kind of person had a white rug? She was bound to spill red wine over it. She needed to be surrounded by clutter and colour right now.

Quickly she set Basil down on the coffee table and

got out her snow globe collection and arranged all twenty of them on one of the shelves. Then she got out the photographs of her friends and family, displayed in a variety of silver or crystal-encrusted frames, and plonked her branch of cherry-tree lights in a vase on the mantelpiece. She plugged them in and was immediately reassured when they gave off their friendly pink glow. Finally she sat in the armchair and surveyed her new home, calmed by the infusion of colour and stuff.

It was a first-floor flat in the highly desirable Sussex Square – a stunning Regency crescent of elegant white stuccoed houses built around a beautiful private garden. Marcus had given her three facts – one that Sir Laurence Olivier once had a house here; two that Lewis Carroll was inspired to write *Alice in Wonderland* by the secret tunnel that led from the garden to the sea, and three that the beach directly opposite her was reserved for nudists. Carmen got up and peered out of the window, wondering if she would catch a glimpse of a bare arse bobbing around on the pebbles. The steely sea and banks of orangey-brown pebbles and chilly October air certainly did not invite one to take one's kit off. Even in blazing sunshine it was hard to imagine wanting to strip off on such an exposed beach. Surely nudism should only be entered into on some exotic island paradise, with white sand and a turquoise sea that would be warm to the skin?

There was something deeply soothing about looking out to sea, the feeling of space uninterrupted by people, buildings and traffic. This was her new start. She could almost feel some of the tension of the past weeks leave her. Almost. She still felt terrible about Will. She hadn't followed up her apology, in spite of Marcus and Sadie nagging her. But it was pointless thinking about him now; she really had burned all her bridges and it was futile to wish things were different. Things were as they were. The harsh, insistent cry of a passing seagull interrupted her reverie. God, they were noisy! Almost as intrusive as the beep-beep of the fire station doors opening. The noise reminded her of the time; she was due at Jess's for dinner in twenty minutes.

Jess lived in a residential area of Brighton, which she had assured Carmen was within walking distance. Carmen enjoyed the stroll along Marine Drive, which ran by the sea. It was lined with Regency-style houses and flats, many fetchingly accessorised with wrought-iron balconies and pillars. A short distance away the brassy Palace Pier squatted in the waves, shadowed by the ghostly iron skeleton of the ruined West Pier. *Ha*, the iron structure seemed to say, *this is what you could end up as one day*. In the meantime the Palace Pier was going for it with its flashing neon lights, booths selling doughnuts and chips and fortune telling, an assortment of scary rides, and candy-striped helter-skelter. However, Carmen did not enjoy the uphill climb to Jess's house and her shoe boots had definitely been a mistake. It was a chilly evening, but by the time she had climbed up the one-in-ten gradient hill, (okay, it probably wasn't as steep as that but it felt it) she was red-faced and out of breath.

'Oh my God, Jess!' she exclaimed as her friend

opened the front door to her terraced house. 'You could have warned me about the hill.'

'You've been here before!' Jess replied, giving her a hug.

'Yes, but I always got a taxi! And now I'm in the grip of credit-crunch-no-salary scenario I had to walk and my feet are killing me!'

They both looked down at Carmen's killer heels. 'It's UGGs for you, baby. Brighton has hills. UGGs in winter, Birkenstocks in summer. That is the rule,' Jess told her. Ah well, Carmen thought, it could have been worse, Jess could have said Crocs.

Carmen followed Jess along the hall and downstairs to the basement kitchen/diner, carefully avoiding the detritus that seven-year-old Harry had left in his wake, the assorted pieces of Lego that Carmen knew from bitter past experience really hurt when you trod on them barefoot, the skateboard, football and folded-up scooter. Jess poured Carmen a more than generous glass of red wine.

'Easy, Jess,' Carmen joked, 'I've got to write tomorrow, and whereas I could always bluff my way as an agent, I've found out the hard way that I absolutely cannot write with a hangover.'

'Oh, get it down you,' Jess insisted, plonking the glass on the worn oak table which was covered with Harry's elaborate drawings of space ships and spindly aliens patrolling their planets.

'Where is Harry?' Carmen asked, carefully clearing a space for her wine. She didn't want to be the bad grown-up who ruined Harry's precious artwork with a red wine stain.

'He's away with Sean for the weekend – they've gone to see Sean's sister in London.'

'Didn't you want to go?'

Jess shook her head. 'Nope, I've got a mountain of marking to do and I wanted to see you. I could do with a break from both of them, if you must know.' She held up her glass. 'Anyway, cheers, Carmen.'

Carmen held up her glass. 'Cheers.'

'I know you've been through it, but you look good, girlfriend,' Jess told her.

'Thanks,' Carmen replied, 'I guess misery must be good for the cheekbones and stomach. I've been feeling so stressed I've hardly eaten anything, apart from Oreos and Hula Hoops.'

'God, I hate you!' Jess shot back. 'If I'm stressed I always end up eating even more, it's like my body goes into survival mode and has to stock up.' Jess was a very attractive woman with long chestnut-brown hair. Her most striking feature was her beautiful hazel-coloured eyes framed by well-shaped dark eyebrows. Carmen had frequently suffered eyebrow envy when looking at Jess. Jess also had a pale complexion, which she had loathed for years until everyone realised that baking your English rose skin in the burning sun was not such a good idea. And a lovely, voluptuous figure that she was always hiding under jeans and smock tops. Carmen had given up telling her to define her waist.

'I'm bloody starving now, though, what's for dinner?' Carmen asked expectantly. Jess was a great cook who usually could be relied upon to lay on a feast. Carmen had been looking forward to it all afternoon, having no food in the house save the aforementioned Oreos and Hula Hoops.

Jess looked slightly guilty. 'Sorry, Carmen, I haven't cooked. D'you mind if we order pizza?'

They moved from the kitchen, upstairs to the living room. Carmen flopped on the sofa next to Kitty Kitty, a fat, bordering on obese ginger cat, while Jess expertly lit a fire. Over a bottle of red wine, and a large American hot, the two caught up on what had been happening with their lives. Carmen couldn't help noticing that Jess was knocking back the wine, getting through two glasses for every one of hers. But fair enough, she reasoned, Jess probably didn't get many nights off as Sean worked as a lawyer in London and didn't get back till late, which meant the bulk of childcare, running of the house and everything else fell to Jess on top of her own career.

During a lull in conversation, as Jess put more logs on the fire, Carmen idly surveyed the room. Jess was the polar opposite to Marcus in interior design and the living room was an explosion of different colours, red velvet sofas, fuchsia cushions, a multi-coloured rug, burgundy curtains. Every available inch of wall was covered in pictures. There were photographs of Harry, from tiny scrunched-up-faced newborn to chubby-faced toddler, to winsome-faced seven-year-old. There were pictures of Jess and Sean from their many travels BH (before Harry), mixed with Harry's early artistic endeavours to draw people, who all resembled giant eggs with enormous stick hands and no legs. The mantelpiece was crowded with bronze candlesticks, pebbles and shells. The bookshelves were bulging with novels, everything from Dickens through to chick lit, and more pebbles.

'I love your house, Jess,' Carmen declared dreamily. 'It's like a proper grown-up's, you know, with the fire and the cat and the child and the husband.' It was intended as a compliment, which made Jess's reaction all the more shocking.

'I'm not Doris fucking Day! What about the mortgage and the damp wall upstairs that needs fixing and the leaking shower and the husband who's never here, and on the rare occasions he is, is a moody git? What about being trapped in a loveless, sexless marriage?' Jess sounded so bitter.

'Is he? Are you?' Carmen sat up, her fantasy dashed. She was used to Jess talking about life with a dry sense of humour making anything seem bearable. But funny Jess seemed to have gone on vacation.

Jess poked rather aggressively at the fire, and stared at the greedy yellow flames as they curled round the logs. 'Yeah – it's been no bed of roses lately. Frankly I envy you being single quite a lot of the time. You can do exactly what you want and you haven't got someone on your back nagging you, saying you're a bad person and a lousy wife.'

Carmen had never seen her friend like this before. Usually they laughed and gossiped their way through a night, but then, since Jess had moved to Brighton three years ago, Carmen supposed she had seen less of her. But she couldn't imagine Jess not getting on with Sean. They had been a couple since their second year at university, falling in love in a student production of *The Importance of Being Earnest*. Jess played Lady Bracknell, Sean, Algernon, and he always joked that she had him at 'A handbag!' Admittedly there had been that blip when they were on a break and Sean ended up in bed with Sadie, but they'd got through that and married a year later. A year after that they had Harry. That made them the longest married couple Carmen knew after her parents. But maybe there were things going on that she had no idea about.

'Sorry,' Jess seemed to snap out of it, 'I sound like some embittered crone, it's just Sean and I had a bit of a row before he left and I hate parting on a quarrel. So go on, make me jealous, tell me all about your fabulous single life.'

Carmen gave a wry smile. 'Well, I managed to totally alienate the man I fancied at work by insulting him in front of his close friends, and I also managed to be horrible to a pregnant woman at the same time. So, fabulous single life? Or total shite?'

Even mentioning the Will scenario caused a fresh wave of mortification. Jess wanted all the gory details and Carmen duly obliged, though she glossed over how very much she had liked Will and how much she missed him.

'Forget about Will – I know an absolutely gorgeous single man who would be perfect for you.' Jess's face took on a dreamy expression. 'Daniel Garner, officially the most beautiful man I have ever seen.' Now dreamy turned businesslike. 'I'll have to orchestrate a meeting for you. Maybe I'll have you both round for dinner. You won't be disappointed.'

'Who are you? My pimp?' Carmen joked back; however gorgeous Jess's single man was, she wasn't interested.

'If I got you two together, you would get down on your knees every day in prayer to thank me. You'd probably have to set up a shrine for me.'

'Whatevah!'

'Oh God, don't say that! It's what I get from my students, it drives me mad! Anyway, you haven't mentioned the bitch whore from hell. Every time I switch on Radio Four she seems to be on it. I've had to go over to Radio Two about ten years before I should, and I swear I'm in the wrong demographic for it.'

'Don't you think enough water has gone under enough bridges and you could actually forgive Sadie?' Carmen asked cautiously. 'It would be so good if we could all get on again.'

Jess shrugged. 'Sometimes I think it would be better if she had gone off with Sean.'

'I'm sure you don't mean that,' Carmen replied, but Jess didn't answer.

By now it was after midnight. Carmen suddenly felt exhausted. 'D'you want a cup of tea?' she asked. Jess shook her head and poured herself another glass of wine. Carmen couldn't help thinking that tea might have been a better option. She was only gone a few minutes making her peppermint tea, but when she returned Jess was fast asleep on the sofa. Carmen leaned over her. 'Jess, don't you want to go to bed?'

Jess batted her hand up and mumbled something unintelligible, so Carmen went upstairs intending to grab a duvet to put over Jess.

She switched on Jess's bedroom light and froze in her tracks as she saw two empty bottles of wine on the dressing table. Surely Jess wouldn't have knocked those back on top of the bottle and a half they'd shared? Downstairs Jess was still out for the count. Carmen gently laid the duvet over her friend and sat on the rug by the fire watching the last dying embers. She felt as if she had been in the grip of a mini whirlwind and was only now emerging from the other side. But she was going to be strong, she was going to focus on her writing, she was not going to obsess about Will or about the baby thing. She turned and looked at her friend again, and not wanting to leave her on her own when she was so out of it, tracked down a sleeping bag and went and slept on Harry's bunk bed.

Harry's current obsessions were Dr Who and dinosaurs, and the walls around the bunk were plastered with pictures of a variety of prehistoric beasts and daleks. As a child Carmen had been petrified of the daleks. The only thing that had stopped her having even worse nightmares about them than the ones she already did was the constant reassurance from her dad that daleks were (a) not real and (b) could not climb stairs. Thank goodness she wasn't a child now and confronted with the *über* upgraded flying daleks. She would never have slept again! She was just dropping off to sleep when she quite clearly heard the voice of a cyberman saying, 'You will be deleted.' WTF! She sat up and cracked her head on the bunk. Swearing profusely, she tracked down the source of the sound to Harry's toy box, the culprit, a Cyberman mask. She picked it up. 'You will be upgraded,' intoned the mask.

'Oh shut it!' she shot back, switching it off. 'You were never as good as the daleks.' Back in her bunk she slept badly and dreamed she was being pursued by a herd of creatures who were scarily half velociraptor and half dalek, but was rescued in the nick of time by David Tennant. *Damn*, she thought, emerging from sleep, *I'd much rather it had been Christopher Eccleston.* No disrespect to David, who was a very good actor, but she'd always had a soft spot for Eccleston. It seemed to be the story of her life right now that even her dreams let her down. She gave herself five minutes to indulge in her favourite fantasy – the one where Will had forgiven her, they'd moved beyond the flirtation stage and were lovers. It was all lovely scenes of them lying in bed together, blissed out in each other's arms, though she did have some saucier versions, then hanging out by the sea in Brighton or strolling along the South Bank with Van Morrison's 'Have I Told You Lately that I Love You' providing the soundtrack to their affair. Okay, so maybe the Van Morrison was a bit predictable, but it was *her* fantasy. A clattering in the kitchen down-stairs disturbed her and reluctantly she got up.

Jess was already dressed, in yet another tunic and jeans combo, and tidying the kitchen in something of a frenzy.

'Hey!' she exclaimed when Carmen shuffled in, 'Coffee and toast? Sorry to fall asleep like that – I was just knackered.'

'Nothing to do with the amount of wine we drank?' Carmen said carefully.

Jess laughed. 'Yeah, we did cane it a bit, didn't we? I definitely can't drink as much as I did in my twenties.' Jess didn't look great. There were dark shadows under her eyes and her pale skin had a slightly sweaty sheen. When she poured out a coffee from the cafetiere, her hand shook. Carmen wanted to reply that no *we* didn't, but maybe she was being unfair, maybe Jess was just kicking back after a full-on week. *Maybe*.

'I've just texted Daniel, the gorgeous man I mentioned last night, and he's up for coming to dinner on Friday, so keep that date free,' Jess told her.

Carmen groaned. 'You didn't make it out to be some kind of blind date, did you? That's so cringey.'

'No, no, I just said I was having a few friends round, including my very sexy, single friend who has just moved down from London. I had to get in quick, Carmen, he's in demand. I just hope no one gets their claws into him before my dinner.'

Carmen treated her to a major eye roll.

'You'll thank me for it,' Jess told her.

Carmen shook her head and tucked into a bowl of muesli.

After breakfast Jess said she had to get on with her marking, so Carmen had no excuse not to go home and continue work on her sitcom.

8

'Leo has just blown me out, he's got to be in New York for some high-profile corporate something-or-other. Please say you'll come to the Comedy Awards with me. *Please!*' Marcus sounded in a complete panic. For all his confidence on stage and on TV, he absolutely hated going to big events without Leo. 'It's on Friday, and I know it's short notice, but I will be eternally grateful.'

'I'm supposed to be going to dinner at Jess's. She's lined up some sexy single man for me.'

'Please, Carmen, I really need you to come.'

Carmen groaned inwardly. Along with letting down Jess, who wouldn't be impressed, if she agreed to go with Marcus it would mean a whole day out of her writing schedule, maybe even two, as she'd have to do that whole pre-event preparation malarkey of having her hair blow-dried, getting key bits of her body waxed, plus finding the right dress to wear. More importantly, Will was bound to be there and she really didn't know if she was up to seeing him. She'd still not heard from him and she hadn't felt up to contacting him again. But if she didn't go Marcus would be gutted, and she was dependent on his charity right now, because without Marcus she would be homeless, since her Hornsey flat was on the market and already had a buyer.

'Please, Carmen,' Marcus repeated. 'I'll sort out the frock.'

'Designer?'

'I thought you were channelling Gok, patron saint of the high street,' Marcus said sarkily. 'I was going to recommend a little number from the house of Top Shop, or isn't New Look coming into its own these days?'

'Bollocks to that! If you're paying I want designer all the way!'

'I can't believe you're so shallow,' Marcus shot back. 'Have you suddenly morphed into Sadie? I thought you would become less shallow now you lived in Brighton and were away from all the temptations of London town.'

'In my heart I'm still a Londoner.' Then she laughed. 'It's okay, you don't have to buy me a dress. I'll come anyway.'

'Buy? I'm going to call in some favours from that designer boutique I go to all the time, and as this is TV they should be glad of the publicity.'

How could Carmen possibly say no after that? She cancelled Jess, who as predicted was narked and told her she'd be lucky to get another chance with Daniel, booked her blow-dry, got waxed and tried not to obsess about seeing Will again. The reality was of course that she spent much time wondering what she would say if she saw him again, and how she would look. Cool, calm and sexy would be her motto for the night, she decided.

On top of the lure of a free outfit, the other good thing about going to the Awards with Marcus was that Carmen got to indulge in one of her all-time favourite fantasies – the I-live-in-Mayfair one. Marcus and Leo owned a flat on the highly prestigious Mount Street. Addresses didn't come much posher: off Park Lane, with the swish Scott's Restaurant at one end – (such a hit with A-listers) and the impressively grand Connaught Hotel at the other. When she'd lived in London Carmen got to indulge in this fantasy on a weekly basis as she'd go round for dinner with Marcus, usually when Leo was visiting his daughter. It had been one of their traditions that they'd eat Thai food, which Marcus loved and Leo didn't, and then slob in front of the TV watching comedy series – everything from *Ab Fab* to *Green Wing* – and eating sweets from M&S. Carmen had her Wobbly Worms, the green ones saved for Will, and Marcus tucked into Percy Pigs and Pals.

Leo was far too sophisticated to eat sweets. The only sweet ever to pass his lips was no doubt some wildly expensive piece of bitter dark chocolate. Carmen liked Leo on the rare occasion she did see him – he was always working – but he was very different from anyone she knew. He was so much more grown up – literally, being in his late forties, but also in his mindset. He had actually been married for seven years and had a daughter, before coming out and falling for Marcus. He had a very high-powered career in finance working for a Japanese bank, but though he had explained more than once to Carmen what he actually did, she never understood it – a little like Daisy explaining the difference between goths and emos. Leo had told her she reminded him of Dory, the fish in the film *Finding Nemo* who keeps forgetting everything she is told. Carmen would like to think that he said it affectionately, but she wasn't entirely sure.

As soon as Carmen turned off Oxford Street, which was heaving with shoppers, and walked down New Bond Street, past the designer shops, it was like entering a different world. It was so posh that even the blades of grass in Berkeley Square and the trees seemed to be standing to attention, striving to be the best. Even the air smelt fresher: less McDonald's mixed with exhaust fumes, more the smell of money, which seemed to consist of wafts of expensive perfume and leather, with no hint of the sweat of the workers who had helped create that wealth – well, that was what her dad, a staunch socialist, would have said. Carmen reached Mount Street. Rich old ladies swanned about in Chanel suits; sleek black cars cruised by like designer sharks. She passed antique shops with unfeasibly grand items displayed in the window that wouldn't looked out of place at Versailles. She paused briefly outside Christian Louboutin. Even the memory of cruel Tiana couldn't dispel the magic of the red-soled wonders.

*   *   *

'How do I look?' Marcus asked anxiously as soon as he opened the door to her, struggling to do up his cufflinks.

'Beautiful,' Carmen was able to say truthfully, taking over and quickly fastening the silver and onyx cufflinks which had Marcus's and Leo's initials intertwined. Marcus was in a black tuxedo, and while he looked good in everything, he was especially stunning in his suit, as if he had stepped out of a lavish 1920s costume drama, with his timeless beauty and high cheekbones. But Carmen knew that beauty had its price: often in the past, people (for that read TV executives) had not taken him seriously, dismissing him as male-model-lite.

'But intelligent as well,' she added hastily.

'Leo hasn't phoned or texted. I thought he would have by now.'

'He's probably tied up in one of those meetings that go on through the night and they order Chinese food in and eat it from cartons and wave their chopsticks around aggressively, and everyone is so macho they pretend they don't need sleep and say things like we work best under pressure and we're giving a hundred and fifty per cent.' Carmen had a horror of people who said they worked best under pressure. She herself wilted under pressure.

Marcus didn't look entirely reassured but changed the subject: 'Come through, Cinders, and I'll show you your dresses.'

Carmen actually clapped her hands in delight – well, who wouldn't at the prospect of free designer clobber?

But she resisted giving a jig with glee – she knew where to draw the line. She followed Marcus into his bedroom, which looked as if it was straight out of the pages of a style magazine with its silver wallpaper with exotic metallic lilies, an exquisite chandelier and a four-poster bed with a white silk canopy. Laid out on the bed were two sumptuous dresses, glowing like precious jewels, one crimson, one emerald.

'Oh Marcus, did I say what a lovely fairy godmother you made?' Carmen exclaimed, drinking in the rich colours and the exquisite cut of the garments.

'I'll pour you a glass of fizz while you decide which one to wear,' Marcus said, discreetly leaving the room.

Carmen quickly pulled off her clothes and slid into the crimson dress, the cool silk swishing against her skin. She considered herself in the mirror. It was very sexy, maybe a little too sexy, with a plunging neckline that would have Carmen paranoid about possible wardrobe malfunctions. 'It could be you,' she mused, 'or it could be you,' she pointed at the emerald. In the event it was the emerald, which was strapless with a fitted bodice that said timeless chic to Carmen, whereas the crimson was a little too attention-grabbing, and she was most definitely not Liz Hurley to Marcus's Hugh Grant.

'Why, Cinders, you shall go to the ball!' Marcus declared when Carmen strutted her stuff into the living room. He handed her a glass of champagne and looked at his watch. 'In four hours' time it will all be over, thank God.'

'I don't get you,' Carmen declared, sinking into Marcus's luxurious charcoal-grey leather sofa, soft as butter to the touch. 'You might even win tonight.'

'It's all that gruesome back-slapping and networking that goes on. You know me, I like to do my show and then slink off into the night. But thanks for coming, it makes it bearable. And you might even see Will.' He said this as if it was a good thing.

Carmen winced. 'I really hope I don't. I still feel awful about what I said. But equally he was unfair about Matthew.'

'Carmen, I know you're completely blinkered where Matthew is concerned, like an old faithful shire horse, but Matthew, in spite of his many virtues, was a crap administrator, and you just can't afford to be like that any more. Will is right on that score. If Fox hadn't taken him over when they did, Nicholson would have gone down and everyone would have lost their jobs.'

Carmen stuck her tongue out.

'Now, now, don't get petulant with me. If you're very good you might be able to keep that frock.'

Carmen zipped the attitude.

She had been to some five Comedy Awards over the years, so it was no big deal seeing all the giants of comedy and all the TV stars in the flesh, here a Lee Evans, there an Eddie Izzard, here a Stephen Fry, there a Paul Merton, but walking up the red carpet with Marcus was a new experience. She had imagined following after him like the faithful shire horse he'd called her, but instead Marcus wanted her arm-in-arm with him to face the barrage of cameras. The press had a double-edged relationship with Marcus. They couldn't deny that he was incredibly funny and talented, but he was ferocious in guarding his personal life which they bitterly resented. Nor was he a cosy, camp gay man whom they could pigeonhole, being more of a maverick. And as Marcus was always telling her, 'The press love you so long as you don't remind them that you like having sex with men.'

'Bloody hell,' Carmen exclaimed, intimidated by the press pack, 'I'm not Liz Hurley, you know.'

'Oh, shut up and think of the dress,' Marcus whispered to her as they paused to pose for a shot that Carmen just prayed would not turn up on *Heat*'s 'What Were You Thinking?' page. Except in this instance, because she wasn't a celeb it would be what was Marcus thinking having a shire horse dressed in green on his arm?

Thankfully, once they were in the studio they had to take their seats immediately at one of the many tables, which was fine by Carmen, even though they were sharing with, among others, Dexter, Marcus's terrifying agent, who was American and had the teeth to prove it, and his equally scary script editor wife Fi, so *über* thin that she made Twiglets look as if they were packing too much weight. The less time spent milling about and 'oh darling'ing everybody, doing the double air kiss routine, the less chance she'd have of running into Will. Her cool, calm and sexy motto had deserted her on the red carpet; she was nervous, and felt as awkward as a teenager. She quickly scanned the tables around her. They seemed to be Will-free, and she was both disappointed and relieved in equal measure.

Russell Brand, fresh from making yet another movie in LA, was compering. Carmen found herself staring at his Sass & Bide skinny jeans and open-to-the-waist shirt showing off his yoga-toned hairy chest. A couple of years ago she'd spent a torrid summer fantasising about him in the manner of a teenage crush, but no longer. It was a pity not to have the crush still as the night was very dull, big on people gushing onstage, and not enough clips of funny bits. It always looked so glam on TV, and so hilarious, but really the hardest part was trying not to yawn or laugh at inappropriate moments, just in case the camera was on you. Marcus was next to her, fidgeting incessantly with his cufflinks. He was up for the Best Comedy Entertainment Personality.

He gently nudged her in the Dolce & Gabbana-clad ribs during a round of applause, for the Best Newcomer in Comedy Award. 'I've just seen Will over there.' He nodded in the direction of one of the tables to their far left.

'Really?' Carmen tried to channel cool, calm, sexy, but could only come up with hot, jittery, jelly. 'Has he seen me?'

'I don't think so.'

Carmen tried to resist looking over. Russell was doing the preamble to the next award, which Marcus was up for; she should be giving it her full attention in case the cameras were on the table. But she found herself looking away from Russell's yoga-toned bod and scanning the room for Will. She caught a glimpse of him in profile, but then the winner of the award was announced and it was Marcus!

Carmen threw her arms round Marcus, applauded wildly and then wolf-whistled as he made his way to the stage. And it was just as she had removed her fingers from their wolf-whistling position that she saw Will staring directly at her. Great, so he had seen her with her cheeks inflated like one of those fish that puff up when they're under attack! Of course he'd also seen her passed out and possibly drooling in his bed, but hey, that didn't count as she couldn't remember it. She instantly sucked her cheeks back in to remind him that actually she did have cheekbones and nodded as he smiled back. Then she directed all her attention to the stage, where Marcus was receiving the award from Jimmy Carr. Did that man ever sleep? He seemed to be on TV *all* the time.

Marcus was very self-deprecating as he accepted the award, but Carmen knew he was thrilled and she was thrilled for him. She had seen him go from doing stand-up at some real dives to being one of the hottest talents on TV. 'Not bad for a bender from Balham,' he was always saying, though thankfully he did not say that now.

Marcus's award was the last to be announced, which meant the audience could commence their milling and oh-darling-kiss-kiss rituals. At first Carmen clung to Marcus's side like a designer-dressed burr, but eventually she conceded defeat: she was going to have to do some milling of her own.

She had just finished catching up with Lottie and Dirty Sam, when she turned round and there was Will. Immediately Carmen felt as skittish as a pony on speed and she couldn't help but notice how Lottie practically got Dirty Sam in a headlock and marched him away.

'Miller, I thought you had forsworn such superficial and trivial events for the discipline and rigour of a writer's life.' Will looked damn fine in his black tie, but knackered too; there were dark shadows under his eyes and his pale skin was paler than usual. In fact, he could probably have given Robert Pattinson from *Twilight* a run for his money in the paleness stakes – and in the looks stakes, it had to be said. Although stakes was maybe not the word you would use to a hot vampire if you wanted to be a fangbanger.

Carmen was secretly thrilled to note that, one, Will had deliberately sought her out, and two, there was a definite dash of flirtation in his tone. Maybe he had forgiven her for her outrageous comments. Maybe they could pick up where they had left off. And as soon as she thought that, she felt a great lifting of her spirits. 'I did it for Marcus,' she replied, 'And I can't say that I've missed these events. The white wine was as acidic as ever, I swear it's been stripping the enamel from my teeth. And Fi, the wife of Marcus's agent, only ate one edamame bean all night and sipped mineral water. I felt like a bloody great porker next to her.'

Will smiled, a smile which instantly turned him from knackered to sexy.

'But you're looking good. I can't fault the dress. I declare you a mutton-free zone.'

'So how are you?' she gabbled, fiddling self-consciously with her charm bracelet.

'Okay, full-on busy but surviving.' He frowned. 'Actually, let's not talk about work. Trish told me you've moved down to Brighton.'

And why haven't you been in touch? Do you hate me? There were so many questions Carmen wanted to ask.

Instead she went for, 'Yep, it's been really good for me to have a change of scene and make progress with my writing. I find being by the sea very inspiring.' Oh no! She sounded so stilted and pompous! This would not do. She took a deep breath and rallied. 'Will, I'm really sorry about that night when I was rude to you and to your friends. It was unforgivable. I can only say that I had a lot of stuff going on.'

Will's smile faded. 'It was quite an evening. I had no idea you had such a low opinion of what I do – nothing about talent and integrity, only caring about money, and you wouldn't trust your work with me. Remind me never to ask you for a reference.'

Carmen's cheeks burned with embarrassment. 'I don't have a low opinion of you and I didn't mean what I said about your work.'

Will lowered his voice. 'It's okay, I guessed there must be other stuff going on. It's forgiven and forgotten.'

He paused. 'But did you mean the other thing you said?'

A lot had happened since they'd met, but Carmen just knew he was referring to the shag comment and her cheeks burned redder still. 'What other thing?' she asked, feigning ignorance.

'Miller, you know exactly what I'm talking about.' Will's tone took a definite flirtatious edge. 'You said I was a good kisser and that you could probably shag me.'

He was about to continue when he was joined by a stunning, willowy woman with long, honey-blonde hair who was a good two inches taller than him, all long limbs and artfully tousled hair, with an effortless English beauty like the model Laura Bailey. Immediately she slid her arm into his. 'I wondered where you'd gone off to.' She looked directly at Carmen, her grey-violet eyes coolly appraising, then back at Will. 'So who wants to shag you, darling? Should I be worried?' she demanded.

Carmen thought her cheeks might actually combust. Will didn't exactly look thrilled as he muttered, 'Just reminding Carmen of one of her old clients, Karl Fraser, and all his shag jokes.' He looked appealingly at Carmen.

She backed him up, 'Yeah, Karl, our least favourite knob, shag-gag comedian.'

Will had a girlfriend. A spectacularly good-looking girlfriend. He was obviously a quick worker, or maybe he'd had her all along? Maybe the flirtation had all been in her head?

'Tash, this is Carmen, Carmen, Tash,' Will did the introductions. 'Tash is a TV producer, Carmen used to work with me as a comedy agent and is now a writer.' Not just spectacularly good-ooking, also in possession of a good career. Carmen now felt about as skittish as a horse on its way to the knacker's.

'What kind of writing?' Tash asked with the characteristic directness of a TV producer.

'Well, actually I'm sort of writing a sort of comedy drama slash sitcom,' Carmen replied, doing a mental d'oh for sounding so uncertain.

'Oh? I'm always interested in new writing, give me the premise.'

It seemed less a request and more of an order.

Carmen hated being put on the spot like this. She found it hard enough describing her drama to her close friends, never mind to someone who was looking at her with disdain and who also happened to be going out with Will. 'Sorry, I've got a thing about talking about work in progress, so all I can say is it's about two sisters and their children who share a house. One sister is widowed, the other divorced, so they both have baggage, but funny-tragic baggage, not moany baggage.' She couldn't believe how much of a loser she sounded.

That comment earned her a condescending look from Tash. 'I wouldn't steal your idea, Carmen. I'm up to my eyes in comedy dramas.'

Will caught Carmen's eye and gave a reassuring smile. 'I don't think Carmen means it like that, Tash.

It's sort of like you don't want to jinx it by talking about it. Am I right?'

Carmen nodded, grateful for the intervention.

'I see,' Tash replied, with the same tone of voice she might have used for 'whatever'. 'It was lovely to meet you, Carmen, good luck with the writing. I must go and talk to Graham.'

'As in Norton,' Will told Carmen, clearly expecting to carry on talking to Carmen, but Tash remained where she was.

'And you need to come too, Will.'

'So email me,' Will said over his shoulder as Tash led him away. 'I've got a backlog of Wobbly Worms for you. I've discovered that you trained me too well – I only like the green ones and I don't know what to do with the others. Not even Trish likes them.'

'Is she okay?' Carmen called back, relieved Trish hadn't been sacked.

'Yep, she and the tropical fish are hanging on in there. See you, Carmen.'

Carmen gave a wry smile and held up her hand in farewell, trying to ignore the unexpected torrent of jealousy that was making its way through her at the fact that Will had a girlfriend. Correction, Will had a hot, super-talented, bloody gorgeous girlfriend. And what did she have? An unfinished sitcom and a cupboard full of green worms that she'd been saving for Will, not forgetting a cactus called Basil.

As Marcus had won an award there was no way that Carmen could make a quick exit; she was in for the long haul and had to spend the next hour doing the oh-darling thing, every now and then catching glimpses of Tash and Will as they worked the room, looking every inch the successful dynamic couple. Every glimpse afforded Carmen a fresh stab of jealousy, so painful that even drinking copious amounts of the evil acidic white wine failed to obliterate the feeling.

'There, it wasn't so bad seeing Will again, was it?' Marcus asked as he sprawled out on the back seat of the limo, the winner's prerogative, as they were whisked smoothly back to Mayfair. 'He looks bloody gorgeous in black tie. Truly scrumptious.' He ignored the filthy look Carmen shot him.

'It was okay,' she replied, being economical with the truth to the point of deceit. She did not want to admit to the complex mix of emotions seeing Will had aroused in her. She was definitely not going to reveal that she was green with jealousy, as green as the wobbly green worms, as green as her designer dress which she would never want to wear again as it would forever remind her of tonight. 'D'you know his girlfriend Tash?'

Marcus wrinkled his nose, 'Oh God, is he going out with her? I thought he had better taste. She's so hard you could cut diamonds on her.'

'Aren't you being sexist just because she's a forthright woman and good at her job? I bet you wouldn't say that if she was a man.' Carmen didn't know why she was defending her; frankly she hadn't warmed to Tash one little bit. She tried to tell herself that was because of Tash's personality and not because she was Will's girlfriend.

'No, she's just hard.' Marcus paused. 'I bet he's only seeing her because you knocked him back.'

'I'm sure he's not,' Carmen replied truthfully, looking out of the window at late-night London rushing by. She had one of those moments when she suddenly felt very small. The kind of moment that called for her Victoria Wood CD with a sketch about Bunsen burners and a hot chocolate, but she suspected Marcus had neither.

Marcus wanted Carmen to spend Saturday with him in London, but after a late breakfast she felt she wanted to return to Brighton and force herself back to reality. She had been harbouring thoughts of Will, had extended the fantasy where they were lovers to include wildly romantic trips to New York, to moving in together. It was where she retreated to avoid thoughts of Nick and his baby. But now she was going to have to let go of it. The sad truth was that the Sinatra song 'One for My Baby', which she'd danced to with Will, had nailed it. All she and Will had shared was a brief episode. And it was over now. She'd had the clearest possible signal seeing him with Tash that there was nothing doing. So she would rather be out of London to clear her head. If she stayed with Marcus, she'd only obsess about what Will and Tash were up to. Had they made love in the morning when they were both still half asleep and full of dreams? Had he then made her tea and toast? No, scrap the toast, Tash did not have the look of a carb eater. She probably had something *über* healthy like a broccoli and spinach smoothie and then went for a ten-K run.

Arriving at Brighton station, Carmen went first to M&S to arm herself for a Saturday night on her own without the Will fantasy to sustain her. She planned to watch a DVD, maybe a French film, something challenging that pushed the boundaries, sip a glass of red wine and eat something healthy. She grabbed a pack of Singapore prawn noodles and a bottle of red wine. This was absolutely fine, she told herself, but then she found herself in the checkout line with tears in her eyes as she surveyed the packets of Wobbly Worms next to her, each and every one reminding her of what she had lost. She tried to tell herself not to be so pathetic. It was hardly up there with the greatest romantic moments of all time, was it? Romeo calling out beneath Juliet's balcony; Cleopatra killing herself after learning of Mark Antony's death; Orpheus rescuing Eurydice from the underworld; Carmen crying over a packet of worms. But it made no difference.

Forget the French film, there was only one thing for it – *Gladiator*. She needed the distraction that this film could deliver. It was Carmen's guilty pleasure, which just a select few of her friends knew about – she didn't want everyone thinking she was a total nutter. But still, didn't some people watch *Dirty Dancing* two hundred and fifty times? When she and Nick were going through the IVF hell she'd had to watch *Gladiator* at least once a month. Yes, she had an all-consuming passion for Russell Crowe, which had abated over the years some- what − mainly due to his penchant for choosing chal- lenging roles where he had to pile on the pounds and often behave quite badly or madly or both − but it was more than that. *Gladiator* offered a world view of black- and-white values, where you had to be brave and get on with things, however bad they were, and in fairness having your wife and son murdered and being forced into slavery and to fight to the death was probably as bad as it could possibly get.

By the time the credits rolled, even though Carmen had fast-forwarded the traumatic scene where the aforementioned son and wife get murdered and some of the gladiatorial combat − once you've seen one arm being hacked off you've probably seen them all − she felt drained. To cheer herself up she watched *Some Like it Hot*, another of her all-time favourites. In conse- quence she got to bed after two a.m., slightly sozzled from the red wine (the one glass had become three- quarters of the bottle) but nicely numb, thoughts of Will thankfully blunted by the alcohol. It possibly wasn't the most mature way of dealing with the situation. *But still*, she told herself, tucking the duvet under her feet to guard against the foot monster, *nobody's perfect*.

161

9

October became November. The weather turned cooler. Carmen fulfilled Jess's prophecy and bought a pair of black UGGs, which she now lived in. She fulfilled her own prophecy and spilt red wine on Marcus's white rug, which no amount of stain remover would shift. She had better make a success of the comedy in order to earn enough money to buy him a new rug. She had finally settled into a routine of sorts. She'd discovered that morning was her best time for writing, that she had to do some kind of exercise, otherwise in the afternoon she wanted to fall asleep, and that she also had to see someone during the day for lunch so as not to go stark raving mad. She met up with Jess several times a week for lunch, usually just a quick sandwich as Jess rarely had time for anything longer. For exercise, she took to alternating running by the sea with swimming in her local pool, where she frequently suffered pool rage from people who swam in the wrong lane. She would spend the rest of the day smelling faintly of chlorine and worrying that she had a verruca.

Swimming was now the only time she allowed herself to think about Will, but thoughts of him crept in when she least expected it. When she'd written a scene she particularly liked she thought about what his reaction would be. When she got dressed up for a night out in London with Marcus and Sadie, both of whom had yet to come to Brighton, she wondered how Will would have rated it on the muttonometer. But on the whole she thought she was handling the whole Will-having-a-girlfriend scenario rather well, which was why she was thrown when a package arrived one Friday morning containing five packets of Wobbly Worms all de-greened with a note, 'As promised. Enjoy. Hope the writing is going well. Will x'.

It was a sweet gesture – no pun intended. Tash did not have the look of a woman who would enjoy a Wobbly Worm. She would no doubt have sophisticated tastes like quail eggs and caviar, and drink detoxifying nettle tea and pretend to like it when everyone knew it tasted like goblin vomit. Oh well, Carmen sighed, Tash and Will would be very happy together. They'd buy a loft in Shoreditch, go to all the achingly cool places, be in with the in crowd, in fact *be* the in crowd. Then when Tash had her first child, an adorable golden-haired girl called Octavia, they'd buy somewhere in the country, say the Cotswolds, to spend weekends. Tash would continue to make award-winning TV, but be slightly softened by motherhood, Will would be every inch the fantastic dad and he would start his own agency and go stateside.

Carmen paused to bite the head off a red worm and chewed it vigorously until the feelings of jealousy receded. In fact, she felt she had worked through her feelings enough to call Will and say thank you. It was two weeks since she'd last seen him; she could do this grown-up, mature, I'm-completely-over-you thing. She had been all set to email, but knew that if she did that she'd spend the next few hours obsessing about whether he had replied or not, and if not why not. So she was not *that* over him. She would go for the direct approach.

'Thanks for the worms,' was her opener. She hoped she wasn't opening a can of them by calling him. 'It's Carmen, by the way.'

'There is only one person I know who would thank me for worms,' Will said drily. 'And there'll be plenty more where they came from. I'm completely addicted to them. I'll probably have to go to Wobbly Worm rehab to break the habit – do you think they do a twelve-step programme for confectionery? Hello, my name is Will and I'm a wormaholic?'

'Hello, Will,' Carmen put in.

'Trish tried to tempt me the other week with some Haribo bears but it just wasn't the same. I felt as if I was betraying the worms.'

'You ate a Haribo bear! That's even more uncool than the worms!' Instantly they were back into banter.

'Carmen, confectionery cannot be cool or uncool. And anyway, I've never said I'm cool, I quoted "Lady in Red" to you, remember? And I'll admit right now that Chris Rea's "Driving Home for Christmas" is one of my favourite Christmas numbers of all time.'

The reference to 'Lady in Red' opened the floodgates of memory in Carmen. Who'd have thought a song by Chris de Burgh would have that effect on her? The night where she and Will had so nearly got it together, the night he had said she was gorgeous ... Well, he surely didn't think that any more now he had Tash, future mother of Octavia. She needed to get in the canoe and paddle away from that memory as quickly as she could. So she didn't pick up on the reference but said instead, 'I bet Tash doesn't eat Wobbly Worms, does she?'

A pause. 'No, Tash doesn't eat sweets. She doesn't eat sugar at all. She has the will power of a ...' He was searching for the comparison.

'An ox in the form of a beautiful gazelle?' Carmen put in for him, and got a brief moment of pleasure from imagining said gazelle being chased and then savaged by a lion on the savannah.

'Something like that.'

Carmen was on a roll now. 'So how's it going with Tash?' In a minute she would be able to forget all about dancing with Will and about how good his kisses had been, forget that there had ever been any hint that they could be more than friends.

'It's going fine, thanks.' He paused. 'I want you to know that it's second time round. I was seeing her at the beginning of the year for a few months, then we broke up and then we got together just after you left London.' Will sounded cautious, which Carmen took to mean that he didn't want to upset her by gushing about the full force of his feelings for the beautiful gazelle-like Tash. 'What about you?'

'Oh, I'm just focusing on writing at the moment, no time for relationships. Besides, finding an available straight man in the gay capital of Europe may well prove challenging, especially now I'm the wrong side of thirty. Though one of the OAPs I see when I go swimming did wink at me the other day and said he liked my costume. So I reckon there's life in the old girl yet.'

Will laughed. 'Don't put yourself down, you're a very attractive woman, Carmen.'

'But?' Carmen demanded, accustomed from their days of banter to Will delivering a compliment only to destroy it with a cheeky jibe. 'A bit mutton, I expect you're thinking.'

'I was thinking nothing of the sort, and anyway, I've only ever said mutton in relation to the zebra print and the wet-look leggings, and they were actually quite hot in a trashy, dirty kind of way. And as for the shorts, you know I loved the shorts, we all loved the shorts, Dirty Sam especially. I think he's still in mourning for them.'

This easy conversation was too painful. It only served to remind her forcibly of how Will was now out of bounds. 'Well, thanks again for the worms,' she said, falsely bright.

'Any time, Carmen. So what are you doing for Christmas?'

God, why was he asking more questions? It was only prolonging the agony.

Oh, spending it with Marcus; my parents will still be in Australia with my brother. You?'

166

'Going skiing with Tash and her family. I hate skiing, but I guess I'll get lots of work done when the others are out showing off on the black run or whatever it's called.'

'Maybe while they're on the piste you can be on the piss.' A lame joke at the best of times.

'I wish, but too much to do.'

'Well, you should learn to ski because Octavia is bound to want to do it.' Oh bloody hell, she hadn't just mentioned Will's imaginary daughter, had she?

'Who's Octavia?' Will asked, sounding bemused.

Carmen tried and failed to think of a suitable reply and could only come up reluctantly with the truth. 'Okay, this is going to sound mad, but Octavia is the daughter I imagined you might one day have with Tash.'

A pause where Will no doubt was struggling to process the madness of Carmen. 'You're way ahead of me on the whole imagination thing. It must be the difference between men and women, I only ever get as far as imagining women without their clothes on and you've imagined a whole next generation!'

'Sorry – I guess I'm spending too much time on my own these days.'

'And Octavia – what kind of name is that? It's the name of a car by Skoda; you could at least have called her Mercedes or Lexi after a Lexus, I'd love a Lexus.'

'Actually, I was thinking of Shakespeare, Octavia wife of Antony in *Antony and Cleopatra*. Mercedes would be a bit flash, don't you think?'

'So did you skip the whole imagining-me-naked bit,

or aren't women like that?' Will, always such a tease. 'I mean, Octavia has to get here somehow.'

This conversation had started out with Carmen thanking Will for the Wobbly Worms and now she was practically in bed with him, which would have been fine in the old days, but there was already someone next to him, someone in an *über* chic Chanel ski suit, who would one day give birth to Octavia/Mercedes/Lexi, so much as Carmen was tempted to flirt back, she didn't.

'Women aren't like that, Will.'

'Shame, I've had *many* enjoyable moments imagining women naked.'

'Thanks again for the worms, Will.'

'Is this you dismissing me?'

'Yep, I've got work to do, and you've probably got lots of pervy fantasies to work through.'

'They're not pervy. I'll tell you about them if you want.'

'Maybe you should be telling Tash. I've really got to go now.' Carmen was suffering from an acute sense of humour failure and really needed the call to end.

'Hey, I didn't mean to offend you, Carmen,' Will replied, reverting to serious. 'We always used to banter like this.'

'That was when you didn't have a girlfriend,' Carmen said quietly. 'See you. Good luck with the skiing.'

It took all Carmen's will power to return to her writing. If Tash had the will power of an ox, Carmen was way down the food chain, say a floppy-eared bunny rabbit. What she had hoped would be a polite but friendly call had left her feeling decidedly unsettled. It had indeed opened a can of worms, as she suddenly realised how very much she missed having Will in her life. She plucked out some worms from the bag and bit their heads off to the chant of likes-me-likes-me-not, until she realised that she was making herself feel sick.

She grabbed her coat and went for a walk by the sea. It was a glorious sunset, the sky streaked with rosy pinks and oranges, and hundreds of starlings were already performing their roosting spectacular over the old pier, swooping across the sky in a tightly packed formation so it was almost impossible to see that they were individual birds. They looked more like clouds of iron filings forming different pulsing and undulating, shifting shapes in the sky, which she had found out was called a murmuration. It was a beautiful, mesmerising sight and Carmen suddenly wished very much that she had someone to share it with. She leaned against the railings looking out to sea, trying not to think about this time a year ago which had seen her final cycle of IVF fail and her and Nick realise that they had reached the end of the line, both with trying for a baby and with their marriage. By her reckoning Nick's baby was twenty-two weeks old, and she had been following her progress on an online pregnancy calendar. It wasn't perhaps the best thing for her mental health, but she was irresistibly drawn to it. She knew that the lines on the baby's fingers were formed, so she already had her own individual fingerprints and a firm handgrip. Her eyelashes and eyebrows were forming. Marian would feel her move. At first she would feel a fluttering or bubbling, or a very slight shifting movement. Later she would see the baby kicking about and be able to guess which bump was a hand or a foot. Lucky Marian, lucky Nick. What could be done in the face of such painful knowledge? She supposed if she believed in God she could have gone to church. Instead she planned to go her local off-licence, appropriately called Wine Me Up, to wine herself up, and maybe even watch *Gladiator* again. And yes, she did know that she was drinking far too much these days.

She was halfway to her destination when her mobile rang. It was Marcus: 'I'm at the station, with Sadie; we'll be with you in fifteen minutes.'

'Brighton?' Carmen asked, confused. Had she forgotten about a date with the two Londoners?

'Yep, a surprise visit. We'll see you in a bit.'

Half an hour later Carmen was pouring out glasses of cava for her friends and hoping against hope that Marcus would not notice the pinkish stain which remained defiant on the white rug, in spite of her frequent attempts to remove it.

'So why have you come down?' Carmen asked. It wasn't like Sadie to leave the capital without a great deal of fuss and forward planning.

'We suddenly remembered what this time last year meant for you,' Sadie said simply.

Carmen was touched. What would she be without her friends?

'And we couldn't bear to think of you on your own,' Marcus put in, 'drinking red wine and' – here Marcus's tone became less sympathetic – 'appearing to spill most of it on my white rug!'

Carmen groaned. 'Oh God, I knew you'd notice, sorry.'

'I'm kidding, it's just a rug, a very expensive rug, but a rug when all is said and done.'

Carmen looked at her friends. 'Thank you, you have saved me from spending all my money in Wine Me Up and from watching *Gladiator* again.'

'You can't possibly watch it any more. Three times is permissible, any more than that is borderline mentalist.' Marcus could be so hard-line at times.

'Remind me, how many times have you seen that porn film *Lucky Dick*?'

'It's not the same and you know it. So tell us what you've been up to. Have you got to meet that sexy man of Jess's yet? I was looking forward to hearing about someone other than Sadie's sexual exploits.'

Carmen shook her head and looked at Sadie. 'How goes it with the shipping forecast shagger?'

'Same old, same old. I did suggest that we played back a recording because I'm getting bored of saying it during the act. And also I got told off at work because I delivered the late-night shipping forecast in a sexually suggestive way.'

Both Marcus and Carmen exploded into laughter. 'What do you mean?' Carmen wanted details.

Sadie sighed. 'I just forgot where I was for a few minutes and thought I was in bed with bloody Dom. My Rockall had definite erotic overtones, as did my Dogger.'

'Are you sure it isn't time to find another comic?' Carmen put in, though she would miss hearing about hapless Dom.

'He may be on the way up, Carmen; he had a meeting with Will the other week. According to him, Will seemed really keen.'

Carmen found that hard to believe, but Dom, like so many other comedians, probably only heard what he wanted to hear.

'Oh, please don't talk to me about Will,' Carmen groaned. 'I had this really embarrassing phone call with him earlier.'

'It's only embarrassing because you fancy him. I don't know why you won't admit it and tell him while you're at it. He'd drop that Tash in a heartbeat, I bet.' Marcus, always so successful in love himself, expected the same level of success for his friends.

'No, he wouldn't. He's going skiing with her and her family at Christmas. I can just imagine the ravishing Tash with her firm but slender thighs hurtling down the piste, her honey-blonde hair flowing behind her like a silken banner, all in expectation of some après-ski with Will.' She suddenly became aware that she sounded a little too concerned and drew back, 'There really is nothing doing there, Marcus.'

'Damn, I would so much rather hear about hot Will than desperate Dom – no offence, Sadie.'

'None taken,' Sadie replied. No one ever liked any of her boyfriends.

'So, Carmen, remove those dreary UGGs – which I will burn if I see you in them again – and slip on your heels, because we're going for dinner at Hôtel du Vin and then we're going clubbing,' Marcus declared. 'I know a gorgeous little gay club on the seafront. I want us to dance the night away. Leo's abroad again and Sadie and I plan to crash at yours if that's okay.'

It was more than okay. Her friends had saved her from the downward spiral and by the time they all got to bed at five a.m. her feet were aching from all the dancing but her spirits were high. She planned to have a long lie-in and then take her friends for brunch, but a phone call from Jess at ten a.m. put paid to that. 'Carmen, can you do me a huge favour?'

'Sure,' Carmen croaked in a voice as deep as Marge Simpson's.

'It's the burning of the clocks workshop and I've got the student assessments to do before tomorrow, and Sean has gone to football. Is there any way that you could take Harry?'

'Is that really a suitable workshop for a seven-year-old boy?' Carmen, who had misheard, asked. 'I mean, won't that make him anxious about being a boy?' God, Brighton had some wacky traditions. It must be the sea air.

'Of course it's suitable!' Jess replied, sounding puzzled. 'All his friends are doing it. There's a big parade through Brighton on the winter solstice and then there are fireworks and an enormous bonfire on the beach. It's intensely moving, very primal, you know, connects us to the seasons kind of thing.'

'Sorry, you lost me there, earth mother. I'm a bit hungover – I went out last night with Marcus and Sadie.'

'*Please* can you take him? It will only be a couple of hours at the most, and by then I might be able to meet you for lunch. And I think you'll really enjoy the workshop.'

That seemed unlikely – Carmen wasn't gifted in the arts and crafts department and Jess must be desperate; she hadn't appeared to notice that Carmen had mentioned Sadie.

'Okay, I'll be round in a bit.'

Harry opened the front door to her half an hour later, good to go in his dayglo orange anorak. Fortunately Carmen felt remarkably okay after a Red Bull and a couple of painkillers. She'd left Marcus and Sadie sleeping soundly. 'Hey Harry,' Carmen said cheerfully, 'are you going to give me a hug?'

Harry looked appalled but allowed Carmen to bend down and put her arms round him, keeping his own arms firmly at his side, tolerating rather than enjoying the contact.

'So where's Mum?'

'In the kitchen.'

Carmen went downstairs, where Jess was sitting at the kitchen table surrounded by files. Instead of working, however, she was reading the style section of the *Sunday Times*. She looked up guiltily when Carmen walked in. 'Just having a break for five minutes. Thanks for taking Harry. Call me when you're done and we'll go out for lunch.' Jess looked slightly coy as she added, 'Enjoy yourself.'

'It's a workshop in a community hall – just how much enjoyment can there be in that?' Carmen demanded.

'Oh, I think you'll be pleasantly surprised. See you later,' Jess said breezily.

Just as Carmen left the kitchen she caught sight of the recycling box. It was full to the brim with wine bottles. 'Blimey, Jess, you and Sean have been putting it away.'

Jess saw what she was looking at and said rather defensively, 'There's several weeks there. Sean keeps forgetting to put it out.'

Walking to the nearby community hall where the dubious workshop was being held, Harry insisted on giving her a blow-by-blow account of the plot of *Dr Who* which he'd watched the night before, and then questioned her in forensic detail about who was her favourite doctor and why, and which was the scariest monster in her opinion. She had forgotten how demanding children could be, especially after only five hours' sleep.

Carmen hadn't really thought that clothing would be an issue in the workshop and so had simply put on what she intended to wear for lunch with Sadie and Marcus later: black skinny jeans, a black jumper with bronze-studded shoulders, a scarlet-and-black leopard-print scarf, her Alexander McQueen biker jacket which she was still paying for and her black patent shoe boots. She had wanted to wear her ever-faithful UGGs but Marcus seemed to have hidden them somewhere. She felt she had gone for the casual look, but as soon as she walked into the community hall, she realised she was wildly overdressed. Quite obviously there was a casual look which had some thought to it like hers, and there was a casual look as in, I don't care a fig about what I'm wearing, clothes are functional and anyone who cares about them is superficial. There were around fifteen people, all accompanied by one or more child, all wearing a uniform of either combats or jeans and puffer jackets, in black, khaki and brown, clothes so resolutely plain they could have given the Amish a run for their money. Carmen seemed to be the only woman wearing make-up.

'Harry,' she whispered, 'do I look silly?'

Harry turned and considered her with his clear, candid child's gaze. 'Nah, you look like you always do. But don't you have to take your shoes off?' He pointed at the sign on one of the walls asking people with heels to remove them, to prevent marking the floor. Carmen looked down at the floor in horror. It was filthy. The hall was clearly used for a toddler group and there were breadstick crumbs scattered everywhere, along with raisins, bits of apple and the remains of a chocolate muffin squished into the floorboards – at least, she hoped it was chocolate muffin. Her lovely spiky-heeled boots were the only thing between her and tetanus. She shook her head. 'These boots won't leave a mark.' Both she and Harry looked down and saw the series of small but nonetheless visible grooves said boots were making. Harry raised his eyebrows and said nothing.

At that moment a striking woman with long auburn hair strode into the middle of the hall. There was no danger of her making any holes in the floor as she was wearing black sheepskin-lined Crocs – a style of footwear that Carmen abhorred. Truly Crocs must have been invented by someone who hated feet and wanted to make them look as ugly as possible, a kind of anti-foot fetishist. Carmen could not imagine slipping her dainty size four and a half pair into such a monstrosity. Croc lady had accessorised the Crocs with black leggings, a black miniskirt and a black North by Northwest jacket. She also had a pretty face, with big brown eyes and thick lashes which Carmen would have loved. Carmen put her at late thirties.

'Hiya, my name's Violet and I'm going to be leading this workshop where we're going to make the wicker and paper lanterns that we'll use in the procession on the twenty-first of December. But before we start, is this anyone's first time?'

Rats! The last thing Carmen wanted to do was draw attention to herself. She was all set to ignore the question but Harry nudged her in the ribs. Damn children and their honesty! She'd have to fess up. She put up her hand.

'Okay,' Violet replied, 'I'll keep an eye on you and make sure you don't fall behind.' Unfortunately said eye was suddenly drawn to the boots. 'I'm sorry, but you'll have to take those off. I can lend you a pair of Crocs.'

She was about to protest, but Violet had such an air of evangelical zeal about her that Carmen felt she would be deaf to her argument that forcing her to wear Crocs would be a violation of her human rights. She sat down on one of the worn orange plastic chairs at the side of the room, after first brushing away the pieces of mouldering apple, and unzipped her boots. Violet marched towards her holding up a bright yellow pair of the horrors. They were such a lurid yellow, it almost hurt Carmen's eyes to look at them.

'Thanks,' she whispered, taking the shoes. Her very soul recoiled at the prospect of putting them on, never mind her soles! But Violet was already waving pieces of willow enthusiastically and Carmen knew if she didn't get her arse into gear and follow the demon-stration she would be utterly lost. She did not have the artistic gene. Gingerly she inserted her feet into the plastic monstrosities. Then she stood up and shuffled over to Harry. The Crocs were at least three sizes too big for her, but surprisingly comfortable, not that she was *ever* going to buy a pair, not even to wear at home on her own in the dark.

'Come on,' Harry said cheerfully, 'we've got to get the pieces of willow first.' He marched purposefully over to one of the trestle tables set up around the hall and grabbed a handful of willow branches.

Carmen turned and watched Violet, who was creating some kind of pyramid shape with the strips of willow. It seemed an unlikely shape if it was supposed to represent the male member. Maybe it would be decorated with phallic symbols?

She was just going to ask when her attention was taken up by the arrival of a stunningly beautiful man, well over six foot, with luminous brown eyes, regular features, and tanned – not a spray-tan tan but an outdoors, glowing, healthy tan. He looked just like the French actor Olivier Martinez with his dark good looks. In fact, he was so gorgeous Carmen was prepared to overlook the complete style no-no in her book – *long* black hair, pulled back in a ponytail. Plus he was accessorised with a small child, also not so good.

'Daniel!' Violet exclaimed, rushing over and hugging him. Pretty tightly, Carmen noted, maybe she was the girlfriend. Lucky girlfriend.

'I'm so glad you and Millie could make it. You haven't missed anything, we've only just started, but I know you could do it with your eyes shut anyway!' She laughed, showing off a gold tongue stud – which was right up with Crocs on Carmen's list of things she didn't get.

Carmen was continuing to have a good old look at Daniel, well, borderline leer – pickings were thin on the ground in the hall, let's face it – when Daniel turned in her direction and gave a broad smile, showing off white, even teeth. *Well, hello*! Carmen thought in delight, she might be surrounded by the Amish and wearing the hideous Crocs but she hadn't lost her touch! As Daniel walked towards her, she could almost feel herself blush, and when he stopped in front of her she gave him her most flirty smile. Unfortunately it was lost on him as he bent down and said, 'Hiya, Harry, how's it going?'

Harry! He was smiling at Harry! Buggeration!

'Give me five!' Harry shot back. Daniel obliged and Carmen watched as the pair enacted a high-five routine that seemed to go on for ages.

Finally Daniel stood up and looked directly at Carmen. 'Hi, I'm Daniel, and this is Millie, she's in the same class as Harry.' He pointed to a little girl with long blonde hair and a sweet face. 'Jess said you'd be coming, nice to meet you.'

Ah, so this was why Jess wanted her to come to the workshop? There was a small pause when Carmen wondered if she should kiss him, as she was used to doing in old London town, but Daniel stuck out his hand, so she shook it, thinking, *My, my, what a firm grip you have*.

Carmen was about to ask him if he'd lived in Brighton long – unoriginal, but a start of a conversation – when Violet clapped her hands and shouted, 'Okay, people, get lashing!' and Daniel strode over to grab some pieces of willow and began expertly lashing them together. Carmen followed his lead with considerably less success. The willow seemed to have a will of its own and slid and slithered out of her hands; even Harry was better at lashing than she was. 'So have you lived in Brighton long?' she managed to ask.

180

'Practically all my life. I wouldn't want to live anywhere else.' Daniel spoke quietly and seriously. 'How are you settling in?'

'I like it here. Of course it's much smaller than London and I do miss the city.'

Daniel frowned. 'Yeah, but London's so busy, so full-on, no space, no room to breathe.'

Carmen was a Londoner by birth and loved the capital, thought it the best city in the world, second only to New York, but she detected that this might not win her brownie points with Daniel. 'And it doesn't have the *sea*. I love the sea.' She said it with enthusiasm, hoping the comment would make Daniel realise that she was not a shallow urbanite, that she could appreciate nature.

'I love it too.' He rewarded Carmen with a smile.

She smiled back, and at that moment one of the pieces of willow she was trying to wrestle into place sprang back and nearly took her eye out. She was about to come out with an entirely justified *Fuck!* but Daniel put down his own pyramid-shaped construction and took the willow from her.

'Tell you what, I'll do yours and Harry's, so long as you put the paper and the designs on it; it will still count.'

It took Daniel some five minutes to polish off the two shapes. Carmen supposed she should have been planning the design, but she was riveted by the sight of his strong, manly fingers working so quickly and expertly lashing – lashings and lashings of lovely lashing.

Oh dear, she really had been spending too much time on her own.

'All done,' Daniel said, and Carmen looked at the two pyramid shapes in front of him.

'Um, great, but they look absolutely nothing like a cock, do they?' It was unfortunate that at that moment a random hush fell across the hall, so Carmen's clearly enunciated 'cock' rang out clear as a bell.

Daniel looked at her in bemusement. 'Why would they? That's the structure for the lantern. The candle goes in the base and the whole thing will be covered in white paper decorated with designs relating to time.'

Harry and Millie were in fits of giggles, though Harry had first managed to splutter, 'Carmen said the C word.'

Carmen wanted to retort that it wasn't *that* C word, in case any of the Amish got the wrong idea and lashed *her* to the willow structures and burned her.

Carmen looked at Daniel. He must think she was such an idiot. 'But I thought it was the burning of the cocks? Isn't that why we're here? It's some kind of pagan, I don't know, end-of-the-year ritual. I've only just moved down here, remember.'

'It's *clocks*,' Daniel said quietly, his mouth twitching. 'Burning of the clocks. It's to celebrate the winter solstice.'

'Well, that's a relief,' Carmen quipped back, though she was mortified by her mistake. 'I was a bit worried that there might be some mass removal of children in Brighton by social services, because their parents forced them to make phallic symbols.'

'So you're all sorted now?' Violet asked, advancing on Carmen. 'It was good of Daniel to help you. Usually we expect people to make their own lanterns, it's part of the ritual. And then when you come to burn it at the end of the procession, you can invest it with your hopes for the future and the things you want to let go of.' She was smiling, but her eyes were not.

'Put it this way, if Daniel hadn't helped me, there would be no lantern to invest with anything. The last thing I made was a papier mâché lighthouse, painted red and white, with a washing-up liquid bottle for a base, when I was at primary school. My parents have still got it, not because it has any artistic merit whatsoever but because it's practically the only thing I ever made that you could see what it was. It would be fair to say, Violet, that I am challenged in the artistic area.' Yes, make her feel guilty for criticising her; she was bound to be so right-on she would hate upsetting anyone, even a lipstick-wearing Londoner.

Violet did not look guilty. 'Why don't you make a start on covering the willow structure with paper?' She held up a lantern which was already covered in white paper and had a hook at the top for ease of carrying. 'Here's one I made earlier. Surely you can do *that* without enlisting Daniel?' She seemed very possessive around the delicious Daniel; perhaps she really was his girlfriend.

Carmen looked over at the trestle table covered in sheets of black-and-white paper. That looked like a no-brainer. It was just a matter of slapping a bit of glue on the paper and then sticking it on the structure. Or not, as she found out a few minutes later when she managed to stick the paper everywhere but the lantern, including on the arm of her Alexander McQueen biker jacket. And she couldn't take the jacket off as both her hands were covered in glue.

'Harry!' she hissed, flapping her arm around like a deranged bird. 'Can you pull that paper off?'

Harry did his best but only succeeded in getting it to stick more firmly to the delicate leather.

'Here, shall I have a go?' Daniel came to the rescue. Carmen held out her arm, hardly daring to look as Daniel deftly removed the paper with those very lovely, strong fingers. 'It's alright. It should come off, shouldn't it?' he said as they both looked at the sticky residue of glue which had left a snail-trail on the leather.

Carmen wanted to stamp her foot and shriek, 'It's Alexander McQueen, goddamit! Of course it's not alright! I haven't even finished paying for it yet!' But she instinctively felt that Daniel might not approve of such an obsessive love of clothes. And she had to admit that, though Daniel was emphatically not her type – the long hair told her that – she *did* want him to approve of her. There was something incredibly sexy about him. Or maybe it was just those stunning good looks in the sea of Amish and that delicious hit of some woody aftershave that she kept getting whenever he was near.

'I'm sure it'll be fine,' Carmen said with more certainty than she felt. 'So what's next?' she asked Harry briskly, trying to put on a brave face and channel all the women who had done amazing things in history – for instance, that suffragette who had jumped in front of the King's horse and been killed, all in the cause of women getting the vote. She did not lay down her life so women like Carmen could witter on about leather jackets.

'We have to cut out shapes from black paper and stick them on to the lantern,' Harry informed her.

'And that will be of *clocks*,' Daniel said cheekily, maybe even flirtatiously.

'Or anything inspired by time and space,' Violet added pompously. 'Like a constellation, stars scattered across the paper reflecting the enormity of the universe, and how we are just a small part of it.'

'I'm going to do a rocket blasting off into space,' Harry informed them enthusiastically. 'Carmen, can you help me?'

'Fine.' Even she should be able to manage a rocket.

Some twenty minutes later Harry and Carmen had completed their lanterns – Carmen with stars and half moons, Harry with his rocket man theme. Carmen was a little concerned the rockets did look somewhat phallic. Daniel meanwhile had drawn and cut out shapes of a tall grandfather clock on one side of the lantern with the hands pointing to one, while black mice scampered up and down each side of the pyramid, each holding a number in their mouths. It was really striking.

'Wow, Daniel – is that supposed to symbolise how time can run away with us?' Violet asked earnestly.

'Nope, Millie wanted me to do it. It's Hickory Dickory

Dock.' He turned to Carmen and, grinning, said, 'That would be dock, I said.'

Enough of all the cocks already! Carmen thought. She was starting to seriously overheat in her jumper, even though it was freezing in the hall.

'Great,' Violet said, a little tersely. 'Well, perhaps we can tidy up now. Carmen, if you could be in charge of sweeping the floor that would be helpful, the broom's in the corner. We really should leave the hall as we expect to find it.'

What, with a ton of crap on it? Carmen was so tempted to reply, but Violet was hot Daniel's friend and Carmen did not want to upset her. So she shuffled off in her Crocs to get the broom. About two years' worth of dust rose up to greet her as she started manhandling the practically bald broom across the worn floorboards. Jess was going to owe her for this big time. Everyone else had cleared everything away before Carmen was even halfway across the room and had collected a pile of dirt and dust and toddler detritus. She looked down at her black jumper and saw that it was attracting a dust colony all of its own, as were her skinny jeans. God knows what her face looked like.

'Let me take over,' Daniel came over. 'You've had the worst job.'

Carmen blew her fringe off her forehead. 'Thanks, are you sure?'

'No problem.' Daniel flashed his broad smile at her.

He was seriously lovely. Thoughtful, too. Maybe she could ask him for lunch, find out if he was connected to Violet or if there was another lady in his life. This really would be a fresh start, and then maybe she could stop thinking about Will, who might have short hair but was not as gorgeous as Daniel and was probably rubbish at lashing willow, and anyway had Tash. Carmen decided to nip to the loos and check on her appearance. She was smiling to herself as she shuffled out of the hall and headed for the Ladies.

Violet met her halfway there. 'Finished already, Carmen? That was speedy.'

'Actually, Daniel's just finishing off for me.'

'So you're at a bit of a loose end? In that case, can you just clean the loos? Give the seats a quick wipe and squirt some bleach down them.' She thrust a bottle of bleach at Carmen and a mangy-looking cloth. *Eeow*! Carmen was so shocked that she didn't even protest but raced into the Ladies. Thankfully the loos were in pristine condition. Violet was obviously just trying to wind her up. Carmen threw the mangy cloth in the bin, did the bleach thing and scrubbed her hands. She caught sight of her reflection in the mirror. Thank you, Coco! The lipstick had stayed in place. She even had quite a healthy glow – it must be all the physical exercise, that and the delicious Daniel. She actually had an extra spring in her Crocs as she walked back to the hall where Daniel had finished sweeping.

He smiled as she joined him and said quietly, 'I was wondering if you and Harry wanted to go and grab some lunch. I don't know about you, but I'm starving.'

'Sure, and is it okay if I ask Jess and my friends along

who are staying with me? They're Londoners but they're okay, honestly.'

Daniel looked a little confused – maybe he didn't do her kind of humour – but said, 'No problem.'

Carmen was so thrilled by the lunch invitation from Daniel that she was halfway down the hill leading into town before she realised that she was still shod in the evil crocs.

'Shit, shit, shit!' she exclaimed, adding 'Sorry,' to Daniel as Harry and Millie shared another giggle. 'I'm not used to being around kids, you've probably gathered.'

'Don't worry,' Daniel replied, 'I'm sure they've heard worse.'

'Like Daddy,' Harry piped up. 'He's always using the F word to Mummy.'

Carmen frowned, that didn't sound like Sean. 'I'm sure he's not.'

'Oh he does,' Harry said cheerfully. 'Last night he called her a fucking drunk.'

Carmen exchanged a worried glance with Daniel and wondered what to say in reply; she felt as if she was in uncharted territory. She was going to have to say something to Jess.

'Sometimes grown-ups say things they really don't mean,' Daniel replied calmly. 'Even though I think Carmen really did mean the S word.'

Although Carmen was shocked by Harry's comment, Daniel had reminded her of the unbearable Croc situation. She simply could not have lunch with hot Daniel in plastic shoes more befitting the feet of garden gnomes. How on earth could he see her as a sexual being, unless he had a thing about garden gnomes in garish shoes, in which case would she really want to have sex with him? She sneaked another look at him and was treated to his perfect profile. Yes, probably.

'I really must get my shoes.'

Daniel shook his head. 'I've just seen Violet drive past us, she'll have locked up. Don't worry, I can get your boots tomorrow.'

Again Carmen tried to channel great women from history. Queen Elizabeth I, leading her troops into battle, giving her great, *I know I have the body of a weak and feeble woman, but I have the heart and stomach of a king*, speech. It still didn't work; even Elizabeth could not have delivered such a rousing speech in dayglo plastic footwear. Never mind Burning of the Clocks, if she had her way it would be burning of the Crocs. 'So shall we go to Wagamama's and have noodles?' Daniel put in. As Millie and Harry whooped their appreciation, Daniel added, 'Would that be okay with you?'

'Perfect, and I'll text Jess and my friends and ask them to meet us there,' Carmen answered. 'But promise me no one will eat the big flat noodles in front of me, they really remind me of earthworms.'

'They're my favourites!' Millie exclaimed. 'And anyway, earthworms are great, Daddy's always telling me.'

Drat, cannot cross the child of the hot man. Carmen managed a smiled, 'You're right, earthworms are very useful. Where would we be without them?'

Wagamama's was heaving. It seemed to be the rule that every long canteen-style table had at least two babies clipped on to it in child seats. Carmen did what she always did when in proximity to babies, she looked away. Sadie and Marcus were going to join them for dessert as they were yet to get up, and Jess was on her way.

Millie was busy twirling a large earthworm-shaped noodle round and round on a chopstick, impressing Carmen with her dexterity. Carmen had to use a fork to eat her chicken chilli noodles; she could use chopsticks but didn't want to risk food falling down her face in front of the *über* gorgeous Daniel. Of all the places to eat with a gorgeous man you didn't yet know but wanted to, a noodle restaurant would be bottom of her list. But Daniel, like his daughter, was having no trouble neatly spinning his (thankfully thin) noodles round on his chopsticks.

So far Carmen had discovered four important facts – not easy as Daniel was quite reserved:

- Daniel ran his own garden design business.
- There was a Mrs Daniel but they were separated and had been for two years. Mrs Daniel was living in San Diego with her boyfriend. Sounded promising.

- Violet was not his girlfriend but a friend who had a child the same age as Millie.
- She, Carmen, really fancied Daniel, a feeling which she hadn't experienced in real life outside of Will and fantasising about Russell Crowe in a very long time.

And maybe there was even a fifth:

- Daniel seemed to quite like her too.

She based number five on all the eye contact they'd had over the noodles, and by the way he seemed very interested in her and what she did, and wanted to know what she thought of Brighton, apart from it being smaller than London. She couldn't say it was in the style of flirtatious banter she was used to, but it was still exciting knowing she had the attention of this handsome man. And then over miso soup he asked a question which surely clinched it, 'So are you living on your own down here?'

'Yes, I separated from my husband about a year ago and I haven't really seen anyone since.' Oh God, why had she said that? It made her sound a complete saddo! Of course there had been the flirtation with Will, but it was probably best not to go there.

Daniel was about to reply when Jess finally walked in. She planted a kiss on Harry's head then sat on the wooden bench next to Daniel, who put his arm round her and kissed her. Lucky, lucky Jess, to be the recipient of such a manly arm and a kiss.

'So, did you enjoy the workshop, Carmen?' Jess had a knowing smirk on her face. 'I thought you might find it interesting.'

Carmen ignored the implication. 'It was great, except for one thing.' She slowly raised her left leg in the air, displaying the offending Croc in its full glory.

'Uggh! Crocs! You're wearing Crocs! I didn't mean for this to happen!' Jess loathed the plastic monstrosities nearly as much as Carmen.

'Well, they're very comfortable, aren't they?'

Jess covered her eyes as if to protect them from the glare of the yellow. 'It's like the end of *Invasion of the Body Snatchers* when Donald Sutherland is practically the only human left, and he stumbles across that woman who was a friend of his and he thinks that she's still human too, but she's been taken over and she betrays him. That's how I feel about seeing you in Crocs. I think you'd better move back to London right now, the sea air is obviously affecting you. Quick, get on the train before it's too late!'

Daniel smiled uncertainly at the two women's banter – maybe, and please let this not be so, he was a lover of Crocs.

As the kids tucked into vanilla ice cream and mango sauce the three adults chatted, all small talk really, but Carmen was struggling to keep her eyes off Daniel. His beauty was mesmerising and every time he smiled at one of her jokes she felt as if she'd won the Nobel peace prize.

'Oh look!' Carmen exclaimed, waving. 'It's Marcus

and Sadie.' She turned to Jess. 'Now play nice, please.'

'Sadie shagged Sean,' Jess couldn't resist saying to Daniel, who looked rather taken aback by the comment.

'They were on a break,' Carmen clarified. Would Jess ever forgive and forget? But then again, would she in Jess's position? It was a tough one.

'Everyone's done things they regret, I'm sure,' Daniel said diplomatically.

There then followed a flurry of introductions, where Carmen was acutely aware of Marcus and Sadie appraising Daniel and of Jess giving Sadie the glacial treatment.

Before they could embark on a proper conversation, however, Daniel and Millie had to leave. 'But you're the best-looking man I've seen in Brighton, you can't go!' Marcus exclaimed. The best-looking man in Brighton looked rather mortified.

'Just ignore Marcus, he says that to all the boys,' Carmen jumped in to Daniel's rescue.

'Oh right,' Daniel replied. He seemed unsure of how to react. 'Anyway, I have to take Millie to a party.' He got up and pulled on his battered brown leather jacket. 'Tragically my seven-year-old daughter has a more exciting social life than me.'

Carmen liked his self-deprecating quality; she did so hate an uptight man. Now if he could just do something with the hair, which was actually longer than hers . . .

He turned to Carmen and said quietly, 'So, I'll get your boots from the hall tomorrow if you like, I'm working round there, and I could drop them at yours tomorrow afternoon.'

Oh yes. Carmen had a little frisson at the thought of being alone with Delicious Dan. Marcus caught her eye and winked. Carmen ignored him and quickly wrote down her address and mobile for Daniel.

Daniel and Millie were barely out of earshot before Marcus leaned forward and said excitedly, 'Can I just say, fucking gorgeous, Jess! Madam here had led me to believe that there are no straight men left in Brighton. And here I am confronted by a magnificent specimen.'

'Less of the F word, Marcus,' Jess replied, looking over at Harry, who was fortunately engrossed in his Nintendo DS.

'Shit, sorry,' Marcus answered.

'Or the S word!' Jess again.

'Bloody hell, it's like a minefield being around children.'

Jess gave up. She looked at Carmen. 'So what did you think? Don't you love me for arranging the meeting? You're going to owe me big time.'

'He *is* gorgeous. Definitely not my type, though. You only have to look at the hair. And we come from such different worlds. He probably thinks I'm really shallow.'

'You *are* really shallow,' Jess shot back. 'But loveable too, and I reckon Daniel would be very interested because you are different to him. Opposites attract and all that jazz.'

The two women did the finger-clicking thing they always did when one of them mentioned a line from a musical. It used to drive Sadie mad when she lived with them.

She rolled her eyes now but let it pass.

Then Carmen said, 'Nothing's going to happen.'

Jess leaned forward. 'He's very shy and can be hard to talk to, but there are compensations.' She lowered her voice, 'He's supposed to be an amazing lover.' Jess's voice dropped a couple of octaves at '*amazing*'.

Carmen gave a snort of laughter. 'How do you know?'

'Because he had a brief fling with a friend of my friend's, and she said it was the best sex of her life.'

Jess, Carmen, Sadie and Marcus all looked into the middle distance. Best sex of her life, versus no sex. Carmen knew which one she would rather have.

'Oh Carmen,' Marcus added wickedly, 'you know you want to. And finally I can get to hear about something other than a man who can only climax to the shipping forecast.'

'What!' Jess exclaimed.

And Sadie was forced to recount the whole sorry saga of Dom's sexual preference, which was big of her, seeing as how Jess was laughing at her rather than with her. But maybe, Carmen reflected later when she'd waved her friends off at the station, that was what it would take to get Jess and Sadie to be friends again.

10

After the encounter with Daniel, Carmen's writing routine was shot to pieces. Remembering Harry's comment about Jess's drinking, she texted her friend the following morning asking her to phone her when she got the chance. Jess replied that she was teaching all day and had drama club that night. It would have to wait until tomorrow. Carmen then found every possible excuse not to sit down in front of her lovely MacBook. It sat on the table by the window, looking all sleek and reproachful, next to Basil, who definitely had a new spring to his spikes since the move, while she procrastinated.

First she performed fifty sit-ups, followed by twenty abductor lifts (the ones that made her want to cry) mindful of the lithe Violet who undoubtedly had her big brown eyes on Daniel and no doubt wanted her slender thighs round him as well. She then painted her nails, even though she had a feeling Daniel was a strictly natural nail man and she'd gone for a deep harlot red, she plucked her eyebrows and straightened her hair, but by eleven she had run out of excuses. She sat down and switched on the Mac and opened up her drama.

She had recently read an article where writers talked about their writing routine. They were all such swots!

They started work at eight, often earlier, and wrote all day, sometimes so absorbed in their work that they forgot to eat. Or if they did break for a snack they'd have something simple like an oatcake and an apple. Not even a Hobnob to get through that creative slump? The moment Carmen had finished a short scene she was ravenously hungry, even though she'd had porridge for breakfast, which should have meant slow release of energy and all that, and therefore no picking. She wrote a few more lines, but now the thought of a snack kept bobbing up to the surface. And surely she had burnt off some calories in the sit-up frenzy. Toast and coffee was what was called for. Toast and coffee was duly made and consumed while she googled Daniel's gardening company.

The photographs of his gardens were stunning, all with strong, visually arresting designs, and reading the blurb it seemed as if wherever possible he tried to source local materials and always used sustainable timber. So he was ethical and sexy. Well, she was quite ethical, wasn't she? She always bought Fairtrade coffee and chocolate and she recycled all her wine bottles. Ten further minutes were wasted by her having a quite involved fantasy of what exactly she would like to do to the ethical and sexy Daniel and what she would like him to do to her. Perhaps she could even tie him up in some S&M-inspired scenario and cut off his hair, but nicely, not in a Delilah I am trying to emasculate you Samson vibe, more of a I am trying to make you look even hotter . . . But then would ethical, sexy Daniel approve of S&M, and was there such a thing as ethical

S&M? And what was she doing going down an S&M cul de sac? It had never interested her before.

To put a stop to the rampant thoughts she logged on to the *Guardian* online. There was bound to be some passion-killing story about the economy and how we were all going to hell in a handcart, or about some atrocity. But no, as she ploughed her way through the articles she realised she wasn't taking in a single word; instead she was imagining what Daniel would look like with short hair. *I really am shallow*, she reflected, logging off. *Shallow and desperate for sex.*

It was now midday. She checked her emails. There was a flirty one from Will asking her what else she had imagined for him and if possible could she imagine him a new job because he was having a bloody hard time at Fox Nicholson. Carmen was all set to reply, then an image of Tash hurtling down the ski slope straight into Will's arms and then on to a passionate embrace in front of an open fire, where Tash was deftly unzipped from her ski suit, popped into her head. He could bloody well get his girlfriend with her slender but firm thighs to imagine him something. She had been very stern with herself about Will and had given all the Wobbly Worms to Harry.

Marcus had also sent her an email wanting an update on Daniel. She might have guessed that he'd be on her case. Daniel was all Marcus could talk about on the walk back to the station last night. She reached for the phone.

Marcus answered on the first ring. 'What news?'

'Give me a chance!' she exclaimed. 'I haven't seen him yet.' And here she sighed, 'It doesn't matter anyway because I know I'm not his type. I bet you anything he likes his women au naturel – not a scrap of make-up on their tiny heart-shaped faces, their hair with that just-got-out-of bed look. You know I don't do that. The last time I didn't wear make-up I was twelve, and have I ever had tousled hair in my life?'

'No,' Marcus said drily. 'In fact, I imagine you entered the world with a sharp bob. But I saw the looks he was giving you and I definitely think that gardener boy was interested.'

'You think?'

'I know. He is ripe for the plucking, and I'd love to talk more but I've got to go. I've got a t'ai chi session in twenty minutes, then I'm seeing my therapist at two, I'm doing an interview with *Grazia* straight after and then I start filming at four.'

'Oh, you and your celebrity lifestyle,' Carmen shot back in a voice heavy with sarcasm. 'And you said fame would never change you.'

'I *never* said that. Did you see that I was in *Heat*'s Spotted section? Bastards took it from my bad side. Laters.'

Carmen reread the last two scenes she'd written but her attention kept wandering. She really must learn to cultivate will power. And she absolutely must not think of words like cultivate, which only took her straight back to her hot gardener. She decided to go for a walk and clear her head to allow the creative thoughts in and the lustful ones out.

Several weeks into her new life in Brighton she still received a jolt of pleasure when she saw the sea stretching out in front of her. Today in the weak November sunlight it was a cheeky green like the inside of an old-fashioned glass marble, and there were white horses foaming across it whipped up by the jaunty wind. High above her head the gulls shot up on the breeze and then drifted nonchalantly, showing off, shrieking the equivalent of *Come and have a go if you think you're hard enough*. They were truly the skinhead bully boys of the avian world. If she'd seen one draped in a St George's flag, swigging from a can of Special Brew, it would not have surprised her.

She took a deep breath of sea air to blow those cobwebs of procrastination away and started walking briskly towards town. She'd have a half-hour walk by the sea and then return and write with purpose, determination and vigour. She should be able to write at least four scenes. She was actually thinking about the sitcom and the interplay between the lead women when she remembered that she hadn't decided what to wear when she saw Daniel later that day. She went through her clothes, mentally discarding the different combinations only to arrive at the crisis conclusion that she had absolutely nothing to wear! Immediately she made a sharp left into the Lanes. What she urgently required was a slouchy off-the-shoulder top in a tee-shirt material, which would be sexy but not in an obvious way, to wear with her skinny jeans.

Understated, that was the kind of thing someone

like Daniel would go for. She found exactly the right top in a little boutique. However, she also found exactly the right midnight-blue silk dress. She really, *really* should not buy the dress, or in fact the top. Should not. Her savings were not going to last long at this rate. But the dress was perfect. *It's an investment piece*, she reasoned. *If I wear it ten times that means it will only have cost me fifteen pounds a time, hang on, that's still a bit much, how about twenty times?* She did a quick calculation, £7.50. What an absolute bargain! Carmen was always doing these calculations to justify purchases, neglecting to think that it only worked out if you didn't buy anything else. But feeling as if she'd only spent £7.50 on the gorgeous dress and practically nothing on the top, she trotted back home, very pleased with herself. *It's important for me to experience* life *as a writer*, she told herself. *I can't just sit at home, I have to embrace experiences, people, lovely dresses.*

The MacBook was waiting patiently for her. God, the amount it cost her, she'd expect it at least to have written half the comedy! She really should sit down and get going. But first she had to check out the I'm-not-making-much-of-an-effort-but-still-sexy top again.

It was just the look she had wanted – the charcoal top falling off the shoulder to reveal a hint of still-tanned skin from the summer and her red satin bra strap. She checked the time – half past three – Daniel wouldn't finish work so early, she reckoned, and quickly put on her new dress. Its sexy temptress impact was slightly marred by her wearing red and black stripy socks, but nonetheless she slipped her feet into her black stilettos with the wickedly high heel and considered her reflection in the mirror. Oh yeah, baby! She thought, turning from side to side, it really was a dress with va-va-voom. She was just imagining going on a date with Daniel – she bet he scrubbed up well – when her doorbell went. She clattered across the wooden floorboards, thinking it was most probably her order from Amazon. Instead it was Daniel.

'Delivery for Ms Miller.' He held up the boots in one hand and a bouquet of vivid orange roses in the other. 'The flowers are to make up for any emotional scarring caused by the Croc experience.'

It was so sweet, but Carmen was mortified by her appearance. Daniel must think she was a total loon trotting around in a cocktail dress at three-thirty in the afternoon. He looked as gorgeous as she'd remembered from the day before, even though his clothes were caked in mud and his hair was still long. He was without doubt one of the most beautiful men she had ever seen.

'Thanks, come in,' she mumbled. 'Would you like a cup of tea?'

'Or isn't it time for something more sophisticated?' He took in the dress and then smiled. 'Lovely dress, looks good with the socks, very Dennis the Menace.'

This was deeply embarrassing. No woman wants to be caught out trying on her new clothes like a teenage girl or be associated with Dennis the Menace. She could either fess up or pretend that she always dressed like this, but then he would think she was some freaky Miss

Havisham type figure. And if she recalled her Dickens, Miss Havisham never got shagged.

'I've just bought it and I admit that instead of working, I tried it on. It's one of my many displacement activities. So, tea?'

'You haven't got a beer, have you?'

'I'll check.' On the way to the kitchen Carmen nipped into her bedroom and took off the shoe-sock combination, then padded barefoot into the kitchen.

'It's a great place you've got here,' Daniel said, coming in. He'd removed his work boots so she hadn't heard him and she was checking her reflection in the shiny stainless-steel kettle, doing a highly unattractive gurn to make sure she didn't have lipstick on her teeth. It just got worse. Why didn't she wear a badge announcing the fact that she was a vain, shallow woman and be done with it?

'I'm borrowing it from Marcus.'

'I love the fact that it's so minimalist. My house is so cluttered, but this is lovely.' At this, he stretched up his arms causing his tee-shirt to ride up and show off some impressive abs. They must feel so good.

It was with some difficulty that she turned her mind to the conversation. 'Yeah, I love the minimalist look myself,' she lied. Carmen found it a form of torture to be so relentlessly tidy and had done her best to introduce some colour into Marcus's ferociously white temple.

They settled in the living room, on each end of Marcus's white leather sofa, which Carmen had covered with an indigo throw. Somehow the silk dress made the moment feel charged, as if they really were on a date.

'So how's the writing gone today?' Daniel asked.

Carmen sighed, 'Undoubtedly not as well as your gardening. I'm starting to think I've got zero will power.'

Daniel grinned. 'I'm sure that's not true, weren't you some kick-ass comedy agent?'

'Kiss-ass, more like,' Carmen replied. 'I'm so glad to be out of it, but I have got to get on with writing.'

'D'you need me to go?' Daniel asked.

That hadn't been her intention. 'No way! Seeing you is about the nicest thing that's happened all day.'

Maybe that sounded a little too enthusiastic. Pull back.

'Same here,' Daniel said quietly. 'You left quite an impression on me.'

Wow! Carmen's heart went pitter-patter-yay! But she couldn't take the compliment, had to make a joke. 'Was it the Crocs?'

Daniel smiled. 'Maybe the Crocs played their part. It's like you were so sexy from the feet up and then whenever I looked down I would see the Crocs.'

'So you like Crocs?' Typical, sexy Daniel was a weirdo Croc fetishist after all. But maybe to have the best sex of her life she would just have to put the cursed Crocs on. That would be a pleasure-pain moment for sure.

Daniel laughed. 'They're just shoes, aren't they?'

Just shoes! But Carmen knew that if she launched into a full-scale attack on Crocs it might well be hammering home just how shallow she was. So with great difficulty she kept quiet.

'Actually, I don't really like them.' Daniel again.

Oh, sweet relief!

'But I think you can carry them off.' Daniel treated her to his gorgeous smile. 'I reckon you could carry anything off.'

Carmen's libido was bouncing around like the Labrador puppy who has just got hold of the Andrex and is whizzing dementedly round the house.

'I should get them, Violet probably misses them.' She got up and headed for her bedroom where she retrieved the Crocs from the back of her wardrobe. She turned to discover Daniel leaning against the door frame. He was frowning. 'Sorry, was that comment too full-on? I'm really crap at this man-woman flirting thing. Really much better with plants.'

'You have sex with plants? How d'you manage that?'

'I'm not that hard up.'

'Sorry, I know what you mean.' Carmen looked at him, clutching the Crocs. 'I'm filling in the awkward moments with throwaway lines; it's what I do best. But I feel the same. A bit rusty.' *At this point I absolutely must not say that I could do with a good oiling.*

'So,' Daniel continued, 'I wanted to ask if you could come out for dinner with me sometime, Crocs not compulsory.'

The Andrex puppy performed a triple back somersault. Very agile, that Andrex puppy.

'I would really like that.'

205

'I know this is going to sound presumptuous, but it's only because I think I can get a babysitter – is there any chance of this Saturday night?'

Carmen wondered if she could even wait that long, but she stuck with 'Lovely.'

After Daniel departed, Crocs in hand, Carmen was buzzing but forced herself to return to her desk and continue writing until six, and then she had a sudden longing to see Sadie and have a debrief.

So it was that Carmen caught the 6.49 to Victoria and met Sadie at a bar just off Regent Street. It was packed but Sadie knew the barman, who was in thrall to her voice, and he had found them a table in the corner. Sadie had just finished a shift at Broadcasting House, which was nearby, and was due to meet Dom in an hour. She was going through one of her why can't I get an acting job phases; or to be more precise, why can't I get a part in *Spooks*, which Sadie adored. 'I have been going to the gym a lot, I'm definitely getting more muscle definition.' She held up an arm in a strongman pose, which to Carmen looked as slim as ever; there wasn't even a hint of a biceps.

'Yeah, but sweetie, you're only five foot three and you've got that lovely curly hair. The female agents in *Spooks* are always tall and they have straight hair. It probably makes them more aerodynamic when they run.'

'I could do that running to defuse a bomb in twenty seconds, I really could. And look at me, I can poker-face, don't mess with me.' She gave Carmen a steely stare.

Carmen resisted the temptation to laugh. Sadie was wearing an electric-blue dress with a big bow on the front, a bright pink plastic Alice band, turquoise false eyelashes and hot-pink lipstick. Scarily fashion forward, yes. Menacing, don't mess with me, no.

Sadie sighed and looked quite disheartened. A businessman from the nearby table had overheard her talking and as he was leaving paused by their table. 'Can I just say that I love the voice, I'm a huge fan. I adore the way you say BBC Radio Four – really you're the best, my favourite. I wonder if I could take you for dinner sometime?' He held out his card. 'Just call me if you fancy it.' He looked hopefully at Sadie. He was in his early forties and had a pleasant enough face, with greying black hair.

'Sorry,' Sadie put extra velvet in her voice, 'but I have a boyfriend.'

Carmen took the card and read the name, 'But I'm sure Charles has somewhere lovely in mind. Somewhere like the Ivy?'

Charles nodded enthusiastically. 'The Ivy or Marcus Wareing at the Berkeley.'

'And remind me where Dom took you last?' Carmen raised an eyebrow at Sadie, who kicked her with her fashion-fast-forward pointy electric-blue shoe but took the card anyway.

Once Charles had left, Sadie turned on Carmen, 'Why did you do that? I don't fancy him, I've got Dom!'

'I just thought it might be useful ammunition, i.e. when Dom next offers to take you for dinner you could point out the other offers you've had, force him to raise his game.'

'As it was KFC last time, him raising his game will mean Pizza Hut.' But Sadie was smiling. 'I know you find it hard to believe, but I do really like Dom, he makes me laugh.'

Ah, and if only it was with him and not at him, Carmen thought. But at least the businessman interlude had put Sadie in better humour and now she was ready to hear all about Carmen's encounter with Daniel.

'Well, he's sounds very interested,' Sadie pronounced when Carmen had finished her description. She paused and said cheekily, 'So someone's getting lucky on Saturday night.'

Carmen groaned. 'It's been nearly a year! Do you think I will have lost my mojo and just lie there rigidly like a Victorian heroine in a white neck-to-ankle nightie?'

Sadie showed off her dimple as she grinned and said, 'Something will be rigid but it won't be you! And anyway, it's like riding a bicycle.'

Wrong analogy. 'Don't you remember the last time I went mountain biking I fell off and twisted my ankle?'

'Okay, forget about the bikes.' Sadie switched to a ludicrous French accent, 'Just remember, *ma chérie*, what Jess told you, Daniel is a really *très bon* lover, a skilful, practised lover who will want to make *lurve* to you all night and will know how to bring you to the most fantastic climax with his beautiful hands and his beautiful mouth and his beautiful tongue and his exquisite member.'

They were still giggling when Dom joined them.

'What's so funny?' he asked. Dom only ever wanted people to be laughing at what he said.

'Just about a certain gardener Carmen is going to test drive on Saturday night.'

There was a slight pause where Carmen could see that Dom was trying to come up with a witty reply. 'Is he going to use his tool in your lady garden then?' He beamed at the two women, who groaned in unison.

After that, conversation revolved around Dom giving them a blow-by-blow account of what gigs he had lined up. At one point he noticed the card Charles had left. 'Just someone who wants to take me out to dinner, apparently they love my voice,' Sadie told him. Dom looked uneasy. '*I* love your voice, *I* want to take you out for dinner. In fact, I was going to suggest the Indian round the corner.'

'The eat-as-much-as-you-like for £8.99 buffet?' Carmen enquired sweetly. 'I think Charles had the Ivy in mind.'

But compared to KFC the eat-as-much-as-you-can Indian buffet probably did seem like a huge improvement. Carmen left Sadie gazing lovingly at Dom, having turned down the offer to stay the night at Sadie's studio flat. She didn't think she was up to hearing Sadie perform the shipping forecast for Dom.

On the train back to Brighton she received a text message from Daniel: 'i have a babysitter for Saturday and booked a table for half eight. Can't wait to see you x.' A message which put a smile on her face all the way back home.

11

For the rest of the week Carmen alternated writing with emailing Marcus and Sadie and going on Facebook, as that was the only way she could contact Matthew, who had become a convert. She really might have to step away from the technology, it was just another method of procrastination. When she wasn't doing that she was daydreaming about Daniel, a hottie and a goodie, she had decided – sexy and green. So she could have great sex and save the planet – yee-hi! Well, maybe not. At this rate the heat generated by her lustful thoughts would significantly add to global warming.

She had tried to meet up with Jess but Jess claimed to be flat out at work with end-of-term assessments and couldn't meet her, and even seemed in a rush to get off the phone. Carmen couldn't help feeling that her friend was avoiding her.

In spite of all the interludes, Carmen was making progress on her drama at last, and hopefully by Christmas she would be halfway through. She received a boost from Marcus when he told her he loved the first three episodes that she'd sent him. She didn't think he was just saying that to be nice. Marcus never said things just to be nice, not even to his closest friends. It inspired her to press on. Hopefully, by March she would have finished. Then she would really have to think about how to support herself, but for now, she wouldn't – at certain times it was best to channel the ostrich in order to preserve one's sanity.

She was to meet Daniel at a multi-award-winning vegetarian restaurant. He had asked Carmen if that would be okay with her as he was a little tired of eating out and ending up with asparagus to start with followed by mushroom risotto, as he was a vegetarian himself. Now, Carmen had dabbled with vegetarianism while at university and it always seemed to her that it was simply code for eating spectacularly badly with vast quantities of carbs and dairy, and Carmen was convinced she'd put on weight. The phase ended when she met Nick, who was a fantastic cook, but not of vegetarian food. He had her at roast chicken, organic, of course. Since then she had always been vegetarian-food-averse – so a romantic meal in a veggie restaurant with the sexy Daniel didn't exactly do it for her. But her reservations went out of the window when she walked into the pleasantly decorated restaurant, not a piece of hessian in sight. Instead it had vibrant burnt orange and maroon walls and felt airy and sophisticated. She sniffed the air cautiously and was relieved not to detect any aroma of nut roast. She was shown to a cosy corner of the restaurant where Daniel was already sitting, a glass of red wine in front of him. He was like a beacon of loveliness and sexiness, even with the long hair – maybe she *could* grow to love it.

'Hey,' he stood up and lightly kissed her cheek. 'You found it okay?'

I didn't, Carmen thought, *the taxi driver did*. As if she could walk a mile in her killer heels! It had taken every ounce of stamina to make it across the restaurant. But she had a feeling Daniel would not approve of the wanton use of taxis to travel short distances, and the defence of the heels would probably not swing it for her. She might be shod in exquisitely pretty shoes, but that wouldn't make her carbon footprint any smaller. She nodded and, sat down.

A pretty, twenty-something waitress, with a pierced nose and long pink hair, in plaits, dyed hot pink, approached and handed Carmen a menu. She hovered by the table, staring at Daniel. 'So can I get you guys any olives or bread while you're deciding? Another glass of wine?'

'We'll get a bottle, shall we?' Daniel asked.

Thank God for that. Carmen was definitely more of a half-bottle-of-wine girl than a glass with her meal.

The waitress whisked off in a swirl of pink plaits, then whisked back with the bottle of wine. She reminded Carmen of a pretty Russian doll, with her perfect pale skin, pink blusher and sweet rosebud mouth.

For a few minutes conversation was on the slightly awkward lines of, How was the rest of your week? How was Millie? How was Jess? How was the writing going? The superficiality was slightly disappointing, as Carmen was sure there had definitely been more than a spark of attraction between them and on her part at least a strong desire to rip Daniel's clothes off. But maybe it had all been in her head. She looked at the menu, expecting a selection of wholesome stodge, so she was taken aback by what she was reading.

'What's Smoked Sakuri Soba?' she asked, bemused. It was like stumbling across another language.

Daniel shrugged. 'No idea, really, but it's all great, I promise, and you won't want to rush home and eat a rare steak or whatever it is you carnivores get off on.'

At this Carmen had the wicked thought that she certainly did fancy a bit of meat inside her later, and hopefully it would be big and juicy, but it wasn't steak. *Oh Carmen, clearly from the Benny Hill school of humour*. She bit her lip to stop herself grinning.

'I suggest we share the tapas for starters and then you have the pasta, which I've had before and I know it's delicious,' Daniel continued. 'It's pasta, but not as you know it.' He might be a vegetarian with long hair but she liked the certainty.

The pretty waitress returned and took their order, enthusing about Daniel's choice and once again directing all her attention at him.

'Wow, that waitress has the hots for you!' Carmen exclaimed when she was out of earshot. 'I thought she was going to arrange herself on a plate!'

Daniel gave a self-deprecating smile, and muttered, 'No way.'

'Or are you used to women throwing themselves at you?'

'Um, maybe it happens every now and then.' So Daniel was not so modest that he didn't realise what a hottie he was. 'But it's only flattering if you want that woman to throw herself at you. So what about you, Carmen? You must get lots of male attention?'

Carmen fleetingly thought of her flirtatious banter with Will and almost felt a pang for those lost days before replying, 'Well, I don't want to boast, but I think I could have had Rico at my favourite café in London, and there was Connor the postboy.' She couldn't bring herself to mention Will.

'I'd like it very much if you threw yourself at me,' Daniel said quietly, so quietly that Carmen wasn't sure she had heard him. She did a double take. 'You heard me right.'

Whoosh! The Andrex puppy went into orbit. Daniel reached across for her hand and lightly held it in his. *My, what lovely strong fingers you have*, Carmen was tempted to say. They both looked at the white band where her wedding ring had been; still, at least she hadn't had Nick's name tattooed there, that would have been a whole lot harder to shift.

'Do you miss him?' he asked quietly.

'Not any more. He's moved on and I have as well.' Carmen had no intention of introducing the whole baby thing into the conversation. 'How about you?' *Please* let him say that he had moved on too.

He looked serious. Maybe this was not the question to ask him. 'Well, Imogen is always going to be in my life because of Millie, but yeah, I've moved on.

I'm ready for something else.' They held each other's gaze. It was an intoxicating moment, broken only when the pretty waitress practically slammed the plate of whatever it was in front of them.

'D'you want me to talk you through the tapas?' she asked in a slightly shrill voice.

Without looking at her, Daniel shook his head. 'I'm sure they're all delicious, thanks.'

Carmen was feeling far too twitchy to eat more than a few mouthfuls. Food was not on her mind right now, but Daniel managed to polish off the plate of whatever it all was plus all the focaccia. 'Sorry,' he said, 'I'm starving, I've been working on a garden all day.' And thus, thought Carmen, the empty plate summed up the world of difference between men and women – men were never too loved up not to eat. And he ate most of her main meal as well as his. Still, at least he would have plenty of energy for later. She made a quick dash to the loo, hoping that they could just pay and go. As she clattered down the stairs she practically bumped into the pretty, sulky waitress, who was coming up the stairs. 'Sorry,' Carmen said automatically.

'D'you mind me asking you a question?' the waitress asked, fiddling self-consciously with her plaits

'Er, okay,' Carmen said uncertainly, wondering what was coming up.

'Is Daniel your boyfriend?'

Carmen hadn't expected that question. 'Um, no, we're just having dinner. Sorry, do you know him?'

'In a manner of speaking. A brief fling in the summer.

Never heard from him again. I got the feeling he gets through women. He has this great act about being a put upon, right-on single dad, but actually he's out to get what he wants for himself.' She paused. 'Sorry, I probably shouldn't have said that.' She switched to waitress mode and said in a sing-song voice, 'Enjoy the rest of your meal.'

Why oh why was nothing in her life ever straight-forward? Carmen continued on her way to the bathroom at a significantly slower pace. And what was the explanation for Daniel not acknowledging the waitress? That he couldn't remember? (Carmen remembered all of her lovers, some of them a little too well.) That he had deliberately ignored her? Neither exactly showed him in a good light.

By the time she returned to their table Daniel had asked for the bill. Carmen reached for her bag. 'How much is it?' she asked, feeling as flat as day-old champagne, although in her present precarious financial state it would have to be cava.

'I'll get it; you can get the next one.'

So Daniel thought there would be a next one. Carmen wasn't so sure. The waitress's revelation had taken some of the spring out of her step. Maybe she was one in a long line of women who wanted him to cultivate their lady gardens. Oh, for goodness' sake! She couldn't believe she'd thought that!

Outside Saturday-night Brighton was in full swing with a succession of hen parties traipsing along East Street towards the seafront clubs. There was a gang with matching hot-pink tee-shirts with 'Julie's hen party posse' plastered across them in pink glitter, and pink glittery cowboy hats – *how matchy-matchy!* Carmen thought to herself to try and cheer herself up. She and Daniel were nearly mown down by a group of bunnies, some of whom should have stepped well away from the black corsets, which were straining to contain their ample figures, followed by a gang dressed up as nurses, in very short white uniforms and fishnets. It was like a tidal wave of fake-tanned limbs coming at you, all with a slightly purplish-blue tint from the bitter wind that was whipping down the street.

'Bloody hell!' Carmen exclaimed in appalled fascination.

'It's the cheeky, kiss-me-quick side of Brighton,' Daniel said. 'So what now?' He steered her into the doorway of L.K. Bennett as another group bowled past them in tiaras and veils, hell-bent on hitting the clubs.

Carmen had a flashback to Will steering her into the doorway on Great Portland Street, and look where that had ended. Perhaps she was only good for doorways. 'The sanctuary of beautiful shoes,' Carmen said, gazing in the window at the deep-aubergine patent-leather stilettos and the delicate silver pumps. 'One can always rely on shoes.'

Daniel frowned. 'Is it my imagination or have you gone a bit funny on me?'

'Um, I kind of lost my zing on the stairs.'

'Your what?'

'That waitress, *our* waitress, said she knew you, said

217

that you'd had a fling and that you got through a lot of women.' The words came out in a rush. Carmen hadn't realised how shaken she had been. It was possibly irrational but the revelation had made her feel stupid. She'd thought that she was special, but apparently she was just one of many. The whole I'm-not-used-to-this-flirting-business act that Daniel had been putting on was just that – an act.

Daniel frowned. 'I've got no idea what you're talking about.' There was a pause then he came out with, 'Oh hang on, shit, that must have been Kirsty.'

Carmen glared at him.

'Don't give me that look!' Daniel appealed to her. 'When we had our fling, which was only twice if I remember, she had black hair. I thought it was nothing more than a fling, I didn't really have anything in common with her, but she kept calling me. I didn't handle it very well.'

Carmen wanted to ask where the pretty waitress fitted in with Jess's friend's friend, but it was probably none of her business.

'Shit,' Daniel said again, looking serious under the glow of the L.K. Bennett lights. 'She must think I'm such a bastard. No wonder she gave me a funny look when I walked in, but I honestly didn't recognise her.'

To believe or not to believe, that was the question, though actually, did it really matter if Daniel had had a fling with a woman he didn't recognise? Carmen wasn't his keeper.

'Has that killed the moment?' Daniel asked. 'I'll go

218

if you'd rather but I'd rather not, because I really like you, Carmen.'

A beat. Did Carmen want the night to end now?

Daniel was nice, Daniel was hot, Daniel was very sexy. Daniel had selective amnesia about the women he'd slept with but he might be just what she needed to feel happy again. She took a deep breath. 'Do you want to come back to mine?'

Daniel smiled. 'Yes, shall we get a taxi?'

Daniel was not as green as he made out.

Carmen had expected to ease into the whole seduction scene. Earlier on she had activated her inner control freak and remembered her Girl Guide motto of Be Prepared. She had set up Miles Davis, *Kind of Blue* (a timeless classic, everyone liked it, didn't they?) on the CD player, had a choice of red or white wine ready and had stashed condoms in the bedroom and living room. But as soon as she shut the front door Daniel put his arms round her and kissed her. And oh, what a kiss. A perfect, seductive, caressing kiss that even had Carmen's toes curling up in delight, whilst other areas experienced a rush of tingling pleasure that seemed to have been absent for a very, very long time – well since her last kiss with Will, actually, but that had ended with the kiss, and Carmen was pretty sure there was going to be more going on here.

At first they were both cautious in their caresses and then as their kiss grew more intense it freed something in both of them. Daniel unbuttoned her shirt and

219

caressed her breasts, those lovely deft fingers grazing across her nipples in a most tantalising way. She slid her hands under his tee-shirt and felt those abs, and they did not disappoint, nor did subsequent explorations. Daniel groaned as Carmen boldly caressed him through his jeans, then he was inching up her skirt and sliding his fingers into her silk briefs and then everything went on fast forward as they pulled each other down to the floor — on to Marcus's hard stripped wooden floor — but Carmen didn't care as her head banged against the wooden boards. She was heading for the best sex of her life, and what were a few splinters and possibly mild concussion compared to that? Daniel might have claimed to have been in a sexual wilderness himself but he certainly had not lost his touch, as his knowing caresses of her body proved.

'I want you,' she murmured as Daniel kissed her neck, her lips, and then, when it seemed he was still intent on the starters, she took matters into her own hands, pulled down his jeans and boxers and wriggled into him. She was a woman on a mission. She had not had sex for nearly a year, she needed to have sex, right now. The hall was the one place she had not thought to stash any condoms, which seemed something of an oversight. Never mind, she thought as Daniel thrust inside her, she would get some in a minute, but right now, right now, this was so good, it was unfettered pleasure, it was desperate, frantic and delicious. Carmen was teetering on the brink of an orgasm that was so pleasurable that it almost hurt. She kissed him harder and slid her arms down his back. All she could hear was their breathing, the rhythmic pounding of their bodies against the wood and a mobile phone playing the theme from *Star Wars*. Now that didn't seem right.

'Oh no!' Daniel exclaimed, coming to an abrupt halt, whereas Carmen was well on the way to a crescendo. 'I'm going to have to get that.'

'No way!' Carmen exclaimed, winding her arms tightly round his neck. She was so close, he mustn't stop now! Sexual nirvana was in her sight and she really couldn't let it slip away.

But slip away it did. 'I'm really sorry, I've got to.'

With a feeling of disbelief Carmen let go of him as Daniel disengaged, and scrabbled in his jacket pocket for his phone and flipped it open. Carmen sat up and attempted to straighten her clothes.

'Yeah, I'll be right back,' Daniel said tersely. He looked at Carmen as he pulled up his jeans. 'I'm really, really sorry, but Millie's had an asthma attack and I've got to go home.'

There was no comeback to that really, was there? Okay, your child is sick but I still need to finish what we started was not going to go down well.

'God, I'm sorry,' Carmen replied, clambering up from the floor but forgetting to hold her skirt, so it fell down, unintentionally giving Daniel a final opportunity to see what he was missing.

'I've got to go, I'll call you tomorrow.' He gave her an awkward kiss then he was gone.

* * *

221

Carmen did what any right-thinking woman would do under the circumstances; she poured herself a glass of Pinot Noir and phoned a friend.

'Jess, I know it's late but please pick up,' she implored Jess's answerphone.

Damn it! She just had to speak to someone! Just as she was about to hang up, Sean answered. 'Hi, Carmen, sorry, I was just with Harry. Jess is actually asleep in bed – she had a really bad headache so I don't want to wake her if that's okay.' Sean sounded uncharacteristically subdued. Really low.

'Sure, sorry, I just needed to offload about something.'

'You can tell me if you like.'

Carmen thought of the frenzied passion in the hallway, and decided it was probably a good idea if she didn't go into details.

'Best not to, Sean. By the way, I've been meaning to ask, is everything okay between you and Jess?'

'Fine.' Sean didn't sound fine.

'It's just something Harry said last week.' Carmen left a pause, she was really hoping Sean would get it without her spelling it out.

'Oh?'

She was going to have to come out with it. 'It's about Jess.' Another pause. 'About her drinking too much.'

'Yeah,' a heavy sigh from Sean, 'it's been going on a while. She's in complete denial about it, though, won't listen to me when I suggest that she cuts back or gets help. Says it's all to do with being stressed at work and how she'll give up in the New Year. To be honest, Carmen, I'm not sure I can go on like this. It's getting worse and worse, and she didn't fall asleep this evening, she passed out. I'm worried about what she'll do. What if she drives with Harry in the car? I just can't trust her at the moment.'

'God, Sean, I'm sorry. I had no idea it had got this bad. Shall I try and talk to her about it?'

'You can try; she'll be defensive, just to warn you.'

Carmen ended the call determined to speak to Jess as soon as possible; she couldn't bear to think of her friend getting into such a state. She ran a bath and added relaxing essential oils. After the encounter with Daniel she felt as tightly coiled as a spring, as if the slightest touch would cause her to bounce off the walls. Man, she was tense. It seemed there was only one thing worse than being out in the sexual wilderness; it was being tantalised with the best shag of your life only to find it whipped away from you. The essential oils did bugger-all to relax her, so she watched TV, convinced that every single actor, chat-show host and comedian had had more sex than her in the last twelve months.

The next dilemma was to text or not to text Daniel to see if everything was okay. If she sent one, did it make her sound too keen? That ridiculous playground chant went through her head: treat them mean to keep them keen. Or did it just say mature woman who didn't need to play games and was just checking his daughter was okay? She decided not to, knowing that if she did she would then spent the next three hours obsessing about whether he was going to reply or not. She would text him in the morning.

But actually, she reflected at five a.m., when she'd woken up still feeling strung out, maybe she should have texted him that night, maybe it looked as if she wasn't concerned about Millie? In so many ways, wasn't it easier being in the sexual wilderness? At least one knew where one stood.

She had just emerged from the shower the following morning when the doorbell rang. She wrapped a towel round her, padded to the door and opened it to Daniel.

'Millie's with her gran, I just wanted to say sorry.' He looked knackered and was unshaven, but still oh so gorgeous. They stood staring at each other for a few seconds as water dripped from Carmen on to the hall floor.

She felt self-conscious after the unbridled passion of the night before. It had been so intense and here they were behaving like polite strangers.

''S'okay – d'you want a coffee?' When in doubt offer a hot beverage.

Daniel nodded and followed her in. 'I'll just get dressed,' Carmen said, diving into the bedroom.

She was about to whip off the towel and grab her clothes when Daniel walked in. 'Actually, can't we pick up from last night? I promise my phone's not going to ring. And by the way, I didn't choose the *Star Wars* ringtone, it was Millie. Just in case you're having second thoughts about getting close to someone who has that on their phone.'

He walked towards her. Carmen decided to be bold and let the towel fall from her body. And they did indeed pick up from last night, except this time on the bed, not on the hard wooden floor, but as Daniel began kissing her body, starting with her neck, moving to her breasts and then continuing his delicious exploration, Carmen would have gladly lain on cold concrete to be the recipient of such intense pleasure, and even if he'd had the ringtone of 'Agadoo', she would have done it all again.

Afterwards they both lay staring up at the ceiling. Carmen didn't know how to begin to frame a sentence expressing all the emotions colliding in her head. In the end it was easier than she thought as Daniel turned to her and simply said, 'Thank you.'

'Thank *you*,' she replied, staring into his brown eyes which were flecked with gold and reminded her of sunlight dappling through the autumn leaves. Ah, didn't post orgasm make one come out with the sweetest things?

'So?' Daniel continued. 'Can I see you again? I don't want you to think that this is just a physical thing, although that was pretty amazing. You're like no one I've ever met before. You're so funny and warm and sexy. Very sexy.'

Carmen turned over and propped herself up on her elbows to consider Daniel, who looked like a handsome Roman soldier with his strong profile and black hair fanned out on the pillow, then checked herself.

I absolutely must not think of the Roman thing, it's just a small step from there to Gladiator. 'So this isn't just in the pretty-waitress category?' she asked. 'You won't forget who I am next time we meet?'

Daniel groaned. 'No.'

'Promise?'

'Promise,' Daniel replied, pulling her to him and kissing her.

And frankly, Carmen thought, even if it was just a fling maybe she could live with that.

'Oh my God! You got to shag hot dad!' Jess exclaimed when Carmen finally caught up with her in the late afternoon after spending a good three hours in bed with Daniel.

Carmen now knew a few more facts about Daniel:

- He was indeed a very good lover, so good that when they made love she forgot all the bad stuff.
- He closed his eyes when they made love.
- He had a tattoo of his wife's name on his shoulder which he said he wanted to get rid of.

Thinking of the last point, Carmen wondered why he hadn't done it ages ago. Actually, so what? If he could make her feel like she did right now, which was sexy, powerful and satisfied, let him keep the tattoo. She gave an enigmatic smile and stirred her latte.

'I have so got to tell all the other mums! They'll go mentalist!' Jess continued.

The enigmatic smile vanished. 'Have you reverted to Harry's age? Strangely enough, Jess, I don't want everyone to know. I'm not just a piece of playground gossip!'

Jess looked suitably shamefaced. 'I'm so sorry, I just forgot myself. If you knew how very few nuggets of gossip there are in the playground you would understand, and Daniel is like a shining star of beauty in a sea of fairly unattractive men – not that I fancy him, of course. I don't shag other people's boyfriends – not like the bitch whore from hell.'

She was like a dog with a bone! Carmen glared at her friend. 'Do not pop my post-orgasm bubble with your bitterness!'

Jess looked at her watch; she just had twenty minutes before she picked Harry up from skateboarding club. 'So come on, give me the low-down, I haven't got long. Is he as good as legend has it?'

A slight nod from Carmen confirmed this.

'No further details?' Jess asked regretfully.

'Nope.' And to prevent any further interrogation she asked, 'Are you feeling okay now?'

Jess looked blank.

'When I phoned last night Sean said you had a terrible headache and had gone to bed.' The blank look became slightly guilty. 'Oh yeah. I did have a headache. I took these really strong painkillers and I must have just zonked out.'

Carmen dipped a spoon into her latte and scooped up a layer of froth. Clearly Jess was not going to admit drinking too much. Carmen wondered how best to get her friend to open up. And she was convinced that she could smell alcohol on Jess now.

'So it wasn't a hangover?'

Jess shook her head, immediately seeming defensive as she snapped, 'No, a headache. I told you.' And before Carmen could come up with a follow-up question, Jess quickly changed the subject. 'So,' she said brightly, 'when are you next going to see sexy Dan?'

'He's asked me round for supper on Tuesday, and I guess I'll have to do the whole engaging-with-small-person routine.' Meeting Daniel's daughter again was a nagging source of anxiety. Yes, her godson Harry seemed to think she was okay, even if she did hug him too much for his liking, but then again she was not getting up close and personal with Harry's dad.

'Oh, come on, you're great with kids and Millie is sweet. She's not a girly girl, and even Harry likes her – in fact, she's the only girl in his class that he does like.'

'Um,' Carmen was not convinced and she knew that however sweet Millie was it was still going to give whatever she had going with Daniel an added layer of complication. 'And there's something else.'

Jess looked at her enquiringly. 'Go on.'

'Don't you think that Daniel's out of my league, looks-wise? I've never been to bed with a man as gorgeous as him before. He's like A-list good looks; I see myself more as a B- or C-list. B-list on very good days and going right down to an E on bad days. I bet his wife is really beautiful, isn't she?'

Jess frowned. 'I can hardly remember what Imogen looked like. Even when she lived with Daniel and Millie he did most of the childcare and school pick-ups. She was always engaged in one of her artistic endeavours. And anyway, sweet cheeks, you're not B- or C-list on the looks front, you are A-list. You're super stylish and sexy.'

'Only with a lot of assistance from Mademoiselle Coco Chanel, combined with flattering lighting,' Carmen said gloomily.

'Oh, pull yourself together! You never used to be so insecure about your looks!' Jess told her.

'That was when I was the right side of thirty, married and looking forward to having children. Now I'm the wrong side of thirty, separated and . . .' – she paused, some of the glow left over from her passion with Daniel dispersing with these thoughts – '. . . barren.'

'Don't say that,' Jess implored her. 'Come on, focus on the good. This is your fresh start in Brighton. Don't be tied to your past, Carmen. It's time for you to move on.'

Carmen sighed and took a sip of coffee. Logically she knew Jess was right, it was just that the past was like a thorn lodged deep inside her and she didn't think she would ever get away from the sadness of not having a child, however much she could rationalise it.

12

Daniel lived a few streets away from Jess. It was very different from the red-brick, rather imposing houses Carmen was used to in North London. Here, many of the Victorian terraced houses were painted in pastel colours – pink, purple and blue seemed to be popular – and so the area had a cheerful, laid-back vibe. Daniel's terrace house was no exception. It was a brilliant Mediterranean blue with a sunshine-yellow door and window frames. Even though it opened directly on to the pavement Daniel still had several large pots of plants outside and Carmen noticed a rose bush and a hydrangea cut back for the winter. She had rocked up at quarter to nine, keeping her fingers crossed that Millie would be safely tucked in bed. She needed more time with Daniel before she got to know Millie. She felt a mixture of anticipation, nervousness, excitement and lust – that Andrex puppy was working overtime.

Daniel opened the door. He had come straight from the shower. His hair was damp and he was naked except for an orange beach towel wrapped round his waist with the word 'hot!' emblazoned across it in red letters. *I should say so*! Carmen thought, taking in his beautiful, smooth brown skin, the colour of mocha. Hang on, she really couldn't be channelling a Ricky Martin song could she? Lust could do most unsettling things to a girl, and right now on a scale of one to ten her lustometer was set to ten. 'Hi,' she murmured.

'Hi,' Daniel murmured back as he dipped his head down and kissed her, at which point Carmen was mightly relieved to have swapped the Chanel red lipstick for the sheer cherry lip gloss, otherwise the Chanel would have gone all over Daniel's lovely manly chin and there would have been that awkward moment when she rubbed it off and wondered what the state of her own chin would be. But never mind about the lipstick, there was a much more interesting stick on her mind right now, actually not on her mind but making its presence known against her. Daniel was not unmoved by her arrival. Carmen kissed him more deeply while his hands slipped under her sexy, understated off-the-shoulder tee-shirt and caressed her bare skin. This was so hot. And then suddenly not, as Carmen took a step to the side and found herself on a skateboard. Before she could get off she shot down the hall, crashed into a table, fell off and landed with a heavy thump on her backside.

'Ouch!' she wailed, having suffered a severe bash to her coccyx and an even worse dent to her pride.

'Why the fuck is there a skateboard here?' she exclaimed, forgetting about the no-swearing protocol in the house of a small person. 'Have you got a teenager you haven't told me about?'

Daniel walked towards her and reaching out his hand hauled her to her feet. 'Um, actually it's mine,' he said sheepishly.

Carmen shot him her most withering WTF look. 'But you're over thirty! Isn't there a law that all skateboards have to be abandoned when a man enters his twenties?'

'I'm really good at it, so I'm afraid not.'

Carmen took a minute to register the thought that the man she wanted to shag senseless, the man who had given her one of the best orgasms of her life, must also at times be a complete tit. 'Just tell me that you don't go around wearing your trousers halfway down your thighs and showing off your pants.'

'Only occasionally.' Daniel laughed as if this was a laughing matter!

Was he in arrested development? A man-child? Was he going to suggest they smoked pot out of a bong (Carmen hated pot, *hated* it!) and listened to Dizzee Rascal? The lustometer went down to five, further still when Millie appeared on the landing and called out, 'Daddy, will you come and tuck me in?'

Daniel shot an apologetic look at Carmen before scooting up the stairs. 'Go downstairs and pour yourself a glass of wine. I'll be down in a bit. I promise.'

Gingerly rubbing the base of her spine, Carmen took a few minutes to survey her surroundings. The house had a similar layout to Jess's and reminded Carmen of the Tardis, in the sense that it looked deceptively small

on the outside while being spacious inside, and not in
the sense that it was a time-travel machine. Directly
opposite her was the bathroom, a Victorian roll-top bath
taking pride of place. Carmen did love a Victorian
bath – so much better to lounge in with your lover. Its
size meant that one could lie back seductively and not
constantly obsess about whether one's stomach was
sticking out, as was always the case in a smaller bath,
where you were forced to sit up and breathe in.
Evidently Daniel had an out-there approach to decor,
as the bathroom was painted a deep cobalt blue, the
fireplace was painted silver and the floorboards were
purple. She peeked round the door to the small front
living room, whose walls were painted orange, and
took in a battered pink velvet sofa covered in purple
cushions, a futon and a guitar, but fortunately no bong.
The whole effect screamed bohemian artist. But never
mind the decor and furnishings! Carmen's attention
was riveted by a painting above the fireplace. And not
just any old painting. This was a huge portrait of a
naked man, lying on a bed with his arms behind his
head. A naked man who bore more than a passing
resemblance to Daniel – in all departments. Wasn't
it a little strange to have it hung above your fireplace
for the world to see just how well hung you were?
She moved closer, trying to decipher the artist's signature, only to find herself eyeball to private parts, like
some pervert, at the exact moment Daniel walked in.
She immediately turned round guiltily. Great, so now
she probably had a penis sticking out of her ear.

Perhaps she would need that bong after all. She moved sharply to the window.

'Oh God, you've seen it! I keep meaning to take that down,' Daniel said apologetically. He was now dressed in a baggy navy jumper and faded jeans, and looked as gorgeous as he had in the towel. 'Imogen painted it.'

Carmen wasn't sure that this revelation made it any more reasonable to have the picture in such a prime position. 'So is she an artist, then?'

'Artist, potter, knitter – you name it, she's tried her hand at it. She's not bad at painting but she was terrible at ever sticking at just one thing, which is no doubt why she chose to leave Millie and me.'

He sounded bitter, as if the memory of his failed marriage was still raw. Carmen thought he'd said they had split up two years earlier, and would have expected a little more distance. He was probably still in love with her. This certainly wasn't turning out to be the seductive evening she had hoped for. She looked at Daniel, who seemed lost in his thoughts, none of them good given the frown causing a deep furrow on his forehead. Then he smiled. 'Sorry, let's go downstairs and have that glass of wine. Millie will be asleep in a bit.'

Carmen followed him along the hall, painted a hot Barbie-pink, and down the wooden staircase, painted gold. She was getting a headache from the clashing colours and was beginning to think that Marcus was on to something when it came to white minimalism. At the bottom of the stairs Daniel turned to her and said,

'Imogen painted the house; she hates white but I love it. I've managed to decorate the top floor but haven't got round to the lower floors.' And so in the meantime Imogen's love affair with colour continued in the kitchen/diner/living room, which was painted a shocking lime green.

Carmen wished she could rewind to their earlier passion. While Daniel opened a bottle of Rioja she strolled over to the fireplace where an impressive fire was blazing away and did another survey of the walls. Thankfully there were no more naked pictures of Daniel, which really would have made him a class-A narcissist, but something worse perhaps – a whole wall was devoted to family photographs. Imogen might have been crap at sticking to things but she was absolutely drop-dead gorgeous. She had long blonde hair and the high-cheekboned, perfect featured, heart-shaped face of a model, striking blue eyes and luscious long lashes. Your basic nightmare actually. There she was on her wedding day with Daniel, in a white silk sheath dress that clung to her slender figure as tightly as she was clinging on to Daniel, as the pair of them smiled their beautiful smiles to the camera; there they were posing on a beach, arms round each other, Imogen gazing at the camera, Daniel gazing adoringly at her. There was Imogen heavily pregnant and still managing to look gorgeous; there she was with a newborn Millie lying in her arms a few minutes old, looking knackered but radiant; paddling in a white bikini with a chubby toddler Millie in the sea at Brighton, her body snapped back into pre-baby top form. They were such intimate pictures that Carmen almost felt as if she was snooping. And as she gazed at the photographs, especially the ones where Imogen was cuddling Millie, she wondered what kind of woman would leave her child? What kind of man, for that matter? But somehow it seemed worse that Imogen was the mother and had left.

Daniel walked over and handed Carmen a glass of wine and obviously noticed she was staring at the photographs. 'I left them up for Millie. After Imogen went I took them all down, but that made Millie even more upset, so I had to put them back up again. So now I have to live with them. But please don't think I haven't moved on because I really have.' He was gazing at her, his hazel eyes warm and passionate. Carmen felt a reignition of the lustometer. 'Come and sit by the fire.'

They sat at either end of the tatty orange velvet sofa and sipped their wine. It felt as if they were biding their time. They chatted about the kind of day they'd had – Carmen revealing that she was now nearly halfway through her sitcom, Daniel talking about the high-maintenance client he had who kept changing her mind about what kind of stones she wanted for her patio, but throughout the polite conversation all Carmen could think was how much she wanted him, wanted him so it was like a pulse, a throb, a beat going through her as if she was standing too close to the speakers at a rock concert.

'I'm just going to see if Millie is settled,' Daniel

said, getting up from the sofa two glasses of wine later and padding across the stripped floorboards. He was barefoot and Carmen couldn't help noticing that even his feet were attractive, and usually men's feet, however much you fancied the man, looked like those of Bilbo Baggins in *The Hobbit*. She took another sip of wine. She was determined not to look at the self-esteem-crushing gorgeous pictures of Imogen and so instead gazed at the fire. A few minutes later Daniel returned. This time he sat down next to her and put his arm round her. 'All quiet on the Millie front, she's zonked,' he said. He ran his hand along her neck. 'You've got a beautiful neck. You look like that twenties film star Louise Brooks, all seductive and mysterious.' Carmen shivered at the lightness of his touch and thought, *You've got a beautiful everything*.

Then Daniel moved closer and kissed her neck, gently pushing Carmen back on the sofa so she was lying down. 'How's the bruise?' he murmured.

'I think I'll survive,' she murmured back.

'I can kiss it better.'

And then it was on fast forward again as Daniel unzipped her jeans. 'What about Millie?' Carmen asked anxiously, as he slid the jeans down her legs. She didn't want to be responsible for a childhood trauma.

'Once she's asleep she never wakes up.'

Carmen took his word for it, and after a few anxious moments when she was straining to hear a footfall on the stairs, she surrendered to the feelings – to Daniel's delicious caresses of her body that were slowly driving her wild, to the feel of his body, to the feel of him inside her, and then it was intense and quick as if they both had to get the desire out of their systems and damn the rest of the world. Afterwards Daniel lay back and pulled her on top of him so her head rested on his chest. 'That was so good. I've been thinking about you all day, and kept forgetting what I was supposed to be doing. It was all your fault.'

'I've been thinking about you too. I couldn't believe it when you opened the door in that towel – I just wanted to rip it off you and jump your bones.'

Daniel smiled. 'Yep, that's the thing about children, spontaneity goes out of the window. But I hope you thought the wait was worth it.' He kissed her again. 'You hungry? I was going to make tagliatelle con funghi. I remember you saying you liked it.'

The night just got better.

After supper, in which Carmen discovered Daniel was an ace cook, they returned to the sofa. By now it was after eleven and Carmen expected to have one more drink then hit the road. She had, however, packed her emergency overnight kit just in case: if on the off-chance she stayed she did not want to wake up in the morning looking like the Bride of Frankenstein. Her thirty-three-year-old skin had needs, expensive Dermalogica skin cream needs. But Daniel insisted that she stayed: 'I want to spend the night with you.'

'Aren't you worried about Millie?'

'I'll make sure we're up and dressed before she is.'

They tiptoed upstairs to a colour-free zone. The walls were white and bare, the carpet a neutral oatmeal. They passed Millie's bedroom door which was ajar, a night light giving out a comforting yellow glow, and on to Daniel's bedroom. In contrast to the clutter of downstairs it was as if everything had been stripped down to the bare minimum – just a bed, wardrobe and chest of drawers, all of which were painted white along with white walls. There was a single framed Picasso print of a woman's back, from his blue period, but thankfully not a photograph of Imogen to be seen. Carmen quickly slipped under the white duvet. The heating had gone off and it was freezing, so she kept her tee-shirt on. She fervently hoped this hadn't been the marital bed; she didn't want to think of the lovely Imogen lying in it, with her lovely limbs entwined round Daniel.

After doing a last-minute check on his daughter, Daniel got in beside her, switching off the light next to him. This was always a telling moment in Carmen's experience. Would he be a holder or would he roll over and go to the opposite end of the bed? Right now she was so cold she was really hoping he was a holder. And all the pictures of Imogen downstairs and evidence of his life with her made her long for reassurance. Daniel slid his arm over her and curled his body round hers, giving her a blast of heat from his bare skin. A holder. Carmen breathed a sigh of contentment and snuggled into him. She expected that they would talk for a while, but after a murmured goodnight, Daniel fell straight to sleep. Well, it was fair enough, the man had been working outside all day. But he was awake at the crack of half-six the next morning, awake and good to go. Carmen had never especially cared for sex before breakfast but for Daniel she made an exception.

A quick scout to the bathroom and Carmen was dressed and downstairs before Millie had even stirred, while Daniel got on with making his daughter's packed lunch and Carmen made coffee. She felt uncertain if she should be there and was not at all sure she was ready to be in the midst of such a domestic scene.

'You could walk to school with us if you like,' Daniel told her. 'It's on your way home.'

Carmen was about to say that hadn't she better leave before Millie woke up when Millie herself appeared on the stairs, bug-eyed with sleep, her hair wildly sticking up. There was no escape now. She tootled downstairs and slid on to one of the chairs. 'Can I have porridge with honey, Daddy?'

'Aren't you going to say hi to Carmen?' Daniel asked, walking over and planting a kiss on Millie's head.

'Hi,' Millie said shyly. 'Did you have a sleepover?'

'Yep,' Carmen replied and steeled herself for further comments.

Millie looked at her and her gaze fell on the silver charm bracelet. 'That's like Sara's.'

Carmen's antennae were alerted. 'Is Sara one of your friends?' she asked.

Millie shook her head. 'One of Daddy's. She had a sleepover here too.'

At that Millie reached for the pot of felt pens and began drawing a picture of a mermaid. Daniel hadn't caught the exchange as he'd been rustling up porridge and Carmen could hardly interrogate him in front of his daughter about who he may or may not have had over. But in her head she couldn't help thinking that was three women in the last year, and Daniel had made out he was rusty on the dating thing. Was she just another in a long line? Were there more? She pushed her own bowl of porridge away, suddenly not hungry.

Daniel sat down opposite her and attacked his bowl with gusto. Millie took a few mouthfuls of her breakfast and then looked again at the charm bracelet.

'I like the swallow best,' she said shyly.

'I like the swallow too,' Carmen replied. 'It's probably my favourite.' *Where are you now, Will?* she wondered. *Having breakfast with Tash, chatting about her latest production, planning when to have the gorgeous blonde-haired Octavia?*

She sipped her coffee and tried to tell herself that it didn't matter how many women Daniel had over.

'I think I'll head off now,' she told Daniel after he'd sent Millie upstairs to get dressed. How did Millie feel about having a stranger at her breakfast table? Maybe she was used to seeing women there. That was not a good thought.

'We're going in a minute anyway, let's leave together,' Daniel replied.

There was suddenly a frenzied hammering on the

front door, combined with the sound of a little boy yelling 'Daniel, Millie,' through the letter box, loud enough to be heard three streets away.

Daniel rolled his eyes. 'Damn, I thought we'd have left before they came round.' He turned to Carmen. 'Prepare to get scrutinised.'

Carmen looked at him blankly as he went on, 'We always walk to school with Violet and her two kids.' He paused. 'You'll probably find her a little surprised to see you.'

Surprised and jealous about summed it up when Daniel opened the door and Violet caught sight of Carmen pulling on her black suede UGGs in the hall. Her jaw didn't quite hit the pavement, but it wasn't far off. Meanwhile her children were on scooters and whizzing up and down the pavement like mad dervishes.

Daniel did the introductions, 'Violet, you remember Carmen from the workshop?' There was a 'hi' from Carmen and a muttered 'hi' from Violet.

'You got the Crocs back okay?' Carmen asked, desperately making conversation. Today Violet was Croc-free in biker boots, leggings, a denim mini and black fake-fur jacket. Violet's 'um' did not encourage further conversation.

There followed a chaotic few minutes while Daniel tried to locate Millie's book bag, she grabbed her scooter and Carmen waited outside, next to a silent, brooding Violet. She clearly had issues – issues with Carmen seeing Daniel.

Finally Daniel had the book bag, had persuaded

Millie to put on her coat, she was on her scooter and had joined the other children. Violet had a ten-year-old daughter who was a mini me and was dressed just like her, a big no-no in Carmen's book, while her seven-year-old son was dressed like a teenager in skinny jeans, Converses and a sweatshirt with a retro picture of Jimi Hendrix on it. Carmen had a thing about children wearing tops with trendy pictures or slogans, which were always more about the parent than the child – like saying, 'Look at my cool kid, everybody! Aren't I such a cool parent?'

'I bet OAPs avoid going out during the school run,' Carmen joked as the three scooters whizzed past, narrowly missing her.

It was meant as an observation rather than a criticism, as Carmen thought it looked like great fun scooting to school. But Violet took it as a negative. 'Yeah, well, I think it's good for the kids to get some exercise first thing, that way they'll concentrate much better in class. So much more preferable to those mothers in London who drive their children to school in four by fours.'

'I'm sure you're right; I don't know any, though, so I can't comment,' Carmen replied neutrally. Blimey, she could do without the hostility first thing in the morning! Then thankfully Daniel had locked his front door and they set off. The path was too narrow for them to walk in a row of three, so Carmen and Daniel went ahead with Violet bringing up the rear. Carmen was convinced her leather jacket must be smoking with Violet's eyes boring holes into it.

'So what are you up to today?' Daniel asked, leaning towards her.

'Just writing,' Carmen replied. 'I've really got to get on; I've been a bit crap.'

Daniel smiled and reached for her hand. 'I'm sure you're not, I bet it's really good.'

He gazed at her with his gorgeous hazel eyes and the lustometer sprang right back into action. It really shouldn't matter how many other women he'd seen. But the moment was shattered when from behind her Violet shrieked, 'STOP AT THE ROAD, BYRON!'

Byron screeched to a halt, did an about-turn and headed back to his mum. He was so intent on his mission that he banged into Carmen, the metal scooter colliding painfully against her ankle. And at that moment Carmen had many bad thoughts about children on scooters and what she would like to do to them, especially ones with names of dead Romantic poets.

'Ouch!' she exclaimed, stopping to rub her ankle – really, UGGS were no protection against scooters.

She expected at least a 'sorry', if not from the monster Byron then from his mother, but Violet was busy praising her son for having listened to her. 'Thumbs up, Byron,' Violet said and Byron took off again. Carmen flattened herself against a wall to avoid another bash. Great, first her coccyx, then her ankle. Brighton seemed to be a very dangerous place.

'Are you okay?' Daniel asked.

'Yeah,' Carmen replied, limping slightly.

Finally Violet spoke. 'Oh, sorry, did Byron hit you?

We think he may have slight dyspraxia, and so has coordination problems. I'm sure he didn't mean to.'

Damn, Carmen couldn't possibly say anything critical now. If she did she would be dissing a child with a special need. As they continued on their journey to school they saw more families setting off and Carmen couldn't help but be aware that she was the focus of many curious looks, especially from the women. It made her feel like a teenager who has just spent the night round her boyfriend's for the first time, and she didn't know quite how to play it. In fact, so vivid was the feeling that she found herself instinctively checking her neck in case she had the teenage love bite to match. Some twenty minutes later, which seemed longer because of Violet's brooding presence, and after several more shrieks from Violet to Byron which Carmen was convinced had given her tinnitus, they arrived at the school, an unremarkable seventies-style flat-roofed series of buildings, but whose windows were decorated with colourful artwork which gave it a cosy, welcoming feel.

The playground was packed with children running around or swarming over the various climbing frames while their parents gossiped with their friends. Carmen looked out for Jess in the scrum but couldn't see her. She left Daniel to say goodbye to Millie and went to stand on the edge of the playground, well out of the way of scooters and nosy mothers. There were plenty of toddlers in buggies and babies in prams, but Carmen did what she always did when she saw a pram and looked the other way. It was admittedly harder in this situation, as practically everywhere she looked there was a pram with a perfect baby wrapped up snug as a beautiful bug inside, but she did her very best. A teacher blew a whistle, the shrill sound cutting through the parents' chatter and the shouts of the children larking around. What was it with the noise overload first thing in the morning? Instantly there was an order to the chaos as the children assembled into some ten lines and line by line filed into school.

Daniel walked over to her. He smiled. 'Was it too much coming with us?'

'No, it was fine,' Carmen replied, thinking she needed a strong cup of coffee and a lie-down to recover.

Daniel draped his arm round her as they walked out of the playground. 'I wish we could just go back to bed,' he murmured in her ear, causing the lustometer to flicker into action again. Outside the high iron railings he paused and pointed down the hill. 'I'm going this way, and you're going that way,' he gestured in the opposite direction.

'Okay,' Carmen replied, trying to ignore the parents trooping by who were ogling them. Daniel moved in closer and put both his arms round her. 'D'you fancy coming round tonight? Say nine? I can cook again.' He lightly kissed her on the lips and it would be true to say that food was the very last thing on her mind.

'I can bring something if you like?'

'Just bring that hot body.' Another kiss. The lustometer hit a perfect ten.

However, it suffered a slight decrease when Carmen

watched Daniel adjust the height of the handlebars on Millie's pink scooter and then take off down the hill at top speed. There was just something not quite right about the sexy man you fancied the pants off scootering, especially not on a girl's scooter.

And when she called Marcus from her mobile as she walked, checking first that no parents were in earshot, and filled him on practically all the details, he agreed.

'Bloody hell, Carmen, you really are going out with a man-child! I said you should have stuck with Will — he's a real man.'

Where did that come from? Carmen was taken aback by Marcus mentioning Will; in fact, she was pretty annoyed. 'There was nothing to stick to, if you remember. Will has got a girlfriend. Nothing ever happened between us except *that* kiss. And anyway, Daniel is hot. And nice and sexy and green and a good cook.'

'Good cock, more like,' Marcus shot back.

'Stop it!' Carmen warned him. 'Or I'll tell Leo about your Percy Pig habit, and it won't be pretty. And he'll realise what a shallow slut you are and not the sophisticated man-about-town you pretend to be.'

'Okay, okay, truce. Really, I'm glad you're finally getting some.'

'It's not just about sex!' Carmen exclaimed, thinking, was it wrong that it actually seemed to be entirely about sex? And that she really knew very little about Daniel.

'And promise me you're not rushing into something because of the Nick baby thing?'

'Marcus! Give me a break! When I wasn't seeing anyone you nagged me about seeing someone, and now I am you're saying I shouldn't be?'

'I just don't want you to get hurt, is all.'

'Thanks for your concern, but really I'm fine. More than fine. I'm great. Don't worry about me.'

Carmen had a spring in her step all the way to Sussex Square, in spite of the bruise on her bum which was still tender, as she thought about Daniel. She would just forget about the skateboarding and the riding on a girl's scooter. All men had annoying habits, but not all men were as gorgeous and sexy as Daniel. Just as she reached her flat, Daniel sent her a text: 'Can't stop thinking about you. What have you done to me? Can't wait for tonight d x.' It gave the rest of her day a glow and she even managed to avoid looking on the pregnancy diary for an update on Nick's baby, and that had to be a good thing.

Man-child or not, Carmen thought when Daniel opened the door to her that night, he was certainly hot. Before she kissed him this time she did a quick reconnaissance to ensure there weren't any rogue skateboards lurking, waiting to trip her up. Thankfully it was all clear. 'Hi,' she murmured and fastened her lips to Daniel's. So what if he skateboarded and rode a girl's scooter when he had a body like this?

'Hmm,' he murmured back, coming up for air. 'I should just warn you that Violet's here, I can't get rid of her. It's like trying to winkle a limpet off a rock.

Her ex has got the kids for the night and she's decided that I'm the shoulder she wants to cry on.'

Carmen, who'd had visions of heading up to Daniel's bedroom and getting straight down to it, was not impressed.

Daniel caught sight of her sulky expression and said quietly, 'I'm sure she'll get the hint when she sees you.'

Carmen trailed downstairs after Daniel, consoling herself with the sight of his broad shoulders. He had the body of a swimmer, she reckoned, with those shoulders, narrow waist and long, lean legs – at least, she hoped it was from swimming and not from skateboarding. Violet was curled up in the zebra-print armchair by the fire, holding a glass of wine. Her face visibly fell when she saw Carmen. She wondered if Violet was in the habit of coming round to Daniel's when her ex had the kids. 'Hi,' Carmen said as casually as possible. 'How are you?'

Violet twirled a long strand of hair round and round her finger. 'Well, I could pretend that everything's fine or I could tell you how I really feel, which is incredibly low.'

Carmen would have infinitely preferred it if Violet could have pretended everything was fine. Couldn't she go and feel low somewhere else? Daniel handed her a glass of wine while he carried on with cooking, and Carmen sat on the sofa and got to hear the whole story of Violet's divorce – how she'd been trapped in her marriage, bored by her partner, how she had filed for divorce, because, like, she was only thirty-eight and life was too short, wasn't it? How he was saying he might have to reduce her maintenance and she would have to get a job as his business was going through a bad patch, but like, how was she supposed to get a job when the children were so little, and anyway, she didn't know what she wanted to do right now and didn't want to rush into anything just to pay the bills.

Now usually Carmen's every sympathy would have been on the woman's side but frankly her ex-husband didn't sound that bad – she was the one who had left. Then of course there was the main reason for her sympathy bypass: she didn't especially like Violet and she suspected that Violet didn't like her either. 'Well, I guess that's what everyone else has to do, isn't it?' she couldn't stop herself from saying.

Violet turned her huge brown eyes on Carmen. 'What do you mean?'

'Just that we all have to make money somehow to pay the bills.'

'Yeah, well, I'm a mother. I need to be there for my children, perhaps when you have kids you'll understand where I'm coming from.'

There was of course no comeback from that one. Carmen looked at Daniel, who had stayed well out of the conversation and was now busy doing something with a wok. Carmen would much rather he'd been doing something to her. He just shrugged. Right now Carmen could have done with him being a teensy bit more forceful, like telling Violet that he and Carmen had plans – plans which did not involve Violet.

'Supper's nearly ready,' he called over. 'There's enough for three, so you're welcome to stay, Violet.'

'It's okay, I should get going and I'm sure I've got some rice cakes in the house, I could have Marmite on them. I'm not that hungry, though, I don't think I've actually eaten all day. I've been so stressed about everything,' Violet said, getting up and radiating an aura of the-world's-against-me. She should bottle it and call it *eau de burning martyr*, Carmen thought.

'Don't be silly, you must stay and eat with us,' Daniel replied. Carmen gritted her teeth, but in fairness she knew there was no other response to Violet.

Violet smiled faintly. 'Okay then, I'll just have a little.'

It was an awkward meal. Violet was milking being a victim for all it was worth, alternating with throwing longing glances at Daniel and extolling his virtues: 'Have you seen any of Daniel's gardens, Carmen? They're wonderful.'

Carmen was forced to admit that she hadn't.

'Oh, of course you haven't known each other that long, have you?'

No, but I have shagged him four times, and that's four times more than you, I'm guessing, Carmen resisted saying, tempting as it was.

'I do admire Daniel for actually making a difference to the environment and his community. Did you know he worked on the community garden for nothing?' Carmen shook her head. 'Well, maybe you should get him to give you a tour – I think you'll be seriously impressed. So you see, Daniel is not only kind, good-looking and a brilliant dad, he's also incredibly talented.' Violet did not say this ironically – her sincerity was almost scary. There was only one thing more unsettling than the fulsome praise coming from Violet, and that was that Daniel seemed to take it in his stride, not once shrugging it off – either he had heard it all before and it went right over his head, or he was enjoying it.

Carmen took a large sip of wine. She would be calm and gracious – she had the promise of great sex in an hour at the most. She could get through this. Focus, look at Daniel's lovely broad shoulders and just imagine pulling off his jumper and kissing his beautiful bare skin. And to speed up her arrival at that scenario she wolfed down her stir-fry, even though it contained tofu and she usually gave that a wide berth, while Violet seemed to be taking tiny mouthfuls, intent on extending her stay. At this rate she'd be here till breakfast. Carmen looked at her – *you will finish your stir-fry and go*, she willed her, *finish and go*. Carmen's mind-bending techniques obviously needed more work, as after making her stir-fry last half an hour Violet had a peppermint tea, and it wasn't until quarter to eleven that she finally made a move. Even then she stayed on the doorstep yacking away to Daniel. Carmen was alarmed to see that by now Daniel was yawning. Violet must have known that he would have put in a hard day's labour and that he would be flagging. This could not be! She'd had to endure the poisonous Violet for a whole evening, there just had to be light at the end of the tunnel, or

Daniel in her tunnel, and, oh God, what kind of analogy was that? The lust was seriously affecting her mind.

Another ten minutes dragged their heels until Daniel at last closed the front door on Violet and made to go downstairs, but Carmen stood in the hallway, arms folded. She meant business. 'There's no need. I've cleaned everything up, so now I want you to get your talented gorgeous body upstairs.'

'Yes, miss!' Daniel said smartly and took the steps two at a time, with Carmen in pursuit. In the bedroom Carmen felt there was no time for niceties as she pushed Daniel back on the bed, unbuttoned his fly and straddled him before you could say *oh baby, that feels so good*. Hang on, she *was* saying 'Oh baby, that feels so good', possibly a little too loudly, as Daniel had to put his hand over her mouth. But what the hell, she got there in the end. Carmen sexually rapacious Miller: one; Violet burning martyr: nil.

13

Carmen was completely smitten with Daniel. She almost got a pain in her chest every time she looked at him, he was so beautiful. She could hardly believe that she was with him. She was intoxicated by her feelings for him; her desire was like a drug. She pushed thoughts about other women out of her head. What did it matter about his past, about the Saras, about the Kirstys and the whoevers? He was with her. That was all that counted. Her days were punctuated with frequent fantasising about him, the feel of his kisses, the feel of his skin, the feel of him inside her; maybe she had better abandon the comedy and write a bonkbuster . . .

Within a matter of weeks her world had suddenly contracted to revolve around his – something she had always vowed would never happen to her, but somehow she had fallen into it. Since leaving London and her job and finding out about Nick's baby news, her life had been terrifyingly free of structure and certainty. Daniel and his ready-made domestic routines filled that void. Now Carmen knew what was happening day by day and week by week. They seldom if ever went out together because of Daniel not wanting to leave Millie too often with a babysitter as her asthma was bad in the winter. On Saturdays Daniel was taken up with ferrying Millie to ballet and tae kwon do. Carmen felt she was gradually getting to know Millie, who fortunately seemed to like her, and they bonded over *High School Musical* which Daniel refused to watch and didn't approve of. He thought it too saccharine, worried that Millie would become obsessed with her looks, but Carmen felt it was pretty harmless. She herself had had Barbies as a little girl and it hadn't turned her into a pink-wearing, blonde-haired, fake-tanned bimbo. If she recalled, she'd mainly used her Barbie in combat with her brother's Action Man, hacking off Barbie's long blonde hair into a more practical bob.

If ever Carmen suffered a pang that she would never have a daughter herself, she pushed it away. She felt she had spent enough time mourning what she couldn't have. The three of them would spend Sundays together going for walks by the sea, Millie scooting beside them, ending up at Morocco's Italian café in Hove for divine ice cream (Millie strawberry, Daniel chocolate fudge and Carmen pistachio). Or working on Daniel's allotment. Allotment was not a word Carmen had ever had cause to use before. To her it conjured up retired men with Jack Russells, smoking roll-ups, growing sprouts and keeping pigeons, but apparently that was an outmoded, even stereotyped concept – allotments were happening in Brighton, full of families and couples growing their own and not a pigeon in sight. And Daniel made even planting spuds feel sexy . . . What's more, she'd spent one afternoon watching him skateboard at one of the skate parks and found that she wanted him just as much that night. She gave him the first three episodes of her comedy, but somehow Daniel never got round to reading it – but that was okay.

She continued to be concerned about Jess, who was doing a very good job of keeping Carmen at a distance, only occasionally meeting her for lunch and rarely for a night out, still claiming to be busy with work. Carmen saw the latest George Clooney film with her, where even gorgeous George appeared not to work his magic on Jess, who seemed subdued and made a big show of ordering a Diet Coke at the bar at the art-house cinema, as if to prove she didn't have a problem.

Will sent through another batch of worms, but this time Carmen put them straight in the bin and didn't bother to contact him. Let sleeping worms lie. Will belonged to her past. Right now she wanted to enjoy her present.

November became December, her second least favourite month since the last two Christmases had been characterised by bitter rows with Nick. Carmen was in denial about the festive season. She'd taken to wearing her iPod on all shopping trips, playing Rufus Wainwright, who seemed to be the only singer who suffered the same exquisite agonies of desire as she did, on a loop, to drown out the noise of back-to-back playing of Christmas hits including 'Driving Home for Christmas'. She definitely could not listen to that as it reminded her of Will. She intended to have the lowest-key ever Christmas with Marcus and Sadie in Mayfair, pigging out, drinking Baileys and watching *It's a Wonderful Life* while Leo spent the day with his daughter. Daniel had already said that he and Millie were going to his sister's and were expecting that Imogen would fly back at some point. Carmen was doing her very best not to think of the beautiful Imogen spending time with Daniel. Say he saw her again and realised that he loved her? She couldn't bear to lose Daniel. She became determined to do everything she could to make sure that he became as obsessed with her as she was with him.

She would have to raise her game in her seduction technique, she decided one night. Because she spent practically every night round his she had fallen into the habit of dressing casually in her jeans, jumper, UGGs combo. So she decided to surprise him by wearing a sexy black dress, hold-up fishnet stockings and her highest heels. She had toyed with the idea of simply wearing her black trench mac with nothing on underneath it, very *Belle de Jour*, but Brighton could be extremely windy and she didn't want to flash any unsuspecting passers-by. Plus knowing her luck she would arrive and Millie would still be up, or Violet would be there, which would kill the moment. She was just about to order a taxi, though she would pretend to Daniel that she had walked, when her mobile rang. It was Sean – a very stressed-sounding Sean.

'Carmen, is there any way you could come and babysit Harry tonight?' Something in his tone of voice stopped Carmen from saying that she had a hot date with a hot gardener and babysitting was definitely not on her agenda. And she was so glad she hadn't when Sean went on, 'I've got to go to the hospital; Jess has just been taken in.' A sickening feeling of fear wiped out everything else.

'Oh my God, Sean! What's wrong?'

'She was found unconscious in Pavilion Gardens. They think it's drink-related but they don't know for sure.' Sean was trying to be calm but she could hear the anxiety in his voice.

'I'll get a taxi, I promise I'll be with you as soon as I can.'

An ashen-faced Sean opened the door to her some fifteen minutes later. 'I'm afraid Harry picked up the upstairs phone when the hospital rang and he heard quite a bit of the conversation, he's really upset.'

On cue Harry appeared at the top of the stairs looking anxious. 'Can't I come with you, Daddy?' he called down plaintively, his little face pinched with worry.

'You stay here with Carmen. I'll be back as soon as I can and I'm sure Mummy will be fine.' He turned to Carmen. 'I'll call you when I know what's going on, thanks for coming round.' Then he was gone.

Carmen went upstairs where Harry was still standing on the landing, looking utterly forlorn. 'So, Harry, how about we have a hot chocolate and maybe watch a bit of *Dr Who*? Then I'll read you a story, and then I bet

Mummy and Daddy will be back.' Harry nodded and while he went off to track down the DVD, Carmen quickly called Daniel and filled him in.

Daniel was typically calm in his reaction, and re-assuring. 'I'm so sorry to hear that. I hope Jess is okay, I've thought for a while that she's been drinking too much. And if they get back tonight, come round, it doesn't matter how late. I miss you.' See? No wonder she was so infatuated. Daniel was perfect boyfriend material.

While Harry seemed engrossed in the antics of the daleks, who were once more intent on extermination and world domination, (didn't they ever learn from their past mistakes?), Carmen fretted about her friend. Just how much had she been drinking to end up unconscious? She should have been on Jess's case more, in spite of Jess being so evasive.

An hour later there was still no news from Sean. Carmen felt tormented with worry. Say Jess had fallen and hit her head? And now had brain damage? Carmen always had an unerring ability to think the worst, but she couldn't afford to do that right now. She had to be the calm, rational grown-up for Harry's sake.

'When are Mummy and Daddy coming back?' Harry said, clearly not that distracted by the DVD after all.

'Soon, I'm sure. Why don't you choose a story for me to read to you?'

'Will Mummy and Daddy be back by then?'

Damn, why had she given him that scenario? 'I hope so.'

But even though they went up to Harry's bedroom and Carmen read him three chapters of his favourite *Horrid Henry* and did all her best impressions, she could tell that Harry wasn't listening to a word. She was running out of options and also feeling pretty freaked herself with the lack of news when Sean finally rang.

'She's still out of it but the doctors are convinced it's alcohol. I'm going to stay with her until she comes round. Would it be okay if you stayed tonight? I might even need you to take Harry to school.'

'Of course. Harry's desperate to speak to you, though.' Harry had practically glued himself to Carmen's side in his urgency to talk to his dad. She handed the phone to the boy, and tactfully left the room.

A few minutes later she returned to find Harry curled up under his duvet, looking exhausted. 'Shall I just read one more story?'

Harry nodded and Carmen picked up *Horrid Henry* and began reading, but by the time she had reached the end of the page he was fast asleep. Carmen on the other hand felt totally on edge, unable to settle. She phoned Daniel and told him she wouldn't be coming over. He sounded like he was already in bed and Carmen had a longing to be there with him, to feel his warm skin next to hers. She rattled around the kitchen making herself a cup of tea, jumping when Kitty Kitty squashed her orange bulk through the cat flap and looked utterly disgusted to see Carmen in her kitchen. Her ginger tail shot up like an orange periscope as she strutted across the floor and took up position on the stairs, where she observed Carmen through the banisters with a palpable air of scorn.

'So you don't want any food, Kitty Kitty?' Carmen asked, opening a succession of cupboards in search of cat food. When she located the bag of dried food she shook some into a bowl: 'Here, Kitty Kitty.' Kitty Kitty stayed put. Clearly when it came to cats, Carmen did not have the touch, but that was fine with her, as she had always preferred dogs. They were loyal and wore their heart on their sleeve, not like cats, who Carmen had the feeling only ever tolerated humans, and actually thought that they were the master race.

She made up the sofa bed in the living room, borrowed a tee-shirt of Jess's and curled up under the duvet. Sleep was out of the question, she was just too worried about her friend. There was only one thing for it – a spot of Jane Austen. She got up and wandered over to the bookshelf where she reached for Jess's copy of *Persuasion*. While the whole world seemed to have gone *Pride and Prejudice* bonkers a few years ago, Carmen and Jess had remained loyal to their favourite Austen – the story of Anne Elliot, who suffered had a wretched family life then had a chance of happiness when she fell in love with dashing Captain Wentworth, only to see that chance ruined when her miserable family stopped her marrying him. Poor Anne lost her bloom and then had to endure the sight of Wentworth flirting outrageously with a succession of silly women.

But Anne stayed true to herself, Anne had integrity. Anne had got her bloom and her man back in the end. Carmen began reading the first chapter, but even the exquisitely polished prose of Austen could not soothe her. Instead she reached for *Marie Claire*. She was clearly a woman of no substance, and no integrity, but hey, if she ever lost her bloom she could just whack on more blusher – presumably a course not open to Anne Elliot. But then again, perhaps what Austen was referring to was a bloom of the soul, and no amount of blusher could make up for that.

Carmen read about the perfect Christmas party outfit – sequins were in again, blah blah blah, were they ever out? Then she turned the page to read a shocking account of the dangers of women drinking too much. There was a heartbreaking case study of a mother of three in her forties who had died from liver disease after drinking two bottles of wine a night for ten years. Great, there was no escape. She picked up Austen again, no binge-drinking women there. It wasn't until after two that she finally fell asleep. She had a horrific nightmare that she was being smothered to death but she was powerless to move. She opened her mouth to scream and woke up to discover Kitty Kitty lying practically on her head – by opening her mouth she had just ingested a mouthful of ginger fur.

'Uggh!' She spat the fur out in disgust. Kitty Kitty gave her a what's-your-problem look. Honestly! A dog would never try and sit on your head.

Blearily Carmen fumbled by the side of the bed for

her watch. Buggeration! It was quarter to eight! She checked her phone and found a text from Sean saying that they wouldn't be back until after ten but that Jess seemed okay, and so could Carmen get Harry to school and make his packed lunch?

She leaped out of bed and raced upstairs, where it took her some five minutes to rouse Harry. Then she dashed downstairs, made him toast, slammed some ham between two pieces of bread, grabbed a Penguin biscuit and an apple and shoved then in the *Dr Who* lunch box. Took the toast up to Harry in bed, raced to the bathroom. There was no time to shower, so she just borrowed some of Jess's Clarins face wash and cleaned her teeth with her finger. And then it dawned on her that she would have to walk Harry to school wearing her seduction outfit from last night, including the heels, which were supposed to say f*** me and were now most likely to say 'ouch'. The trouble was, Jess's feet were a size six and Carmen's were a four and a half – there was no way she could walk in Jess's shoes. There was nothing for it, she was going to have to look like a ho touting for business on the school run.

As Sod's Law would have it, outside was blowing a gale. As soon as Carmen and Harry started out, a strong gust of wind whisked up Carmen's flimsy skirt, causing her to reveal her stockings and lacy French knickers to the family behind them. Though the indecent exposure had one advantage of making Harry laugh, and Carmen reflected that helping him lose his old-man worried expression was worth any transient humiliation. There were two further knicker-flashing incidents before they reached their destination – well, at least she was wearing some – and Carmen's feet were indeed killing her. Once they were in the playground Harry shot off with his friends, while Carmen folded her arms and hopped from one poor blistered foot to the other to keep warm. She was relieved when she saw Daniel and he came over, just as she was having a flashback to childhood and remembering how busy playgrounds can seem like the loneliest places in the world when you are on your own.

'Hey,' he leaned in and kissed her. 'What's the news?' As Carmen filled him in she was again aware of other mothers eyeballing them.

She could feel tears prickling her eyes. 'So I really hope Jess is going to be okay. I should have made her do something about it. What kind of useless friend am I?'

Daniel draped his arm round her shoulder, 'It's not about you and what you did or didn't do, though I'm sure you've always been a good friend – it's about her and her addiction. Only she can do something about it.'

Hearing Daniel say those words out loud made Carmen feel even worse. Just then the whistle went, and it was the usual frantic scramble as kids got into their lines and Carmen tracked down Harry. She could tell he was trying with all his seven-year-old might to put a brave face on things but his little chin wobbled when she said goodbye. 'Daddy will pick you up later. Have a great day and don't worry about Mummy, I'm sure she'll be fine.'

Harry nodded and Carmen moved to the side to watch his line file into school. Harry's shoulders were hunched up in an effort not to cry.

Carmen looked for Daniel but he was surrounded by a gaggle of women, *Talk about bees round a honey pot*, she thought, walking slowly out of the gates. And then, as she did a survey of the dads trooping out of the playground with her, she reckoned that she would have been one of the bees. The other dads were a motley crew compared to Daniel. They were either wearing clothes so nondescript they made no impression whatsoever, or they were making way too much effort in clothes that would have better suited a teenager – she counted several pairs of low-slung jeans with the pants out, which might have been forgivable in a sixteen-year-old, but on a thirty-something was nothing short of a fashion outrage. There was bizarre facial topiary, plenty of long hair, some multiple piercings of ears and noses, and some of the dads looked like they needed a good bath. It was a no-brainer that Daniel had so many admirers. Seeing him in the midst of such examples of manhood was akin to seeing the sun rise when you'd been living in the Arctic Circle for three months in total darkness. Finally Daniel managed to extricate himself from the women and head over to Carmen.

'So I meant to say, that's quite an outfit you're wearing

265

for the school run. Really, why don't more women make the effort.' Daniel grinned at her.

'I didn't know I was going to be doing the school run when I put it on last night, if you remember!' Carmen exclaimed.

'So it was all for me?'

'I guess so.'

Daniel looked at his watch. 'I've got forty minutes before I need to start. You could come back to mine and the outfit won't have been wasted.'

Carmen's eyes were scratchy with lack of sleep, she felt consumed with worry about Jess, and actually the last thing on her mind right now was a shag with Daniel, however gorgeous he was. She couldn't help thinking that it was slightly insensitive of him, but maybe she was feeling oversensitive.

'How about tonight? I'm expecting a call from Sean and I'd like to see Jess if possible.'

Daniel's face fell. 'I've got the book club at my house tonight and I can't get out of it.'

Carmen did a double take. 'You've got a book club? I can't imagine a group of men sitting round each other's houses discussing fiction!'

Daniel looked slightly embarrassed. 'Actually, I'm the only man. I just needed to do something when Imogen left me and I've never been one for going out to the pub with the lads, and so Violet suggested I join their book club.'

I bet she did! Carmen thought, giving Violet full marks for resourcefulness. *Hell, she probably started up* the book club just so she could get Daniel to come and I bet it wasn't anything to do with Violet wanting to share her love of great works of literature with him.

'But why don't you come along?' Daniel went on. 'We're doing *Atonement*.'

Carmen hesitated. She had read *Atonement* and seen the film; she could think of something to say, couldn't she? So when she agreed, it had nothing to do with wanting to police the other women, did it? And catching a glimpse of Violet, Carmen gave Daniel a smouldering kiss on the lips, even raising one stocking-clad leg coquettishly behind her.

Back home she quickly showered and changed, anxious not to miss any call from Sean. By eleven she had heard nothing and felt compelled to phone him. He was apologetic not to have rung, but they'd only just arrived home. Carmen was all set to bombard him with questions but he said, 'Why don't you speak to Jess?'

Her friend was uncharacteristically subdued. 'I've just got a terrible headache. Thanks so much for looking after Harry,' she said quietly.

'Shall I come round and see you?' Carmen asked.

'Yeah that would be great – Sean's got a meeting and he's probably sick of the sight of me after sitting up with me all night.'

It was still windy as Carmen walked to her friend's house. The sea was being whipped up into a frenzy, frothing and foaming like a gigantic coffee machine. She wondered what she should say to Jess. Probably best to listen, she reflected, and let Jess do the talking. Or ranting, she discovered some twenty minutes later. She had expected a repentant Jess, but what she got was angry Jess.

'I mean, fucking hell!' Jess exclaimed as she aggressively spooned coffee into a cafetiere and managed to spill most of it on the kitchen surface. 'I don't know why Sean made such a big deal! I had a few drinks and fell down, but I'm fine. It could have happened to anyone.'

Carmen stared at her friend in disbelief. She was so far in denial. How could she think that getting so drunk you passed out in a park equalled fine? Jess looked like death, she had a purple bruise on her forehead from where she'd fallen, her skin was blotchy and her eyes were bloodshot. Carmen was about to point out that she didn't seem fine, as diplomatically as possible – that's if you could be diplomatic about telling your best friend that you thought she was quite possibly an alcoholic – when Jess ploughed on: 'Sean's going on and on about how I need to admit that I have a problem with alcohol and go to rehab, but I think that's his problem! Not mine. I know I need to cut back, but who doesn't?'

'So are you going to rehab?' Carmen asked, wincing as the lyrics to Amy Winehouse's song popped up in her head. How shallow was she?

About as shallow as Jess apparently, as Jess sang back, 'They tried to make me go to rehab, I say no, no, no.' Or maybe it was gallows humour.

Jess snapped out of it. 'I've promised to cut back and we're going to see how it goes. I just hate the way Sean puts it all on me. He doesn't get that one of the reasons why I drink is because he is so miserable to live with.'

Carmen inched one foot on to the minefield. 'Are you sure he isn't miserable because of you drinking too much?'

It was carnage. The comment blew up spectacularly as Jess went off on one. 'God, Carmen, I thought you would be on my side! My best friend! And you drink loads as well, so don't come all moral fucking high ground with me!' She shoved the cafetiere plunger down so violently that coffee spurted up like a geyser. 'Oh fuck!' Jess yelled as hot coffee went all over her jumper. Carmen went to help her. 'No, it's okay, I'll get changed. Could you just pour me a coffee – or do you think I drink too much coffee as well?' Jess sniped. And with that she stormed up the stairs.

Kitty Kitty shot past Carmen like an orange cannon-ball, clearly put out by the noise, and, pausing only to glare at her, squeezed her offended orangeness through the cat flap. Carmen shrugged and said out loud, 'So shoot me, I'm a dog person.' She mopped up the coffee and poured a mug for herself and Jess, and then sat down at the table. She was beginning to wish she'd had that quickie with Daniel if Jess was going to bite her head off like this.

She had almost finished her coffee when Jess returned, looking more upbeat. 'Sorry I yelled at you,' she said as she breezed in, smelling of Clinique's Happy. She sat down opposite Carmen and reached for her coffee. 'I had such an ear bashing from Sean and I think I felt ashamed of getting so drunk, but it really is not going to happen again. I was so stressed at work. And anyway, it's not like I make a habit of it.'

Carmen didn't want to risk another outburst so did not remind her that practically every time she had seen her recently she had been drunk, or on the way to being drunk, or recovering from a killer hangover. She stayed for another coffee and then walked back home.

She was at her front door when she got a call from Daniel. 'I'm two minutes away, how about I call by? I don't think I can wait until tonight.'

'Come on round,' Carmen replied, thinking that was bound to cheer her up.

But afterwards, as she watched Daniel getting dressed, she couldn't stop herself from asking, 'Is it just about sex, then?'

Daniel stopped buttoning up his shirt. 'No way! I really like you, Carmen.' And he walked back to the bed and kissed her.

'Is it just about sex for you?' he asked as they both came up for air.

'Definitely!' Carmen joked back.

'Oh.' Daniel looked genuinely rattled.

Carmen sat up, holding the sheet to her body. 'Oh Daniel, I was teasing, I really like you too.'

Daniel looked relieved. 'Sorry, I can't do the joking thing about feelings, not after Imogen.'

Shit! Why did all roads lead back to her? 'No, I'm sorry,' Carmen said softly, and wrapped her arms round Daniel's neck. 'I mean it, I really like you.'

'You too,' Daniel murmured back. 'Sorry, I've got to go. Mrs McDonald's patio waits for no man. I'll see you at eight.'

After he'd gone Carmen flopped back on the pillow, wondering if she and Daniel had missed the moment to reveal that they were in love with each other. 'Like' didn't seem to cover her feelings for Daniel, but then again, did she love him?

271

14

'Everybody, this is Carmen,' Daniel said as Carmen walked into the living room. It was like walking into an antenatal class as Daniel pointed out the women in turn: 'Ilsa, Julie and Gemma. And of course you know Violet.' Carmen smiled weakly. Ilsa (wild chestnut curls and a smiley, open face) was about to pop; Julie (blonde bob, good bone structure) was breastfeeding a tiny baby, who Daniel informed her was called Florence, and Gemma (long black hair, petite, looked like a former ballet dancer) was about six months pregnant – and Violet looked like she wanted to dance on Carmen's grave.

The women, except Violet, smiled back at Carmen. 'Oh no! I'm never going to remember all your names,' Carmen groaned as she sat on the one remaining chair, in front of the two sofas, so she felt a little bit as if she was being interviewed.

'Well, we all know who you are!' Julie exclaimed. 'We've seen you in the playground.'

This was so not what Carmen needed. She looked appealingly at Daniel – *Save me from trial by the mummy mafia*, her eyes pleaded – but at that moment Millie called out and he disappeared upstairs.

'So we finally get to meet hot Dan's girlfriend,' Ilsa put in. 'Oh sorry, I shouldn't have said that, it's my hormones.' Ilsa pushed her wild curls out of her face and gave Carmen an apologetic smile.

'It's okay, he is hot.'

'He is the only hot man in the playground!' Gemma declared. 'Some mornings I forget to say goodbye to my son because I'm too busy staring at him.' Carmen laughed. The women weren't so bad after all. She had been expecting clones of Violet, and they seemed infinitely more friendly.

'So where did you meet him?' Julie asked.

Carmen had barely replied before Ilsa piped up with a follow-up, then Gemma.

'Of course, we've all seen the picture,' Ilsa said conspiratorially, gently rubbing her bump. 'So we know that Daniel is way more than a pretty face.'

There was a pause while Carmen wondered how to respond. Clearly these women didn't do small talk.

'And there I was thinking we were going to be discussing *Atonement*!'

'I just need to know one thing,' Ilsa again. 'Is he as good as we all think he is? He is, isn't he? He's my in-case-of-emergency fantasy, just if Gorgeous George isn't working.'

She caught sight of her friends and Carmen staring at her, all wearing identical expressions of shock.

'I'm a pregnant woman! My brain cells have turned to mush, I want to pee all the time and my ankles have swollen up to the size of a baby elephant's legs. Carmen could surely take pity on me and tell me,' Ilsa said defiantly. 'It would be doing a public service.'

'He's so much better,' Carmen confided.

And everyone laughed again, except Violet, who clearly thought a change of subject was in order. 'So, how are you feeling about the birth, Ilsa?' she asked briskly. 'Have you been listening to the relaxation tape I gave you?'

Ilsa stopped laughing, 'To be honest, all that whale music makes me feel even more uptight – the Kings of Leon is much more my thing. And I can't help feeling nervous after what happened last time.'

Julie interpreted for Carmen: 'Thirty-six hours of labour, with forceps followed by emergency Caesarian.'

'Josh would like me to book in for an elective C section,' Ilsa continued.

'But haven't you read the email I sent you which listed the statistics and experiences of women who have a natural delivery after a C section? Honestly, Ilsa, you can do it!' Violet sounded as if she was coaching a netball team, which Carmen thought quite wrong under the circumstances – it wasn't her vagina in peril!

'Violet is really into natural birth – she had her two at home,' Julie said. She looked down at the baby still attached to her breast. 'God, haven't you finished yet? I'd like to say that breastfeeding has helped me lose weight, but because she is constantly feeding, I've been eating even more. I need individual, low-calorie meals to be delivered to me, like a Hollywood star, and for my house to be empty of all other food. What chance have I got with a seven-year-old son who can't live without Monster Munch and chocolate chip cookies, and a husband who has to have more cheese in the house than bloody Wallace in *Wallace & Gromit*, even though he knows that I can't, I simply can't resist a piece of cheese?'

Violet was still on at Ilsa. She was such a bully, Carmen thought, why couldn't she just drop it? What business was it of hers if Ilsa had a C section?

'And you'll recover so much better if you have a natural birth and be up and about in no time.'

'Actually, I'd quite like to be flat on my back so that Josh might actually pull his finger out and do something! That was the only good thing about having a C section last time.'

Violet narrowed her eyes and turned her attention to Gemma. 'What about you, Gemma? Have you thought any more about the home birth?'

'I'm just not up to it, Violet. I know it worked for you, but I'm too scared. I want to be in a hospital surrounded by doctors and a shedload of drugs, like last time.'

'I understand,' Violet replied, looking as if she did not understand at all, 'but I think you are missing out. There is something so wonderful about having a baby at home. And it is after all the most natural thing in the world giving birth. Hospitals turn it into a medical procedure.'

Carmen had recently read an article about the shockingly high number of women in Africa who die in childbirth because of the lack of medical facilities and thought that Violet was being rather too evangelical about something which was surely a personal choice. And now Violet thought Carmen needed drawing out. 'So, how about you, Carmen? What kind of birth do you think you'll have?' The cruel assumption of the fertile that everyone was similarly blessed.

'I really haven't thought about it,' Carmen replied flatly. Of all the topics, why did it have to be this one? 'But if I did have a baby I really wouldn't mind how it was delivered, just so long as it was healthy, and I definitely wouldn't think that my birth experience was lessened if I had to have a C section.' She could see Ilsa giving her the thumbs up behind Violet's back. 'I don't think that you're a better mother just because you had a natural birth.' But her confident statement was not going to deter Violet.

'Imogen had Millie at home. Daniel was brilliant, apparently.'

'Did he cut the umbilical cord with his teeth? Roast the placenta and serve it up for tea?' Carmen's voice was laced with sarcasm; it was self-preservation. It didn't help that she was sitting opposite the wall of photographs, testimony to a life that would never be hers.

'He was just very on the ball,' Julie said quietly. 'Imogen's labour progressed rapidly and the midwife wasn't there when Millie was crowning.'

'That's when the head is visible from the vagina,' Violet said to Carmen. 'Breathing is everything during that stage so you don't tear.'

276

'However you bloody breathe your vagina is never the same again,' Julie said bitterly, 'whatever anyone says.'

'Pelvic floor exercises,' Violet said sweetly.

'Take more than that after delivering a ten-pound whopper. I asked Tony did it feel different, you know, when we finally had sex again,' Julie commented.

'Nine months later!' Gemma exclaimed.

'A year later!' Ilsa put in, causing all the women to cackle, giving the witches in *Macbeth* a run for their money.

Julie continued, 'And he said "Oh no," but he was definitely lying. He was just desperate for me to shag him again.' More cackling.

'I know Daniel is desperate for a sibling for Millie.' Bam, Violet's comment was like a punch in the guts. 'He's really close to his brother and sister and wants Millie to have the same experience.' She was looking directly at Carmen.

Carmen shrugged, trying her hardest to look unconcerned. Channel all the good things, she urged herself, you have Daniel, she doesn't. But would Daniel want her if he knew the truth about her?

'I'm just going to call the babysitter,' Violet said, taking her mobile out of her bag and going upstairs.

Julie waited until she was safely out of earshot before saying quietly, 'She's okay most of the time but you have to remember she is deeply insecure.'

'And totally obsessed with Daniel,' Carmen said gloomily. Violet's comment had really got to her.

'Well, I think she thought their fling would lead to something more.'

Her *what*? No wonder Violet was so possessive. Why the hell hadn't Daniel told her?

'So when was this fling?' Carmen asked, speaking very carefully and trying not to betray any emotion.

'Oh Lordy!' Julie exclaimed, 'I thought you must know! It was last year; I don't think it was serious, at least not on Daniel's part.'

'I can't believe I'm asking you this, but have there been many others?'

Julie looked anxious, clearly realising that she was entering a danger zone. 'Three that I know about, but Daniel's never seemed as close to anyone as he does to you. Please forget I said anything. I didn't mean to upset you.'

At that moment Daniel came back downstairs. All eyes turned to him. 'So how are you getting on? I thought *Atonement* was thoughtful, provocative and moving,' he said as he walked over to where Carmen was sitting and sat cross-legged beside her. 'I got that from a review I googled,' he added.

'We hadn't actually started talking about the book,' Carmen said quietly.

Daniel smiled, 'I bet you were gossiping.'

If only you knew, Daniel. Violet returned and then for some ten minutes *Atonement* was discussed (in a nutshell they all loved it, except Violet, who was very angry about the ending being ambiguous) and then conversation turned to Christmas and what was everyone doing, and which children believed in Father Christmas and which didn't, and was it right to pretend that a man in a red-and-white outfit squeezed himself down your chimney on Christmas Eve? Carmen nodded and forced herself to smile and look animated, but how she longed for them to return to Ian McEwan's tragic story because, painful and heartbreaking as *Atonement* was, it had the virtue of being fictional.

She felt subdued, a dull ache taking over. First the whole baby thing and then the revelation about Violet. Daniel was sweetly attentive to her, trying to draw her into their conversations whenever possible, but as they had turned out to be all about children, that wasn't easy. She could feel herself slipping into the dark place, never more so than when Julie wanted to nip to the loo and asked Carmen to hold baby Florence. Baby Florence felt surprisingly solid as she nestled in the crook of Carmen's arm; she was just two months old, dressed in a white sleepsuit with cute brown bears printed on it, with an absolute peach of a face, and she broke Carmen's heart. It was her survival strategy never to look at a baby and definitely not to touch one, but baby Florence was gazing up at her with her clear blue eyes; Carmen had no choice but to return the gaze.

I should not be holding a baby, Carmen wanted to say. *Don't you understand? This is very, very bad for me*. Everyone was of course oblivious to the battle being waged within her, and when Julie reappeared she whisked baby Florence out of Carmen's arms as if it had meant nothing.

279

She couldn't wait for the women to leave, but it wasn't until eleven that they did. She confronted Daniel in the kitchen. The fire had gone out and it was cold. Carmen got straight to the point: 'Why didn't you tell me you had a fling with Violet?'

'Oh', came his reply, 'who told you?'

'Does it matter? Why didn't *you* tell me? It explains why Violet is so funny with me all the time.'

'I just didn't think you needed to know. It was something that happened last year and since then we've just been friends.'

'I think Violet's feelings for you are way more than those of a friend!' Carmen retorted. 'Anyone can see that! I think she's in love with you.' Her arms were folded against the cold and as a defence. She had never felt so angry with Daniel before.

It was clearly a sentiment he shared as, after a brief pause where he seemed stunned that Carmen should be questioning him, he exclaimed, 'Don't be ridiculous, Carmen, you're completely overreacting. I don't ask you about your past, so why this intense scrutiny of mine? I fucking hate this kind of thing.'

Daniel's handsome face was screwed up with anger, he almost looked plain. He seemed a complete stranger to her. What did she know about this man?

She shook her head. 'I'm not having a go at you, Daniel, I just think it would have been good if I'd known about Violet. I mean, God! The poor woman! I had no idea.'

She thought back to the times she'd been snippy with

Violet, the times she had flaunted her relationship with Daniel, and felt awful. 'But d'you know what, if it's such a problem, I'll go.'

She reached for her jacket and the fight seemed to go out of him. He walked over to her. 'I'm sorry, Carmen, I shouldn't have snapped like that. I should have told you about Violet. I guess I feel slightly ashamed. For about a year after Imogen left I did have quite a few affairs, but I want to put all that behind me now with you. I'm sorry.'

He was back to being the Daniel she thought she knew. 'Please don't go.' He put his hand on her shoulder and said softly, 'You look so gorgeous tonight, I kept thinking how much I wanted you, couldn't wait for the others to go.'

Half of her wanted to storm dramatically out into the night, but the other half was already imagining being next to Daniel in bed. Self-righteousness was never going to win in a battle with lust. And she did want Daniel so very much.

In the week that followed Carmen tried to push away thoughts of Violet and Daniel – maybe he was right and that was his past and nothing to do with her. But she couldn't get Violet's comment about Daniel wanting more children out of her head. And on Thursday night as they lay in bed together she realised she had a question to ask, a question that was burning into her consciousness. She knew she absolutely shouldn't go there but couldn't stop herself. She had to put the children question to him. 'So, Violet said you really wanted to have more children?'

There wasn't even a beat before Daniel replied, 'Yeah, of course – it's why we're all here, isn't it? I couldn't imagine life without Millie; she gives my life meaning. I know several couples who've chosen not to have kids and there's always something a little precious about them. They seem inward-looking to me, fussing over each other, going on expensive holidays, getting pets, just to fill that void.'

Carmen thought she might throw up. 'Perhaps those people haven't chosen not to have children, perhaps they can't have them,' she said in a small voice.

'Perhaps – but there's always a way, isn't there – what with IVF and things like that.'

'Only one in three IVF cycles results in a successful pregnancy.' The statistic was etched on her consciousness forever.

'Hmm,' Daniel said vaguely. The statistic of course would mean nothing to him. 'You want kids, don't you, Carmen? You're a complete natural with Millie and Harry. And you were great with Florence.'

'I do really want kids,' Carmen replied truthfully and felt the tears prickle her eyes.

'Are you okay?' Daniel asked.

Oh, how to answer such a question? With the truth? *Well, Daniel, no I'm not okay. I'm a woman who can't have children and according to you my life has no meaning, and believe me when I say that I have spent a long time thinking the same thing, and only after a great deal of expensive therapy, tears and support from my friends, I know that it does. It's something I'm having to take one step at a time, but my life does have meaning.* She couldn't bear to tell him THE TRUTH. So she told him something else painful instead.

'It's just the build-up to Christmas. It really isn't my favourite time of year. It reminds me of breaking up with Nick. We'd already decided to split up before last Christmas but didn't want to upset his parents as his dad was recovering from a stroke. So we went to Nick's parents and put on this act that everything was okay. And it was just so sad.' That was an understatement. It had also been gut-wrenching, heartbreaking. She and Nick could hardly bear to be in the same room together. The only way that they had got through it was to drink from the moment that they arrived at his parents' to the moment they went to bed on Christmas Day. Carmen drank a bottle of cava and half a bottle of Baileys and passed out during *The Pirates of the Caribbean*; Nick drank a bottle and a half of cava, a bottle of Merlot and half a bottle of Jameson's. They both had the mother of all hangovers on Boxing Day but at least neither could actually remember Christmas Day.

'So why did your marriage end, Carmen?'

If she told him now it would surely ruin everything. And just lately so many things seemed to have been ruined – her career, whatever she had going with Will, her friendship with Jess – Daniel was the one bright star in her life right now.

'Oh, so many reasons, but I guess the biggest one was that we had just fallen out of love – but it's okay between us now, and maybe one day we can even be friends.' The words came out as a rush. 'How about you and Imogen?' Carmen was not at all sure that she wanted to hear about the lovely Imogen, but anything to deflect attention away from herself.

There was a pause. 'What can I say? She broke my heart. I don't think we can ever be friends. Anyway, let's not talk about it, it's so depressing and it belongs to the past.' He slid his hand inside her tee-shirt and caressed her breast. It felt more as if he wanted the conversation to end, but her traitorous body was quick to respond to his touch and then they were having a fast, furious, silent fuck. It was if they could both exorcise the demons of their past. But even as Carmen lost herself in their passion, she thought that the past had a nasty little habit of catching up with you . . .

15

The small comedy venue below the pub in Camden was crammed and steaming hot. Everyone had stripped off coats and jumpers down to tee-shirts, and there was a pervading smell which Carmen always associated with comedy gigs of wet dogs, lager and cigarette smoke, even though no one could smoke inside any more. She herself was ferociously hot and bitterly regretted wearing her UGGs.

She had just endured two open-mic spots where both comedians or rather wannabes died, and it had been excruciating watching their efforts. Though one positive side-effect of their appalling acts had been to make Dom appear quite funny, even though his material was a highly predictable succession of anecdotes about schooldays, wanking and sex, and Carmen felt she had heard it all a million times before. But Sadie had begged her to come and see Dom, and as Sadie had made what was for her the incredible effort of going from London to Brighton more than once, Carmen thought she had better return the favour. Also, after the children conversation, she felt she needed a little time out from Daniel. She had yet again tried to meet up with Jess, to have a frank talk with her about her drinking, but, as if Jess had some sixth sense about why Carmen wanted to see her, she had cancelled her twice, blaming pressure of work again.

During the interval Sadie was required to perform her duty as a comedian's girlfriend and go and massage Dom's ego – in other words, lie outrageously about how hilarious he had been, along the lines of yes of course she could easily see him occupying the chair next to Paul Merton on *Have I Got News for You*, except that he was so funny Paul might feel threatened by his comedy genius. Carmen was spared the lie-fest as she pushed her way towards the upstairs bar to get the drinks in. She needed alcohol and fast if she was to last through any more routines. 'Ouch!' she exclaimed as someone trod on her toe.

'Sorry,' the someone said. Except it wasn't any old someone. It was Will.

'Carmen Miller, what are the chances?'

Those blue blue eyes, that face, that teasing tone. Carmen straightened her back and hoped that her make-up hadn't slid off her face in the furnace downstairs. She only liked to see Will when she was her sparkly best, especially after the night of the passing out where he had undoubtedly seen her at her worst.

'I was dragged here by my friend who has the misfortune to be going out with a comedian – Dom, I think you might have met him. Why are you here? Shouldn't you be practising ski jumps on the dry run?'

He grimaced. 'Don't remind me about the S word. But here I am talent-spotting, a slave to my work. I haven't seen any so far, but hey, I've seen you, so the night's looking up.'

'That is such a woefully bad line, Will,' but Carmen smiled in spite of herself. Daniel didn't do flirtatious banter. Carmen missed that.

'Actually, I knew you were going to be here, Dom told me. So will you have a drink with me and save me from returning to the hellhole downstairs, where nothing has made me laugh? *Please.*'

Carmen reflected. The last time she had seen Will, at the Comedy Awards, she had been decidedly flustered; the time before that she had insulted him; and the time before that she had insulted him; and the time before that she had ended up in his bed. It would be good to draw a line under all that erratic behaviour and show that she was a woman in control.

The two of them sat upstairs in the pub, which was largely deserted. They were sitting opposite each other at a small table tucked to the side, Carmen with her vodka and tonic, Will with his pint of Guinness. It reminded Carmen of all the many hours they had spent in the Ship together with their colleagues, and she felt a pang of nostalgia for those days. As always with Will there was no small talk: 'So how's it going with the writing and with the new man? Marcus mentioned a certain sexy gardener. I guess that's why you didn't bother to reply to my email and to my last consignment of worms.'

'Oh sorry, I thought I had said thank you.' Carmen was such a bad liar, she could have given Pinocchio a run for his money.

'Must have been too taken up with your gardener. How very Lady Chatterley of you to hook up with a man of the land.' Will's tone was as playful as it used to be, but Carmen wondered if she was right in detecting an undercurrent. Then again, she'd been wrong quite a few times about Will.

'Well, it makes a change from being married to a comedian and being a comedy agent,' Carmen said drily. 'At least I don't have to spend every night at a gig like this watching some terrible routine and pretending to like it, not that Nick's routine was bad.'

'So what do you do?'

'He, Daniel, is a single parent so we don't go out much. We cook. Well, actually, he cooks, I wash up; I'm a terrible cook. We drink wine, I'm very good at that, we sit by the fire which he's made, and—'

Carmen was about to say work our way through various box sets, but Will interrupted her and held up his hand: 'It's okay, I don't need to hear about how you have great sex with him.' As so often in the past with Will all roads led back to this. 'Isn't it enough that you taunted me with Connor the postboy? I swear he's lost some of the swagger to his step since you left. God knows who he's going to snog at the Christmas party this year.'

'I was going to say that we watch *The Sopranos*, but since you've brought it up, yes to the other.' Carmen tilted her chin up defiantly. Yes, she was in control! For once she was not going to say something she regretted. 'And how about you and Tash?' She stumbled over her words, 'I meant how's the relationship going, not do you have great sex.' Damn, it only took one mention of the slender but firm-thighed one for her control to weaken.

Will sighed. 'Fine. We're always out at something – some gig, some show, some dinner, so actually *we* don't always have great sex because we're both knackered. And she gets up at five to go to the gym, so mornings are out.'

Carmen couldn't resist being cheeky: 'You could have it at four fifty-five a.m.'

'Oh, you reckon I can go for five minutes, do you, Miller? As much as that? God, I'd forgotten what a wind-up you were. I'm going to have to get the muttonometer out and say that denim skirt is very short, foxy admittedly, but borderline mutton, lucky you've got the legs to carry it off.' His face assumed an exaggerated look of horror, 'But what are you wearing on your feet? I never thought that I would see Carmen Miller in UGGs! Have you taken leave of your senses? I'm surprised sexy gardener wants to have sex with you after seeing you in them.'

'They don't seem to put Daniel off; I've lived in them since I moved down. Of course I don't wear them in bed.' Oh God, she was already losing the I'm-in-control edge.

'Well, he's from Brighton, what can I say? But I always liked seeing your pretty feet and slender ankles, Miller. You should let him see them sometimes.'

'You like my feet?' Carmen asked with some surprise.

'You have lovely feet. I don't usually like feet, but I make an exception for yours. Tash was a ballet dancer and I feel disloyal saying this, but her feet are seriously ugly, kind of gnarled and bumpy.'

Carmen arched an eyebrow. 'I bet she's very supple, though.'

'Very. Not that I get to appreciate that quality, as I'll refer you back to my earlier comment about the lack of great sex.'

Phew! Carmen suddenly felt even hotter, all this talk of sex and Will liking her feet. The flirtatious banter. It was delicious, intoxicating and, yes, exciting. The bell rang, indicating the end of the interval and Carmen started to get up. Will lightly touched her arm. 'Don't go, stay and talk to me.'

'Don't you need to see the acts? Sign someone up and snatch them out of the jaws of comic obscurity?'

Will grimaced. 'I feel like I've seen it all before. Work's been shit anyway, I don't owe them anything. I'd rather see you.'

'Even with the UGGs?'

'Even with those sheepskin monstrosities. So how are you?' Will leaned forward on the table, his arms folded. Carmen got a hit of Amber and Lavender. Damn, why was her heart suddenly racing and the lustometer, which was supposed to be reserved for Daniel, springing into action? Was she *that* fickle?

'I mean *really*, how are you? And don't give me one of your fob-off flippancies, like you always do.'

Wow, Will was being very direct, she was a little uncertain about how to respond. 'Do I?'

An eye roll from Will. 'The moment I ever felt I was

getting close to you, you would put up the keep-out signs. And I know there's something you're hiding. You are really frustrating, Miller.'

This was news to her and she wasn't sure if she liked being put on the spot.

'Is that what you do with the gardener? Or is it all about great sex so you never have to let him in?'

'Bloody hell, Will, what is this? Tonight I'm supposed to be watching bad comedy and drinking too much, listening to Sadie witter on about whatever Dom has or hasn't done, most likely not, knowing him. I didn't expect to be psychoanalysed when I got on the 5.49 tonight and sat opposite the woman who alternated talking loudly on her mobile and doing her nails. She was using nail clippers, a disgusting habit in public if you ask me, and a piece of nail shot across the table and nearly landed in my latte!'

'You're doing it now, but I think you know exactly what I mean.' The blue eyes challenged her, told her that she had no hiding place.

'Okay,' she conceded, 'maybe I do know what you mean.' For a while they held each other's gaze and Carmen wondered what might have been if, on Will's birthday night all those weeks ago, she had gone beyond the banter.

Then in true comedy bad timing Dom came bounding over, completely oblivious to the intimate scene he was gatecrashing. 'Hey, Will, glad you could make it, what did you think of the act? I'd appreciate any pointers you could give me.'

'I think your timing could be better,' Will said drily.

And that was the end of the intimate scene. Dom was followed by Sadie, so then came all the introductions.

'So you must be Sadie of the sexy voice,' Will said. 'I've long been an admirer of your work on the radio. I bet people are always asking you to recite the shipping forecast.' Oops, Carmen had forgotten that she had told Will about Dom and his fetish for hearing about gales when he was in flagrante with Sadie.

'You'd be surprised,' Sadie said, putting extra velvet into her voice.

'Oh, I don't think I would,' Will replied. 'I've heard your German Bight is unparalled and as for your Dogger, well what can I say?' Carmen had to take a big sip of vodka and tonic to avoid catching Sadie's eye.

'Ha ha,' Dom gave an uneasy laugh, as he caught on to what they were saying. 'I was going to put that in my routine but Sadie felt it wasn't appropriate.'

'I think that would definitely constitute grounds for being dumped,' Will agreed. 'Best stick to wank jokes.'

Dom looked stricken at the prospect of being dumped by Sadie, as well he might seeing as she was now bankrolling him and against the advice of all her friends she'd let him move into her tiny studio flat in Islington. But he quickly regained his composure and was back to doing what all comedians do best, talking about themselves. Maybe you simply couldn't have too much self-awareness if you were a comedian because of the awfulness of going onstage and being heckled? And all the while Dom babbled on about how this gig had gone or that gig, Carmen thought about what Will had said to her. She knew he was right, but what did that matter? When it came to it, Will had Tash, and she had Daniel. They had made their choices. It was only as the pub was closing that Will and Carmen got to be alone again.

'So, another ultimately frustrating encounter, Carmen,' Will said outside, as they waited on Camden High Street to hail a taxi. It was a bitterly frosty night and their breath came out in white clouds. Will had his hands shoved into his black wool jacket and his collar turned up. Carmen was shifting from UGG foot to UGG foot to keep warm. 'I've just had a text from Tash wondering where I am. I expect your gardener is tucked up in bed, dreaming of an UGG-booted girl with beautiful green eyes.'

'Who is wearing a mutton skirt,' Carmen replied, but was highly tuned to the compliment.

Will shook his head, and said, 'You're doing your distance thing again.'

'And Tash, your girlfriend, is wondering where you are,' Carmen reminded him, doing her distance thing. It was, after all, what she did best with Will. Always one step forward two steps back. Except that seeing him again was such a bitter-sweet pleasure she didn't know if she wanted to go two steps back. Will was reminding her of a time when she could be funny, flirty Carmen.

At that moment a taxi went by and Will hailed it for her. 'Take care, Carmen. Maybe one day we'll get our timing right.' He gave her the lightest of kisses on the cheek and Carmen had to resist the temptation to throw her arms round him. Where did that impulse come from? She really was fickle.

Back to banter: 'Have fun on the piste. Don't forget you'll be doing it for Octavia slash Mercedes slash Lexi. But I think I prefer Octavia; I really do think Mercedes is too flashy, unless you're Spanish.'

A resigned shake of the head from Will. And then she was alone in the taxi travelling back to Mayfair, where she was staying with Marcus. Why had Will said those things to her, hinting at deeper feelings between them? He'd had a dash of devil-may-care about him tonight. Maybe things were going badly at work or with Tash, and Carmen had just been a welcome distraction. Maybe that was what she always had been to him – a distraction.

16

'Well, I love the first three episodes,' Marcus declared the following morning, as they sat having tea in their pyjamas (well, Carmen was in PJs, Marcus was in a luxuriously fluffy white robe, the kind you get in really expensive hotels). Leo had left for work at the ungodly hour of four forty-five. Carmen so rarely saw him that sometimes she thought it might be possible that he was a figment of Marcus's imagination. 'I think it's time you got someone else's input on it, someone who is an expert in this.' He paused, 'Someone like Will.'

Carmen groaned. 'Why do you persist in mentioning Will?'

'Because he's a great agent and he knows his stuff. And because I've agreed that we will meet him for breakfast at Rico's' – Marcus checked his Omega watch, he really was a watch whore – 'in an hour, so go and get ready.'

Carmen remained sitting on the sofa.

'It's not enough to write a good drama – you know that, you need contacts. Will's a good contact, now go and get ready.'

She still sat.

'And because I may be starting a production company

and I just may be interested in new up-and-coming writers of comedies, but only if they do exactly as I say.'

That shifted her. 'Really?'

'Really. Leo thinks it's a good investment, I've just got to get the talent together. I've already asked Will if he'll consider joining as executive producer, and he's thinking about it. So you see, as one of my best friends, your future is inextricably linked with Will.'

'He's with Tash,' Carmen said through gritted teeth, 'and I'm with Daniel.'

'A man who's into skateboarding, has a tattoo of his supposedly ex-wife's name on his shoulder, has a picture of himself naked above his fireplace, has photographs of his supposedly ex-wife all over his walls. Are you sure?'

In spite of being one of her best friends, Marcus had a cruel streak which made him say things which he probably shouldn't, all in the pursuit of getting his own way. Carmen suddenly felt an all-too-familiar feeling of insecurity invade her. She called it the wobbles, a horrible, sickening feeling. She'd had it constantly when she and Nick were going through IVF, feeling that she was balancing on the top of a very high building and that any minute she would lose her grip and tumble. She had hardly discussed Imogen with Daniel, took him at his word when he said he was over her, but it was more than possible he wasn't, more than possible that she, Carmen, was yet again just a distraction.

Marcus saw the look on Carmen's face and realised he'd gone too far. 'Sorry, I didn't mean it. I just want what's best for your work. *Please* come and meet Will. Forget what I said about Daniel. He's got baggage, so what? We've all got baggage. I could bloody fill bloody Terminal Five with mine and so could you.'

Rico looked as if he might possibly burst with happiness when Carmen walked into the café, which was in full festive swing, adorned with garish gold stars and red and green tinsel hanging in loops from the ceiling and an enormous fibre-optic Christmas tree which kept changing colour. He actually abandoned his post behind the counter to rush round and give her three kisses on the cheeks, though there was the briefest moment when he looked as if he might kiss her on the mouth, but then Mamma Mia's voice boomed out, '*Carissima Carmen!*' and he hastily redirected his lips.

Will had walked in just after Carmen. 'What is it with you and men wanting to kiss you all the time?' Will asked, amused. But then he found himself the subject of one of Mamma Mia's bear hugs and her hefty kisses and so Carmen didn't need to answer.

'It's great what you've written so far,' Will told her when he was finally free of Mamma Mia and the trio were installed in one of the booths with coffee and croissants. Mamma Mia had also insisted on having a photograph taken with Marcus, something he usually resisted at all costs, but she was not a person to be resisted. Her will was stronger, and if that failed she had the look of a woman from a James Bond movie, circa Sean Connery's era, who would gladly sit on a man with her meaty thighs wrapped round his neck until he acquiesced to her every demand.

Will was in work mode and there wasn't a trace of last night's flirtation. The blue eyes were serious, businesslike, she could read nothing more in them. That was the downside to blue eyes: they could be so cold. Carmen registered the disappointment and instantly felt guilty.

'I've got a few suggestions which we can go through, but what we really need to think about is casting, and I've got some suggestions for that as well.'

'Would you like to perhaps finish the drama as well?' Carmen put in. While she was pleased by Will's praise, she had forgotten what a forceful presence he had. She was half in awe, half in rebellion that he should have ideas about her work. She would say her baby, but she never used that word any more when she could possibly avoid it.

Will shrugged. 'You're the creative one, I'm just someone who can help make it happen. You can't be precious; you know that I'll only make suggestions that will improve it.'

Carmen set her mouth in a stubborn line. 'But I'm not joining Fox Nicholson, and anyway I doubt Tiana would want me on her books.'

'Who said anything about Fox Nicholson? If I worked on your drama it would be if I joined Marcus's production company.'

Instantly Marcus perked up and Will nodded at him. 'I'll have an answer for you at the end of the week, I promise. And if I do join, I want to bring some colleagues from Fox Nicholson with me, as I explained the other day. I think it could work if we were both a production company and an agency.'

'Shouldn't it be in twenty-four hours?' Carmen asked. The two men looked at her. She was forced to explain herself: 'Well, in movies whenever something big happens the hero or heroine – invariably hero, movies are so sexist except for Lara Croft and Linda what's-her-name in *Terminator* – only ever has twenty-four hours to save the world from a meteorite, a tidal wave, a virus or a demented loon who can close down the entire mobile phone and power systems and so render mankind helpless because no one can remember phone numbers any more.'

A perfectly arched eyebrow from Marcus, 'Sweetie, this is real life; Will can take as long as he wants.' He looked back at Will. 'I'm having doubts about her temporary relocation to Brighton. I think she's been watching too many DVDs with the gardener.'

'And the UGG boots have got to go,' Will put in. 'She must realise that they are the most unsexy piece of footwear ever created.'

'Hello!' Carmen raised her hand. 'I am sitting here. My relocation may be permanent, Marcus, and UGGs are not the most unsexy piece of footwear ever created; that accolade goes to Crocs. Obviously.'

'I bet come next summer you'll be wearing them. It's a slippery slope from UGGs.'

Carmen had no intention of ever wearing Crocs again and was irked by Will's critique of her footwear.

Being with the two men, both such strong personalities, made her dig deep for her feminist streak. 'So what would you rather? That women's feet were enslaved in toe-pinching stilettos, or worse a high slingback that offers no support and is notoriously difficult to walk in?'

'If it was a choice between them and UGGs, the painful ones every time. Anyway,' and finally the blue eyes had lost their glacial quality, 'I give good foot massage.'

Carmen was sure he did.

'I bet the green-fingered one is good at them too.' Marcus had put on a deliberately pervy voice.

'Yuck! Don't say it, just don't say it!' Carmen knew that the pervy voice was a prelude to Marcus coming out with her all-time least favourite word.

'And I bet he's especially good at peeling off your p-p-p-panties!'

The bastard had said it!

'I hate you, Marcus! You should never have made it. You should still be in Balham performing to homo-phobic old men in a pub stinking of urine and broken dreams and Cheesy Wotsits!'

Will was looking at the pair in bemusement. 'What happened there?'

'It's all because Carmen hates the word—' but before he could come out with it again, Carmen pressed her hand over his mouth.

'Oh, panties,' Will put in. 'Carmen hates the word panties. I see. Any particular type of panties? Silk panties? Cotton panties? Synthetic panties? Satin panties? Leopard-print panties, lacy panties, crotch-less panties? I could go on.'

'All panties!' Carmen was forced to say it to shut them up. 'What's wrong with saying knickers or pants or, if you must wear them, even though no one looks good in them, a thong!' Her anti-pantie speech had become heated and other customers had paused in their coffee drinking to stare at her.

'Just not as good as saying panties,' Will replied, as usual determined to get in the last word. And treated her to his most wicked smile. Goddamn him for being the man who could wind her up more than anyone else and yet whose approval she always wanted!

At that moment Will's BlackBerry vibrated with an incoming text. 'Shit!' he exclaimed as he read it. 'I'm due to meet Tash at the hospital, I'll have to go.' He stood up, 'Marcus, I'll be in touch. Carmen, keep your panties on, less hot sex with the gardener, more focus on finishing the comedy. And I've got something important to tell you, but it'll wait till next time.' And with that he was gone, though not before Mamma Mia had got him in another of her embraces.

There was no chance for further discussion with Marcus as Carmen was due at Millie's nativity play in the afternoon and had to dash off to Victoria and get the train. Christmas was just over a week away. In Carmen's old life that would have meant a steady stream of Christmas parties in the run-up, which required one to have the constitution of an ox and drink a lot of Red Bull the morning after, culminating in the office party where

Matthew would take them all out for dinner at Rico's restaurant and they would go back to the Ship and down quite spectacular amounts of alcohol and dance wildly and very badly. It was all about getting merry and deriving much pleasure from seeing who got off with whom. Oh, and trying to avoid Connor, the postboy. But now she had a different life and Christmas was all about being a grown-up, and not disgracing oneself by throwing up in one's handbag (two years ago) on the Tube home, or stealing flowers from outside a very swish hotel (three years earlier). Christmas was about doing grown-up things like going to your boyfriend's daughter's nativity play, even though, much as you liked his daughter, it was the very last thing you wanted to do.

It was only when she was installed on the train in a window seat (tick), not in front of anyone clipping their nails (tick), that she thought about Tash's hospital appointment. And suddenly all the verve and sparkle went out of Carmen's day when she came up with the conclusion, the only possible conclusion for a healthy thirty-something to be having a hospital appointment, given that Will didn't seem upset, and that was this: Tash must be pregnant. Octavia was real! Tash was texting Will to remind him to turn up at the first scan. It was so glaringly obvious! Plus hadn't he said that he had some big news for her? No wonder he needed time to consider Marcus's offer – he had to weigh up the pros and cons of leaving Fox Nicholson knowing that he was having a baby; maybe that was why he had said those things last night – a man on the brink of becoming a father remembering his last great flirtation and what might have been. That would be just like a man. Nick was having a baby and now so was Will; Daniel wanted one but as long as he was with her, zero chance of that. Carmen caught sight of the smartly dressed elderly lady sitting opposite her looking at her sympathetically and couldn't work out why until a tear sploshed down on her copy of *Grazia*.

The school hall was already packed with proud parents and grandparents, all vying for the best position from which to view, film and photograph their progeny.

'Hey, you made it,' Daniel said as she found him standing at the back, digital recorder at the ready. Carmen longed to put her arms round him and not let go, but she was too aware of the inevitable eyeballing they were attracting and had to make to do with a quick kiss on the cheek.

'Millie will be so pleased; she was worried you might not come.'

'I'd never let her down!' Carmen exclaimed.

'Not like her mother,' Daniel muttered, 'who still hasn't said if she is coming back for Christmas or not.' His handsome face took on a sombre, brooding expression.

'I'm sorry,' Carmen replied, unsure of what else to say. *Have yourself a merry little dysfunctional Christmas* didn't seem entirely appropriate under the circumstances.

Daniel hugged her shoulders. 'You've got nothing to be sorry for.'

303

Carmen scanned the rows looking for Jess. It had been over a week since she'd seen her friend, though she had texted her every day. Jess's replies had all been bland, reiterating 'I'm fine', so Carmen had no idea how things really were. She didn't manage to locate Jess, but Ilsa caught her eye and indicated that there was a seat free next to her.

'Sit with Ilsa,' Daniel told her. 'It gets crammed at the back.'

Ilsa looked not unlike humpty-dumpty, sitting precariously on a tiny red plastic child's chair, as all the adults were forced to do. Carmen sat next to her and felt uncomfortably like Goldilocks. Any minute she expected the chair to give way under her weight, for a tiny voice to shout out, *Look who's been sitting on my chair! And she's broken it with her massive buttocks!*

'Lucky you, seeing the Christmas concert,' Ilsa said. 'It must be love.' She managed to turn round and look at Daniel wistfully. 'Not that I can blame you.' Then she frowned. 'Sorry, I really must stop saying things like that. I feel as if there is no filter between me and the rest of the world right now; I keep coming out with absolutely outrageous comments.'

'It's okay,' Carmen replied, 'I promised Millie I'd come.'

Ilsa moved nearer to her so she could whisper, 'And looking round, do you get why Daniel is such an object of desire?'

Carmen did a quick scan of the hall. It confirmed her impressions from the playground that many of the dads could have done with a good wash and brush-up, a haircut

304

and a change of clothes. She counted only two dads in a suit. The rest were all staunchly casual, and while there were a couple of cuties, neither was in Daniel's league.

'I see what you mean,' she whispered back, wondering if it was entirely appropriate to be cruising the dads at a children's concert.

'And look at that specimen over there!' Ilsa exclaimed, pointing at a man with wild black curly hair. He hadn't shaved for several days, had a slightly hangdog expression and he was wearing a huge, baggy black-and-white striped jumper with holes in the elbows, ripped jeans and a pair of battered Adidas trainers. 'I mean, would you want to shag that?' Ilsa continued.

'No way!' Carmen replied. 'He looks like he needs a sheep dip, never mind a bath!'

Ilsa did one of her cackling laughs, causing the surrounding parents to look at her with raised eyebrows. 'He certainly does! That's my husband.'

Carmen was mortified. 'I'm sorry, I didn't mean it.' Oh God, how did she get out of this one? She could hardly say, actually I do want to shag him, as she now knew who he was.

'No, I'm sorry, Carmen, I was just teasing you. You have to allow a vastly pregnant woman her bit of fun, especially when she is with a man who looks more like Stig of the Dump with every day that passes.' She lowered her voice, 'He'll look like that until I can finally bring myself to shag him again. Sorry,' she said again, 'too much information. I just can't stop myself, it's that no-filter thing again.'

At that moment Stig of the Dump caught sight of Ilsa and made his way over. He managed to navigate his way along the rows of parents and then sat down next to Ilsa. As he passed by her Carmen caught a whiff of stale roll-ups. Stig definitely did need a bath and a change of clothes.

'Josh, this is Carmen,' Ilsa introduced them. Carmen and Josh leaned forward so they were both looking at each other across the mini mountain of Ilsa's bump.

'Hi,' Carmen said, hoping that Stig, sorry, Josh couldn't lip-read.

'Hi,' Josh replied. 'So you're the minx going out with Daniel.' He smiled and actually had a sweet face under that four-day-old beard. 'Just make sure you're never alone with the other mums or they will probably torture you to find out what Daniel's like.'

'Oh, she's already told us!' Ilsa exclaimed. 'He's absolutely fantastic and brilliant at—

Josh cut across her, 'Okay, Ilsa, maybe this isn't the time to reveal the extent of Daniel's sexual prowess. I think the concert is about to start.' But he was smiling. Josh/Stig didn't seem so bad and Ilsa was smiling back at him.

A young female teacher sat down at the piano and began playing 'Good King Wenceslas' as the children began filing in, dressed as kings, shepherds and sheep. The sheep were wearing jerkins covered in cotton wool, and white bobble hats, and raised a laugh as they made a few random bleats on their way in. Carmen smiled and gave a little wave at Millie who was dressed as a king, in a long red velvet cloak and gold crown which kept slipping into her eyes, and looking incredibly solemn. Harry was also a king and looked equally solemn. Carmen looked around and saw Jess and Sean sitting at the opposite side of the hall. Jess gave her a brief smile. The music stopped and then, after a signal from their teacher, some forty children chanted in unison, 'Good morning everybody, welcome to our show.' It was very sweet. Carmen loved seeing the look of complete concentration on the children's faces as they remembered the actions to the songs and the words. She tried not to dwell on her situation but it was hard, because as she watched the children she knew how wonderful it would be to be watching her own child. In a few years' time Nick would be watching his child, and Will would be watching Octavia.

The amused expression on Ilsa's face was replaced with one of glowing maternal pride as her little boy, who was the innkeeper and dressed in an apron at least three sizes too big for him, acted his part with gusto. Carmen would be okay so long as they didn't start singing 'Away in a Manger', a carol which had had the power to reduce her to tears even before she'd found out she couldn't have children. Carmen forced herself to think of all the things that made her happy and all the many reasons to be cheerful. She caught sight of Violet gazing across the hall at Daniel, a look of intense longing on her face, and she realised she envied her. Yes, she was the one who was going out with Daniel but Violet had children, Violet could have more children.

And then the children launched into 'Away in a Manger'. She dug her fingernails into her palms. *Be happy, Carmen, be happy, Carmen,* she intoned to herself, trying to drown out the painfully sweet voices of the children.

Somehow by the time she caught up with Daniel at the end of the performance she had managed to put a lid on her emotions; besides, all the parents were too caught up looking at the children to notice her.

'Wasn't she fantastic!' Daniel exclaimed, coming over to Carmen and blowing a kiss to Millie as she filed out of the hall with her class.

'Brilliant,' Carmen agreed, waving at Millie.

Daniel watched his daughter all the way out of the hall and then the joy seemed to go out of his eyes as he said flatly, 'I just wish her mother could have seen her. Every time we have one of these school events I can just see her scanning the rows, a look of hope on her face that maybe, just maybe her mummy might be there.'

Carmen reached out for his hand. 'You were there.'

He held her hand tightly. 'And you were, and I really appreciate that, Carmen. Millie really likes you.' Now why did that lovely comment make Carmen want to cry again? This was exactly why she loathed Christmas, too emotionally loaded for its own good.

Daniel had to dash off to work and Carmen caught up with Jess and Sean in the playground. 'Harry was fantastic!' Carmen told them enthusiastically, but the words died in her mouth as she saw that the couple looked terribly strained. 'Is everything okay?'

Sean glanced at her. 'I'll leave Jess to answer; I've got a train to catch. One of us has to work.' And with that he strode out of the playground. His navy overcoat flapped behind him like a reproof and it hadn't escaped Carmen's notice that he had not said goodbye to Jess.

Carmen looked at her friend. 'What is it, Jess?'

Jess frowned and pulled her red scarf tighter round her neck. 'Not here, can you come round to mine?'

'Sure,' Carmen replied. There was no chance to talk on the way as so many other parents were heading in their direction and it was clear Jess did not want anyone to overhear. It was only when they were inside the house that Jess opened up. She'd been accused of being drunk in class and had been suspended from work.

'Of course it's absurd!' Jess exclaimed, enacting her all-too-familiar routine of denial. 'It's some bloody student who's got it in for me, but because the college are so paranoid about keeping students, so they don't lose funding, it's the teachers who get it in the neck. It's fucking outrageous!' She stomped round the kitchen grabbing a bottle of wine from the fridge and without even asking Carmen, poured out two generous glasses of Pinot Grigio. 'It's fucking Christmas, alright? I'm having a drink, along with most of the population, so don't give me a hard time.'

Carmen had a sick feeling in the pit of her stomach. She could not let this moment go. She had to lay it on the line to Jess about her drinking. 'Are you sure you weren't drunk in class?' Carmen said quietly. 'Daniel says he's been concerned for a while that you were drinking too much.'

Jess froze, wine glass in hand, and glared at Carmen. 'How fucking dare you! What happened to my friend, the one who was on my side? Since you've shacked up with Daniel you've become so unbearably smug. I wish I'd never introduced you. You're so obsessed with him, it's pathetic! And you know you're not the first, don't you? He could fill an entire classroom with the women he's shagged in the last year alone. You're just one in a very long line.' Wine splashed out of her glass as she pointed her hand accusingly at Carmen. 'I feel more betrayed by you than when that bitch whore from hell shagged Sean!'

Her features were contorted and ugly with rage, brown eyes narrowed into slits of hate. Carmen was utterly shell-shocked by the venom pouring out of her friend. She hardly recognised her. 'This has got nothing to do with Daniel!' Carmen shot back, equally passionate. '*I've* noticed how much you've been drinking. For God's sake, Jess, you ended up in hospital! You've got a serious problem and you're in real danger of losing everything.' Carmen got up from her chair. Her voice was shaking with emotion. 'You've got to get help, Jess. Please. I'll do whatever I can; I'll look after Harry if you go to a clinic. I know you can beat this, Jess, you're such a strong person.'

There was a pause when Jess silently glared at her. Then she spat out more venom. 'Oh, you'd love that, wouldn't you? Looking after my son, playing at being his mum, just like you're playing at being Millie's! No wonder you want Daniel so much, you've got your own ready-made family. Everything's worked out so perfectly for you, hasn't it? How lucky for you, Carmen. Well, you can fuck off out of my house. I don't need you in my life. Go on, go back to your pretend family. I don't want you anywhere near mine.'

Somehow Carmen stumbled up the stairs and out of the front door.

She sobbed all the way home, oblivious to the curious looks of passers-by, oblivious to the cold biting wind whipping at her body. Her jacket was open but she was too dazed to do it up. Somewhere deep down she knew that Jess didn't really mean those terrible words, that she was lashing out because of her addiction; but Carmen couldn't be rational now. The things Jess had said had been so cruel, and so wounding.

There was no word from Jess in the days that followed. And Carmen felt too hurt and too battered to contact her friend. She spoke to Sean and he told her that things were very bad, that unless Jess went into rehab he would leave her and take Harry with him, but not even that threat seemed to impact on Jess who was still drinking, stopping only when she passed out. Not wanting their son to see his mother in this state, Sean had sent Harry to stay at his grandmother's as the children had now broken up for the Christmas holidays.

Carmen felt as if she had an icy shard of pain inside

her. She could not get Jess's words out of her head. It wasn't Jess's jibe that she was one in a long line of women. That she could deal with. It was the comments about Carmen wanting to be part of a ready-made family, to be Millie's mum. Those were the words she could not forget. The fact that it was Christmas only amplified the feeling, as every time she was round at Daniel's, Millie was so keen to involve her in the whole Christmas count-down, insisting Carmen help decorate the tree, going through her list to Father Christmas in painstaking detail. Even as she smiled at Millie and went along with the whole Santa fantasy, she felt hollow inside, a fraud. She knew that she would have to tell Daniel the truth. She had been living in a dream, enjoying the moment, pushing out thoughts of the past and of the future. She had reached a turning point.

The twenty-first of December – the winter solstice, the shortest day in the year and the night of the Burning of the Clocks Parade. The workshop where Carmen had met Daniel seemed to belong to another life. She'd moved to Brighton to escape her past but it had caught up with her and she was going to have to deal with it – and soon. She would have preferred to be just with Daniel and Millie on the procession, but she suspected that would be out of the question, and sure enough they were part of a large group of parents and children from school. She felt Jess's absence keenly and had a horrible sick feeling that Jess was never going to stop her destructive behaviour, that her friend was lost to her.

It was a perfect night, with a clear starry sky. There was no wind, but it was bitterly cold, a sharp white cold that got into your bones. The group had to assemble at Brighton Dome, a theatre next to the Pavilion. The children were high as kites, darting about, delirious with excitement, at the combined thrill of staying up past their bedtime and it being so close to Christmas. The adults were caught up in the children's excitement, passing round hipflasks, in between trying to rein in their offspring. There were hundreds of lanterns glowing with candles, and spectacular giant paper sculptures of vast clocktowers, alarm clocks, clocks with wings, time bombs. There were figures too – a King and Queen whose paper arms and heads could be moved by their carriers, like giant puppets. There were jugglers and acrobats on stilts, dressed in white suits and pointed Pierrot hats, drummers beating out a rhythm that got into Carmen's head. A rhythm that told her tonight was the night she had to tell Daniel. She had run out of time.

Finally the procession set off, to the accompaniment of the drums. The streets were packed with people watching, and the city had an air of carnival about it, accentuated by the Christmas lights strung across the streets. Even the weird and wonderful Pavilion, with its cream-coloured towers like a maharajah's palace, was overshadowed by the procession, the lanterns bobbing around like enormous fireflies, the puppets held aloft, moving their arms as if they were orchestrating the event.

'Bit different from how you'd usually spend a

313

Thursday night with your media friends in London I imagine, Carmen?' Violet remarked as she walked beside her. Carmen, who wanted to prepare herself for talking to Daniel, could really do without Violet needling her.

'Yes, usually I'd be hoovering up cocaine while drinking champagne out of a crystal-studded Louboutin and eating the meat of some endangered species.' She paused. 'Violet, I know why you dislike me so much.'

Violet gave her a wide-eyed startled-fawn look of surprise, which Carmen did not buy, and didn't answer as Daniel rejoined them. He was wearing a black fake-fur hat with ear flaps. Any other man would have looked ridiculous. Daniel as usual looked beautiful, striking, like a hunter.

'Look, Carmen, your favourite shoe shop,' Millie said excitedly as they made their way past Kurt Geiger. Yes, even in the short time she had known Millie she had managed to instil a love of shoes in the little girl. Perhaps that was how she could remember her: the woman who couldn't give Daddy what he really wanted but had lovely shoes. And on the procession went into East Street, a narrow road which led to the sea, usually a magnet for shoppers, but now it was the shops which looked out of place against the lanterns. Shoes and beautiful clothes would not save her, would not save anyone. Bloody hell, she was getting maudlin, it must be the brandy. The drumming seemed to get louder, more insistent, as the procession filed across the main seafront road and on to the promenade. Brighton Pier, with its neon lights flashing on and off, looked particularly garish.

The sea was an inky black, perfectly calm, the lights of the pier reflecting on it in pools of gold.

'I am so glad that you went to that workshop,' Daniel told her, as he reached out and held her hand. 'You've been the best thing to happen to me and Millie in such a long time. Millie has already said that she wants to spend Christmas with you next year.'

He smiled at her, and Carmen thought she would shatter as she forced herself to smile back. 'I'm so glad too.' And then, because she knew the truth was going to hurt, added, 'Even if I did ruin my leather jacket, it was worth it. And as it was Alexander McQueen, that is really saying something.' If in doubt go for the cheap gag, make them laugh, because you know that tears are just around the corner, or at the end of Madeira Drive, to be precise.

The procession was now reaching its climax where there would be a huge bonfire on the beach and all the lanterns would be burnt, culminating in a firework display. As they drew closer to the final destination there came the sound of a woman humming, a noise which seemed to hang in the night.

'Daddy,' Millie piped up, 'I don't want to burn my lantern, please can I keep it?' She clutched it tightly, as if fearing it would be forcibly taken from her.

'But you won't be able to make your wish,' Violet said. For a woman with two children, Violet could be breathtakingly insensitive.

Millie looked upset. 'But I need to make my wish that Mummy comes back.'

'Well, you'll have to hand your lantern over,' Violet persisted. 'Only that way can you make a wish, that's the whole point of making it.'

'You can have mine,' Carmen told Millie. 'Keep your lantern.'

'But what about your wish?' Millie asked her anxiously.

'Carmen can wish on mine,' Daniel told her. *Oh Daniel, if only you knew, I have used up all my wishes*, Carmen thought as she gave her lantern to the little girl and watched her hand it to the line of people passing the lanterns on to the bonfire.

'Come on.' Daniel took her hand and Millie's and led them to the edge of the barrier from where they would get a good view of the fireworks. The music seemed to get louder, now the humming had been joined by the plaintive tones of a cello. In front of the bonfire was an enormous paper sculpture of a queen. Her arms were stretched out as if in welcome. Carmen realised that the queen was also on fire, a slow, controlled fire, from inside the structure, turning her white skirt a vivid orange. As the flames took hold she seemed to sway as if dancing. It was a powerful image against the black of the sky and the black of the sea. Carmen found herself offering a silent prayer to the burning queen. *Help me do this thing; help me let go of the past. And help my friend Jess.* The fire around the queen grew more intense; it wouldn't be long before she was consumed by the flames. Behind her the bonfire had been lit, yellow and orange flames leaped out, reaching up to the black sky.

'Did you invest my lantern with your hopes and wishes?' Daniel asked her, ducking his head down so she could hear him over the music. He was clearly expecting a light-hearted response from her by the way he smiled, a quip from Comedy Carmen. She took a moment to take in his beautiful face, his warm eyes, his lips which she adored kissing. *I really can't bear to lose him*, she thought.

'I did. I hoped that Jess would be okay.'

It was true, but she was putting off the moment. *Now, tell him now*, the music seemed to implore her. The queen shifted in the fire, her arms seeming to stretch in supplication as the flames licked around her.

'I made a wish too,' Daniel replied. His face was so close to hers she could feel his warm breath, felt the slight graze of his stubble on her cheek, cold in the December air.

'Do you want to know what it was?'

'Shouldn't you keep it a secret?'

'Not this – it only has a chance if I'm honest. So here goes. I wished you would stay in Brighton, because I've fallen in love with you.'

'You love me?' Carmen asked. 'Really?' She was stunned by the revelation, absolutely had not seen it coming.

'Really.' Daniel smiled at her. Then he took off the ridiculous fur hat. Gone was the long hair, in its place short hair, cut close to his head. If possible he looked even more beautiful than before, as all focus was now on his face, those features, those deep brown eyes. 'I know you prefer short hair, so I did it for you.'

317

This should have been a perfect moment and Carmen was greedy to hold on to it as she put her hand to his face, stood on tiptoes and kissed him. But it was a kiss that felt as if it was under false pretences. 'There's something I have to tell you and I don't want to tell you, but I have to.'

Daniel smiled at her. 'Well, I know your divorce hasn't come through yet, nor has mine, but they will, so that's okay.'

She shook her head. 'It's not that.'

Daniel shrugged. 'What, then? What could be so bad? That you don't want to go to the allotment any more? You don't have to, I know you don't really enjoy it. That you're sick of eating vegetarian food? I'll cook you some meat if you like, so long as it's organic.'

It crossed Carmen's mind that Daniel was just as afraid of hearing what she had to say as she was of saying it.

She shook her head. 'No to all of those. The thing I have to tell you is a big thing. A really big thing.' Oh God, did she have to go ahead and say this? But she knew she had to. 'I can't have children. And I have to tell you because I know you want to have them, and if that's a problem I need to know now.'

A pause, everything hung in the balance, everything depended on his answer. Daniel frowned. 'I didn't mean to freak you out the other night; I just wanted you to know how I felt about children. But we don't have to have a baby yet, I know it's early days.'

Carmen felt cold despair grip her. 'It's not about timing. I can't have them. It's not that I don't want

318

them because I do, more than anything else, but I physically can't have them. I have tried everything and couldn't. And it wasn't my husband, it was me.'

Daniel didn't say anything, just looked at her, a look which she couldn't fathom.

And then further conversation was made impossible by fireworks exploding over the beach. Millie squealed with delight and demanded to be given a piggyback so she could better see the elaborate showers of green and blue, the gold and silver fireworks that bloomed like giant flowers in the sky, jets of white glittering sparkles, silver and gold spirals. How hopeful and optimistic the fireworks seemed, blazing away in the darkness. And then nothing, just smoke and the smell of gunpowder. The darkness was always going to win.

Carmen felt numb. She had done what she had set out to do. It was obvious, Daniel wouldn't want her now – the reject, the defective – and who could blame him? Their romance had been as short and intense as the fireworks, but it was over.

But then, after Millie had slid off his back he turned to her and said, 'What you've told me doesn't make any difference. I love you, Carmen.' There was an urgency to his voice. Carmen so wanted to believe him. Maybe everything would be alright. A tiny spark of hope ignited within her. She had told him the truth and he had said that he loved her. A thought which burned brighter than any of the fireworks . . .

17

Christmas Eve. Carmen was on the train headed for London and Marcus. She'd said goodbye to Daniel and Millie the day before. Imogen still hadn't said if she was coming back or not. Daniel suspected not and had wanted Carmen to come with them, but Carmen felt she couldn't let Marcus down. Leo was spending it with his daughter and his parents who were not accepting of Marcus as his partner. There had been no more talk about her revelation. She was on tenterhooks, analysing Daniel's every expression and the way he spoke to her to see if anything had changed between them, any shift that she could detect. But there was none. Could Daniel have truly meant what he said? That he didn't mind? It seemed too wonderful to believe, too good to be true. Carmen did not trust things that seemed too good to be true.

The train was packed with people travelling home for Christmas. Everyone was in good spirits. Carmen tried to share in it; it was after all a novelty to be on a train where people actually looked happy. Her usual experience of train travel was that every man and woman wanted to be an island, reading their papers, working on their laptops, drinking coffee or clipping their fingernails, and pretending that no one else was in the carriage with them.

She was lost in thought when her mobile rang. It was Sean. 'I just needed to let you know that Jess went to a clinic in Hertfordshire this morning. She especially wanted me to say sorry to you. It will be a while before she can have any visitors except me and I know she feels terrible about the things she said to you. She didn't mean them, Carmen.' The sweet relief of hearing that. Carmen now had a smile to match anyone's in the carriage.

'Tell her it's forgiven and forgotten; all I want is for her to get better. And send her all my love, Sean.'

They talked briefly about Jess's treatment. She would have to spend a month in rehab, with a week drying out and then intensive therapy following the twelve-step programme. Carmen knew that Jess was at the beginning of what would be a long and difficult road to recovery, but at last her friend was on it. As they ended the call and Carmen looked out at fields white and brittle with frost, she reflected that one of her wishes from the Burning of the Clocks had come true.

Victoria Station was heaving. The station forecourt was adorned with a very large Christmas tree, decorated with blue and silver lights, actually quite tasteful, and a Salvation Army band was singing 'Oh Little Town of Bethlehem'. Now it just needed to be snowing and it would be a perfect Richard Curtis film set. Mind you, Carmen thought, as she struggled towards the exit with her suitcase, a character from one of his films would not be getting the number 38 bus, but she had blown December's budget on presents and so could not get a taxi.

'So, champagne or some kind of festive punch which Sadie has concocted, which believe me has one hell of a kick?' Marcus demanded as soon as he opened the door to her. 'Let the festivities for the dysfunctional family begin!' Carmen was too excited about Daniel's saying he loved her and Jess's news to notice that Marcus looked exhausted.

'Both! I have to celebrate,' Carmen said, whirling into the flat, hugging Marcus and Sadie in succession. At last she was going to have a Christmas where she could be happy and not weighed down with the blues, where she would be drinking out of joy and not to escape.

Marcus and Sadie looked at her expectantly.

'Daniel said he loved me and Jess is going into rehab!'

'A declaration of love from skater boy, well, well,' Marcus said, handing her two glasses. Carmen was too excited to consider the possible irony that she was toasting Jess going into rehab by drinking to excess. She took a sip of punch, so strong that it nearly blew her head off, followed by a sip of bubbles to redress the balance.

Marcus carried on, 'I thought he would be the kind who would never give it up. Who said it first?'

'He did,' Carmen replied. 'And I even told him about

not being able to have children. Don't you think that's brilliant?' She flashed a hundred-megawatt smile worthy of Julia Roberts.

'It's fabulous,' Sadie replied, giving Carmen another hug. She looked meaningfully at Marcus. 'Isn't it, Marcus?'

'If that's what you want, Carmen, then I'm happy for you.' Marcus didn't look happy.

Why was he raining on her parade? The hundred-megawatt smile disappeared from Carmen's face.

'I think it's early days and don't want you to get hurt, is all. You have only just met the man. No other reason. Now come on, it's Christmas Eve. And I've got an announcement of my own. You are looking at the man behind Neon Tiger, which is going to be half TV production company, half agency. Will is going to join as executive producer. And one of our first pitches is going to be a comedy drama by an up-and-coming writer, who we just happen to think has a hit on her hands. Yes, I mean you, Carmen! So you'd better pull your lovestruck finger out, because after Christmas you have a month to finish. And then I want you to help me set up the company, maybe even be a shareholder.'

So Will was taking the plunge even with a baby on the way. He must be confident. Carmen could not allow thoughts of Will's impending fatherhood to take her on a downer, so she threw herself into celebrating with Marcus and Sadie. They drank champagne, pigged out on lovely food from M&S as none of them was gifted with culinary skills, and watched their favourite films for the festive season: *Some Like it Hot* (Carmen), *The Wizard of Oz* (Sadie), *It's a Wonderful Life* (Marcus). Everything was bathed in a happy glow, just like being in a Richard Curtis film after all. She had her lovely friends, she had a lovely boyfriend who loved her and told her again on Christmas morning when she called him, and she had the promise of a new career.

'This has been the best Christmas ever,' she said to her friends as she and Sadie ended Christmas Day eating crackers and Stilton, possibly a little too much Stilton, but hey, it was Christmas.

'What time's Leo getting back tomorrow?' she continued.

'He's not.' Marcus was not partaking of the cheese fest. He sat next to her on the sofa, arms folded.

'I thought he was due back on Boxing Day?'

'He's not coming back.'

Surely he couldn't mean that? Marcus and Leo were the perfect couple – well, of course Marcus hardly saw Leo because of his work, but she knew how much Marcus loved him. He was the love of his life, he was always saying.

'He's left me.' A pause. 'For his personal trainer, Darius. Apparently all those early mornings and late nights when I thought he was slaving over the Dow Jones he was shagging Darius.'

'Oh my God, Marcus, I'm so sorry.' She looked across at Sadie, who seemed as shocked as she was. 'You should have said, I've gone on and on about Daniel.'

'I didn't want to ruin Christmas for everyone. Anyway, fuck him, he's made his choice. I hope he'll be very happy with his pea-brained fuck buddy. It's funny, because on New Year's Eve I was going to ask him to marry me. I'd even bought the ring from Tiffany's – what a fucking idiot! How could I have got it so spectacularly wrong?' Everything about Marcus radiated hurt and betrayal. He stood up abruptly. 'D'you mind if I go to bed? I've got the most appalling headache.'

Carmen wanted to put her arms round Marcus, tell him everything was going to be alright, just as he had done for her, many, many times, over the years. But she knew her friend, knew he wouldn't allow it. She waited until she heard his bedroom door click shut. 'You didn't know, did you, Sadie?'

'I had absolutely no idea. Poor Marcus. He's devastated, but you know he won't show it. Well, he might to you, but no one else.'

Carmen hardly slept that night. She lay awake bathed in the orange glow of possibly one of the poshest street lamps in London, thinking of Marcus and wondering how she could possibly help her friend. How she wished she could make things better, as if things like this could be made better.

In the morning Sadie left early to visit her gran in Egham; Carmen had also intended to leave on Boxing Day as she was due to spend the day with Daniel and Millie, but once she'd packed, she realised that she couldn't leave her friend.

Millie answered the phone when Carmen rang. 'I got my wish, I got my wish!' she squealed, almost unintelligible with excitement.

'So Father Christmas did bring the *High School Musical* karaoke set?' Carmen replied, secretly pleased that Millie liked the present that she'd persuaded Daniel to buy.

'No, not that! Mummy has come back! And she says she's going to stay! Thank you for giving me your lantern, Carmen; it's all because of you that I got my wish!'

Carmen suddenly had a horrible sick feeling that she knew could not be blamed on the Stilton. 'I'm so pleased for you, Millie, but can I speak to your daddy now?'

The way Millie described things, it sounded as if Imogen was back at the house, but that surely couldn't be, could it? The little girl must simply mean that her mummy was visiting. Daniel came on the phone. 'So you've heard the news? I imagine half of Brighton has – Millie has been beside herself.' Even Daniel sounded more animated than usual.

'So can you tell me what's going on?' Carmen asked, aware that her voice sounded brittle.

'Christmas Day night we're just back from my sister and there's a knock at the door, and there's Imogen. Oh God, Carmen, I wish you could have seen Millie's face.' Perhaps not the most sensitive of comments under the circumstances, but Daniel probably wasn't thinking straight.

'And is she just back for Christmas or is it more

permanent?' Was it wrong of Carmen to fervently hope that the beautiful one was on a flying visit and very soon would be returning to the land of the free?

A pause. This was not looking good.

'I think she's planning to stay.'

'I imagine she still has plenty of friends in Brighton she could stay with?' But Carmen had a nasty suspicion that she knew where Imogen would be staying.

'Not so many now, Carmen. She left the States in a bit of a rush. She's split with her boyfriend and it's all a bit stressful because she's pregnant. I've said she can stay with us for the time being, until she gets herself sorted.' Daniel was talking quickly, guiltily, as if he knew that what he was saying would cause pain.

'She's staying with you?' Carmen felt the need for clarification.

'Just for a few weeks or so. It really won't affect us. She can have the attic room.'

His not-even-ex-wife was moving back into the house and he didn't think it would affect them? Carmen suddenly felt as if the last few weeks with Daniel had been as unsubstantial as a dream. 'Please don't say that, you know it will affect us,' she said quietly.

Daniel's tone turned defensive. 'Look, what can I say? I'm sorry, but she's Millie's mum and I can't see her out on the streets, can I?'

'So it's nothing more than you thinking of her as Millie's mum, and it's not anything more than that?'

'It's nothing more than that, I swear. I love you; Imogen turning up out of the blue doesn't change that.'

327

But Daniel's *I love you* sounded like a man trying to convince himself, and Carmen could still not bring herself to say it back. How funny that both she and Millie had got their wishes. But she had the strongest feeling that Millie's wish would be the undoing of her and Daniel.

Marcus finally emerged from his bedroom to find Carmen sitting on the sofa. She hadn't moved since her conversation with Daniel.

'You know when I said that this was the best Christmas ever?' she said numbly. 'Can I just rephrase? I think it's the worst. First Leo, and I've just found out that Imogen has moved back in with Daniel and Millie. She's pregnant, by the way. Is it just me, or is everyone pregnant?'

Marcus sat down next to her and put his arm round her.

'He told me he loved me,' Carmen said.

'Leo told me he loved me.'

Marcus didn't say it, but Carmen knew that he thought she should get out of her relationship with Daniel right now.

18

Carmen didn't meet up with Daniel until the day before New Year's Eve. She told herself that she hadn't wanted to leave Marcus, who was doing his best to act as if Leo's departure was no more than an inconvenience, an act which Carmen didn't buy for a second, but also she was putting off confronting the Imogen situation. She supposed that had she been younger or could have children, she might have hotfooted it to Brighton as soon as she heard about Imogen, to lay claim to Daniel. But she had no energy for a fight.

Daniel opened the door to her when she finally went round in the early evening. For a moment they stood there – her on the doorstep, him inside the house – and it seemed to Carmen as if she was the outsider, looking in at a life that would never be hers.

'Hi, good to see you, Carmen, come in.' Daniel kissed her on the lips, but it felt like the kiss of a stranger; Carmen waited for the kiss to become more passionate, for Daniel to take her in his arms. They hadn't seen each other for a week, the longest time they had been apart in their relationship, but Daniel simply said, 'Everyone's downstairs.'

Carmen followed him along the hall. Imogen had

draped her coat over the banisters and left a pair of boots lying by the bathroom as if marking her territory once more in her home. The house even smelt different; she was sure she could detect a woman's perfume, a strong, sweet fragrance, slightly overpowering. Millie and Imogen were sitting on the sofa by the fire. Millie was reading to Imogen from Roald Dahl's *Danny the Champion of the World* – a book which she and Carmen had been reading together only two weeks earlier.

Mother and daughter turned to look at Carmen when she walked into the room. She had never realised that Millie's eyes were the exact blue of her mother's.

'Imogen, this is Carmen who I told you about,' Daniel said. He seemed awkward, not his usual laid-back self. So she wasn't even going to be introduced as his girlfriend?

'Hi, nice to meet you,' Imogen said, reaching out her hand in a gesture which seemed to say, *I'm the lady of the house.* 'I would get up but as you can see,' she gestured at her bump, 'it's easier if I sit.' She was probably around six months pregnant by Carmen's reckoning and was wearing a khaki-coloured wrap dress that would have made anyone else look dreary but on Imogen simply made her look like a pregnant supermodel.

Carmen shook the beautiful one's hand. Pregnancy had made Imogen's beauty even more radiant, her skin looked glowing, her eyes were bright, her blonde hair seemed to shimmer in the firelight. Carmen tried to cheer herself up by imagining that the shimmering was down to extensive and expensive highlights and that really Imogen had mouse-brown hair. And then there was something to cheer Carmen as she happened to catch sight of Imogen's feet. The beautiful one was wearing chocolate-brown Crocs lined with sheepskin. However, she had a feeling the cheer would be short-lived.

Carmen sat down in the armchair and Daniel handed her a glass of red wine and remained standing. And now Carmen noticed that Daniel was wearing Crocs as well − of the navy sheepskinned variety. She gave him a WTF look and pointed at the Crocs.

He looked at her blankly, then registered, 'Oh yeah, they were a present from Imogen.'

Carmen wanted to say that the Crocs were an outrage and what was he thinking, but Daniel turned away from her to ask Imogen if she wanted a glass of wine.

'I'd better not, Dan, but could I have a pink grape-fruit juice? Thanks.' Her voice was low, with a slight Californian drawl. 'I've got the same cravings for it that I had with Millie. God, d'you remember, Dan? You had to go out and buy up all the supplies from the 24-hour Tesco's.'

'I certainly do. And I remember your craving for vegetable juice. But not just any old vegetable juice − it had to be V8, didn't it? And that was a bugger to find.' The two of them were on a cosy walk down memory lane in their Crocs and Carmen still felt horribly excluded. How could Daniel do this to her? Did he have no awareness of how it made her feel?

'How healthy!' Carmen put in. 'I'd have thought

pregnancy was the one time you could get to indulge a love of muffins and sweets. A kind of carte blanche for porking out.' She was half-joking, she knew from her extensive reading that a healthy diet was important.

'Oh my God, Carmen! That's the road to pre-gestational diabetes!' Imogen exclaimed. 'And not good for the baby at all. Luckily I had Dan looking after me, so every time I got an unhealthy craving I'd get him to make me a healthy snack.'

'I was on houmous and crudité-making duty, practically twenty-four seven,' Daniel replied, giving Imogen the benefit of one of his gorgeous smiles. Next they'd be retelling the story of the birth. Carmen didn't think she could take it.

'So,' Carmen said brightly, 'when's the baby due?'

'March.'

The same month as Nick's, Carmen thought with a pang.

'And d'you know if you're having a boy or girl?' She was good at asking these questions, wasn't she? Imogen would never know how much it pained her.

'I *really* hope it's a girl!' Millie exclaimed, bouncing up and down on the sofa. 'I'd love to have a sister! If it's a girl can we call her Ruby? That's my favourite name for a girl.'

'I kind of want the surprise,' Imogen replied. 'But yeah, I quite like Ruby. Your dad and I nearly called you Ruby.'

'And where are you planning on having the baby?' Carmen had to know.

'That sort of depends on a few things.'

'Oh stay here, Mummy, please! I'll help you with the baby and so will Daddy.'

It was like watching yourself being airbrushed out of a picture. Any moment now Carmen would have disappeared altogether.

Daniel walked over to Imogen and handed her a glass of juice. 'Thanks, Dan. I still can't believe you cut your hair. It looks so much better long, you'll have to grow it back. I love it when it's long. Short is so severe.'

Daniel gave an embarrassed laugh and sat on the armchair opposite Carmen. 'I don't think Carmen would agree.'

'Oh?' Imogen directed her beautiful blue-eyed gaze at her.

Carmen shrugged. 'I am a short hair kind of girl.'

'And you're a writer, Dan says. I'm hoping to finish my novel before I've had the baby. I'm so nearly there.' So Imogen could add writer to her list of accomplishments, was there no end to them?

They were treated to a detailed synopsis of the work in progress as they sat down to a healthy supper of lentil moussaka, cooked by Daniel, of course. Imogen liked the sound of her own voice very much. No one got a word in edgeways. The novel sounded dire, about a thirty-something woman who falls in love with a vampire.

'So, chick lit with fangs?' Carmen commented, which didn't raise a smile from anyone.

'It's a serious love story, think *Wuthering Heights*, but set in LA,' Imogen snapped back, and Carmen didn't add that wasn't the whole vampire genre like totally bled dry at the moment? She toyed with her food. She was no lover of lentils at the best of times, and right now she had absolutely no appetite. It was torture sitting there with the beautiful one and seeing Millie and Daniel hanging on her every word.

After they'd eaten Millie was desperate to sing to them with the *High School Musical* karaoke set.

'Oh, Millie, you're not into that rubbish!' Imogen exclaimed. 'I'll gladly listen to you sing something of your own, but not that! Dan, I can't believe that you would allow this. It's so stereotyped and cheesy.'

'I agree,' Daniel said, 'but it's what Millie wanted.'

The little girl looked utterly crestfallen. Clearly she was longing to impress her mum.

'How about you sing one of the carols from your concert?' Carmen said quietly, wanting to make things better for Millie.

But Millie shook her head and Carmen felt like the bad guy for encouraging Millie in her HSM passion.

After supper Imogen discovered she'd run out of ginger tea, could Dan be an absolute star and go and get some for her? She found it impossible to sleep without it. Dan dutifully went off to the nearest Tesco Metro while Imogen put Millie to bed, a first time for everything, Carmen thought bitterly. She stayed in the living room flicking through a day-old *Guardian*. As soon as Daniel returned she would go back to her flat. There was no way she could remain in the same house as Imogen – Daniel's promise that Imogen's presence wouldn't affect their relationship was simply absurd. She and Daniel had some serious talking to do and she wanted to be as far away from Imogen as possible when they did. A creak on the stairs alerted her to Imogen sashaying down. She had changed into a pair of white silk pyjamas with a pale pink pashmina flung over her shoulders. She looked like Claudia bloody Schiffer.

'Would you like another glass of wine, Carmen?' she asked, again making it clear that she was the lady of the house.

Carmen shook her head.

'I meant to say I was so sorry to hear that you can't have children. You must have thought me terribly insensitive to be going on about my pregnancy. But I didn't want to say anything in front of Millie − she would be so upset for you.' She tilted her beautiful face towards Carmen. 'It's great that you've got your writing, though − art can be incredibly fulfilling.'

It was, Carmen decided, one of those defining moments. It felt like the very worst kind of betrayal by Daniel to tell his pregnant wife about his barren girlfriend. There could be no going back from this. It was a jumping into the deep end kind of moment.

'So Daniel told you?'

'Yes, the other day. I am truly sorry, Carmen.'

Carmen got up out of her chair and grabbed her coat and bag. 'It *is* sad that I can't have children, but d'you know what's sadder? A woman who can walk out on her five-year-old daughter and leave her wondering every day whether her mummy is ever going to come back. Asking herself what she might have done wrong to make her mummy go away.'

'Now hold on a minute,' Imogen's voice was sounding less laid-back LA drawl, more uptight English. 'You don't know what was going on. I had my reasons, very good reasons, which are absolutely none of your business.'

Carmen looked back at her; she was intimidated by Imogen's beauty no longer – she would never want to look like or be like her.

'And they outweighed the needs of your child? You're obviously a deeply selfish woman, but I hope for Millie's sake that you're staying. Tell Daniel I've gone.'

And before Imogen could reply, Carmen practically ran up the stairs and out of the house.

She was halfway down the road when she bumped into Daniel returning from his errand. 'Hey, where are you going?' he exclaimed, his face concerned under the orange streetlight, but his looks no longer had a hold on her.

'You told Imogen about me not being able to have children, how could you?' She was bubbling over with a sense of hurt and betrayal.

Now he looked awkward. 'Well, she was asking me about you and it just sort of came out; I didn't realise it was this great secret.'

'And you didn't stop to think how I would feel about you telling your pregnant wife that I, your girlfriend, can't have children? Never mind let her move back into your house and pretend that it won't make a difference to our relationship!'

'Imogen was really concerned for you. And I don't see why her staying with me will change anything.'

Just hearing Daniel try and justify himself killed any feelings Carmen had for him. He was so deluded she almost wanted to laugh. 'Daniel, why don't you just admit that you're still in love with her?'

He shook his head. 'No way, I told you, I'm in love with you.'

He went to take her arm, but Carmen brushed him away. 'I would have so much more respect for you if you told me the truth. Goodbye, Daniel.' She turned to go.

'Carmen, what are you doing? Don't go; come back to the house. We can work this out.'

She spun back and faced him. 'What, a cosy little chat between you and your wife and me? I don't think so. Goodbye, Daniel,' she repeated. 'Just promise that you won't let her hurt Millie again.'

Daniel looked as if he was going to say something else, but Carmen's expression was resolute. She turned again and began walking swiftly away. There was nothing more to be said. She had been Daniel's distraction, while he tried to pretend that he wasn't still in love with Imogen. But if she was honest, and brutal honesty was what was called for now, he had been hers. She had been so desperate to push away thoughts of Nick and his baby and of Will that she had hurled herself into the relationship with Daniel. For the last few weeks she had been living a lie, not thinking straight, not being true to herself. The one thing she felt truly sorry about was not saying a proper goodbye to Millie, and she determined that she would go round and see her in the New Year. It wasn't Millie's fault that her dad was deluded.

'There is no way you are spending New Year's Eve on your own!' Marcus declared when she finally got round to calling him the following day. She hadn't been up to speaking to any of her friends the day before as once back at the flat the steely resolve had deserted her and she had spent two hours sobbing in the bath.

'I'll be fine, Marcus. It will be good for me to draw a line under this year. I'll have half a bottle of champagne, watch Jools Holland, look at the fireworks and go to bed.'

'*Please* come up to London. I'm only having a small party, you don't have to put on a brave face or anything. You can even wear your UGGs, and you know I loathe them as much as Will does. And speaking of Will, he's coming tonight.'

'I can't come, Marcus; I just need to be on my own. But say hi to Will and say congratulations.'

'What for?'

'On Tash being pregnant.'

'Is she? That's news to me.'

'Yeah, I mean Will hasn't told me yet, but it's obvious.'

'Well, I'm surprised. Will came back early from skiing as they were rowing so much.'

'Perhaps he's feeling nervous about fatherhood. It can affect men like that.' Carmen sounded surprisingly calm; perhaps she could have an alternative career as a relationship counsellor. Marcus pleaded some more but eventually told her he would call her again at regularly hourly intervals to see if she would change her mind.

I will not wallow, Carmen told herself as she switched on her MacBook. *This will be the day that I finish episode five of my sitcom. This will not be the day that I remember for ending my relationship with Daniel.* And in one of those creative spurts where things start coming together, she did indeed finish, writing until nine o'clock at night, not even stopping to eat. Oh my God! She was turning into a proper writer at last. Next she would be nibbling an oatcake and an apple in place of her usual salt and vinegar Hula Hoops and Oreos. Marcus had phoned every hour as promised, but each time Carmen had declined, and finally he had conceded defeat. But she had to celebrate the fifth episode; there was only one more to go. She would nip to Wine Me Up and buy a bottle of champagne.

Just as she was about to walk out the door she looked in the hall mirror. The jeans, jumper, UGG combo did not reflect the Carmen she wanted to be; they were a reminder of the Carmen she had been with Daniel. Quickly she slipped them off and put on the midnight-blue silk dress she had bought to impress Daniel, but never worn, and her heels. Outside the temperature had dipped below freezing and Carmen walked briskly, but in spite of the cold she enjoyed being out after hours of sitting at her desk. Daniel and Imogen and Millie would all be at Violet's New Year's Eve party by now. Carmen allowed herself a small smile as she thought of how Violet would respond to the return of the beautiful one and then reflected that she actually felt sorry for Violet for being in love with Daniel, a love that was surely doomed.

She bought the most expensive bottle of champagne and a large packet of pistachios (well, she had to keep her strength up) and headed back. The pavements glinted with frost and the stars were out in force. It was a beautiful night. She would miss Brighton but she realised with a sudden clarity that she wanted to go back to London as soon as she'd finished the sitcom. This had been time out from reality, but she needed to return to her friends and help Marcus set up the production company. She was so lost in thought that she didn't notice the figure standing by the door.

'Miller, where the hell have you been? I'm freezing my bollocks off here.'

Carmen nearly dropped the bottle of Veuve in her surprise at seeing Will.

'What are you doing here?'

'Come down to see you, of course. I had to walk from the bloody station as there was no taxi to be had for love nor money.' Will was shivering, he was only wearing a jacket over a black shirt.

'But what about Tash?' And the baby, she wanted to add.

'I'll explain everything, but can we go inside before I expire from hypothermia? I know you'd be a terrible nurse, too busy looking at yourself in the mirror in your uniform to minister to me – even though I have to admit that the thought of you in a nurse's uniform

is quite appealing on a pervy level. I can feel my extrem-
ities warming up now just thinking about it. You haven't
got one, have you?'

Carmen ignored him and opened the door.

As soon as they were inside in the living room
Carmen put her hands on her hips like she meant business. 'Well? What's the explanation? Marcus sent you,
didn't he? Honestly, I'm fine. I'm an independent
woman; I'm not going to wither just because I'm alone
on New Year's Eve and because I've just dumped my
lover. Yes, I dumped him, he didn't dump me.'

Will meanwhile was standing by the fire, rubbing his
hands together; he really did look frozen, 'Any chance
of a brandy? See, I was right that you'd be a terrible
nurse, no bedside manner whatsoever.'

Carmen rolled her eyes and followed Will's instruc-
tions, pouring each of them a more than generous
measure. Will took a large gulp. 'That's better, maybe
hypothermia isn't quite so imminent after all. Shall we
start again?' He walked over to where Carmen was
standing and kissed her on the cheek. His lips felt ice-
cold against her skin and she inhaled the familiar scent
of Amber and Lavender which seemed to awaken the
butterflies who had gone into hibernation but were now
flexing their wings and seemed rather sprightly.

'Now come and sit down and tell me how you are.
I hope you're not giving that gardener a second thought
for how appallingly he treated you?' Will's tone was
light but his eyes had their serious, searching look as
he tried to detect Carmen's mood.

341

'I'm fine, actually.' As soon as Carmen said the words she realised that she was. Daniel didn't have the power to hurt her because she had never really let him in.

'get back to London and Tash, especially as it will be your last New Year's Eve without the baby. This time next year you'll be suffering from sleep deprivation and wondering why you wasted the New Year's Eve pre-children seeing me when you could have been clubbing all night and taking shitloads of drugs. And you'll never be able to go out on New Year's Eve again, well maybe when Octavia slash Mercedes slash Lexi is fourteen. Or I guess you could have a party round at yours, but it's not the same, is it? It will just be couples like you moaning about the fact that they never get to go out any more and treading peanuts into your carpet. No, hang on, Tash probably prefers expensive oak floors.'

Will was staring at her as if she had gone completely mad. 'There are so many things wrong with what you've said I don't know where to start. First off, I don't take drugs, I never have, which I know may sound a bit unlikely for someone who works in the media but there you are. Secondly, what baby? I thought Octavia slash Mercedes slash Lexi was in your over-vivid imagination; why are you talking about her as if she's real?'

God, he wasn't going to make her spell it out for him, was he? 'Because I know Tash is pregnant, you idiot! Though going skiing at Christmas seems reckless of her, but maybe she took medical advice.'

'Tash is most definitely not pregnant. Or if she is I

am not the father. We broke up on Christmas Day night, which was extremely awkward given that I couldn't get a flight home for two days and all the hotels were booked up.'

It was Carmen's turn to stare at him. She'd had it all mapped out in her head, had been so sure. 'But you went to the hospital, wasn't that for the scan? You said so when we were at Rico's.'

Will looked blank then said, 'Tash was having an X-ray. They think she might have broken her toe when she dropped a weight on it at the gym and she wanted me to keep her company as she hates hospitals.'

'What about you saying you had some important news for me as you left?' Carmen was determined to prove that she had not been a loony tune by jumping to the pregnancy conclusion.

Will burst out laughing. 'Carmen, you are priceless, a ruby, a diamond among women. I was going to tell you that M&S seem to have stopped making Wobbly Worms and replaced them with Colin the Caterpillar, and how did you feel about confectionery that had the same name as our former accountant?'

Tash wasn't pregnant? She and Will had broken up? There was just too much to take in. Carmen put her hands over her face and laughed so hard that she cried. Will put his arms round her and pulled her to him and she put her arms round his neck and for a while they just held each other until the tears had run their course. As soon as she stopped crying Carmen registered that the butterflies were going ballistic, especially when Will kissed her neck and then her lips and Carmen kissed him back. No kiss was ever sweeter or sexier or held such a promise. And this time Carmen knew exactly where the kiss was leading, didn't want it to stop. 'I'm still cold,' Will murmured.

'Come to bed then, I'll warm you up.'

And so it was that instead of sitting alone and surveying the wreckage of her love life, Carmen took Will into her bed and Will had his eyes open all the time they made love and it was even better than she had once anticipated that it might be.

'That was even better than I thought it would be,' Will said afterwards.

'Even though I lack Tash's balletic suppleness,' Carmen teased.

Will looked at her and put his finger on her lips. 'No teasing. I feel bad about Tash, I only went out with her again on the rebound, all thanks to you. There I was gearing up to declare my feelings to you and you knocked me back. I used Tash to repair my battered ego but it was wrong of me. And then when I found out about Daniel I was so jealous of the skateboarding gardener.'

Carmen turned over and propped herself on her elbows to look at Will. She still couldn't quite believe that he had ended up in her bed, though it felt right as well, as if he belonged there.

'Why were you jealous of him? You've got a great career and I bet you don't even like skateboarding. You'd be rubbish at it anyway, I reckon.' Carmen was trying to keep it light because she couldn't quite believe what she was hearing.

'I wasn't jealous of that, I was jealous because . . .' Will hesitated. 'Oh, for God's sake, Carmen, I thought as a woman you were supposed to be blessed with powers of intuition. I was jealous because he had you.' Will ran a hand over his short black hair, suddenly less sure of himself than usual. 'Don't you get it, Carmen? I really like you, I mean *really* like. Don't laugh but I think I love you, Carmen Miller. I don't mean I think, I mean I know I love you. You've been wrapped around my heart since you first walked into my office in your foxy mutton outfits. It was the denim shorts and high heels that did for me.'

Carmen punched him on the arm (on the very satis-fyingly muscular arm, she was pleased to notice – in fact, everything about Will's body was satisfyingly muscular).

'Don't hit me, I've just said I love you. It's a big moment.' It was a big moment. Carmen looked at Will and knew that she loved him. It was in a different league to what she had felt for Daniel, which she now realised was infatuation. She loved Will because he understood her, understood the person that she wanted to be, well, nearly.

At that a series of loud bangs signalled fireworks exploding over Brighton to bring in the New Year. 'I didn't plan that,' Will said, pulling her to him.

'It would have been a terrible cliché if you had.' Carmen was so close to telling Will that she loved him, but something stopped her.

'I'll get the champagne.' If in doubt, reach for alcohol.

19

Walking into Marcus's production company Neon Tiger was like stepping back in time as Carmen saw first Trish, then Daisy, Lottie and Dirty Sam, all of whom had needed very little persuasion to take redundancy and leave Fox Nicholson.

'Oh my God!' she exclaimed, hugging each of them in turn, even Dirty Sam, and usually she kept him at arms' length as he was a terrible groper. 'It's so good to see you all! You can let go now, Dirty Sam,' she added, extricating herself from Dirty Sam's overly passionate embrace – if he was a dog he'd be one of those pesky little mongrels who was forever trying to mate with your leg. It was the first time Carmen had visited the company. She had spent the last month working flat out to finish the sitcom, discovering that there was nothing like a deadline to stop all the random acts of procrastination and focus the mind.

Marcus had managed to rent an office in a prime location just off Tottenham Court Road. He'd got it at a bargain price as it was slightly run down and wasn't built to the high-tech spec so many companies demanded. But that was a plus as far as Carmen was concerned. She was delighted to see that all the windows opened, there was no hideous overhead lighting that made one want to put one's head in a bag to escape its penetrating glare, and there were no glass cages, though Will had his own office tucked in the corner, as did Marcus, both of which had glass doors with venetian blinds. Trish had already made herself at home and had surrounded her desk with her cacti collection and aquarium.

'This is going to be your desk,' Trish told her, pointing out a work station adjacent to hers. Carmen was going to work part-time for the company developing scripts while they waited to see what would happen with her sitcom. Will was training up Daisy to be an agent, as he reckoned she had a killer instinct and was wasted as a receptionist. With characteristic dark humour she had decorated her work station with a red-and-white triangular warning sign: 'Touch my stuff you die, yes, I mean you, Dirty Sam.' Lottie's desk had a vase of cheery sunflowers on it, a present from her girlfriend congratulating her on her new job, and Dirty Sam's had at least three coffee mugs that needed washing and a large cardboard figure of Megan Fox.

'It's the closest he gets to a real woman,' Will told her as they walked past on their way to his office.

'We know what you're up to!' Dirty Sam called out after them.

Will fixed him with his big boss look. 'Missing Tiana?'

Dirty Sam pretended to be working on a very important document.

'We're going through Carmen's sitcom, not that it's any of your business.'

Will could be very masterful when he chose to be, Carmen reflected as she followed him. As soon as Will had shut the door he pulled down the venetian blind. 'But now Dirty Sam will definitely think we're up to something,' Carmen protested.

'We are up to something,' Will said, putting his arms round her and kissing her. 'I've always wanted to have carnal knowledge with one of my colleagues in the workplace, and now I'm the boss I really feel there's nothing stopping me.'

'I'm not having sex with you in here,' Carmen said when she surfaced from the kiss. 'I just couldn't, knowing that everyone was out there.'

'You mean you don't want to slip out of your panties and straddle me while I sit at my desk playing at being a big executive.' Will gave her a wicked grin.

'Not now you've said that word. I'll never forgive Marcus for telling you.'

Will sighed theatrically. 'Shame. Come on, Miller, let's get to work. I'm going to be pitching this to Channel Four in three weeks and it's got to be perfect.'

And they did just that. Carmen knew that once Will had set his mind to do something, he would not be deflected. She watched him frowning with concentration as they went through the scenes, running his hands through his short hair, and her heart flipped over.

The four weeks since New Year's Eve had been some of the happiest she had ever known, passing in a whirlwind of passion, laughter and work. She had moved back to London on New Year's Day and was staying in Marcus's spare room until she could get enough money together for a deposit. Will wanted her to move in with him but it felt too soon after everything that had happened. She had rushed into things with Daniel, and look where that had got her. Besides, she told Will, she couldn't leave Marcus on his own. He was still mourning Leo, and Carmen felt that only her presence in the flat stopped him embarking on a self-destructive fuck-fest, which was what he kept threatening to do. Will didn't push it, but Carmen could tell that he was waiting for her to move their relationship on. She still hadn't told him she loved him, knowing that when she did she would have to tell him about not being able to have children. Will would be very understanding, she was sure, but the pity would creep in and then he would be looking for an exit.

'So what's the plan for tonight?' Will asked when they'd been working for some three hours, sustained only by quantities of Colin the Caterpillars, which neither thought were a patch on Wobbly Worms, and interrupted at least four times by Dirty Sam with spurious questions, desperate to see if they really were up to anything.

'We're taking Marcus out for his birthday at Rico's. I thought he'd want to go somewhere posher but he said he wanted low-key. Last year Leo flew him to the Four Seasons in New York, and I imagine that Rico's is probably about as far away from the Four Seasons as you can get. I'll meet you there, I've got to go and buy his present.'

'Ah, the life of a part-time worker.' Will leaned back in his chair. 'Are you sure you won't move in with me? Then I could come home to you cooking supper, wearing a cute little apron, maybe with nothing on under the apron.'

'That would be dangerous in the kitchen, don't you think?'

Will was lost in his fantasy. 'My slippers warming by the fire as you pour me a glass of wine.'

'If that's the life you've imagined for us then let me tell you I am never moving in with you, and if I ever see any slippers in your flat, they won't be warming by the fire, they will be in the fire. Slippers are the anti-dote to passion,' Carmen declared, gathering up her things.

'How can an UGG-wearer diss slippers? My West Ham pair are very fetching, I'll have you know. I'm sure you'd find me just as irresistible if I was naked and only wearing them and a smile.'

'No way!' Carmen shot back.

'Yes way.' Will got up and grabbed her arm, forcing her to sit on his lap, at the very moment Dirty Sam came in on one of his leering missions.

'I knew it!' he declared, punching the air and prac-tically skipping back to his desk, shouting, 'Lottie, you owe me a fiver. They were at it.'

Carmen looked at Will. 'And you employed Dirty Sam why?'

'Evidently not for his social skills. He's very good at spotting comic talent, and in an ideal world he would do just that and the rest of us would never have to interact with him.'

Carmen slid off his lap and straightened her skirt.

'We may as well do it, don't you think, now that they all think we have?' Will said hopefully.

'I'll see you later,' Carmen replied, walking out of the door and glaring at Dirty Sam who still looked as if he had won the lottery. She wondered if there was a course he could go on to learn people skills, then reasoned it was probably too late.

She spent a pleasant couple of hours mooching around the shops trying to find a suitable present for Marcus – the man who really did have everything. In the end she went for a collection of Oscar Wilde's fairy stories. As she walked back to Mount Street she thought about the last month. Being with Will was a revelation – it was like having a lover and a best friend all rolled up. Carmen had never attached much weight to the idea that there was a person out there who would be 'the one'. But with Will she was having to revise that idea, maybe he was her one. The trouble was, for how long? She knew she was living on borrowed time and felt that any moment there would be a wake-up call, and she would be forced to say goodbye to a happiness that seemed all the sweeter as she knew it couldn't last.

'Happy Birthday, Marcus!' Mamma Mia declared, folding Marcus into one of her bear hugs and giving him a series of hefty kisses which indicated the depth of her affection for him, almost as great as her feeling for Will if the tightness of her grip and passionate smack of her kisses was anything to go by. 'The first celebrity to dine at Rico's! I am so proud. See, I have already put your picture up on the wall.' She pointed over to a poster-sized framed photograph of herself and Marcus she'd had taken the last time he'd visited, and which was decorated with gold tinsel to ensure it stood out from the others. 'I know you are used to the very best and I will give you the VIP treatment, I promise, my darling boy.' With that she exited in a flurry of black skirts to boss the waiters around.

'I thought this was going to be low-key,' Marcus said, looking accusingly at Carmen.

'It is,' Carmen insisted. She appealed to Will, Sadie and Dom (yes, miraculously Sadie still hadn't dumped Dom), for back-up. 'Mamma Mia's always like this. She's not putting on anything special just for you.' At this Carmen crossed her fingers as Mamma Mia had excelled herself in the birthday arrangements by making a cake and decorating it with a picture of Marcus's face made out of icing, which she was going to carry to the table while the entire restaurant burst into a rendition of 'Happy Birthday', accompanied by Mamma Mia's grandson on the accordion. Carmen hadn't had the heart to tell Mamma Mia that Marcus had an irrational hatred of the accordion – even the sight of one set his teeth on edge.

'Well, just so long as there is no cake and no singing of "Happy Birthday", you know I hate that kind of thing.'

'More Barolo, anyone?' was Carmen's reply, as Will winked at her.

The meal got underway with plenty of laughter, then Sadie said she had an announcement to make. There was an expectant hush. *Please, please, please don't say that you're going to marry him,* Carmen thought. Cohabiting with Dom was surely punishment enough, and she had never expected that Dom would last this long. Maybe there were hidden depths to his shallowness? Maybe he had actually paid for something?

'I no longer have to recite the shipping forecast in bed,' Sadie declared.

'Damn!' Marcus exclaimed. 'I've been dining out on that for ages, it's been comedy gold. You'll have to give me something else, Dom. Surely you've another sexual peccadillo you could share with me?'

Anyone else might have been offended by Marcus taking the piss out of their bedtime activities, but Dom was so thick-skinned and so in awe of Marcus, as a successful comedian at the top of his game, while he languished somewhere in the foothills, that he took it all in his stride. 'I'm afraid not, Marcus,' and his tone was apologetic. 'But there is a chance that Sadie might land a role in *Holby City* as a nurse.'

'Really?' Will had perked up at this. 'Sadie, with that voice you'll give all the male patients heart attacks. It'll be carnage on the ward!'

'I predict a whole new role-play for you two,' Marcus said drily. 'But alas, it's not as good as the shipping

353

forecast; the whole nurse–patient dynamic is very well-charted territory. You know the sort of thing: Nurse, "It's only a little prick." Patient, "That's what my wife says!" Boom boom! It just doesn't work for me in the same way, I'm not that kind of comedian.'

Now Dom visibly wilted as he took on board the bitter knowledge that there is only one thing worse than being talked about by a celebrity, and that is not being talked about by one. 'Perhaps we could have a monthly shipping forecast?' he said, looking at Sadie hopefully.

She shook her head and snapped a breadstick for emphasis. At last, Sadie seemed to be learning to say no.

'D'you remember when we came here for *my* birthday?' Will said quietly while Sadie and Dom chatted to Marcus.

'Of course I remember – Dirty Sam nearly dropped his trousers, it quite put me off my tiramisu.'

Will shook his head. 'I was going to say that I remember looking at you across the table and thinking I wanted you so much, and that when we kissed it was one of the best kisses of my life. But I knew then that you were holding something back from me and you still are, aren't you?'

Not this, not now. Carmen shrugged. 'I don't know what you mean.'

Will was prevented from pressing his case further as suddenly the lights were dimmed and Mamma Mia's twelve-year-old grandson, dressed in a smart black suit, with a severe side parting, marched proudly into the restaurant playing 'Happy Birthday' on his accordion. Marcus glared at Carmen, who in turn pretended to be captivated by the little boy's performance. She was never more grateful for the distraction. Then Mamma Mia strode triumphantly into the room bearing the cake in her arms as it blazed with sparklers. 'Happy Birthday to you!' her voice boomed out as she indicated to the diners that they should join in. Everyone present knew that Mamma Mia was not to be trifled with if they wanted to dine there again and gave it their best shot.

Marcus had a fixed smile on his face and a glazed look in his eyes as he muttered out of the corner of his mouth, 'I'll pay you back for this, Carmen, maybe not tonight or tomorrow, but one day in the future.'

As the cake drew nearer he stared at it in appalled fascination. 'Why's Dale Winton on my cake?'

'It's not Dale Winton, it's supposed to be you.' She and Marcus were getting very good at this talking-out-of-the-side-of-their-mouths.

'Shoot me now.'

'Happy Birthday, dear Marcus!' Mamma Mia had reached her destination. The cake looked like a fire hazard and the sparklers were beginning to melt the gold icing, causing the face to take on a most macabre appearance, as first one eye disintegrated then the mouth. Marcus flashed his best always-look-on-the-bright-side-of-life smile at Mamma Mia. 'Thank you, Carla, this is spectacular.'

'I'm so glad you like it!' Mamma Mia swooped down on him and plastered him with kisses.

'And now we must toast Marcus with Strega!' she declared.

'The night just gets better!' Marcus replied, visibly wilting under the Mamma Mia experience. Carmen bet he didn't get this treatment in the Four Seasons. 'I know Carmen has been looking forward to the Strega all night, make sure you pour her an extra large measure.'

Somehow they all managed to finish their glasses of the liqueur, watched over tenderly by Mamma Mia, who also insisted that Marcus have two pieces of birthday cake. Will wasn't able to say anything else personal to Carmen, who fully intended to whisk him back to his place and get him into bed before he knew what had hit him.

Will had just asked for the bill and there was a general feeling of contentment around the table when there was a chorus of beeps from Carmen's mobile, Marcus's mobile and Sadie's, which seemed odd.

Marcus was first to access his. Instantly he frowned. 'Was it from Leo?' Carmen asked, poised to check hers. She was expecting to hear from Jess.

Marcus shook his head and looked over at Sadie, who had just read hers and appeared equally troubled.

'Don't look at the message,' Marcus said quietly. 'I think it's been sent to you by mistake. I'm sure he didn't mean to.'

'Why not? Is it porn? I bet it's Dirty Sam.' Ignoring his advice, Carmen opened her inbox. And then froze.

The message was from Nick. It was a picture message of him with his arm round Marian, who was holding a tiny newborn baby. 'Introducing the wonderful Noah, born a month early, we're all doing great but knackered!!' was the accompanying message.

'He must have done one of those group text things,' Sadie said. 'Marcus is right, I'm sure he didn't mean to send it to you.'

Carmen was falling down one of those cracks again, falling, falling, falling. She stared down at the red-and-white tablecloth, not even registering that Will had put his arm round her. 'Well, it doesn't matter,' she said, 'I'm impressed that anyone can do a group text message, I've never worked out how to.' When in doubt make them laugh. No one was laughing. 'I'm really happy for them,' Carmen went on, 'I just need to go to the bathroom.' And without looking at anyone, she got up, but instead of going to the Ladies she ran up the steep stairs, pushed open the door and rushed into the street.

It was a bitterly cold February night – the forecasters had kept saying it was going to snow – but Carmen was oblivious to the cold as she walked blindly along Great Portland Street without an idea of where she was going. She just knew that she couldn't sit there and pretend everything was alright. She could hear Will calling her name but she kept on walking.

'Carmen, wait, please!' He had caught up with her. He grabbed her arm, forcing her to stop. Carmen looked down at the icy pavement and her shoulders sagged. She suddenly felt incredibly weary, resigned;

this would be it, the moment she said goodbye to Will. It had been bad enough telling Daniel, it would be a thousand times worse telling Will.

'Before you tell me what's going on, I just want to say that I love you. And there is nothing you could say to me that could ever change that,' Will said passionately.

Carmen still couldn't look at him. 'If only I could freeze time to half an hour ago when we were all so happy,' she said.

'You can't do that, Carmen, and I wouldn't want to. I want us to move forward together. It's time to go beyond the banter, don't you think? I've been very patient while you've continued to do your distance thing. You've never quite let me in, have you?'

'Because you wouldn't want to be let in if you really knew me.' Carmen's voice was flat, as flat as her flat-lined spirits. There was no hope.

'I do really know you, Carmen,' Will insisted.

'I can't have children.' There, she'd blurted it out, quickly ripped that plaster off the wound.

She felt him slip his jacket round her and she realised she was shivering. She continued to look at the pavement. *On Great Portland Street I sat down and wept* – that almost had the right poetic ring to it.

'I know,' Will said quietly. 'I've known for ages. I guessed that's why your marriage must have broken up and then I saw Nick at a gig and he told me. I know, and it doesn't make any difference. I love you. I don't even want children, why did you ever think I did? I've got loads of nieces and nephews and I've got an adopted child in Africa.'

Still Carmen stared at the ground. 'You only say that because you're thirty-five. I bet when you turn forty, when all your friends have got children, you'll be desperate for them and then you'll start resenting me, and then finally leave me or I'll leave you because I can't bear to see you so unhappy.'

'Oh, and you know everything, do you, Carmen? Well, do you know that you have made me happier than anyone else, ever, that the days I don't see you are the days that don't feel as bright? That you make it all mean something?'

'I can't do it again, Will, really can't. I can't open myself up only to be rejected.' She was crying now. Why did the most wonderful thing in the world, Will telling her he loved her, seem like the saddest?

Will wiped away the tears with his thumb, so, so gently. 'Then you won't be living, Carmen, you'll just be existing. I promise you that I will never reject you because you can't have children. Maybe,' and here his tone became lighter, 'because of your mutton tendencies and your relentless teasing of me, and because you so far have refused to tell me you love me.'

He had his arms round her now and had pulled her close to him. He was so warm against her.

'I want to be with you, and maybe one day if things change and we did both want children we could adopt. Anything's possible; you've just got to be open.'

Finally Carmen looked at him. Something gave inside

her and she did the bravest thing she had done in a very long time. 'I do love you, Will.'

She gazed into those blue eyes and he said, 'We're even, then.'

For a while they just held each other until Will said, 'Now please, can we go back to the restaurant? I'm freezing. And look, it's snowing!' All around them tiny snowflakes were swirling down.

Downstairs in Rico's they were met with cheers and applause from the diners and from their friends. 'What's going on?' Will asked, bemused by the attention.

'Mamma Mia was watching you on her CCTV screens and reporting to us what you were doing,' Marcus told them. 'It was very exciting, and also disturbing as I know it was a terrible invasion of your privacy, but we take it she's finally said it.'

Will nodded.

'About bloody time, Carmen.' Marcus's tone was teasing but his brown eyes were warm.

Mamma Mia came over and enfolded both Will and Carmen in a hug. 'Oh my darlings, you are the perfect couple. How would you feel about having your wedding reception here, and I could make you a wonderful cake?'

Carmen and Will just looked at each other, knowing that where Mamma Mia was concerned resistance was futile.